P9-EMQ-836

the dazzling heights

the dazzling heights

KATHARINE McGEE

HARPER
An Imprint of HarperCollinsPublishers

The Dazzling Heights
Copyright © 2017 by Alloy Entertainment and Katharine McGee

alloyentertainment
Produced by Alloy Entertainment
1325 Avenue of the Americas
New York, NY 10019
www.alloyentertainment.com

Library of Congress Control Number: 2017943576

ISBN 978-0-06-241862-3 (trade bdg.) — ISBN 978-0-06-268853-8 (int.)

Typography by Liz Dresner

17 18 19 20 21 PC/LSCH 10 9 8 7 6 5 4 3 2 1
❖
First Edition

For my parents

PROLOGUE

IT WOULD BE several hours before the girl's body was found.

It was late now; so late that it could once again be called early—that surreal, enchanted, twilight hour between the end of a party and the unfurling of a new day. The hour when reality grows dim and hazy at the edges, when nearly anything seems possible.

The girl floated facedown in the water. Above her stretched a towering city, dotted with light like fireflies, each pinprick an individual person, a fragile speck of life. The moon gazed over it all impassively, like the eye of an ancient god.

There was something deceptively peaceful about the scene. Water flowed around the girl in a serene dark sheet, making it seem that she was merely resting. The tendrils of her hair framed her face in a soft cloud. The folds of her dress clung determinedly to her legs, as if to protect her from the predawn chill. But the girl would never feel cold again.

Her arm was outstretched, as though she were reaching for someone she loved, or maybe to ward off some unspoken danger, or maybe even in regret over something she had done. The girl had certainly made enough mistakes in her too-short lifetime. But she couldn't have known that they would all come crashing down around her tonight.

After all, no one goes to a party expecting to die.

MARIEL

Two months earlier

MARIEL VALCONSUELO SAT cross-legged on her quilted bedspread in her cramped bedroom on the Tower's 103rd floor. There were countless people in every direction, separated from her by nothing but a few meters and a steel wall or two: her mother in the kitchen, the group of children running down the hallway, her neighbors next door, their voices low and heated as they fought yet again. But Mariel might as well have been alone on Manhattan right now, for all the attention she gave them.

She leaned forward, clutching her old stuffed bunny tight to her chest. The watery light of a poorly transmitted holo played across her face, illuminating her sloping nose and prominent jaw, and her dark eyes, now brimming with tears.

Before her flickered the image of a girl with red-gold hair and a piercing, gold-flecked gaze. A smile played around her lips, as if she knew a million secrets that no one could ever guess, which she probably did. In the corner of the image, a tiny white logo spelled out INTERNATIONAL TIMES OBITUARIES.

"Today we mourn the loss of Eris Dodd-Radson," began the obituary's voice-over—narrated by Eris's favorite young actress. Mariel wondered what absurd sum Mr. Radson had paid for *that*. The actress's tone was far too perky for the subject matter; she could just as easily have been discussing her favorite workout routine. "Eris was taken from us in a tragic accident. She was only seventeen."

Tragic accident. That's all you have to say when a young woman falls from the roof under suspicious circumstances? Eris's parents probably just wanted people to know that Eris hadn't jumped. As if anyone who'd met her could possibly think that.

Mariel had watched this obit video countless times since it came out last month. By now she knew the words by heart. Oh, she still hated it—the video was too slick, too carefully produced, and she knew most of it was a lie—but she had little else by which to remember Eris. So Mariel hugged her ratty old toy to her chest and kept on torturing herself, watching the video of her girlfriend who had died too young.

The holo shifted to video clips of Eris at different ages: a toddler, dancing in a magnalectric tutu that lit up a bright neon; a little girl on bright yellow skis, cutting down a mountain; a teenager, on vacation with her parents at a fabulous sun-drenched beach.

No one had ever given Mariel a tutu. The only times she'd been in snow were when she ventured out to the boroughs, or the public terraces down here on the lower floors. Her life was so drastically different from Eris's, yet when they'd been together, none of that had seemed to matter at all.

"Eris is survived by her two beloved parents, Caroline Dodd and Everett Radson; as well as her aunt, Layne Arnold; uncle,

Ted Arnold; cousins Matt and Sasha Arnold; and her paternal grandmother, Peggy Radson." No mention of her girlfriend, Mariel Valconsuelo. And Mariel was the only one of that whole sorry lot—aside from Eris's mom—who had truly loved her.

"The memorial service will be held this Tuesday, November first, at St. Martin's Episcopal Church, on floor 947," the holo actress went on, finally managing a slightly more somber tone.

Mariel had attended that service. She'd stood in the back of the church, holding a rosary, trying not to break out into a scream at the sight of the coffin near the altar. It was so unforgivingly final.

The vid swept to a candid shot of Eris on a bench at school, her legs crossed neatly under her plaid uniform skirt, her head tipped back in laughter. "Contributions in memory of Eris can be made to the Berkeley School's new scholarship fund, the Eris Dodd-Radson Memorial Award, for underprivileged students with special qualifying circumstances."

Qualifying circumstances. Mariel wondered if being in love with the dead scholarship honoree counted as a qualifying circumstance. God, she had half a mind to apply for the scholarship herself, just to prove how screwed up these people were beneath the gloss of their money and privilege. Eris would have found the scholarship laughable, given that she'd never shown even a slight interest in school. A prom drive would have been much more her style. There was nothing Eris loved more than a fun, sparkly dress, except maybe the shoes to match.

Mariel leaned forward and reached out a hand as if to touch the holo. The final few seconds of the obit were more footage of Eris laughing with her friends, that blonde named Avery and a few other girls whose names Mariel couldn't remember. She loved this part of the vid, because Eris seemed so happy, yet she resented it because she wasn't part of it.

5

The production company's logo scrolled quickly across the final image, and then the holo dimmed.

There it was, the official story of Eris's life, stamped with a damned *International Times* seal of approval, and Mariel was nowhere to be seen. She'd been quietly erased from the narrative, as if Eris had never even met her at all. A silent tear slid down her cheek at the thought.

Mariel was terrified of forgetting the only girl she'd ever loved. Already she'd woken up in the middle of the night, panicked that she could no longer visualize the exact way Eris's mouth used to lift in a smile, or the eager snap of her fingers when she'd just thought of some new idea. It was why Mariel kept watching this vid. She couldn't let go of her last link to Eris, forever.

She sank back into her pillows and began to recite a prayer.

Normally praying calmed Mariel, soothed the frayed edges of her mind. But today she felt scattered. Her thoughts kept jumping every which way, slippery and quick like hovers moving down an expressway, and she couldn't pin down a single one of them.

Maybe she would read the Bible instead. She reached for her tablet and opened the text, clicking the blue wheel that would open a randomized verse—and blinked in shock at the location it spun her to. The book of Deuteronomy.

You shall not show pity: but rather demand an eye for an eye, a tooth for a tooth, burn for burn, wound for wound . . . for this is the vengeance of the Lord . . .

Mariel leaned forward, her hands closing tight around the edges of the tablet.

Eris's death wasn't a drunken accident. She knew it with a primal, visceral certainty. Eris hadn't even been drinking that night—she'd told Mariel that she needed to do something "to help out a friend," as she'd put it—and then, for some inexplicable reason, she'd gone up to the roof above Avery Fuller's apartment.

And Mariel never saw her again.

What had really happened in that cold, thin air, so impossibly high? Mariel knew there were ostensibly eyewitnesses, corroborating the official story that Eris was drunk and slipped off the edge to her death. But who were these eyewitnesses, anyway? One was surely Avery, but how many others were there?

An eye for an eye, a tooth for a tooth. The phrase kept echoing in her mind like cymbals.

A fall for a fall, a voice inside her added.

LEDA

"WHAT ROOM SETTING would you prefer today, Leda?"

Leda Cole knew better than to roll her eyes. She just perched there, ramrod-straight on the taupe psychology couch, which she refused to lie back on no matter how many times Dr. Vanderstein invited her to. He was deluded if he thought reclining would encourage her to open up to him.

"This is fine." Leda flicked her wrist to close the holographic window that had opened before her, displaying dozens of décor options for the color-shifting walls—a British rose garden, a hot Saharan desert, a cozy library—leaving the room in this bland base setting, with beige walls and a vomit-colored carpet. She knew this was probably a test she kept on failing, but she derived a sick joy from forcing the doctor to spend an hour in this depressing space with her. If she had to suffer through this appointment, then so did he.

As usual, he didn't comment on her decision. "How are you

feeling?" he asked instead.

You want to know how I'm feeling? Leda thought furiously. For starters, she'd been betrayed by her best friend and the only boy she'd ever really cared about, the boy she'd lost her virginity to. Now the two of them were *together* even though they were adopted siblings. On top of that, she'd caught her dad cheating on her mom with one of her classmates—Leda couldn't bring herself to call Eris a friend. Oh, and then Eris had *died*, because Leda had accidentally pushed her from the roof of the Tower.

"I'm fine," she said briskly.

She knew she'd have to offer up something more expansive than "fine" if she wanted to get out of this session easily. Leda had been to rehab; she'd learned the scripts. She took a deep breath and tried again. "What I mean is, I'm recovering, given the circumstances. It's not easy, but I'm grateful to have the support of my friends." Not that Leda actually cared about any of her friends right now. She'd learned the hard way that none of them could be trusted.

"Have you and Avery spoken about what happened? I know she was up there with you, when Eris fell—"

"Yes, Avery and I talk about it," Leda interrupted quickly. *Like hell we do.* Avery Fuller, her so-called best friend, had proved to be the worst of them all. But Leda didn't like hearing it spoken aloud, what had happened to Eris.

"And that helps?"

"It does." Leda waited for Dr. Vanderstein to ask another question, but he was frowning, his eyes focused on the near distance as he studied some projection that only he could see. She felt a sudden twist of nausea. What if the doctor was using a lie detector on her? Just because she couldn't see them didn't mean this room wasn't equipped with countless vitals scanners. Even now he might be tracking her heart rate or blood pressure, which were probably spiking like crazy.

The doctor gave a weary sigh. "Leda, I've been seeing you ever since your friend died, and we haven't gotten anywhere. What do you think it will take, for you to feel better?"

"I *do* feel better!" Leda protested. "All thanks to you." She gave Vanderstein a weak smile, but he wasn't buying it.

"I see you aren't taking your meds," he said, changing tack.

Leda bit her lip. She hadn't taken anything in the last month, not a single xenperheidren or mood stabilizer, not even a sleeping pill. She didn't trust herself on anything artificial after what had happened on the roof. Eris might have been a gold-digging, home-wrecking whore, but Leda had never meant to—

No, she reminded herself, clenching her hands into fists at her sides. *I didn't kill her. It was an accident. It's not my fault. It's not my fault.* She kept repeating the phrase over and over, like the yoga mantras she used to chant at Silver Cove.

If she repeated it enough, maybe it would become true.

"I'm trying to recover on my own. Given my history, and everything." Leda hated bringing up rehab, but she was starting to feel cornered and didn't know what else to say.

Vanderstein nodded with something that seemed like respect. "I understand. But it's a big year for you, with college on the horizon, and I don't want this . . . situation to adversely affect your academics."

It's more than a situation, Leda thought bitterly.

"According to your room comp, you aren't sleeping well. I'm growing concerned," Vanderstein added.

"Since when are you monitoring my room comp?" Leda cried out, momentarily forgetting her calm, unfazed tone.

The doctor had the grace to look embarrassed. "Just your sleep records," he said quickly. "Your parents signed off on it—I thought they had informed you . . ."

Leda nodded curtly. She'd deal with her parents later. Just

because she was still a minor didn't mean they could keep invading her privacy. "I promise, I'm fine."

Vanderstein was silent again. Leda waited. What else could he do, authorize her toilet to start tracking her urine the way the ones in rehab did? Well, he was welcome to it; he wouldn't find a damned thing.

The doctor tapped a dispenser in the wall, and it spit out two small pills. They were a cheerful pink—the color of children's toys, or Leda's favorite cherry ice whip. "This is an over-the-counter sleeping pill, lowest dose. Why don't you try it tonight, if you can't fall asleep?" He frowned, probably taking in the hollow circles around her eyes, the sharp angles of her face, even thinner than usual.

He was right, of course. Leda *wasn't* sleeping well. She dreaded falling asleep, tried to stay awake as long as she could, because she knew the horrific nightmares that awaited her. Whenever she did drift off, she woke almost instantly in a cold sweat, tormented by memories of that night—of what she'd hidden from everyone—

"Sure." She snatched the pills and shoved them into her bag.

"I'd love for you to consider some of our other options—our light-recognition treatment, or perhaps trauma re-immersion therapy."

"I highly doubt reliving the trauma will help, given what my trauma was," Leda snapped. She'd never bought into the theory that reliving your painful moments in virtual reality would help you move past them. And she didn't exactly want any machines creeping into her brain right now, in case they could somehow read the memory that lay buried there.

"What about your Dreamweaver?" the doctor persisted. "We could preload it with a few trigger memories of that night and see how your subconscious responds. You know that dreams are simply your deep brain matter making sense of everything that has happened to you, both joyful and painful . . ."

He was saying something else, calling dreams the brain's "safe space," but Leda was no longer listening. She'd flashed to a memory of Eris in ninth grade, bragging that she'd broken through the Dreamweaver's parental controls to access the full suite of "adult content" dreams. "There's even a celebrity setting," Eris had announced to her rapt audience, with a knowing smirk. Leda remembered how inadequate she'd felt, hearing that Eris was immersed in steamy dreams about holo-stars while Leda couldn't even *imagine* sex.

She stood up abruptly. "We need to end this session early. I just remembered something I have to go take care of. See you next time."

She quickly stepped out the frosted flexiglass door of the Lyons Clinic, perched high on the east side of the 833rd floor, just as her eartennas began to chime a loud, brassy ringtone. Her mom. She shook her head to decline the incoming ping. Ilara would want to hear how the session had gone, would check that she was on her way home for dinner. But Leda wasn't ready for that kind of forced, upbeat normalcy right now. She needed a moment to herself, to quiet the thoughts and regrets chasing one another in a wild tumult through her head.

She stepped onto the local C lift and disembarked a few stops upTower. Soon she was standing before an enormous stone archway, which had been transported stone by stone from some old British university, carved with enormous block letters that read THE BERKELEY SCHOOL.

Leda breathed a sigh of relief as she walked through the arch and her contacts automatically shut off. Before Eris's death, she'd never realized how grateful she might feel for her high school's tech-net.

Her footsteps echoed in the silent halls. It was sort of eerie here at night, everything cast in dim, bluish-gray shadows. She moved faster, past the lily pond and athletic complex, all the way to the blue door at the edge of campus. Normally this room was locked after hours, but Leda had schoolwide access thanks to her position on student council. She stepped forward, letting the security system register her retinas, and the door swung obediently inward.

She hadn't been in the Observatory since her astronomy elective last spring. Yet it looked exactly as she remembered: a vast circular room lined with telescopes, high-resolution screens, and cluttered data processors Leda had never learned to use. A geodesic dome soared overhead. And in the center of the floor lay the pièce de résistance: a glittering patch of night.

The Observatory was one of the few places in the Tower that protruded out *past* the floor below it. Leda had never understood how the school had gotten the zoning permits for it, but she was glad now that they had, because it meant they could build the Oval Eye: a concave oval in the floor, about three meters long and two meters wide, made of triple-reinforced flexiglass. A glimpse of how high they really were, up here near the top of the Tower.

Leda edged closer to the Oval Eye. It was dark down there, nothing but shadows, and a few stray lights bobbing in what she thought were the public gardens on the fiftieth floor. *What the hell*, she thought wildly, and stepped out onto the flexiglass.

This sort of behavior was definitely off-limits, but Leda knew the structure would support her. She glanced down. Between her ballet flats was nothing but empty air, the impossible, endless space between her and the laminous darkness far below. *This is what Eris saw when I pushed her*, Leda thought, and despised herself.

She sank down, not caring that there was nothing protecting her from a two-mile fall except a few layers of fused carbon.

Pulling her knees to her chest, she lowered her forehead and closed her eyes.

A shaft of light sliced into the room. Leda's head shot up in panic. No one else had access to the Observatory except the rest of the student council, and the astronomy professors. What would she say to explain herself?

"Leda?"

Her heart sank as she realized who it was. "What are you doing here, Avery?"

"Same thing as you, I guess."

Leda felt caught off guard. She hadn't been alone with Avery since that night—when Leda confronted Avery about being with Atlas, and Avery led her up onto the roof, and everything spun violently out of control. She wanted desperately to say something, but her mind had strangely frozen. What *could* she say, with all the secrets she and Avery had made together, buried together?

After a moment, Leda was shocked to hear footsteps approaching, as Avery walked over to sit on the opposite edge of the Oval.

"How did you get in?" she couldn't help asking. She wondered if Avery was still talking to Watt, the lower-floor hacker who'd helped Leda find out Avery's secret in the first place— Leda hadn't spoken to him since that night, either. But with the quantum computer he was hiding, Watt could hack basically anything.

Avery shrugged. "I asked the principal if I could have access to this room. It helps me, being here."

Of course, Leda thought bitterly, she should have known it was as simple as that. Nothing was off-limits to the perfect Avery Fuller.

"I miss her too, you know," Avery said quietly.

Leda looked down into the silent vastness of the night, to protect herself from what she saw in Avery's eyes.

"What happened that night, Leda?" Avery whispered. "What were you *on*?"

Leda thought of all the various pills she'd popped that day, as she'd sunk ever deeper into a hot, angry maelstrom of regret. "It was a rough day for me. I learned the truth about a lot of people that day—people I had trusted. People who *used* me," she said at last, and was perversely pleased to see Avery wince.

"I'm sorry," Avery told her. "But, Leda, please. Talk to me."

More than anything, Leda wanted to tell Avery all of it: how Leda had caught her cheating scumbag of a father having an affair with Eris; and how awful she'd felt, realizing that Atlas had only ever slept with her in a fucked-up attempt to forget Avery. How she'd had to drug Watt to uncover that particular grain of truth.

But the thing about the truth was that once you learned it, it became impossible to unlearn. No matter how many pills Leda popped, it was still there, lurking in the corners of her mind like an unwanted guest. There weren't enough pills in the world to make it go away. So Leda had confronted Avery—screamed at her atop the roof, without fully knowing what she was saying; feeling disoriented and dizzy in the oxygen-thin air. Then Eris had come up the stairs, and told Leda she was *sorry*, as if a fucking apology would fix the damage she'd done to Leda's family. Why had Eris kept walking toward her even when Leda told her to stop? It wasn't Leda's fault that she'd tried to push Eris away.

She had just pushed too hard.

All Leda wanted now was to confess everything to her best friend, to let herself cry about it like a child.

But stubborn, sticky pride muffled the words in her throat, kept her eyes narrowed and her head held high. "You wouldn't understand," she said wearily. What did it matter anyway? Eris was already gone.

"Then help me understand. We don't have to be this way,

Leda—threatening each other like this. Why won't you just tell everyone it was an accident? I know you never meant to hurt her."

They were the same words she'd thought to herself so many times, yet hearing them spoken by Avery wakened a cold panic that grasped at Leda like a fist.

Avery didn't *get* it, because everything came so easily to her. But Leda knew what would happen if she tried to tell the truth. There would probably be an investigation, and a trial, all made worse by the fact that Leda had tried to cover it up—and the fact that Eris had been sleeping with Leda's dad would inevitably come to light. It would put Leda's family, her *mom*, through hell; and Leda wasn't stupid. She knew that looked like a damned convincing motive for pushing Eris to her death.

What right did Avery think she had, anyway, gliding in here and granting absolution like some kind of goddess?

"Don't you dare tell anyone. If you tell, I swear you'll be sorry." The threat fell angrily into the silence. It seemed to Leda that the room had grown several degrees colder.

She scrambled to her feet, suddenly desperate to leave. As she stepped from the Oval Eye onto the carpet, Leda felt something fall out of her bag. The two bright pink sleeping pills.

"Glad to see some things haven't changed." Avery's voice was utterly flat.

Leda didn't bother telling her how wrong she was. Avery would always see the world the way she wanted to.

At the doorway she paused to glance back. Avery had slid to kneel in the middle of the Oval Eye, her hands pressed against the flexiglass surface, her gaze focused on some point far below. There was something morbid and futile about it, as if she were kneeling there in prayer, trying to bring Eris back to life.

It took Leda a moment to realize that Avery was crying. She had to be the only girl in the world who somehow became *more* beautiful when she cried; her eyes turning an even brighter blue, the tears on her cheeks magnifying the startling perfection of her face. And just like that, Leda remembered all the reasons she resented Avery.

She turned away, leaving her former best friend to weep alone on a tiny fragment of sky.

CALLIOPE

THE GIRL STUDIED her reflection in the floor-length smart-mirrors that lined the walls, lifting her mouth in a narrow red smile of approval. She wore a navy romper that was at least three years out of fashion, but deliberately so; she loved watching the other women in the hotel shoot envious glances toward her long, tanned legs. The girl tossed her hair, knowing the warm gold of her earrings brought out her caramel highlights, and fluttered her false lashes—not the implanted kind, but real organic ones; grown from her own eyelids after a long, and painful, genetic repair procedure in Switzerland.

It all exuded a tousled, effortless, glamorous sort of sexiness. *Very Calliope Brown*, the girl thought, with a frisson of pleasure.

"I'm Elise on this one. You?" her mom asked, as if reading her mind. She had dark blond hair and artificially smooth, creamy skin, making her seem ageless. No one who saw the pair of them was ever quite sure whether she was the mother or the more experienced older sister.

"I was thinking Calliope." The girl shrugged into the name as if into an old, comfortable sweater. Calliope Brown had always been one of her favorite aliases. And it felt somehow fitting for New York.

Her mom nodded. "I do love that one, even if it's always impossible to remember. It sounds like it's got . . . spunk."

"You could call me Callie," Calliope offered, and her mom nodded absently, though they both knew she would just call Calliope by endearments. She'd said the wrong alias once, and it ruined everything. She'd been paranoid about making the same mistake ever since.

Calliope glanced around the expensive hotel, taking in its plush couches, lit with gold and blue strands that matched the hue of the sky; clumps of businesspeople muttering verbal commands to their contact lenses; the telltale shimmer in the corner that meant a security cam was watching. She stifled an urge to wink at it.

Without warning, the toe of her shoe caught on something, and Calliope crashed violently to the ground. She landed on one hip, barely catching herself on her wrists, feeling the skin of her palms burn a little with the impact.

"Oh my god!" Elise's legs folded beneath her as she knelt beside her daughter.

Calliope let out a moan, which wasn't difficult given how much actual pain she was in. Her head pounded angrily. She wondered if the heels of her stilettos were totally scuffed.

Her mom gave her a shake and she moaned harder, tears welling in her eyes.

"Is she okay?" It was a boy's voice. Calliope dared tilt her head enough to peer at him through half-lidded eyes. He had to be a front-desk attendant, with his clean-shaven face and the bright blue name-holo on his chest. Calliope had been to enough five-star hotels to know that the important people didn't advertise their names.

Her pain was already subsiding, but still, Calliope couldn't resist moaning a little louder and pulling one knee up to her chest, just to show off her legs. She was gratified by the mingled flash of attraction and confusion—almost panic—that darted across the boy's face.

"Of course she's not okay! Where's your manager?" Elise snapped. Calliope stayed quiet. She liked letting her mom do the talking, when they were first laying the groundwork; and anyway, she was supposed to be injured.

"I'm s-sorry, I'll call him . . ." the boy stammered. Calliope gave a little whimper for good measure, though it wasn't necessary. She could feel the attention of everyone in the lobby shifting toward them, a crowd beginning to gather. Nervousness clung to the front desk boy like a bad perfume.

"I'm Oscar, the manager. What happened here?" An overweight man in a simple dark suit trotted over. Calliope noted with delight that his shoes looked expensive.

"What's going on is that my daughter fell in *your* lobby. Because of that spilled drink!" Elise pointed to a puddle on the floor, complete with a lost-looking lime wedge. "Don't you invest in a *maid* service here?"

"My sincerest apologies. I can assure you nothing like this has ever happened before, Mrs. . . . ?"

"Ms. Brown," Elise sniffed. "My daughter and I *had* planned on staying here for a week, but I'm no longer sure we want to." She bent down a little lower. "Can you move, honey?"

That was her cue. "It really hurts." Calliope gasped, shaking her head. A single tear ran down her cheek, ruining her otherwise perfectly made-up face. She heard the crowd murmur in sympathy.

"Let me take care of everything," Oscar pleaded, turning bright red with anxiety. "I insist. Your room, of course, is complimentary."

———————

Fifteen minutes later, Calliope and her mom were firmly ensconced in a corner suite. Calliope stayed in bed—her ankle propped on a tiny triangle of pillows—holding perfectly still as the bellman unloaded their bags. She kept her eyes closed even after she heard the front door shut behind him, waiting till her mom's footsteps turned back toward her bedroom. "All clear now, sweetie," Elise called out.

She stood up in a fluid motion, letting the tower of pillows tumble to the ground. "Seriously, Mom? You tripped me without warning?"

"I'm sorry, but you know you've always been terrible at a fake fall. Your instincts for self-preservation are simply too strong," Elise replied from the closet, where she was already sorting her vast array of gowns in their color-coded transport bags. "How can I make it up to you?"

"Cheesecake would be a good start." Calliope reached past her mom for the fluffy white robe that hung on the door, emblazoned with a blue *N* and a tiny image of a cloud on the front pocket. She pulled it around her, letting the threads of the tie instantly weave themselves shut.

"How about cheesecake *and* wine?" Elise made a few brisk motions with her hands to call up holographic images of the room service menu, pointing at various screens to order salmon, cheesecake, a bottle of Sancerre. The wine popped into their room in a matter of seconds, propelled by the hotel's temperature-controlled airtube system. "I love you, sweetie. Sorry again for flinging you on your face."

"I know. It's just the cost of doing business," Calliope conceded with a shrug.

Her mom poured them two glasses and clinked hers to Calliope's. "Here's to this time."

"Here's to this time," Calliope echoed with a smile, as the words sent a familiar shiver of excitement up her spine. It was the same phrase she and her mom always used when they arrived somewhere new. And there was nothing Calliope loved more than starting somewhere new.

She headed into the living room, to the curved flexiglass windows that lined the corner of the building, with dramatic views over Brooklyn and the dark ribbon of the East River. A few shadows that must have been boats still danced across its surface. Evening had settled over the city, softening the edges of it all. Scattered flecks of light blinked like forgotten stars.

"So this is New York," Calliope mused aloud. After years of traipsing the world with her mom, standing at similar windows in so many luxury hotels and looking out over so many cities—the neon grid of Tokyo; the cheerful and vibrant disorder of Rio; the domed skyscrapers of Mumbai, gleaming like bones in the moonlight—she had come to New York at last.

New York, the first of the great supertowers, the original sky city. Already Calliope felt a burst of tenderness toward it.

"Gorgeous view," Elise said, coming to join her. "It almost reminds me of the one from London Bridge."

Calliope stopped rubbing her eyes, which were still a bit itchy from the latest retinal transfer, and glanced sharply at her mom. They rarely spoke of their old life, before. Yet Elise didn't pursue the subject. She sipped her wine, her eyes fixed somewhere on the horizon.

Elise was so beautiful, Calliope thought. But there was something hard and a little bit plasticky about her beauty now: the result of the various surges she'd had to change her appearance and go unrecognized each time they moved somewhere new. *I'm doing this for us*, she always told Calliope, *and for you, so you don't have to. At least not yet.* She never made Calliope play more than a supporting role in any of her cons.

For the past seven years, ever since they'd left London, Calliope and her mom had moved constantly from place to place. They never stayed anywhere long enough to get caught. The pattern was the same in each city: They would trick their way into the most expensive hotel in the most expensive neighborhood, and scout the scene for a few days. Then Elise would pick her mark— someone with too much money for his or her own good, and just enough foolishness to believe whatever story Elise decided to tell. By the time the mark realized what had happened, Elise and Calliope were always long gone.

Calliope knew that some people would call the pair of them cheats, or con artists, or swindlers. She preferred to think of them as very clever, very charming women who'd figured out how to level the playing field. After all, as Calliope's mom always said, rich people get free things all the time. Why shouldn't they, too?

"Before I forget, this is for you. I just uploaded it with the name Calliope Ellerson Brown. That's what you wanted, right?" Her mom handed her a shining new wrist computer.

Here lies Gemma Newberry, beloved thief, Calliope thought in delight, burying her most recent alias with a silent flourish. *She was as shameless as she was beautiful.*

She had a terribly morbid habit of composing epitaphs each time she set aside an identity, though she never shared them with her mom. She had a feeling that Elise wouldn't find them quite so amusing.

Calliope tapped at the new wrist computer, pulling up her list of contacts—empty, as usual—and noticed to her surprise that there wasn't a school registration listed. "You're not making me go to high school for this one?"

Elise shrugged. "You're eighteen. Do you want to keep going to school?"

Calliope hesitated. She'd gone to school so many times, playing whatever role their particular scheme cast her in—a long-lost heiress, or a victim of some conspiracy, or occasionally just as Elise's daughter, when Elise needed a daughter to seem attractive to some victim. She'd attended a preppy British boarding school and a French convent and a pristine public school in Singapore, and had rolled her eyes in sheer boredom at each one.

Which was how Calliope had ended up running a few cons of her own. They were never as big as Elise's cons, which netted their real payout; but Calliope liked to do something on the side if she saw an opportunity. Elise was fine with it, as long as Calliope's projects didn't impede her ability to help out her mom whenever she was called upon. "It's good for you to get some practice," Elise always said, and let Calliope keep everything she earned herself—which supplemented her wardrobe quite nicely.

Usually Calliope tried to gain the interest of a wealthy teenager, then conned him into buying her a necklace, or a new handbag, or the latest Robbie Lim suede boots. On a few rare occasions she'd managed to get bitbanc payments—not gifts—by pretending to be in serious trouble, or by finding out people's secrets and blackmailing them. Calliope had learned through the years that rich people did a lot of things they would rather keep buried.

She briefly considered going to high school, doing the same thing as usual, but she quickly dismissed the idea. This time, she would go bigger.

Oh, there were so many ways to hook a mark—the "accidental" run-in, the sidelong glance, the nuanced smile, the flirtation, the confrontation, the accident—and Calliope was an expert in all of them. She'd closed out every con she'd ever started.

Except Travis. The one mark who'd ever left Calliope, rather than the other way around. She'd never figured out why, and it still nettled her, just a little.

But he was just one person, and there were millions here. Calliope thought of all the crowds she'd seen earlier, streaming in and out of elevators, rushing home or to work or to school. All of them preoccupied with their own small worries, clutching at their impossible dreams.

None of them even knew she existed, and if they did know, they wouldn't care. But that was what made this game fun: because Calliope was about to make one of them care, very much. She felt a bright, glorious, reckless rush of anticipation.

She couldn't wait to find her next mark.

AVERY

AVERY FULLER WRAPPED her arms tighter around herself. The wind tore at her hair, yanking it into an unruly blond tangle, whipping the folds of her dress around her like a banner. A few droplets of rain began to fall. They stung lightly where they touched her bare skin.

But Avery wasn't ready to leave the roof. This was her secret place, where she retreated when all the furious lights and sounds down there, in the rest of the city, became too much to bear.

She looked out to the hazy purple of the horizon, which stretched into a deep fathomless black overhead. She loved the way she felt up here, aloof and alone and safe with her secrets. *It's not safe*, a nagging feeling told her, as a pair of footsteps sounded. Avery turned around, nervous—and broke into a smile when she saw that it was Atlas.

But the trapdoor flung open again and suddenly Leda was there, her face suffused with anger. She looked thin and drawn and dangerous. She wore her very skin as if it were armor.

"What do you want, Leda?" Avery asked warily, though she didn't really need to ask; she knew what Leda wanted. She wanted to break her and Atlas apart, and Atlas was the one thing Avery would never, ever give up. She took a step in front of him as if to protect him.

Leda caught the gesture. "How *dare* you," she spat, and reached out to shove Avery—

Avery's stomach lurched, her arms wheeling as she tried desperately to cling to something, but it was all too far away, even Atlas, and the world had devolved into a blur of color and sound and screaming, the ground hurtling ever faster toward her—

She sat up abruptly, a cold sheen of sweat on her brow. It took her a moment to recognize the dim bulkiness of her surroundings as the furniture in Atlas's bedroom.

"Aves?" Atlas murmured. "You okay?"

She curled her knees to her chest, trying to slow the erratic beating of her heart. "Just a nightmare," she told him.

Atlas pulled her close and wrapped his arms tightly around her from behind, so that she was safe in the warm circle of his embrace. "Do you want to talk about it?"

Avery *did* want to talk about it, except she couldn't. So she turned around to silence him with a kiss.

She'd been sneaking over to Atlas's room every night since Eris died. She knew she was playing with fire. But being with the boy she loved—talking to him, kissing him, just inhaling his presence—was the only thing that kept Avery from spinning off the edge lately.

And even here, with Atlas, she wasn't wholly safe from herself. She hated the web of secrets that kept tightening around her, driving an invisible wedge between them, though Atlas had no idea.

He didn't know about the delicate balancing act Avery now found herself in with Leda. A secret for a secret. Leda knew about them, and the only reason she hadn't blasted it to the world was that Avery had seen her push Eris, up on the roof that night. Now Avery was hiding the truth about Eris's death under threat from Leda.

She couldn't bring herself to tell Atlas about it all. The knowledge would only hurt him, and the truth was, Avery didn't want him to learn what had really happened that night. If he knew what she'd done, he might not look at her this way anymore—with such blinding love and devotion.

She wrapped her fingers tighter in the curls at the base of Atlas's neck, wanting to stop time, to disappear into this moment and live in it forever.

When Atlas finally pulled away, she felt his smile, even if she couldn't see it. "No scary dreams anymore. Not while I'm here. I'll keep them away, I promise."

"I dreamed that I lost you," she blurted out, a note of trepidation threading through her voice. Now that they were together, against all odds, losing Atlas was her greatest fear.

"Avery." He put a finger under her chin and gently lifted it, so that she was looking into his eyes. "I love you. I'm not going anywhere."

"I know," she replied, and she knew that he meant it, but there were so many obstacles in their path, so many forces stacked against them, that at times it all felt insurmountable.

She lay back down in the soft, warm space next to his body, but her thoughts were still scattered. She felt like she was coiled too tightly and couldn't be unwound.

"Do you ever wish another family had adopted you?" she whispered, voicing a thought she'd had countless times. If he'd ended up with some other family, if some other boy had grown up as her adopted brother, then Atlas wouldn't be forbidden. She wondered what it would have been like, meeting him in school, or at some party; bringing him home to meet the Fullers.

It would all be so much easier.

"Of course not," Atlas said, startling her with the vehemence of his tone. "Aves, if I'd been adopted by a different family I might never have met you."

"Maybe . . ." She trailed off, but she couldn't help thinking that she and Atlas were inevitable. The universe would have conspired for them to meet, some way or another, pulling them together with a gravitational force that was all their own.

"Maybe," Atlas conceded. "But that's not a risk I'm willing to take. You're the most important thing in the world to me. The day your parents brought me home—the day I first met you—was the second-best day of my life."

"Oh really? And what was the best day?" she asked with a smile.

She expected Atlas to say that the best day was when they confessed their love for each other. But he surprised her. "Today," he said simply. "Which will only last until tomorrow, and then tomorrow will be the best day. Because every day with you is better than the one before."

He leaned over to kiss her lightly, just as a knock sounded on the door.

"Atlas?"

For a terrible instant, every cell in Avery's body was frozen. She looked up at Atlas and saw her own terror reflected on his handsome face.

His door was locked, but here—like everywhere in the apartment—Mr. and Mrs. Fuller had the ability to override.

"One second, Dad," Atlas called out, a little too loudly.

Avery stumbled out of bed, wearing her ivory satin shorts and a bra, and stumbled breathlessly toward Atlas's closet. Her bare feet nearly tripped over a shoe as she ran.

She'd just managed to pull the door shut behind her when

Pierson Fuller strode into his adopted son's room. The overhead lights flicked on with his steps.

"Everything okay in here?" Did she hear a note of suspicion in her dad's voice, or was she imagining it?

"What's going on, Dad?" Typical Atlas, answering a question with a question. But it was a good deflective technique.

"I just heard back from Jean-Pierre LaClos, in the Paris office," Avery's dad said slowly. "It looks like the French might finally let us build something next to that antique eyesore of theirs." His form was just visible through the slats of the closet door. Avery stayed utterly still, pressing back into a gray wool coat, her arms crossed over her chest. Her heart was pounding so erratically she felt certain her dad would hear it.

Atlas's closet was much smaller than hers. There was nowhere to hide, if Pierson came to open the door. There was no possible explanation for why she would be here, wearing a bra and pajama shorts in Atlas's room, except, of course, for the real reason.

Out there in the bedroom, her pink shirt lay on the floor like a glaring searchlight.

"Okay," Atlas replied, and Avery heard the unspoken query. Why was their dad coming over in the middle of the night, for something that didn't sound particularly urgent?

After what was surely too long a silence, Pierson cleared his throat. "You'll have to come early to the development meeting tomorrow. We're going to need to do a full analysis of their streets and waterways, to start prepping."

"I'll be there," Atlas said tersely. He was standing directly on top of the shirt, trying to discreetly cover it with one of his feet. Avery willed her dad not to notice the movement.

"Sounds good." A moment later Avery heard the door to her brother's room click shut.

She leaned back and slid helplessly down the wall to a seated position. It felt like tiny needles were prickling all over her skin, like that time she'd been vitamin-checked at the doctor, except laced with adrenaline. She felt restless and reckless and strangely exhilarated, as if she'd tripped into quicksand and somehow emerged on the other side unharmed.

Atlas flung open the closet. "You okay, Aves?"

The closet lights turned on as he opened the doors; but for an impossibly brief instant, Avery was in the dark while Atlas seemed illuminated from behind—light streaming around him, gilding the edges of his form, making him seem almost other-worldly. It seemed suddenly impossible that he was real, and here, and hers.

And in truth, it *was* impossible. Everything about their relationship kept proving impossible at every turn, yet somehow they had willed it into being.

"I'm fine." She stood up to run her hands up his arms, settling them finally on his shoulders, but he took a reflexive step back and reached for her top, which still lay there on the ground.

"That was *not* good, Aves." Atlas held out the shirt, his features creased with worry.

"He didn't see me," Avery argued, but she knew that wasn't the point. Neither of them mentioned what their dad might have already seen: Avery's bedroom, on the other side of the apartment, her pristine white bedcovers rumpled but decidedly empty.

"We need to be more careful." Atlas sounded resigned.

Avery pulled her shirt over her head and looked up at him, her chest constricting at what he wasn't saying. "There's no more sleeping over, is there?" she asked, though she already knew the answer. They couldn't risk it, not anymore.

"No. Aves, you need to go."

"I will. Starting tomorrow," she promised, and pulled his mouth to hers. Now more than ever Avery knew how dangerous it was, but that just made each moment with Atlas infinitely more precious. She knew the risks. She knew they were walking a tightrope; that it would be so, so easy to fall.

If this was their last night sleeping over, then she was going to make it count.

She wished she could tell him everything, but instead she willed it all into her kisses: all the silent apologies, the confessions, the promises to love him forever. If she couldn't tell him aloud, there was no other way to tell him than this.

Clutching Atlas by the shoulders, she yanked him forward, and he followed her into the closet as the overhead light clicked back off.

WATT

WATZAHN BAKRADI LEANED back in the stiff auditorium chair, studying the chessboard currently displayed over his field of vision. *Move rook three spaces on the left diagonal.* The chessboard, projected in ghostly white and black onto the high-res contacts he constantly wore, changed accordingly.

That wasn't a wise move, pointed out Nadia, the quantum computer embedded in Watt's brain. Her knight immediately swooped forward to capture his king.

Watt stifled a groan, eliciting a few strange looks from the friends and classmates seated around him. He quickly fell silent and focused his gaze forward, to where a man in a crimson blazer stood at a podium, explaining the liberal arts offerings at Stringer West University. Watt tuned him out, just like he'd done all the other speakers at this mandatory assembly for the junior class. As if Watt had any intention of taking a history or English class again after high school was over.

You've been losing to me on average eleven minutes more quickly than normal. I believe it's a sign of distraction, Nadia added, flashing the words over his contacts like an incoming flicker.

You think? Watt thought testily. Watt had good reason to be distracted lately. He'd taken what seemed like an easy hacking job for a highlier girl named Leda, only to fall for her best friend, Avery. Until he'd learned that Avery was actually in love with Atlas, the very same person Leda had hired him to spy on. Then he'd accidentally delivered that secret straight to Leda, who was vicious and high and out for revenge. An innocent girl had ended up *dying* because of it. And Watt had just stood there and let it happen, let Leda walk away scot-free—because Leda knew about Nadia.

Watt wasn't sure how she'd figured it out, but somehow, she'd learned Watt's most dangerous secret. Anytime she wanted, Leda could turn Watt in for possession of an illegal quantum computer. Nadia, of course, would be destroyed forever. As for Watt, he'd go to jail for life. If he was lucky.

"Watt!" Nadia hissed, sending a zap of electric shock down his system. The Stringer representative was stepping down from the podium, replaced by a woman with shoulder-length chestnut hair and a serious expression. Vivian Marsh, the head of admissions at MIT.

"Few of you will apply to the Massachusetts Institute of Technology. Even fewer of you have the grades to get in," she said without preamble. "But for those of you who do, you'll find that our program rests upon three tenets: explore, experience, evolve."

Watt heard a soft pattering of fingers on tablets. He glanced around; some of the kids from his advanced math classes were typing furiously, hanging on Vivian's every word. His friend Cynthia—a pretty Japanese American girl who'd been in Watt's classes since practically kindergarten—was on the edge of her seat, her eyes lit up. Watt hadn't even known Cynthia was *interested* in MIT. Would he have to compete against her for the limited spots?

Watt hadn't really considered what he would do if he didn't get into MIT. For years he had dreamed of attending their extremely competitive microsystems engineering program. It was the research team in that very department that had invented the millichip, and entanglement software, and the room-temperature supermagnets that prevented quantum decoherence.

Watt had always assumed he would get in. Hell, he'd invented a quantum computer *on his own* at age fourteen; how could they *not* take him?

Except that he couldn't exactly talk about Nadia on his application. And as he looked around at the other students, Watt was forced to confront the very real possibility that he might not get in after all.

Should I ask a question? he thought anxiously to Nadia. Something, anything to get Vivian to notice him.

"This isn't a Q and A, Watt," Nadia observed.

Suddenly, far too quickly, the Stanford rep was stepping up and clearing his throat.

Without thinking, Watt shot to his feet, cursing as he stumbled down the row of seats. *Seriously?* Cynthia mouthed as he climbed over her, but Watt didn't care; he needed to talk to Vivian, and anyway, Stanford was at best his safety school.

He burst out the double doors at the back of the auditorium, ignoring the eyes that turned accusatorily toward him as he did, and began sprinting around the corner to the school exit.

"Ms. Marsh! Wait!"

She paused, one hand on the door, an eyebrow raised. Well, at the very least he would be memorable.

"I have to say, it's rare that I'm chased out of a school

auditorium. I'm not a celebrity, you know." Watt thought he heard an edge of wry amusement behind her tone, but couldn't be sure.

"I've been dreaming of going to MIT ever since I can remember, and I just . . . I really wanted to speak with you." *Your name!* Nadia prompted. "Watzahn Bakradi," he said quickly, holding out a hand. After a moment, Vivian shook it.

"Watzahn Bakradi," she repeated, her gaze turned inward, and Watt realized she was doing some kind of search of him, through her contacts. She blinked and focused on him again. "I see that you participated in our Young Engineers' Summer Program, on scholarship. And you weren't invited back."

Watt flinched. He knew exactly why he hadn't been asked to return—because one of his professors had caught him building an illegal quantum computer. She'd promised not to alert the police, but still, the mistake had cost him.

Nadia had pulled Vivian's CV onto his contacts, but it wasn't helpful; all it told Watt was that she'd grown up in Ohio and had studied psychology as an undergraduate.

He realized that he needed to answer her. "That program was four years ago. I've learned a lot since then, and I'd like the chance to prove it to you."

Vivian tilted her head, accepting a ping. "I'm speaking with a student," she said to whoever it was, probably an assistant. "I know, I know. Just one moment." As she tucked a strand of hair behind one ear, Watt caught a glimpse of an expensive platinum wrist computer. He wondered, suddenly, what she really thought of coming down to speak on the 240th floor, even if it was at a magnet school. No wonder she was in a hurry to leave.

"Mr. Bakradi, why is MIT your top choice?"

Nadia had pulled up the MIT guidelines and mission statement, but Watt didn't want to give a safe, canned answer.

"Microsystems engineering. I want to work with quants," he said boldly.

"Really." She looked him up and down, and Watt could tell her interest was piqued. "You know that program receives thousands of applications, but only selects two students per year."

"I know. It's still my top choice." *It's my only choice*, Watt thought, giving his best smile, the one he always used on girls when he and Derrick went out. He felt her softening toward him.

"Have you ever seen a quant? Do you know how unbelievably powerful they are?"

An untruth would be optimal here, Nadia told him, but Watt knew he could dance around the question.

"I know there are only a few left," he said instead. There were quants at NASA, of course, and the Pentagon; though Watt had a feeling there were far more illegal and unregistered quants—like Nadia—than the government would care to admit. "However, I think there should be more. There are so many places we need quantum computers."

Like in your brain? Watt, be sensible, Nadia urged, but he wasn't listening. "We need them now more than ever. We could revolutionize global farming to eradicate poverty, we could eliminate fatal accidents, we could terraform Mars—"

Watt's voice rang overly loud in his ears. He realized that Vivian was looking at him, her eyebrows raised, and he fell silent.

"You sound eerily like the science-fiction writers of the last century. I'm afraid that your opinion is no longer popular these days, Mr. Bakradi," she said at last.

Watt swallowed. "I just think the AI Incident of 2093 could have been avoided. The quant in question wasn't responsible. The security hadn't been properly set, there was an issue with his core programming . . ."

Back when quants were still legal, they'd all been given the same piece of fundamental core programming: that the quant could take no action to harm a human being, no matter what later commands were given to it.

"*His*?" Vivian repeated, and Watt realized belatedly that he'd used a gendered pronoun to describe a computer. He said nothing. After a moment, she sighed. "Well, I have to say, I look forward to personally reviewing your application."

She stepped through the door and into a waiting hover.

Nadia, what on earth do we do now? he thought, hoping she might have a brilliant solution. She usually picked up on situational details that he had missed.

There's only one thing you can do, Nadia replied, *and that is to write the best damn essay Vivian Marsh has ever seen.*

———

"There you are," Cynthia breathed, when Watt finally made his way to their locker. Technically, it was Cynthia's locker: Watt had been assigned one, but it was at the end of the arts hallway, and since he never went that direction, and never carried much stuff anyway, he'd gotten in the habit of using Cynthia's instead. Derrick, Watt's best friend, stood there too, worry creasing his forehead.

"Yeah, what happened? Cynthia says you skipped out early?"

"I went to try to talk to the MIT admissions officer, before she left."

"What did you tell her?" Cynthia asked, while Derrick shook his head, muttering something that sounded like "Should've thought of that."

Watt sighed. "I'm not sure it went well."

Cynthia glanced at Watt in sympathy. "I'm sorry."

"Hey, at least if I tank, it'll increase your chances of getting in," Watt replied, a little too flippant; but sarcasm had always been his defense mechanism.

Cynthia seemed hurt. "I would never think like that. Honestly, I was hoping that we would both end up at MIT. It could be nice, having a friendly face so far from home . . ."

"And then I'll come visit you both, and pester you constantly!" Derrick said, throwing his arms jovially around both their shoulders.

"That would be fun," Watt said cautiously, with a glance at Cynthia. He hadn't realized that they shared the same dream. She was right: it *would* be nice—walking across the leaf-strewn campus together on their way to class, working together in the engineering lab late at night, getting lunch in that enormous arched dining hall Watt had seen on the i-Net.

Then again, what would he and Cynthia do if only one of them got in?

It'll be fine, he told himself, but he couldn't help thinking that this was just one more thing in his life that could end in disaster.

He seemed to be collecting a lot of those lately.

RYLIN

THAT SAME AFTERNOON, Rylin Myers leaned forward on the checkout scanner, counting down the minutes till her shift at ArrowKid was over. She knew she was lucky to have this job—it paid more than her old one at the monorail, and the hours were better—but every moment here still felt like utter torture.

ArrowKid was a mass retailer of children's clothing in the mid-Manhattan Mall, up on the 500th floor. Until recently, Rylin had never set foot in a store like this. Arrow was the kind of place where midTower parents came in packs: wearing brightly colored exercise pants and dragging toddlers by the arm, strollers bobbing through the air alongside them, pulled by invisible magnetic tethers.

Rylin glanced around the store, which was a dizzying kaleidoscope of sound and color. Jarring pop music played on high volume through the speakers. The entire space smelled overwhelmingly of ArrowKid's sickly sweet self-cleaning cloth diapers. And crammed on every display were children's clothes, from pastel-colored baby onesies to dresses in a girls' size fourteen—all of it covered in arrows. Arrow-stitched baby jeans, arrow-printed T-shirts, even little blankets covered in tiny flashing arrows. It made Rylin's eyes hurt just to look at it.

"Hey, Ry, can you help out the customer in fitting room twelve? I'll man checkout for a while." Rylin's manager, a twenty-something named Aliah, sauntered over and flipped her close-cut dark hair. There was a bright purple arrow on her shirt, spinning slowly like the hands of a clock. Rylin had to look away to keep from feeling dizzy.

"Of course," Rylin said, trying not to be irritated that Aliah had started calling her by the nickname she reserved for close friends. She knew her manager just wanted to duck under the counter .and ping her new girlfriend when she thought the employees couldn't see.

She knocked on the door of fitting room twelve. "Just wanted to see how things were going in there," she said loudly. "Any sizes I can grab for you?"

The door swung open to reveal a tired-looking mom perched on a stool, her eyes glazed over as she probably checked something on her contacts. A pink-cheeked girl with a smattering of freckles stood before the mirror, turning back and forth as she studied her reflection with critical intensity. She was wearing a white dress that read BE DAZZLING and was covered in tiny crystal arrows. Her feet were encased in a pair of arrow-printed boots. They already belonged to the girl; if she'd picked them up today, Rylin would have seen a subtle holographic circle marking them as a new purchase, reminding her to ring them up. She thought of the times she and her best friend, Lux, used to shoplift on the lower floors—nothing big, just a couple of tubes of perfume and paintstick, or once a box of chocolate puffs. You couldn't get away with that up here.

"What do you think of this?" the girl asked, turning to let Rylin inspect her.

Rylin gave a watery smile. Her eyes darted to the mom—after all, she was the one who would pay—but the older woman seemed content to stay out of her daughter's shopping habits. "It looks great," Rylin said weakly.

"Would you wear it?" the little girl asked, her nose wrinkling adorably.

For some reason all Rylin could think of were the clothes she and Chrissa used to wear, some of which had been given by the Andertons, the upper-floor family she'd worked for as a maid. Rylin's favorite outfit at age six had been a swashbuckling pirate costume, complete with a feathered cap and a gold-hilted sword. She realized with a start that it had probably once belonged to Cord. Or Brice. The knowledge should have made her embarrassed, yet all she felt was a strange sense of loss. She hadn't spoken to Cord in a month—probably wouldn't even see him ever again.

It's for the best, she told herself, the way she always did when she thought of Cord. But it never seemed to work.

"Clearly not," the girl huffed, pulling the dress back up over her head. "You can go," she added pointedly, to Rylin.

Rylin realized belatedly that she'd made an error. She tried desperately to backtrack. "I'm sorry, I just lost track of my thoughts for a moment—"

"Forget it," the girl said in a single breath, slamming the door in Rylin's face. Moments later she and her mom were walking out of the store, leaving a pile of discarded clothes in the fitting room behind them.

"Ry." Aliah made a disappointed clucking noise as she walked over. "That girl was an easy sale. What happened?"

Don't Ry *me*, Rylin thought with a sudden burst of anger, but she knew better than to say anything; the whole reason she had this job was because of Aliah. She'd been applying for a waitress job at the café next door when she'd seen the shooting arrow display that spelled out HELP WANTED in the holographic window, and stepped inside on a whim. Aliah hadn't even cared that she had no experience in retail. She'd taken one look at Rylin and let out an excited squeal. "You can totally fit into our junior sizes. Your hips are, like, really narrow. And your feet are even small enough for some of the sandals!"

So here Rylin was, wearing the least offensive merchandise she could find in the store—a tank top and her own black jeans, not an arrow in sight—trying halfheartedly to sell clothes to mid-Tower kids. No wonder she sucked at it.

"I'm sorry. I'll do better next time," she promised.

"I hope so. You've been here almost a month and yet you've barely hit the sales minimum for a single week. I keep making excuses for you, saying it's a learning curve, but if things don't change soon . . ."

Rylin bit back a sigh. She couldn't afford to be fired, not again. "Got it."

Aliah's eyes flicked as she glanced at the time in the corner of her vision. Rylin had been surprised that most girls who worked here could afford to wear contacts, even if it was just the cheaper versions. Then again, this was an after-school job for most of them; they didn't have younger sisters to support, or a never-ending stack of bills to pay.

"Why don't you head home, get some rest," Aliah suggested gently. "I'll close up. That way you can start fresh tomorrow. 'kay?"

Rylin was too exhausted to argue. "That would be amazing," she said simply.

"And, Ry, why don't you take one of those"—Aliah gestured toward a display near the entrance, of printed T-shirts in a bright lemon yellow, covered in purple arrows—"to wear to work tomorrow? It might help you feel a little more . . . enthusiastic."

"Those are for ten-year-olds," Rylin couldn't help pointing out, eyeing the shirts with trepidation.

"Good thing you're *super* skinny," Aliah replied.

Rylin held her breath as she grabbed the shirt at the top of the stack. "Thanks," she said, flashing the biggest smile she could manage, but the older girl was already on a ping, her hand to her ear as she whispered something and laughed.

When Rylin waved her ID ring over the touch pad in the door and stepped inside, the comforting smells of batter and warm chocolate rose up to meet her. She felt an immediate stab of regret that Chrissa had beat her home yet again. Ever since Rylin had started working evenings, rather than the crack-of-dawn shift she'd had at the monorail, Chrissa had been handling more of the cooking and grocery shopping. Rylin felt guilty; those had always been her jobs. She wanted to be the one taking care of her fourteen-year-old sister, not the other way around.

"How was work?" Chrissa asked cheerfully. Her eyes drifted to Rylin's new T-shirt and she pursed her lips, suppressing a smile.

"Don't you dare say anything, or your birthday present this year will be nothing but a huge bag of arrow-printed underwear."

Chrissa tilted her head as if considering it. "How many arrows per pair are we talking, exactly?"

Rylin let out a laugh, then fell silent. "Honestly, at this rate, I'll be fired long before your birthday. Turns out I'm not the best salesperson." She came to where Chrissa stood at the cooktop, making the banana pancakes they both loved so much. "Breakfast for dinner? What's the occasion?" she asked, and reached into the bag of chocolate flakes to grab a handful.

Chrissa batted good-naturedly at Rylin's hand, then tossed the rest of the chocolate flakes into the mix and let the infra-powered spoon stir the batter. She looked up at her sister with evident excitement, jerking her chin toward an envelope on the table. "You got some news."

"What is that?" No one sent real paper envelopes anymore. The last one Rylin had gotten was a medical bill; and even that was in addition to her weekly reminder pop-ups with sound, and only because the payment was a year past due.

"Why don't you open it and see," Chrissa said mysteriously.

Rylin's first thought was that the envelope was heavy, which signified something momentous, though she wasn't sure whether to be excited or afraid. There was a familiar blue crest embossed on the back. THE BERKELEY SCHOOL, SINCE 2031, it read in gilded letters along the top. That was Cord's school, Rylin remembered, up in the 900s somewhere. Why would they be sending anything to *her*?

She slid a fingernail beneath the crisp edge of the envelope and pulled out its contents, dimly aware that Chrissa had come to stand next to her, but she was too focused on reading the strange and surprising letter to say anything.

Dear Miss Myers,

We are pleased to inform you that you have been selected as the inaugural recipient of the Eris Miranda Dodd-Radson Memorial Award to Berkeley Academy. The scholarship was established in memory of Eris, to reward unrecognized individual potential in underprivileged students. The value of your scholarship is detailed on the next page. Full tuition is covered, as well as a stipend for academic materials and other cost-of-living expenses . . .

Rylin blinked up at Chrissa. "What on earth is this?" she asked slowly.

Chrissa squealed and threw her arms around Rylin in a breathless hug. "I was hoping this was a 'yes' envelope, but I wasn't sure! And I didn't want to open it without you! *Rylin!*" She took a step back and looked at her sister, her entire being suffused with a happy glow. "You got a scholarship to *Berkeley*. That's the best private high school in New York—maybe even in the country."

"But I didn't apply," Rylin pointed out, to which Chrissa laughed.

"I applied on your behalf, of course. You aren't mad, are you?" she added, as if the thought had just now occurred to her.

"But—" A million questions rippled through Rylin's mind. She seized on one, randomly. "How did you even find out about this scholarship?"

Rylin had known about it, of course; she'd seen it mentioned on Eris's obituary video, which she'd watched dozens of times since that fateful night. The night her whole life turned upside down—when she went to an upTower party, way up on the thousandth floor, only to find the boy she loved with another girl. Then that girl had *died* in front of Rylin's eyes, pushed off the side of the Tower by one of her drugged-out friends, who proceeded to blackmail Rylin, forcing her to keep quiet about what had really happened.

"I saw the obit video pulled up on your tablet. You watched it a lot of times," Chrissa said, and now her voice was quiet and her eyes were searching Rylin's. "You met Eris when you were with Cord, right? Was she a friend of yours?"

"Something like that," Rylin said, because she didn't know how to tell Chrissa the truth—that Eris was someone she'd scarcely known, except that Rylin had seen her die.

"I'm sorry, about what happened to her." The timer beeped,

and Chrissa scooped the pancakes into two fat stacks, handing the plates to Rylin.

"But—" Rylin still didn't understand. "Why didn't you apply to the scholarship for yourself?" Of the two of them, Chrissa was the one with real promise: she made straight As in her honors classes, and would probably play volleyball at the college level. She was the one who deserved a fancy upper-school scholarship. Not Rylin, who hadn't even *been* in school the last few years.

"Because I don't need it like you do," Chrissa said intently. Rylin followed her to the table, carrying the plates of stacked pancakes. One of the legs of their table was broken clean off, causing it to wobble as she set the plates down.

"Between my grades and volleyball, I'm on track to get a college scholarship anyway. You, on the other hand, need this," Chrissa insisted. "Don't you see? Now you don't have to be the girl who dropped out of school to work a dead-end job, for my sake."

Rylin fell silent at the flicker of guilt in her sister's explanation. She'd never really considered what Chrissa had thought, when Rylin had dropped out of school to work full-time after their mom died. She'd never imagined that Chrissa might blame herself for Rylin's choice.

"Chrissa, you know it's not your fault that I took the job I did." And Rylin knew that she would do it all again in a heartbeat, to give her little sister the chance she deserved. Then she thought of another complication. "Anyway, I can't quit work now. We need the money."

Chrissa's smile was contagious. "Didn't you see what it said about a cost-of-living stipend? It's enough to keep us going, and if we get into a tight spot, we can always figure something out."

Rylin looked again, and saw that Chrissa was right. "But why would they pick *me*? I'm not even in school right now. There must have been so many applicants." Her eyes narrowed at Chrissa as she began to think through the odds. "What did you put on my application, anyway?"

Chrissa grinned. "I found an old essay of yours about working at a summer camp, and made some tweaks to it."

Two years before their mother died, Rylin had applied to be a junior counselor at an expensive summer camp. It was all the way in Maine—somewhere with a lake, or maybe it had been a river; the kind of place rich kids went to learn useless things like canoeing and archery and braiding friendship bracelets. For some reason, maybe because she'd seen too many holos about summer camp, Rylin had always fostered a secret desire to attend one. Of course they could never afford anything like that. But Rylin had hoped that maybe, if she worked there as a counselor, she would still have a version of the experience.

She'd gotten the job. Though it quickly became irrelevant, because her mom had gotten sick that year and nothing else mattered after that.

"I can't believe you found that," she said, shaking her head in amused wonder. She would never cease to be surprised by Chrissa's resourcefulness. "Though I still don't understand why they would pick me."

Chrissa shrugged. "Didn't you see the description? It's a weird, nontraditional scholarship, for 'creative-minded girls who would otherwise be overlooked.'"

"I'm not exactly creative-minded," Rylin argued.

Chrissa shook her head so violently that her ponytail whipped back and forth, a dark shadow behind her head. "Of course you are. Stop selling yourself short, or you'll never survive at that school."

Rylin didn't answer that. She still wasn't sure whether or not she was going.

After a moment Chrissa sighed. "I'm not surprised you were

friends with Eris. From the sound of this scholarship, she was really cool. I mean, she clearly wasn't like the other highliers, if this is how her family chose to honor her."

Suddenly Rylin's mind was alit with memories of that night—of breaking up with Cord, then trying to win him back, only to find him with Eris; of seeing Eris on the roof, yelling at the other girl, Leda, then watching in horror as Eris tumbled off the side of the Tower and into the cold night air. She shivered.

"You're going, right?" Chrissa asked, her voice hopeful.

Rylin thought of how it would feel, being at an expensive highlier school with a bunch of strangers who wouldn't give her the time of day. Not to mention Cord. She'd promised herself she would stay away from him. And then there was school itself—how would she handle being in a classroom again, learning and studying and taking tests, surrounded by a bunch of students who were probably a lot smarter than she was?

"Mom would want you to go, you know," Chrissa added, and just like that, Rylin's answer was clear.

She lifted her eyes to her sister's and smiled. "Yeah, I'll go." Maybe something good could finally come of that night. She owed it to herself, and to Chrissa, and her mom—hell, even to Eris—to try.

CALLIOPE

THE TWO WOMEN strode through the entrance to Bergdorf Goodman on the 880th floor, their four sharp heels making satisfying clicks on the polished marble. Neither of them paused at the sumptuously decorated lobby, its holiday-themed display holos dancing around the crystal chandeliers and jewel cases; tourists crying out whenever the reindeer swooped down toward their heads. Calliope didn't even glance in their direction as she followed Elise up the curved staircase. It had been a long time since she was impressed by something as prosaic as a holographic sleigh.

The designer floor upstairs was scattered with clumps of furniture, each of them partitioned by an invisible privacy barrier and equipped with a body-scanner. Real gowns were draped on mannequins in various corners, for nostalgia's sake. No one actually tried on anything here.

Elise flicked her eyes significantly at Calliope before heading toward the youngest, most junior-looking employee: Kyra Welch. They'd already preselected her online, for the simple reason that she'd worked at the store a grand total of three days.

Just a few meters away from the girl, Elise made a show of sinking onto a pale peach settee. She crossed one leg over the other and began scrolling through cocktail dresses on the screen before her. Calliope stood idly to one side and stifled a yawn. She wished she'd gotten one of those honey coffees from the hotel this morning. Or even a caffeine patch.

The salesgirl predictably hurried over. She had alabaster skin and a perky carrot-red ponytail. "Good afternoon, ladies. Did you have an appointment?"

"Where's Alamar?" Elise demanded, in her most dismissive tone.

"I'm so sorry—Alamar is off today," Kyra stammered, which of course Elise and Calliope had already known. The girl's eyes skimmed quickly over Elise's outfit, taking in the designer skirt and seven-carat stone on her finger, so high quality it was almost indistinguishable from a real diamond. Evidently she concluded that this was someone important, someone Alamar shouldn't have upset. "Perhaps one of our senior sales associates can—"

"I'm looking for a new cocktail dress. Something show-stopping," Elise talked over the younger woman, waving at the holographic display to project this season's designs onto a scan of her body. She flicked her wrist to scroll rapidly through the images, then held out her palm to pause at a plum-colored dress with an uneven hem. "Can I see this one, but shortened?"

Kyra's eyes unfocused, probably checking her schedule on her contacts. Calliope knew she was debating whether to abandon her restocking duties in favor of this new, most likely lucrative commission.

She also knew that at the end of the shopping spree, after the various dresses had been instantly woven and sewn by the super-looms hidden in the back of the store, Kyra would haltingly ask for an account number to charge it all to. "Alamar knows," Elise would say, with her *sorry but I can't be bothered* shrug. Then she would walk out of the store, her arms laden with bags, without a backward glance.

Technically, they could have paid for the dresses the normal way—they did have money squirreled away in a few different bancs all over the globe. Though at the rate they spent, it never seemed to last very long. And as Elise always said, why pay for something you can get for free? It was the motto they lived by.

Elise and Kyra dissolved into a discussion of silk panel-ing. Calliope looked up, already bored, and saw three girls her age crossing the store, wearing identical plaid skirts and white button-downs. A slow smile spread across her face. No matter what country they were in, private-school girls invariably made easy targets.

"Mom," she interrupted. Kyra stepped aside for a moment to give them some privacy, but it didn't matter; Calliope and her mom had long ago established a code for situations like this. "I just remembered an assignment that I need to go finish. For history class." History meant a group con. If she'd used biology class, it would have meant a romantic one—a seduction.

Elise's eyes lit on the trio of girls and flashed in instant under-standing. "Of course. I wouldn't want you to lose your place on the honor roll," she said wryly.

"Right. I do need to graduate with honors." Calliope kept a straight face as she turned away.

She muttered "nearby private high schools" under her breath as she moved toward the accessories section, where the girls seemed to be headed. It only took two search results before she found the right one; she could tell since the students on the homepage were wearing the same lame uniform. Bingo.

She stationed herself in the girls' path and began to studiously loiter: picking up various items, studying them as if actually considering them, then setting them down again. She was keeping an eye on the progress of the group, but still, she couldn't help relishing the feel of a cool leather belt or a slippery silk scarf in her hands.

When the girls were only a row away, Calliope stumbled forward, knocking a whole table of purses to the ground. They fell across the polished wood floor like pieces of spilled candy.

"Oh my god! I'm so sorry," Calliope muttered, in the posh British accent she and her mom had been using all week—not the cheap cockney one she'd grown up with, but a refined one she'd mastered after careful practice. She had purposefully tipped the table so that the clutches fell in the girls' direct path; forcing the trio to either step carefully through them or kneel down to help. Unsurprisingly, they did the latter. Rich girls never left something expensive on the ground, unless they'd been the one to toss it there.

"It's okay. No harm done," said one of the girls, a tall blonde who was far and away the most beautiful of the three. She had such an air of sophistication that on her, the ridiculous school uniform was transformed into something almost chic. She stood up at the same time as Calliope, setting the last little beaded clutch on the table.

"You all go to Berkeley?" Calliope asked, in that crucial instant before they started to walk away.

"Yeah. Wait, do you go there too?" asked one of the other girls. She frowned a little, as if wondering whether she'd seen Calliope before.

"Oh no," Calliope said breezily. "I recognized the uniforms

from the admissions tour. We're in town from London—staying at the Nuage—but we might move here for my mom's job. If we do, I'll be transferring schools." The lines rolled easily off her tongue; she'd spoken them many times before.

"That's exciting. What does your mom do?" The blonde spoke again; not pushy, but with a quiet, genuine interest. Her clear-eyed gaze was somehow disconcerting.

"She works in sales, for private clients," Calliope couldn't resist saying, with a deliberate vagueness. "So what do you think of Berkeley? You like it there?"

"I mean, it's school. It's not like it's fun," the third girl finally chimed in. She had tawny skin, and her dark hair was pulled into a chic fishtail braid. She quickly looked over Calliope's outfit, taking in her cream-colored knit dress and brown boots, and her eyes grew warmer in evident approval. "You would like it there, I think," she concluded.

Calliope hid a familiar flash of disdain at these empty-headed girls. They were so easily persuaded of anything, as long it fit within their narrow worldview. She couldn't wait to con something from them—shave off a little of the wealth they hadn't worked for and were clearly not entitled to at all.

"Nice to meet you. I'm Calliope Brown," she declared, holding out a hand laden with stacked enamel bangles and a fresh dove-gray manicolor. After a moment, the girl took it.

"My name is Risha, and this is Jess, and Avery," she told Calliope.

"We actually need to get going," the blond girl—Avery—said, with an apologetic smile. "We have appointments at the facial bar downstairs."

"No way!" Calliope lied, with a practiced laugh. "I have an appointment there in half an hour. Maybe I'll see you on your way out."

"You should just come now, with us. I bet they can take you early," Risha urged. She glanced quickly at Avery for confirmation, and Calliope didn't miss the slight nod of approval that Avery gave at the suggestion. So, Avery was the one who called all the shots. Calliope was hardly surprised.

She'd never been quite as good at faking friendship as she was a romantic attachment. Lust was so delightfully uncomplicated and straightforward, while female friendships were inevitably layered with conditions, and history, and unspoken rules of behavior. Still, Calliope was nothing if not a fast learner. She could already see that Risha would be the easiest of the three to win over, but Avery was the crucial one, so she focused her efforts on her.

"I'd love to come, if you don't mind," she admitted, smiling at each of them in turn, her eyes lingering the longest on Avery.

As they walked through the doors of Ava Beauty Lounge, Calliope took a deep breath, inhaling the glorious scents of lavender and peppermint and spa. Everything inside was done in shades of peach and cream, from the soft carpet underfoot to the delicate sconces hanging on the walls, casting pools of golden light on the girls' faces.

"Miss Fuller," said the store manager, snapping to instant attention. Calliope studied the other girl with markedly more interest. So, she was the type of person who got recognized at places like this. Was it for her beauty, or her money, or both? "I didn't realize you were a party of four today. I'll add another facialette station to your cluster."

He began to usher them all forward just as another girl walked out of the inner lounge and froze at the sight of Avery.

"Hi, Leda." Avery's voice was distinctly chilly.

The new arrival—a thin black girl with wide eyes and darting, nervous gestures—pulled herself up to her full height. It wasn't very tall. "Avery. Jess, Risha." Her eyes lit on Calliope, but she apparently decided it wasn't worth introducing herself. "Enjoy your facial," she said on her way out, managing to turn the innocuous phrase into something almost vindictive.

"Thanks, we will!" Calliope said cheerfully, delighting at the three horrified expressions that whirled toward her. But she didn't give a damn about these girls' intra-clique drama. She was here for a free facial, thank you very much.

Soon the four of them were seated at the gleaming white facial bar, clutching glasses of chilled grapefruit water. A bot wheeled over and handed them each a pink-and-white-stitched apron. "To keep the facial products from splattering onto your clothes," the facial attendant explained, in answer to Calliope's curious look.

"Oh, right. We wouldn't want the girls to ruin their fabulous uniforms," Calliope deadpanned, and was gratified to hear Avery laugh.

A row of lasers on the opposite wall turned on, aiming beams of focused photons toward the girls' faces. Calliope instinctively shut her eyes, though she knew the lasers were too precise to hurt her. She felt nothing but a slight tickle across her nerves as the laser skimmed over the surface of her skin, collecting data on her oil levels and pH balance and chemical composition.

"So," she asked Avery, who was sitting to her left, "what's the deal with that Leda girl?"

Avery seemed startled by the question. "She's a friend of ours," she said quickly.

"She didn't seem that friendly." The lasers began to flash more quickly, signaling that they were almost finished with their dermatological analysis.

"Well, she was a close friend of mine until recently," Avery amended.

"What happened? Was it about a boy?" It usually was, with girls like this.

Avery stiffened, though her face remained immobile as the laser traced across her poreless porcelain skin. Calliope wondered what they would even give her; she was so obviously already perfect.

"It's a long story," Avery answered, which was proof enough to Calliope that she was right. She felt a momentary stab of sympathy for Leda. That must suck, being the girl who had to compete with Avery.

A holographic menu popped up at Calliope's eye level, with treatment recommendations. Next to her, she heard the other girls chatting in low voices as they debated which add-ons to select: a soothing cucumber mask, a hydrogen infusion, a crushed-ruby scrub. Calliope checked the boxes for everything.

A steaming cocoon dropped down from the ceiling before each of them, and the girls leaned forward and closed their eyes.

"Avery," said the brunette girl—Jess, Calliope remembered. "Your parents' holiday party is still happening this year, right?"

Calliope's ears perked up a little at the mention of a party. She turned her head just slightly to the left, letting more of the steam hit the right side of her face, so that she could listen.

"Didn't you get the invitation?" Avery asked.

Jess seemed to quickly back down. "Yes, but I just thought, after everything that happened . . . Never mind."

Avery sighed, but she didn't sound angry, only regretful. "There's no way my dad would cancel. During the party, he's going to announce the completion of The Mirrors—that's what he named the Dubai Tower, since it has two sides that are mirror images."

Dubai Tower? Suddenly Calliope remembered what the sales associate had called Avery when they walked in, and the puzzle pieces clicked into place.

Fuller Investments was the company that had patented all the structural innovations needed to build towers this tall: the ultra-compounded steel supports, the earthquake shock protectors stuffed between every floor, the oxygenated air that was pumped throughout the higher floors to prevent altitude sickness. They had built the New York Tower, the first global supertower, almost twenty years ago.

Which meant that Avery Fuller was very wealthy indeed.

"That sounds like fun," Calliope chimed in. In her lap, she clenched one hand atop the other, then flipped them over again. She'd been to parties far more exclusive and incredible than this, she tried to remind herself: like the one at that club in Mumbai with the champagne bottle as big as a small car, or the mountain-side lodge in Tibet where they'd grown hallucinogenic tea. But all those parties faded in her memory—as they always did—when confronted by the specter of some other future party that Calliope wasn't invited to.

A puff of steam rose from the top of Avery's cocoon as she gave the answer Calliope had been hoping for. "If you're not busy, you should come."

"I'd love to," Calliope said, unable to keep the excitement from her voice. She heard Avery mutter under her breath, and an instant later the envelope icon in the top of her vision lit up as her contacts received the message. Calliope bit her lip to keep from smiling as she opened it.

Fuller Investments Annual Holiday Party, read the scrolling gold calligraphy, against a black starry background. *12/12/18. The Thousandth Floor.*

It was kind of badass, Calliope admitted to herself, that the only address they needed to write was their floor. Clearly they owned the whole thing.

The girls' chatter moved on, to something about a school

assignment, then a boy that Jess was dating. Calliope let her eyes flutter shut. She did love rich things, she thought with unadulterated pleasure, now that she got them for real—and usually on someone else's dime.

It hadn't always been like this. When she was younger, Calliope had known about these sorts of things, but never actually experienced them. She could look, but never touch. It was a particularly excruciating sort of torture.

It felt like a long time ago, now.

———————

She'd grown up in a tiny flat in one of the older, quieter neighborhoods of London, where none of the buildings stretched higher than thirty floors and people still grew real plants out on their balconies. Calliope never asked who her father was, because she honestly didn't care. It had always been Calliope and her mom, and she was fine with that.

Elise—she'd had a different name back then, her *real* name—had been the personal assistant to Mrs. Houghton, a stuffy rich woman with a pinched nose and watery eyes. She insisted on being called "Lady Houghton," claiming that she descended from an obscure branch of the now defunct royal family. Elise managed Mrs. Houghton's calendar, her correspondence, her closet: all the myriad details of her useless, gilded life.

Elise and Calliope's life felt so dull in contrast. Not that they could complain: their apartment should have been adequate, with its self-filling refrigerator and cleaning bots and a subscription to all the major holo channels. They even had windows in both bedrooms, and a decent closet. Yet Calliope quickly learned to see their life as something unforgivably drab, illuminated only by the occasional touches of glamour that her mom brought home from the Houghtons'.

"Look what I have," Elise would proclaim, her voice taut with excitement, each time she walked in the door with something new.

Calliope always hurried over, holding her breath as her mom unwrapped the package, wondering what it contained this time. An embroidered silk ball gown with sequins missing, which Mrs. Houghton had asked Elise to take back for repairs. Or a hand-painted china plate that was one of a kind, and could Elise please track down the artist and have her make another? Even jewelry, on occasion: a sapphire ring or a diamond choker that needed to be professionally cleaned.

Reverently, Calliope would reach out to touch the sumptuous fur shrug, or crystal wine decanter, or her absolute favorite, the supple Senreve shoulder bag in a shocking bright pink. She would look up into mother's eyes and see her own childlike longing reflected there, like a candle.

Always too soon for Calliope's taste, her mom would pack away the treasure with a sigh of regret, to take it to the repair shop or cleaners or back to the store for return. Calliope knew without being told that Elise wasn't even supposed to bring these things home at all—that she did so for Calliope's sake, so that Calliope could get a little glimpse at just how beautiful they were.

At least Calliope got the hand-me-downs. The Houghtons had a daughter named Justine, one year older than Calliope. For years, Elise had brought Justine's discarded clothing home to their flat, rather than taking it to the donation center as Mrs. Houghton instructed. Together Calliope and her mom would sort through the bags, exclaiming over the gossamer dresses and patterned stockings and coats with embroidered bows, tossed aside like used tissue because they were a season old.

When her mom worked late, Calliope would go to her friend Daera's apartment down the hall. They spent hours pretending they were princesses at afternoon high tea. They would put on

Justine's old dresses and sip cups of water at Daera's kitchen table, curling up their pinkies in that funny, fancy way, speaking in a butchered approximation of the upper-crust accent.

"It's my fault you have such a taste for expensive things," Elise said once, but Calliope didn't regret any of it. She would rather see a tiny sliver of that beautiful, charmed world than not know of its existence at all.

Everything came to a head one afternoon when Calliope was eleven. She'd had the day off from school, so Elise was forced to bring her to Mrs. Houghton's house while she worked. Calliope had firm instructions to stay in the kitchen and read quietly on her tablet—which she did, for almost a full hour. Until she heard the little beep of the house comp that meant Lady Houghton had left.

Calliope couldn't help it—she darted straight up the stairs into the Houghtons' bedroom. The door to Mrs. Houghton's closet was wide open. It was just *begging* to be explored.

Before Calliope could think twice she'd slipped inside, running her hands longingly over the gowns and sweaters and soft leather pants. She reached for that bright fuchsia Senreve purse and slung it over one shoulder, turning from side to side as she studied her reflection in the mirror, so excited that she didn't hear the second beep of the house comp. If only Daera were here to see this. "You will address me as 'Your Highness,' and bow when I approach," she said aloud to her reflection, fighting not to giggle.

"What do you think you're doing?" came a voice from the doorway.

It was Justine Houghton. Calliope started to explain, but Justine had already opened her mouth to let out a shrill, blood-curdling scream. *"Mom!"*

Mrs. Houghton materialized an instant later, accompanied

by Elise. Calliope winced under her mom's gaze, hating the way her expression flitted between recrimination and something else, something frighteningly close to guilt.

"I—I'm sorry," she stammered, though her fingers were still closed tight around the handle of the purse, as if she couldn't bear to release it. "I didn't mean any harm—it's just that your clothes are so beautiful, and I wanted to see them up close—"

"So you could get your grubby little hands all over them?" Mrs. Houghton reached for the Senreve bag, but for some perverse reason Calliope held it even tighter to her chest.

"And, Mom, look—she's wearing my dress! Though she doesn't look nearly as good in it as I did," Justine added, nastily.

Calliope glanced down and bit her lip. This was indeed one of Justine's old dresses, a white shift with distinctive black Xs and Os along the collar. It was true that it was a little long and shapeless on her, but they couldn't afford to tailor it. *Why do you care? You* gave *it away*, she wanted to say, resentment rising up in her, yet for some reason her throat had closed up.

Lady Houghton turned to Elise. "I thought I instructed you to donate Justine's used clothing to the poor," she said, her tone clipped and businesslike. "Are you, in fact, *poor*?"

Calliope would never forget the way her mom's shoulders stiffened at that remark. "It won't happen again. Say you're sorry, dear," she added to Calliope, gently prying the purse from her rigid hands and passing it over.

Some deep-rooted instinct of Calliope's rose up in protest, and she shook her head, mutinous.

That was when Lady Houghton raised her hand and slapped Calliope across the face so hard that her nose bled.

Calliope expected her mom to retaliate, but Elise just dragged her daughter home without another word. Calliope was silent and resentful at the time. She knew she shouldn't have been in the closet, but she still couldn't believe Lady Houghton had *struck* her, and that her mom hadn't done anything about it.

The next day Elise came home in a flurry of agitation. "Pack your bags. Now," she said, refusing to explain. When they got to the train station, Elise booked them two one-way tickets to Moscow and handed Calliope an ID chip with a new name. An unfamiliar pouch jangled at Elise's waist.

"What's that?" Calliope asked, curiosity getting the better of her.

Elise glanced around to check that no one was watching, then opened the drawstring of the bag. It was full of expensive jewelry that Calliope recognized as Mrs. Houghton's.

That was when Calliope realized her mom was a thief, and that they were on the run.

"We're never coming back, are we?" she'd asked, without a shred of regret. A sense of limitless adventure was unfurling in her eleven-year-old chest.

"That woman had it coming. After everything she did to me—after what she did to *you*—we deserve this," Elise said simply. She reached for her daughter's hand to give it a squeeze. "Don't worry. We're heading on an adventure, just the two of us."

And from that day on, it was indeed a glorious, nonstop adventure. The money from the Houghtons' jewelry eventually ran out, but by then it didn't matter, because Elise had figured out how to get more: she'd swindled a proposal from a gullible, wealthy older man. She'd realized that Mrs. Houghton had given her something even more valuable than jewelry—the voice, and mannerisms, and overall demeanor of someone entitled. Everywhere she went, people thought Elise was rich. Which meant that they gave her things without expecting her to pay, at least not right away.

The thing about rich people was that once they thought you were one of them, they became much less wary around you—and that made them easy targets.

Thus began the life Calliope and her mom had lived for the past seven years.

———————

"What flavor would you like for your facial cleanser?" a spa attendant asked, and Calliope blinked to awareness. The other girls were sitting up, their skin glowing. A warm, scented towel was curled around Calliope's neck.

She realized that her treatment included a custom face wash, which had been created during her treatment specifically for her.

"Dragonfruit," she declared, because its shocking red-pink was her favorite color. The technician deftly twisted open the jar, revealing a scentless white cream, and tossed in a red flavor pod before holding it up to a metallic wand on the wall. Moments later the jar of bright red face wash spun out of a chute, with a list of all the enzymes and organic ingredients that had been uniquely combined for Calliope's skin. A tiny cranberry sticker completed the package.

When they emerged into the gold-and-peach front room and the other girls started leaning toward the retinal scanner to pay, Calliope pulled the trick she always performed when shopping in groups. She hung back; dilating her pupils, muttering curse words under her breath.

"Is everything okay?" Avery asked, watching her.

"Actually, no. I can't log into my account." Calliope gave a few more pretend bitbanc commands, letting a note of agitation creep into her voice. "I don't know what's going on."

She waited until the gentleman from the front desk was pointedly clearing his throat, making it awkward for everyone, before turning to Avery. She knew her cheeks were bright pink with embarrassment—she'd long ago learned to blush on command— and her eyes were gleaming with a silent entreaty. But none of the girls made any offer to help.

A boy would have paid by now; though out of self-interest, not chivalry. This was precisely why Calliope preferred lust to friendship. *Fine*, she thought in irritation; she would just have to do this the direct way.

"Avery?" she asked, with what she hoped was the right amount of self-consciousness. "Would you mind covering my facial, just till I figure out what's going on with my account?"

"Oh. Sure." Avery nodded good-naturedly and leaned forward, blinking a second time into the retinal scanner to cover the exorbitant cost of Calliope's facial. Just as Calliope expected, she didn't even seem to register the long list of add-ons. She probably had no idea how much her *own* facial had cost.

"Thank you," Calliope began, but Avery waved away the gratitude.

"Don't worry about it. Besides, the Nuage is one of my favorite places. I know where to find you," Avery said lightly.

If only you knew. By the time Avery got around to collecting—if she ever even remembered to—Calliope and her mom would be long gone, living on a different continent under new names, no trace left of them in New York at all.

The many boys and girls who'd known Calliope these past few years, whose hearts she'd left carelessly strewn throughout the world, would have recognized her smirk. She felt sorry for Avery and Risha and Jess. They were headed back to their boring, routine lives, while Calliope's existence was anything but boring.

She followed the other girls out the door, dropping the jar of cleanser into her bag—the special-edition Senreve bag in bold fuchsia, of course—with a satisfying *clunk*.

RYLIN

THE FOLLOWING MONDAY, Rylin stood before the grandiose carved entrance to the Berkeley School, immobile with shock. This couldn't be her, Rylin Myers, wearing a collared shirt and pleated skirt, about to start at a preppy highlier private school. It felt like it was happening to another person, a bizarre series of images that someone else had dreamed.

She adjusted the strap of her tote bag over one shoulder, shifting her weight uncertainly. The world was brightening around her as the timed bulbs subtly adjusted their luminosity to indicate the lateness of the morning. Rylin had forgotten how much she loved the effect; one time she'd sat on Cord's doorstep as the sun rose outside, just watching the slow shift of the overhead lights. Down on the 32nd floor, the lights never shifted from their single fluorescent setting, unless one of the kids on her block threw something to smash out a bulb.

Well, it was now or never. She started toward the main office, following the highlighted yellow arrows on the school-issued official tablet she'd picked up last week. Unlike her normal MacBash tablet, this one worked within the boundaries of the tech-net that surrounded the school, though it could only carry out basic approved tasks, like checking her academic e-mail account or taking notes. And the tablets all shut down during exams, to prevent cheating. There was no hacking the tech-net, Rylin knew; though plenty of kids through the years had tried.

She tried not to stare as she moved through the hallways. This place looked the way she'd always imagined college campuses, with its wide, light-filled corridors and stone colonnades. Directional holos popped up each time she turned a corner. In a courtyard down the hall, palm trees waved in a simulated breeze. A few kids passed, all wearing the same uniform.

Of course, Rylin had seen the uniform before—in the laundry, back when she worked for Cord Anderton.

She had no idea what she would say when she saw him. Maybe she wouldn't see him, she thought with a dubious hope; maybe this was a big enough campus that she could avoid him for the next three semesters. But she had a feeling she wouldn't be that lucky.

"Rylin Myers. I'm here to meet with an academic adviser," she told the young man behind the desk, when she'd finally reached the main office. She still couldn't believe that this school even *had* a human academic adviser. DownTower, things like college recommendations and course assignments were distributed by an algorithm. These people must feel pretty full of themselves if they thought they could do a better job than a computer.

The man typed on a tablet. "Of course. The new scholarship student." He glanced up at her, an unreadable expression on his face. "You know that Eris Dodd-Radson was very beloved here at Berkeley. We all miss her."

It was an odd welcome, to bring up the person whose death had made her very presence here possible. Rylin wasn't sure how to reply, but the man didn't seem to expect an answer. "Have a seat. The adviser will see you in a minute."

Rylin sank onto a couch and glanced around the room, its beige walls decorated with framed teaching awards and motivational holos. She wondered suddenly what her friends were doing—her *real* friends, downTower. Lux, Andrés, Bronwyn, even Indigo. She knew a few people at Berkeley, but they all already hated her.

And just like that, as if she'd summoned him with her thoughts, Cord Anderton walked into the office.

She'd told herself over and over these past weeks that she didn't miss him, that she was doing perfectly fine without him. But it nearly undid her, seeing Cord now; his oxford shirt untucked, his dark hair a little unkempt. So familiar, and so achingly off-limits.

She sat still, letting her eyes drink him in, dreading the moment when he would notice her and she'd have to glance away. It was a cruel cosmic joke, that the *very first* person she ran into at her new school had to be Cord.

His gaze almost slid past her, seeing just another half-Asian girl in the uniform—and then he seemed to register who she was, and did a double take. "Rylin Myers," he said, in the old familiar drawl; the one he used for people he didn't know well. Rylin's heart broke a little when she heard it. It was the way Cord had spoken the first night he met her, when she was nothing but the hired help. Before she stole from him and fell in love with him and everything spun wildly out of control.

"I'm as shocked as you are, trust me," she told him.

Cord leaned back against the wall and folded his arms over his chest. He was smiling, but it didn't reach his eyes. "I have to admit, this is one place I hadn't expected to see you."

"It's my first day. I have to meet with an adviser," Rylin explained, as if it were the most natural thing in the world for her to be here. "What about you?"

"Truancy," Cord said carelessly. Rylin knew that he sometimes skipped school to visit his parents' house on Long Island and drive their illegal old autocars. She thought of the day he'd taken her out there, a day that had ended on the beach in a rainstorm, and she reddened at the memory.

"Is there somewhere we can talk in private?" She hadn't planned on having this conversation with Cord, at least not today, but there was no avoiding it. She was here, in his world—or was it her world now too? It certainly didn't feel like it.

Cord hesitated, seeming torn between his resentment toward Rylin and his curiosity about what she was doing here—and what she had to say. Apparently curiosity won out. "Follow me," he told her.

He led Rylin out of the office and down the hallway. It was getting more crowded as the first bell approached, students gossiping in small clusters, their gold bracelets and wrist-comps flashing as they gesticulated to make a point. Rylin saw their eyes travel curiously over her—taking in her unfamiliar features, her angular beaded earrings, her close-cut blue fingernails and the scuffed flats she'd stolen from Chrissa, because she didn't own any footwear that qualified as "simple black shoes without a heel." She kept her head held high, daring them to challenge her, resisting the urge to look over at Cord. A few people said hi to him, but he just nodded in greeting, and certainly never introduced Rylin.

Finally he turned through a set of double doors into a pitch-dark room. Rylin was startled by the holographic label that popped up as they crossed the door. "You have a screening room at *school*?" she asked, because it was weird and because she desperately wanted to break the silence.

Cord messed with a control box, and after a moment, the track lighting along the stairs flickered on. It was still very dark. Cord was little more than a shadow.

"Yeah, it's for the film class." Cord sounded impatient. "Okay, Myers, what's up?"

Rylin took a deep breath. "I've imagined this conversation at least a hundred different times, and in absolutely zero of those scenarios was I here, at your school."

Cord's teeth gleamed in a hollow smile. "Oh, yeah? Where *did* you imagine this conversation?"

In bed, but that was wishful thinking. "It doesn't matter," Rylin said quickly. "The point is, I owe you an apology."

Cord stepped back, toward the top row of seats. Rylin forced herself to look directly at him as she spoke. "I've been wanting to talk to you ever since that night." She didn't need to clarify; he would know what night she meant.

"I wanted to ping you, but I had no idea what to say. And it didn't seem like it mattered anymore. You were up here, and I was down on thirty-two, and I figured it was just easier not to dig it all up." *And I'm a coward*, she admitted to herself. *I was afraid to see you again, knowing how much it would hurt.*

"Anyway, now I apparently go to school with you—I mean, I'm here on scholarship—"

"The one Eris's parents endowed," Cord said, unnecessarily.

Rylin blinked. She hadn't counted on the fact that so many people would talk to her about Eris. "Yes, that one. And since I'm going to keep seeing you around, I wanted to clear the air."

"'Clear the air,'" Cord repeated, his voice flat. "After you pretended to date me so that you could steal from me."

"It wasn't pretend! And I didn't want to steal—at least, not after the first time," Rylin protested. "Please, let me explain."

Cord nodded but didn't answer.

So she told him everything. She admitted the truth about her ex-boyfriend, Hiral, and about the Spokes—how she'd stolen the custom-made drugs from Cord that one time, the first week she worked for him, to keep her and Chrissa from being evicted. Rylin lifted her chin a little, trying not to falter as she explained how Hiral had blackmailed her into selling his drugs for bail money. How V threatened her, forcing her to steal from Cord again.

She told Cord everything except how his older brother, Brice, had confronted her, saying that unless she broke up with Cord— unless she acted like she'd only dated him for the money—he would send her to jail. She knew how close Cord was with his older brother and had no desire to get in the middle of that relationship. So she made it sound like Hiral did it all.

And she didn't tell Cord how much she'd loved him. How much she still loved him.

Cord didn't say anything until Rylin's last words fell into the silence like stones, causing it to ripple in waves around them. By now it was well into first period; they'd both missed their meetings in the main office. Rylin didn't care. This was more important. She wanted, desperately, to make things right with Cord. And if she was being honest with herself, she wanted so much more than that.

"Thank you for telling me all this," he said slowly.

Rylin took an involuntary step forward. "Cord. Do you think that we could ever—"

"No." He flinched away before she could finish the question. The movement hit her like a blow to the stomach.

"Why?" she couldn't help asking. She felt like she'd ripped her heart open, let its contents spill like sawdust all over the floor, and now Cord was walking carelessly all over it. She somehow held back the tears that threatened to overwhelm her.

Cord let out a breath. "Rylin, after everything that's happened, I don't know how to trust you. Where does that leave us?"

"I'm sorry," she ventured, knowing it wasn't enough. "I never meant to hurt you."

"But you did hurt me, Rylin."

Someone cracked open the door, letting a flood of light into the room, then backed away hastily when they saw Cord. In the brief moment of illumination, Rylin caught sight of his face: distant, cold, closed-off. It terrified her. She would rather that he yell at her, seem angry or wounded, even cruel. This casual indifference was infinitely worse. He was retreating somewhere deep inside himself, where she could never reach him—where he would be lost to her forever.

"I wish I could rewind, do things differently," she said uselessly.

"I wish that too. But that's not how life works, is it?"

Cord took a step forward, as if he was about to leave. Rylin realized in an instant of clarity that she could not let him be the one to walk away from her, not if she were to maintain any semblance of pride. She moved quickly to the door and glanced back over her shoulder.

"I guess it isn't. I'll see you around, Cord," she told him, which was, unfortunately, the truth. She would keep seeing the boy who didn't want her, over and over again.

Later that day, Rylin moved mechanically through the lunch line, wondering how many total minutes she had left at this school. Already she wanted to start a ticking countdown in the corner of her tablet, the way some girls did for their birthdays.

Predictably, the school had launched her on a schedule of entirely base-level classes—including freshman biology, since biology was the one science she'd never taken at her old school. She was actually relieved that she'd shown up so late to her meeting with the registrar, Mrs. Lane, if only because it spared her a full half hour of that woman's incredulous condescension. "It says here you were working at a store called Arrow?" Mrs. Lane had asked with a haughty sniff. Rylin half wished she'd bought a pair of the flashing Arrow rainboots and worn them around school, just to make some kind of point.

As she stepped up to the retinal scanner to check out, Rylin grabbed a shining red bottle of water from one of the dispensers. The scripted logo read MARSAQUA, in letters that looked like icicles against a bright red planet. The cartoon letters repeatedly melted, dripped to the bottom of the bottle, then floated back up to re-form ice crystals.

"Martian water," she heard from behind her.

Rylin whirled around, only to see her worst nightmare standing there. Leda Cole.

"They chip away chunks of the Martian ice caps, then bring it back to Earth and bottle it. It's fantastic for your metabolism," Leda went on. Her voice was frighteningly sweet.

"That sounds harmful to Mars," Rylin replied, proud of how unconcerned she sounded. Leda was like the vicious stray dog that used to lurk near their apartment—you couldn't afford to reveal any weakness before her, or she would never lay off the attack.

"Come sit with me," Leda commanded, and started off without waiting to see whether Rylin would follow.

Rylin didn't bother hiding her sigh of irritation. Well, she might as well get all her shitty conversations over with on the first day. It could only go upward from here, right?

Leda had planted herself at a two-person table near a flexiglass window that overlooked an interior courtyard. Rylin saw kids out there playing with flying video-cams and chatting around an enormous fountain. There was so much real sunlight flooding in from the ceiling, filtered by mirrors from the roof, that it felt like they were outdoors—if outdoors was ever this clean and symmetrical and perfect.

She sank into the seat across from Leda and dunked one of her sweet potato fries in aioli. Leda obviously wanted her to feel intimidated, but Rylin wouldn't give her the satisfaction.

"What the hell are you doing here, Rylin?" Leda demanded, without preamble.

"I go to this school now." Rylin gestured down at her pleated skirt and lifted an eyebrow. "We're wearing the same uniform, in case you didn't notice."

Leda didn't seem to have heard. "Did the cops send you?"

"The cops? Do you realize how paranoid you sound?" The idea was ludicrous, that Rylin Myers would become some kind of undercover police spy.

"All I know is that you're a walking reminder of a night I'd rather not think about." *That makes two of us*, Rylin thought. "And now, for some inexplicable reason, you're here at *my* school, instead of down on the twentieth floor where you belong!" Leda's voice quavered, and Rylin realized with pleasure that she sounded just a little bit . . . afraid.

"Last I checked, Leda, it didn't say your name on the arch out front. So no, this isn't *your* school. And I live on the *thirty-second floor*," she corrected, "but I'm here on scholarship."

Understanding flashed in Leda's eyes. "The Eris scholarship," she breathed.

"That's the one," Rylin said cheerfully, and took a bite of her enormous cheeseburger, relishing the look of disgust that flitted over Leda's face. "Now, unless you have more threats for me, I'd suggest you back off and let me enjoy my lunch in peace. I'm not here to mess with your perfect life." She put just a little emphasis on *perfect*, as if to indicate that she didn't quite buy into the notion that Leda's life was so perfect after all.

Leda stood up abruptly, scraping her chair across the dark walnut floor. She grabbed her uneaten spinach salad and tossed her hair over one shoulder. "Let me give you some free advice," she said, a fake smile pasted on her face, and glanced again at Rylin's burger. "Girls don't ever eat the grill special."

Rylin smiled back, just as wide. "That's funny. Because I'm a girl, and I just did. Guess you don't know everything after all."

"Be careful, Myers. I'm watching you."

What a great first day it was shaping up to be. Rylin leaned back in her chair and took an enormous sip of the overpriced Martian water, because why the hell not.

LEDA

"WHERE'S MOM?" LEDA hesitated in the doorway of her family's dining room, keeping the toes of her boots lined up with the ivory carpet of the hall. Her dad was sitting at the table alone, tapping his fingers absentmindedly on its ultramodern glass surface as he read something on his contacts.

He glanced up. "Hey, Leda. I think she's running a little late."

"Dad, what dates do we have the Barbados house in January?" Jamie asked without preamble as he sat down. Leda cautiously ventured inside and pulled out the chair across from him. The table had no legs: it floated unsupported in the air, the ultimate centerpiece of their home's spare, minimalist décor. Leda thought it was tacky and impersonal, but then, it was fitting that their apartment should feel more like a hotel than a home. A home would imply that the people who lived there actually cared about one another.

Matt Cole cleared his throat. "Actually, we released the Barbados time-share."

"What?" Leda was stunned. They'd had the time-share in Barbados for ages: a sprawling, serene house atop a hill, with a tiny cobblestone path directly to the beach. Leda had always loved how relaxed her parents were there, as though they became the best, purest versions of themselves, freed of the grime of New York.

"We thought we'd take a year off, maybe do something new," her dad explained, but Leda wasn't buying it. She wondered if he'd lost a lot of money recently. Maybe he'd spent too much on Calvadour scarves for his teenage mistress, she thought resentfully, thinking of the exorbitant present he'd given Eris before she died.

"That sucks. I wanted to see if I could bring friends," Jamie said, and shrugged. "I'm starving. Can we eat?" Typical Jamie; he was never really bothered by anything for very long.

"Let's wait for Mom," Leda said quickly, but her dad was already pushing a discreet touch-screen pad at the center of the table. Their chef, Tiffany, appeared, pushing a wide cart laden with dishes.

"Mom said to start without her. She's held up in a meeting," their dad explained. Leda pursed her lips and reached for the bowl of pasta without comment. She saw that it was her favorite, a kale-noodle penne with crumbled soy protein and phenerols. Her mom had totally picked this menu to cheer Leda up. A stubborn, contrary part of her was determined not to like it.

"How was school, Leda?" her dad asked. That was his version of parenting: asking scripted questions that he'd gotten from some *How to Talk to Your Teenage Daughter* book. Leda wondered if they shelved that one next to *How to Hide Your Teenage Mistress*.

"Fine," she said curtly, and started to take a bite of the penne, only to put down her fork with a clatter. "Although, there was a new girl at school today. Isn't that weird, that she was able to start mid-semester like that?"

"I think I saw her," Jamie chimed in, for once. "The scholarship student?"

Leda glanced at him in surprise. Jamie usually never noticed anything, unless you could smoke it or drink it or had given it to him as a present. Then again, Rylin *was* pretty, if you could look past her disrespectful attitude.

"Exactly. She moved here from the *twentieth floor*," Leda said dramatically, wrinkling her nose at the thought. "Can you imagine?"

"Sort of like how you felt, when we moved here from mid-Tower," her father said, which shocked Leda into silence.

"No, not at all like me," she countered after a moment. She didn't appreciate being compared to an arrogant lowlier. "This girl is rude and insulting. She thinks the rules don't apply to her."

Jamie burst out laughing. "Look who's talking. Leda, you've *never* thought rules apply to you!"

Matt Cole tried to stay impartial, but amusement danced across his features. "Leda, I think you should give this girl the benefit of the doubt. I'm sure she had a tough first day, starting at a new school in the middle of the year. Especially as a scholarship student."

This was her opening. "You're right," Leda said, her voice dripping with false sympathy. "And I imagine it's been extra hard on her, because she won Eris's scholarship, and of course we all miss Eris *so* much."

Silence settled over the room. Leda's family knew she'd been on the roof, of course; they'd picked her up from the police station that morning after everyone provided their witness statements, and had reviewed it with their lawyer in excruciating detail. Eris's death was one of those things they seemed to have collectively decided not to talk about. As if all their family's dirty little secrets could be wrapped up and buried, just the way Eris herself had been, and then they would disappear.

Leda watched her dad's face closely. Looking for what, she wasn't quite sure. An acknowledgment of his relationship with Eris, she supposed.

She saw it right away. He flinched at Leda's words, just barely, but it was enough. She quickly looked down.

Leda had expected to feel pleased at seeing the proof, right there on her dad's face—yet all she wanted, suddenly, was to cry.

For the rest of the meal she pushed her food around, letting her dad and Jamie talk about lacrosse and some great save Jamie had made and whether or not the school would hire a new coach next year. As soon as she could, she mumbled an excuse and escaped down the hall to her bedroom.

A knock sounded at her door. "Leda?"

"What?" she snapped, wiping at her eyes. Didn't her dad understand that she had no desire to see him?

He tentatively pushed the door open. "Can we talk?"

She swiveled her desk chair around but stayed where she was, her legs crisscrossed beneath her.

"I just wanted to check on you," he said, fumbling. "You haven't spoken about Eris much, since she died. And then what you said, at dinner . . ." He trailed off awkwardly. "I just want to make sure you're okay."

Of course I'm not okay, Leda thought. She almost pitied how clueless her dad was. She'd mentioned Eris at dinner because she wanted to *provoke* him, because she was sick of pretending that everything was fine, that a cozy pasta dinner could fix things the way it had when she was little. He was the one who'd started sleeping with her friend, and had betrayed everything their family was built on.

But more than that, Leda was disgusted with herself. She'd been keeping it a secret too, and that made her as culpable as he was.

So many times since Eris's death she had wanted to confront her mom with the truth. She would march up to Ilara, ready to spill it all: that Dad was a two-timing scumbag and that they needed to leave him. "I have something to tell you," Leda had said, on more than one occasion, "something important—"

Yet Leda could never bring herself to actually say the words. Eris was already gone, she told herself; what good would it do to tear her family apart now? Each time Ilara looked at her with those dark eyes, so full of love, Leda wavered and fell silent. She didn't want to be the one to break her mom's heart.

The child in Leda couldn't bear the thought of her parents splitting up. Her family might be riddled with secrets and betrayals, but it was still *her family*. And she would rather keep them together, even if it meant sitting on this secret for the rest of her life.

She had earned this, she thought darkly. This twisting, tormenting guilt was her penance, for what she'd done to Eris.

"I'm fine," she said tightly, in answer to her dad's question. What else could she say to him, anyway? *Hey, Dad, remember how you were having an affair with my friend, and then she fell off the roof? Guess what? I'm the one who pushed her!*

"You and Eris were close, right?" her dad persisted. God, why couldn't he just go away? And why did everyone keep *asking* that? Just because she and Eris had some friends in common didn't mean they were attached at the hip.

"We were friends, but not best friends." Leda was ready to end this conversation. "Actually, Dad, I have a lot of studying to—"

"Leda," her dad interrupted, and now he was the one who

seemed to be desperate, "There's something I want to tell you about Eris—"

No, no, no. "Sorry!" Leda stood up abruptly, knocking her chair to the floor, and began frantically throwing items in her massive tote bag. She was wearing floral yoga pants and a black zip-up, but it didn't matter; she needed to get the hell out of here. She absolutely could *not* stay and listen to her dad's fucked-up confession about how he'd been sleeping with her so-called friend. "I'm late to study at Avery's. Can we talk later?"

Understanding, and a little bit of hurt, flashed in her dad's eyes. Maybe he knew that she knew. "All right. We'll talk another time."

"Thanks! See you later!" she said with false brightness, and ran blindly out of the apartment.

Only after she'd slipped inside a hover did Leda realize she had no idea where she was going. Of course she couldn't actually head to Avery's. It was too late for a workout class at Altitude, though she could go to the coffee bar there . . . but then she might see Avery or, worse, one of Eris's parents . . . Leda was far too angry and shaken up for that.

The hover started beeping angrily, indicating that it would charge her for the delay if she didn't enter a destination soon, but Leda couldn't be bothered to care. God, what had her dad been thinking, bringing up Eris? Why would he make that kind of confession to his own daughter?

Leda felt like everything was spinning wildly out of control. If she hadn't sworn never to touch drugs again, she would be searching for a xenperheidren right now; but it had become a matter of pride, and Leda's pride was matched only by her stubbornness.

She hated thinking about that night. Of course, Leda knew that she was safe: no one could prove what she'd done to Eris.

There'd been no cameras on the roof, no way for anyone to find out that it was Leda's fault. Nothing except her three witnesses.

Come to think of it, maybe she should check in on them, make sure they were sticking to their story.

Suddenly Leda knew exactly where to go. She entered an address in the hover's system and leaned back, closing her eyes. This would be fun.

WATT

WHAT IF YOU *compose the first draft, then I tweak it to sound like me?* Watt begged Nadia for at least the tenth time.

"May I remind you that last fall, you gave me firm orders never to write anything for you again. These are instructions from your past self."

Last fall Watt had been called into the school office for plagiarism, because Nadia's essay had come out a little too perfect. He'd been more careful since then. *These are extenuating circumstances*, he thought huffily.

"I'm just the messenger. Take up the fight with your past self."

"Nadia—"

"That's it. Per your past instructions, I'm turning off. Wake me up when you have a draft," Nadia replied, and beeped into silence.

Watt stared at the blank monitor uncertainly. It was true; he had definitely told Nadia to turn herself off if he kept begging her to write his papers. Past Watt was too damned clever for Present Watt to want to deal with right now.

He began speaking aloud, his dictation-screen picking up the words as he said them.

"The reason I want to work with quantum computers is . . ."

He paused. There were a million things he could discuss in this essay: that quants were faster and smarter than people, even though people had made them, of course; that they could solve problems that humans never dreamed of. God, just a hundred years ago, it took a digital computer several hours to factor a twenty-digit number. Nadia could do it in four seconds flat. Watt couldn't even imagine what she would be capable of if she were linked to other quants—and put in charge of international trade, or the stock market, or even just the operations of the U.S. food bank. Nothing would go to waste anymore. Human error would be virtually eliminated.

But none of that had to do with Watt on a personal level, or why the program should choose him over the other thousands of applicants.

If only he could write about Nadia, about how unerringly good she was. *She can't be good; she's a machine*, he corrected himself. But Watt knew that at his core, he believed in Nadia's good intentions as if she had a human conscience.

He thought of what Vivian Marsh had said, that she wanted to personally read his application essay, and felt his heart sink.

"Watzahn!" His mom knocked at his door. "Your friend is here. For your group project."

"Cynthia?" They had a video to make for English class. He wondered why Cynthia hadn't warned him that she was coming over. "You should have pinged, we could have met at the library," he added, opening the door—only to see Leda Cole standing there, wearing pink floral yoga pants and a self-satisfied smirk.

"We could've," she said smoothly, "but I wanted to use your computer. It's so much better than the ones at the library, you know?"

"Of course. Watzahn is so proud of his computer. He works on it all the time!" Watt's mom pronounced, beaming.

Quant on, Watt thought frantically, feeling disoriented and blindsided. What the hell was Leda Cole doing here?

"Thank you, Mrs. Bakradi," Leda said sweetly, her eyes wide and innocent. She stepped into Watt's room and swung a tote bag onto the floor, kneeling as if to get out the fictional homework assignment. Watt stared in shock at his mother. He couldn't believe she was even letting a girl *into* his bedroom. But Shirin just nodded and smiled at Leda, reminding them to let her know if they needed anything. "Don't work too hard!" she said, and shut the door quietly behind her.

"Sorry I'm not Cynthia," Leda purred. "Though I'm glad to hear that one of us has moved on from the Fuller siblings."

"She's just a friend," Watt shot back, then felt ashamed that he'd risen to her bait.

"Too bad." Leda's fingers kept tapping against the floor. He didn't think she was on anything—her eyes were too clear, her gaze steady—yet there was a taut, thrumming nervousness to her movements.

He knelt next to Leda and took her bag from her hands. "Seriously, you need to go."

"Come on, Watt. Be nice," she admonished. "I came all the way down here to talk to you."

"What the hell do you *want*?" he demanded. *Watt, be careful*, Nadia cautioned. He let his hands fall uselessly to his sides, clenching them into fists, and sat back on his heels.

"I thought you knew everything, with your little supercomputer tracking all of us all the time," Leda said acerbically.

Nadia, if you hadn't turned yourself off, I wouldn't have been caught like this!

Perhaps you shouldn't have violated the guidelines you set for yourself, Nadia replied, with ruthless logic.

"What did you tell my mom, for her to let you in?" he asked Leda, to buy time—and because she was right, she shouldn't be able to sneak up on him like this. He wanted to make sure it never happened again.

Leda rolled her eyes. "I was *nice* to her, Watt. You should try it sometime. It often works on people." She stretched her legs out and leaned against his bed, glancing up at the tangle of clothes floating near the ceiling on cheap, disposable hoverbeams.

"I don't have a closet in here. It's the best I could think of," Watt said, following her gaze, not sure why he was explaining himself.

"Actually, I'm impressed." Leda's eyes were still darting around the room. "You've really maximized the space in here. What was this originally, a nursery?"

"No, the twins got the bigger room when they were born." He shifted, suddenly seeing the room through Leda's eyes: the rumpled navy bedcovers, the cheap halogen lighting along the ceiling, the narrow desk littered with secondhand virtual reality gear.

"Twins?" Leda asked, as if she was genuinely curious.

Nadia, what's she doing?

I believe this is the rhetorical tactic of koinonia, *whereby the speaker gets the opponent to talk about himself instead of tackling the subject of the debate.*

No, I mean, what does she want?

Watt stood up, losing patience. "You didn't come over here to make small talk about my family. What's going on?"

Leda unfolded herself in a slow, graceful movement to stand next to him. She took a step closer, tipping her face up to look at him directly. Her eyes were darker than he remembered, her lids dusted with a smoky powder. "You aren't even going to offer me a drink before I go? Last time you gave me whiskey," Leda murmured.

"Last time you seduced and drugged me!"

She smiled. "That was fun, wasn't it? Well, Watt"—she reached up to tuck a stray hair behind his ear and he yanked his head angrily away; he was starting to feel very confused—"if you must know, I need you to monitor some people for me."

"Forget it, Leda. I told you, I'm done with all that."

"That's too bad, because I'm not done with *you*." She'd dropped the playful tone, her voice cold with the veiled threat. She had him cornered, and they both knew it.

"Who do you want me to monitor?" Watt asked warily.

"Avery and Rylin, for starters," Leda said. There was a new energy to her voice, as if bossing Watt around somehow lent her strength. "I want to make sure they stay in line, that neither of them is talking to anyone about what happened that night."

He realized she was wearing the same pearl studs that she'd had on the last time she came over here, and the memory caused his anger to bubble up even hotter. "You want me to spy on both of them and report anything unusual?" Watt asked. "Two full-time monitoring tasks. That'll cost you."

Leda burst out laughing. "Watt! Of course I won't be paying you! Your payment is my silence."

Watt didn't need Nadia to tell him he'd better not respond to that. Anything he said would only dig him in deeper. He just nodded once, jerkily, hating her.

"You see, Rylin started at my school today," Leda mused aloud. She'd started circling through his room like a predator, opening various drawers and glancing at the contents, then shutting them again. "It really caught me off guard. I hate that feeling.

The whole reason I pay you is to never feel that way, *ever* again."

"I believe we just established that you don't pay me," he replied evenly.

Leda slammed another drawer shut and lifted her eyes to look directly at Watt. "Where is it?" she demanded. "Your computer."

Nadia. Can you pretend to be an external? he thought, and made a show of pushing a useless button on his monitor. "Right here. Look, I'm turning it on," he said. "And now it's starting up."

"I don't need a running commentary." Leda took a seat on Watt's bed without being invited. Some strange part of Watt realized that was the first time a girl had ever been on his bed. He'd hooked up with plenty of girls before, of course, but he always went back to their places. He shook his head, a little irritated; why was he thinking about sex right now?

"Let's start with Avery," Leda began.

"What? Right now?"

"No time like the present," she said with false cheerfulness. "Come on, pull up her room comp."

"No," Watt said automatically.

"Too painful a memory?" Leda laughed, but it rang hollow to Watt's ears. He wondered what had happened tonight, to send her down here. "Fine, then. Her flickers."

"Still no."

"Oh my god, move *over*," she snapped, pushing him impatiently from his chair. Their legs brushed, sending a strange row of sparks up Watt's body. He quickly edged away from her.

"How do you input commands?" She leaned forward and gazed expectantly at the monitor.

"Nadia, say hello to Leda," Watt instructed, very loudly and slowly. *Use the speakers*, Watt thought, but Nadia was already doing so—using every speaker in the room, including the ones on his old VR gear.

"Hello to Leda," Nadia boomed. Watt barely choked back a laugh. She was using a robotic, monotonous voice, like in old science fiction movies.

Leda practically jumped. "Nice to meet you," she said cautiously.

"Wish I could say the same," Nadia replied.

"What is *that* supposed to mean?" Leda smiled.

Great, go ahead and antagonize her, Watt thought, rolling his eyes.

I'm just following your lead. "You think you can blackmail Watt because you've got something on him? Do you even know what I have on *you*? I see everything you do," Nadia warned, as ominously as she could.

Leda shoved back the chair in a show of anger, but Watt could tell Nadia's proclamation had shaken her.

"You watch it. *Both* of you." Leda pulled her bag onto one shoulder and stormed out without another word.

Watt waited until he heard the front door close behind her before collapsing backward onto his bed, rubbing his hands over his temples. His bedcovers still smelled like Leda's rose perfume, which pissed him off to no end. "Nadia, we're screwed," he said aloud. "Is she going to keep blackmailing us for all eternity?"

"You won't be safe unless she's in jail," Nadia told him, which he already knew.

"I agree. But we've been through this already. How could I send her there?"

He and Nadia had tried everything they could think of. There was no video of Leda pushing Eris: there weren't any cameras on the roof, and no one had been recording on their contacts when it happened, not even Leda, not even *Nadia*—who deeply regretted it, but then, no way could she have predicted that outcome. Hell, Nadia had even hacked all the satellite cams within a thousand-kilometer vicinity, but none of them had picked up anything in the darkness.

There was, unfortunately, no way to prove what had happened on the roof. It was Watt's word against Leda's. And the moment he said anything, he and Nadia were toast.

Nadia was quiet for a moment. "What if you recorded her confessing to her actions?"

"Can we deal in reality and not hypotheticals? Even if she did say the truth aloud, no way would she say it to *me*."

"I disagree," Nadia said levelly. "She would say it if she trusted you."

For a moment Watt didn't understand what Nadia was implying. When he did, he laughed aloud. "Do I need to reprogram your logic functions? Why would Leda Cole trust me, when she so clearly hates me?"

"I'm just trying to explore all possible options. Remember, you programmed me to protect you above everything else. And statistics would suggest that the more time you spend with Leda, the greater your chances of winning her trust," Nadia replied.

"Statistics are useless when your chances of success increase from one-billionth of a percent to one-millionth." Watt pulled up the covers, closing his eyes. "Did you know about Rylin going to school with them?" he asked, changing the subject.

"I did. You never asked me about her, though."

"Have you hacked their school?" An idea was forming in his mind. "What if we messed with Leda a little—put Rylin in all her classes, so Leda can never escape her?"

"Like I haven't already done that. You underestimate me," Nadia said, sounding self-satisfied.

Watt couldn't help smiling into the darkness. "I think the more time you spend in my brain, the more my personality has grafted itself onto you," he mused aloud.

"Yes. I'd venture to say I know you better than you know yourself."

Now *there* was a terrifying notion, Watt thought in amusement.

"Nadia?" he added as he started to drift off. "Please don't ever turn off around Leda again, no matter what commands I've given in the past. I need you, around her."

"That you do," Nadia agreed.

RYLIN

RYLIN STRODE QUICKLY down Berkeley's main hallway, keeping her gaze forward to avoid accidentally making eye contact with Leda—or worse, Cord. At least it was finally Friday afternoon, the end of her seemingly endless first week here.

She followed the directions on her school tablet, past an enormous sandstone bell tower and a shining statue of the school's founder, whose head moved majestically to follow her progress as she walked. She turned left at the athletic center toward the art wing, ignoring the somewhat morbid shrine to Eris that had been erected in one corner of the hallway, full of candles and insta-photos of her and notes from students who probably hadn't even known her that well. It gave Rylin the creeps. Though she wasn't sure whether that was because she'd seen Eris die, or because of the fact that she was here on scholarship, taking Eris's spot in their class, which made Rylin's existence a bizarre sort of living shrine.

When she pushed open the door to Arts Suite 105, a dozen heads whipped toward her—almost entirely girls'. Rylin paused, confused.

"Is this holography?" she asked. The room was black, lined with dark view screens and a velvet charcoal carpet.

"It is," Leda Cole called out from where she sat in the back row, next to the only available seat in the room.

"Thanks." Rylin's heart sank as she took the empty desk, wondering what exactly she'd gotten herself into. She pulled out her school tablet and doodled a few loopy cartoons in its notepad function, but she still felt Leda's eyes on her.

Finally Leda grabbed something from her bag—a blue cone-shaped silencer, inscribed with calligraphied letters that read *Lux et Veritas*. She should get one of these for Lux, Rylin thought sarcastically. Of course Leda was the type of person who would buy branded gear from a university bookstore before she'd even gotten in.

Leda flicked on the silencer, and the rest of the room immediately hushed, the machine distorting sound waves to create a little pocket of silence. "Okay. How did you get in here?" she snapped.

"I thought we'd been through this. I go to school with you now, remember?"

"Look around. These are all seniors." Leda gestured sharply to the other girls in the class. "This is *the* most popular elective at school, with a ninety-person waiting list. The only reason I'm even here is because they reserve a few spots for juniors, and my application essay was best." She clenched the edge of her desk as if she wished she could break it. "What's your explanation?"

"I honestly have no idea," Rylin admitted. "I was just assigned this class. It appeared on my schedule the other day, so here I am." She shoved her tablet toward Leda as if to offer proof. *Accelerated Studies in Holography; instructor, Xiayne Radimajdi.*

"Watt," Leda muttered under her breath, saying it as if it were a curse word.

"What?" Rylin couldn't have heard correctly. Wasn't that the boy from the roof, who'd come with them to the police that night?

Leda sighed. "Never mind. Just don't screw this up for me, okay? I'm hoping to get a recommendation out of it."

"To Yale?" Rylin said drily, glancing at the silencer.

"Shane went there," Leda snapped. At Rylin's confused look, she sighed. "Xiayne Radimajdi. He teaches this class! His name is *right there* on your tablet." She rapped sharply at the evidence, and cut her eyes to Rylin in evident disbelief.

"Oh." Rylin hadn't realized that Leda was saying the name Xiayne. She'd been wondering how to pronounce it. "Who is he?"

"The triple-Oscar-winning director!" Leda exclaimed. Rylin just stared at her blankly. "You haven't seen *Metropolis*? Or *Empty Skies*? That's why this class only meets on Fridays—because he works the rest of the week!"

Rylin shrugged. "The last holo I saw was a cartoon. But those things you just mentioned sound depressing anyway."

"Oh my *god*. This class is *wasted* on you." Leda tossed the silencer back into her bag, turning away from Rylin just as the door swung inward. The whole room seemed to edge forward, collectively holding its breath. And then Rylin understood why the class was composed mostly of girls.

Into the room walked the most incredibly attractive guy Rylin had ever seen.

He was tall, and not much older than they were—in his early twenties, maybe—with deep olive skin and shaggy dark curls. Unlike her other professors, who all wore neckties and blazers, he dressed with shocking disregard for the dress code, in a thin white T-shirt, a jacket with zippers all over it, and skinny jeans.

Rylin glanced around and noticed that she and Leda were the only ones not swooning.

"Sorry I'm late. I just got off the 'loop from London," he announced. "As you all probably know, I just started filming a new project there."

"The royalty one?" a girl in the front row exclaimed.

Xiayne turned. The girl shifted, but then Xiayne gave a devilish smile, and she visibly relaxed. "I'm not supposed to share this, but yes, it's about the final queen of England. A little more romantic than my usual material." The announcement elicited a few gasps and *oooh*s.

"Now, Livya, since you were so eager to volunteer, can you tell me what we discussed in the last class about Sir Jared Sun?"

Livya sat up straighter. "Sir Jared patented the refractive technology that allowed holographs to obtain motion perfectly aligned with the observer, creating the illusion of presence."

The door to the classroom slid open again, and a familiar form appeared there. Rylin instinctively sank lower in her seat, wishing she could sink all the way into the floor—farther, even; into the mechanical jumble of the interstitial level and the floor below, all the way down to the ground itself, littered with trash and god knows what else, it didn't matter—she just wanted to disappear.

"Mr. Anderton," Xiayne said, sounding amused and unsurprised. "You're late. Again."

"I got held up," Cord offered by way of explanation, and Rylin couldn't help noticing that he hadn't exactly said he was sorry.

Xiayne glanced around the room as if searching for some explanation for why he was missing a desk. He seemed to register Rylin's presence with some astonishment. He hadn't singled her out yet, hadn't made her do one of those awful self-introductions that some of the other professors insisted on. What if he did so now, and in front of Cord?

But to Rylin's shock, the professor *winked* at her, in a way that could only be described as conspiratorial.

"Well, Mr. Anderton, it seems you need somewhere to sit." Xiayne pushed a button and a desk rose up out of the floor, directly in front of Rylin.

Cord didn't glance Rylin's way as he took his seat. Only the tension in his shoulders betrayed any reaction to her presence. Rylin sank miserably lower.

"As we discussed last week," Xiayne continued, undeterred, "settings are the easiest aspect of the world to re-create in holographic form, because, of course, they are stable. A far more difficult task is the portrayal of something living. Why is that?" He snapped his fingers, and a cat leapt from behind his desk onto the top of it.

Rylin barely refrained from gasping aloud. She'd seen plenty of holograms before: on their screen at home, and of course the adverts that popped up whenever she went shopping. But those were loud and flashy and low-resolution. This cat felt different. It was rendered in exquisite detail, and moved so realistically in a thousand small ways—the lazy flick of its tail, the way its chest lifted lightly with its breath, the challenging blink of its eyes.

The cat jumped onto the desk of the girl in the front row who'd spoken earlier. She let out an involuntary squeal of shock. "Movement," Xiayne went on, ignoring the scattered laughter. "The movements of anything living must be rendered with perfect relation to any viewer, no matter where he or she is located with respect to the holo. Which is why Sir Jared is called the father of modern holography."

Xiayne went on for a while about light and distance, about the calculations needed to make something seem larger to the viewers who were closer to it, but smaller to those farther away. Rylin tried to listen, but it was hard to focus with Cord's dark head right in front of her. She willed herself not to stare. A couple of times she saw Leda looking at her out of the corner of her eye, and she knew the other girl was missing none of it.

When the bell finally rang to signal the end of class, Xiayne quickly changed tack. "Don't forget that your next project is in pairs, and is due in just two weeks. So you all need to find a partner if you haven't already."

The room burst into a hum as everyone began pairing off. Suddenly, Rylin was seized by a terrible, overwhelming fear that she might somehow end up with Cord. She thought of the way he'd looked at her earlier this week, resentful and hurt. No matter what, she could *not* be partnered with him.

The sounds of the room seemed to be growing louder, making Rylin almost dizzy with the pressure of it. She did the only thing she could think of.

"Partners?" she asked, turning to Leda.

Leda blinked at her in disbelief. "You're kidding," she said flatly.

Rylin forced a smile. She had a feeling she would regret this. "What have you got to lose?" she asked.

Leda glanced from Rylin to Cord and back again. "Fine," she said after a moment, with a flash of reluctant respect. "Just don't expect me to do all the work for you."

Rylin started to reply, but the other girl had already stood up to gather her things.

Rylin bit back a sigh and started toward the front of the classroom. She might as well introduce herself to the professor and ask what this assignment was.

"Professor Radimajdi," she ventured as Cord walked silently out the door. He'd probably partnered with one of the senior girls. That was for the best, Rylin told herself. At least this way she wouldn't look like a fool. "I just joined the class. Can you tell me about the assignment?"

"Rylin, right?" There was something unusual about the way he said her name, as if it were the word for something delicious and wicked in a foreign language. For some reason it made her shiver. "The other students all know this already, but please, call me Xiayne."

"Okay," was all Rylin could think to say. He gestured to the chair before his desk, and she sank into it, pulling her bag awkwardly onto her lap.

"Sorry, it gets so hot in here," he muttered, and shrugged off his zippered black jacket.

Rylin nodded, her eyes widening at the sight of Xiayne's arms. Inktats covered every square centimeter of skin—beautiful, abstract shapes in a dizzying array of colors. They gathered like fabric over his biceps, swirled down his muscled arms to finish in a visual kaleidoscope at his wrists. Rylin found her gaze drawn to those wrists, watching them bend and flatten, the inktats shifting in anticipation of his every moment. They were the kind of inktats that went nerve-deep: the micropigment shards had been blasted into his skin with a fibrojet, lined with astrocytes that would sink deep into his tissue and cleave irrevocably to the nerve cells, enabling them to shift with constant movement. By far the most painful, and therefore the most badass, kind of inktat.

Xiayne leaned forward and she caught a hint of more ink at his neck, disappearing into the collar of his shirt. She felt herself redden as she imagined what the rest of it looked like, on his chest.

"Did you design them yourself?" she ventured, gesturing to the inktats.

"Oh, years ago," he said lightly, "at a place called Black Lotus.

As you might imagine, the school isn't thrilled about them, so I try to wear sleeves during class hours."

"Black Lotus?" Rylin repeated. "You don't mean the one down on the thirty-fifth floor?" Rylin had gone there with her friends once, several years ago, back when her mom was still alive. She'd inked a tiny bird on her back, right at the waistband of her jeans, the one place her mom wouldn't see. The pain was excruciating, but it was worth it—she loved the way the bird responded to her movements; flapping its wings when she was walking, tilting its head beneath a wing when she was asleep.

Xiayne blinked at her in surprise. "You know it?"

Suddenly Rylin wished she were wearing a hoodie and sneakers instead of this starched uniform skirt. She wanted to feel more like herself. "I actually live on the thirty-second floor. I'm here on scholarship."

"The Eris Dodd-Radson award."

"I *get* it, okay?" Rylin snapped—and winced. "I'm sorry," she said haltingly. "It's just that everyone has been saying that all week, like I'm some kind of weird reminder of her. It's already uncomfortable enough for me, that I'm here because a girl *died*. But I'm not here as a sort of"—she swallowed—"replacement for her."

An indecipherable expression darted across Xiayne's features. Rylin realized that his eyes were lighter than she'd thought at first, a deep gray-green that stood out shockingly against the smooth darkness of his skin. "I understand. That must be difficult." Then he broke out into a smile. "But I'd be lying if I said I wasn't a little excited, to be teaching someone different. It's refreshing. Nostalgic for me, even."

Rylin felt puzzled and flattered all at once. "What do you mean?"

"You're from my old neighborhood. I went to P.S. 1073."

"That was my rival school!" Rylin couldn't help laughing at the unexpectedness of it all. For the first time since walking in the front doors on Monday, she didn't feel like she was being judged.

"And what do you think of Berkeley so far?" he asked, seeming to sense her thoughts.

"It's . . . an adjustment," Rylin admitted.

Xiayne nodded. "There are good parts and bad parts, as with most things in life. But I think you'll find that after a time, the good outweighs the bad." Rylin didn't agree, but she wasn't sure she wanted to protest, and anyway, Xiayne was already reaching into a cabinet in the corner. "Have you ever used a vid-cam before?" he asked, pulling out a shining silver sphere, about the size of a grape.

"No." Rylin had never even seen one.

Xiayne opened his hand, releasing the sphere gently upward. It floated to hover in the air a few centimeters above his palm. He twirled his index finger in a circle, and the vid-cam spun, mirroring his movements. "This is a 360-degree vid-cam, equipped with powerful spatial processors and a microcomputer," he explained. "In other words, it records in every direction, no matter which way the viewer turns."

"So you just turn on the camera and it starts recording an immersive holo?" That didn't sound difficult.

"It's harder than you'd guess," Xiayne said, understanding her meaning. "There's an artistry to it—staging the scene, making sure it's perfect in each direction, then removing yourself from it all before you film. Unless you decide to edit yourself out in postproduction."

"You can do that?"

"Of course. Once you really get the hang of it, you can edit different takes together into a single view. That's how I got the midnight sunrise in *Metropolis*. You know, the one that Gloria watches from the rooftop at the end of the movie?" He sighed a little. "I stitched that together from about three hundred takes, pixel by goddamned pixel. Took me two months."

"Right," Rylin breathed, since she didn't know the scene he was talking about. "So, what exactly did we need to film for the assignment?"

"Something interesting." He snatched the camera from midair and held it toward her, palm outstretched. "Surprise me, Rylin."

Maybe I will, she thought, a curious jolt of anticipation in her chest.

CALLIOPE

"SO. THIS IS the thousandth floor."

"I know." Elise echoed Calliope's tone of momentary surprise. "I expected more diamonds."

Calliope and her mom had just been ushered into the living room from the private elevator bank, complete with a real, human elevator attendant—that had to be just for parties, Calliope reasoned; surely he didn't do that job *all* the time. She shook her head in wry amusement. "It's a cocktail party, Mom, not a gala. This isn't the right occasion for diamonds."

"You never know," her mom said, reaching into her purse to trade her enormous diamond bracelet for a more discreet gold one. She always traveled with varying levels of jewelry, ever since the time in Paris that they showed up to a party shockingly overdressed.

No, it hadn't been the lack of carats that prompted Calliope's comment. She'd just expected the Tower's penthouse apartment to feel more, well . . . *more.*

Beneath the festive wreaths and glowing lights festooned around the room, the massive poinsettias and the enormous Christmas tree that took up one whole corner of the living room, the thousandth floor looked to Calliope like any other of the countless expensive apartments she'd seen. It was just another room full of stuffy antiques and crystal candlesticks and wallpaper in muted colors, the same couture heels stepping on the same carpets the world over. And what was with all the mirrors? Calliope loved looking at herself as much as the next girl, but the one time she didn't care about her reflection was this high up. She wanted to look *out*—at the world, the light, the stars.

What a damn shame, to have the best views in the world, only to cover your walls with mirrors and brocade curtains.

"I'm going scouting. Wish me luck," Elise said briskly, her attention already roving restlessly over the various guests.

"You don't need it, but good luck."

Calliope watched as her mom advanced across the room with a near savage intensity, her eyes narrowing as she assessed various potential marks, talking to some of them for a few moments before tossing them aside and moving on. She was looking for the perfect target: rich enough to be worth the effort, but not so rich that it would be impossible to get close to him or her. And of course, foolish enough to fall for the stories she would inevitably tell.

At times like this, Calliope loved watching her mother at work. There was a deliberateness to all her movements—to her laughter, the way she tossed her tawny tousled hair—that drew eyes to her like a magnet.

As her mom dissolved into conversation with a group of partygoers, Calliope drifted toward the edge of the room. In her experience, detaching yourself was the best way to read the intricacies of every party, all the little currents of attraction and alliances and drama. And you never knew who might appear once you pulled yourself away from the action, made yourself a little more approachable.

Almost immediately she caught sight of Avery Fuller moving through the crowds. It was as if Avery had her own personal spotlight trained on her: illuminating her flawless features, making her ivory cheekbones even more pronounced, her eyes an even brighter blue. Calliope would have resented Avery for being so impossibly beautiful, if she weren't so deeply confident in her own charms—which were different, certainly, but no less effective.

She started toward Avery, thinking she might as well thank her for the invitation, only to stop in her tracks as Avery made eye contact with someone across the room. A look of such love suffused her face that Calliope knew she'd blundered into a sacred, private moment. She quickly turned her head the same direction as Avery, piqued with curiosity about who could possibly inspire that level of devotion. But the crowd was too thick and swirling for her to see.

A sharp cough sounded across the room, and even beneath all the cacophony—the exclamations of greeting; the clipped business discussions and liquid, languid flirtations; the shaking of cocktails and strumming of the string quartet in the corner—the sound vibrated through Calliope's consciousness with an electric shock. She responded to that cough more instinctively than she did to her name, real or assumed. That cough meant that her mom needed Calliope for backup. Now.

At least this guy was good-looking, Calliope thought, when she found her mom in conversation with an older gentleman. He had chiseled features and close-cut gray hair, which made him handsome in a distinguished sort of way, even if his plain dark suit was rather staid. Elise was laughing at some joke he'd told, looking exotic and exciting in her bright green dress and vivid smile. Calliope imagined that she could already see her mother sharpening her claws, readying herself to move in for the kill.

"Hello," Calliope said politely as she approached. It was the safest greeting, since she never really knew what role she'd been cast in for this con until Elise prompted her.

"Darling, I'd love for you to meet Nadav Mizrahi," Elise exclaimed, and turned to the man she was speaking with. "Nadav, this is my daughter."

"Calliope Brown. Pleasure to meet you," she said, stepping forward to shake Nadav's hand. She was grateful to be playing a daughter again this time. That was always the most fun.

Sometimes Elise cast her as a cousin or friend instead—or worse, in some completely unrelated role, like a new assistant in the mark's office, or a maid. Elise insisted that she assigned roles based on her read of the situation, but Calliope suspected that she sometimes picked them simply because being the mom made her feel old. Not that Elise was old at all. Hell, she'd only been nine-teen, barely older than Calliope was now, when she got pregnant with Calliope. Now *there* was a sobering thought.

"I have a daughter about your age. Her name is Livya," Nadav volunteered, with a warm smile. Well, that explained it.

"Mr. Mizrahi works in cybernetics. He's only recently moved to New York from Tel Aviv," Elise added.

That was why Elise had homed in on him with such deadly skill. She could smell new blood a mile away. Newcomers were more trusting of strangers, since to them, everyone was a stranger. They were far less likely to notice any missteps.

A hovertray floated past, laden with crystal flutes of some-thing pink and fizzy. Calliope plucked three of them deftly off the top. "Mr. Mizrahi," she said, handing him a drink. "I'm not very familiar with cybernetics. Can you explain the basics?"

"Well, cybernetics is technically defined as the study of sub-systems in both man and machine, but I work in a division that attempts to replicate simple patterns . . ."

Calliope smiled even as she tuned out his monologue. Give a mark the chance to show off, to spout a little bit of specialized knowledge, and he or she automatically felt affection toward you. After all, there was no topic of conversation that people enjoyed talking about more than themselves.

"And how have you enjoyed New York?" Calliope asked at a break in the conversation, taking a sip of her drink. There were sticky sugar crystals on the rim and bright red pomegranate seeds clustered at the bottom.

And so she and her mom went back and forth, settling into their familiar, practiced rhythm. They flirted and teased and peppered Nadav with questions, and no one but Calliope could sense the cold ruthlessness behind it all. She watched how her mother's pale green eyes—not their original color, of course—barely flicked away from Mizrahi's, even when his gaze was directed somewhere else.

It's all about the eye contact, Calliope remembered her mom saying, her first lesson in the art of seduction. *Look directly into their eyes until they can't look away.*

And then, unexpectedly, Calliope heard a familiar voice behind her.

She made a little gesture to her mom and turned slowly, dragging out the moment before he recognized her. It had only been five months, yet he looked older, and somehow sharper. His shadowed beard from the previous summer was gone, his eyes glassy in a way they hadn't been before. She'd never seen him in a suit.

The only boy who'd ever gotten the better of her; and here he was, halfway around the world.

She saw the moment he registered her presence. He looked as stunned as she felt. "Calliope?"

"Travis?" she asked, which was the name he'd given her this summer, though she'd suspected at the time it wasn't real. Then again, neither was hers. Thank god she'd been using Calliope so much lately.

He winced, and looked around as if to see whether anyone had heard. "It's Atlas, actually. I wasn't quite honest with you this summer."

"You lied to me about your name?" she said indignantly, though of course she didn't mind. If anything, she was intrigued.

"It's a long story. But, Calliope . . ." He ran a hand through his hair, suddenly awkward. "What are you doing here?"

She tipped back the rest of her pomegranate champagne, then deposited the empty flute on a passing tray. "At the moment, I'm at a party," she replied flippantly. "What about you?"

"I *live* here," Atlas answered.

Holy. Shit. Calliope prided herself on being prepared for anything, but even she needed a moment to process this turn of events. The boy she'd met this summer, who'd bummed around Africa with her like a pair of nomads, was a Fuller. He wasn't just rich—his family was in its own stratosphere of wealth, so high that they had their own zip code. Literally.

She could work this to her advantage. She wasn't sure how quite yet, but she felt confident that a situation would arise, some way that she could walk away from Atlas richer than when she'd met him.

"All that time we spent haggling over the price of beer, and you live here?" She laughed.

Atlas joined in, shaking his head appreciatively. "God, you haven't changed at all. But what are you doing in New York?" he persisted.

"Why don't you tell me why you were hiding your name, and I'll tell you what brought me here?" Calliope challenged, even as she tried to remember what exactly she'd told him about herself. She smiled—her absolute best smile, the one she held in reserve for special occasions, which blossomed into something so bright and dazzling, that most people had to look away. Atlas held her gaze. She wanted him all the more for it.

The truth was, she'd wanted Atlas from the first moment she saw him.

———

She'd been standing in the British Air lounge at the Nairobi airport, trying to figure out where to go next, when he walked past, a tattered backpack slung over one shoulder. Every instinct in her body—honed to precision after years of practice—screamed at her to *go go go* in pursuit of him. So she did, tailing him all the way to a safari lodge, where she watched him apply for a job as a valet. He was hired on the spot.

She kept watching.

He was a mark, all right, for all that he was wearing a regulation khaki uniform, greeting guests, helping carry their luggage. He came from money. Calliope could see it in his brilliant smile, in the way he held his head, the way his eyes traveled over the room, confident and easy, but somehow not overly entitled. She just hadn't guessed how very *much* money.

She'd showed up at the lodge's employee party that weekend, wearing a crimson silk dress that draped all the way to the floor, hugging the curves of her hips and her chest. She wasn't wearing any underwear and the dress made that fact abundantly clear. But as her mom always said, you only got one good chance to bait the hook.

The party was far behind the lodge, past the enormous shed where they kept the flexiglass safari hovers. It was more crowded than she'd expected: dozens of young, good-looking employees were gathered around one of those fake bonfires—the holographic kind that threw off real heat—all dancing and laughing and drinking a bright lemony liquid. Calliope wordlessly took a cup and leaned back against a fence post. Her expert eyes picked him out at once. He was standing with several friends, grinning at something they had said, when he looked up and saw her.

A few other people approached, but Calliope waved them off. She crossed her legs to better reveal the slit in her dress, her long legs beneath. Calliope never made the first move, at least, not with boys. She'd found that they bought into a romance more quickly when they were the ones that came to you.

"You won't dance?" he asked when he'd finally come to stand near her. He sounded American. Good. She could pass for anything, but she always preferred being from London; and American boys were usually fascinated by that husky, sexy accent.

"Not with anyone who's asked me so far," she replied, raising one eyebrow.

"Dance with me." There it was again, that self-assurance, tinged with just a hint of recklessness. He was acting out of character. He was trying to escape something—a terrible thing he'd done, maybe, or a relationship that had ended badly. Well, she should know; she was running from a mistake herself.

Calliope let him lead her past the fire. The little bell earrings she'd bought in the open-air market that morning jangled with each step. Music blared from speakers; it was instrumental and wild, with a drumbeat pounding relentlessly through it. "I'm Calliope," she decided. It had been one of her favorite aliases, ever since she read it in an old-fashioned play, and she always felt like she had good luck as Calliope. The shadows from the holo-fire flickered over the boy's face. He had prominent cheekbones, a high forehead, a light dusting of freckles beneath his slight sunburn.

"Travis." She thought she heard a falsehood in his voice. He wasn't practiced at lying. Unlike Calliope, who'd been telling lies for so long she'd half forgotten how to tell the truth.

"Nice to meet you," she told him.

When the party drew to a close, Travis didn't invite her over. Calliope found to her surprise that she was glad of it. But as they said good-bye, she realized that her mom had been right: cons were much easier to manage when the mark was ugly. This boy was too attractive for her own good.

Now, as Calliope's eyes traveled over Atlas—the one boy she'd never been able to hook, never even *kissed*—she knew she was tempting fate.

She couldn't predict what he might do, and that made him dangerous. Calliope and Elise didn't like the unknown. They didn't like not being in control.

Calliope tossed her head restlessly, a little bit of a challenge in it. She'd slipped up with Atlas once, but now she was wiser, and determined. There never had been a boy she couldn't get, once she set her mind to it.

Atlas didn't stand a chance.

AVERY

"THE SPARKLING COCKTAIL, please," Avery said, the tulle skirt of her gold lamé dress—which her mom had insisted she wear, "for the holiday theme"—swishing a little as she approached the bar.

The bartender tapped a tall cylindrical beaker on his counter, which re-formed into a round pitcher, its crystals moving along their preprogrammed patterns. Then he grabbed the pitcher by the handle and poured her drink into a glass, adding a festive sprig of holly for good measure.

The walls of Avery's apartment were festooned with bright green garlands and gold twinkle lights. Tentlike bars soared on both sides of the room, flanked by miniature reindeer, which were tethered to a real-life sleigh with enormous bows. Thanks to holo-renderers, the ceiling seemed to disappear into a vast snow-filled sky. The apartment was more crowded than Avery had ever seen it—full of men and women in cocktail attire, clutching their sparkling red drinks and laughing at the holographic snow.

Avery just hoped it was because of people's interest in the Dubai tower, rather than their morbid curiosity about her, and what had happened on the thousandth floor the night Eris died.

Her father threw this holiday party for Fuller Investments every year, to schmooze his stockholders and biggest clients and, of course, to show off. Every December since they were children, Avery and Atlas had been expected to attend these events, to act charming and look perfect. That didn't change as they got older; if anything, the pressure was even greater now.

Back in middle school, Eris used to always be Avery's partner in crime on these nights. They would sneak plates of cake from the dessert bar and listen to all the lavishly dressed adults trying to impress one another. Eris had this funny habit of making up the conversations they couldn't overhear. She would use exaggerated voices and accents, spinning outrageous dialogues full of unearthed secrets and lovers' quarrels and families reunited. "You watch too many trashy holos," Avery would say through her muffled laughter. That had been one of her favorite things about Eris: her wild, sky-high imagination.

Avery felt someone's gaze on her. She looked up to see Caroline Dodd-Radson—Caroline Dodd now, she reminded herself, since the divorce. Eris's mom looked as gorgeous as ever in a screen-printed jacquard dress with a layered skirt. But the glow of the lanterns bobbing in the room picked out silver threads in her red-gold hair, the same bold shade as Eris's; and new lines were etched on her face. Her eyes were staring mournfully into Avery's.

Avery didn't think of herself as a coward, yet in that moment she wanted nothing more than to turn and run—anything to avoid making eye contact with the woman whose daughter Avery had allowed to fall. Because no matter how things had played out on the roof that night, Eris had died at Avery's apartment. Avery was the one who'd opened the trapdoor, and now the worst had happened; and she had to live with the consequences for the rest of her life.

She nodded at Caroline in a silent gesture of remorse, and grief. After a moment, Eris's mom inclined her head in reply, as if to say that she knew what was in Avery's heart, and understood.

"Is that Caroline Dodd? Didn't her daughter *die* in this apartment?" Avery heard a voice murmur behind her. A group of older women were bent together, their eyes cutting furiously toward Eris's mom. They seemed unaware of Avery, who stood there in frozen hurt.

"How shocking," another of them said, utterly placid and calm, the way people are when shocking things do not touch them at all.

Avery's hand tightened around her fizzy pink cocktail, and she retreated toward the library, away from this loud room with its vicious canned gossip and the searching eyes of Eris's mom.

But in the library, she was startled by the sight of another unexpected face. Though it shouldn't have been unexpected, Avery realized, given that she'd invited the girl herself. Calliope was here, wearing a low-cut dress and talking with Atlas in a way that was unmistakably flirtatious.

"Calliope. I'm so glad you made it," Avery interrupted, making her way over. "I see you've already met my brother," she added, and finally turned to the boy she couldn't stop thinking about.

Ever since that near miss with their dad, she and Atlas had tried to avoid each other around the apartment. Avery had scarcely seen Atlas all week. Now she let her eyes travel gratefully over his features, with a wicked sense of having gotten away with something forbidden. He looked as handsome as ever in a navy suit and tie, his hair parted to one side. He'd freshly shaven for the party, which Avery always thought made him seem younger, almost vulnerable. She tried to ignore the way her heart picked up speed at his nearness, but her whole body already felt several degrees warmer, just from knowing he was close enough to touch.

"Oh, you've already met Avery?" Atlas turned to Calliope, who tilted her head back and laughed as if this were some delightful coincidence, a lush, throaty laugh that to Avery didn't feel genuine.

"Avery and I got facials together a few days ago," the other girl said—and Avery realized how deft her wording was, that she made it sound like an organic, planned excursion rather than the truth, which was that she'd tagged along on Avery's afternoon with her friends. "She's the one who invited me tonight." Calliope turned to Atlas, a hand posed confidently on one hip. "You're terrible. You never even told me that you *had* a sister."

Avery was suddenly hyperaware of how beautiful the other girl was, in a scented, silvery way, all curves and bright eyes and smooth tanned skin. And the way she spoke to Atlas was so casual, almost familiar. Avery felt like she was missing something. She looked back and forth between them.

"I'm sorry. Did you two already know each other?"

"Callie and I met last May, on safari in Tanzania." Atlas kept trying to catch her gaze, clearly desperate to convey something.

"It's Calliope. You of all people know how much I hate nicknames! Although, Avery"—Calliope lowered her voice in an attempt at camaraderie—"you should know that James Bond here insisted on using a fake name with me. How utterly mysterious of you, *Travis*. As if anyone was going to track you from Tanzania to Patagonia." Calliope laughed again, but Avery didn't join in.

Patagonia? She knew that Atlas had gone straight from Africa to South America, but she'd always thought he was traveling alone. Maybe she'd misheard.

Just as she was trying to understand, Mr. Fuller's voice reverberated through the party.

"Hello, everyone!" he said, the sound projected by miniature speakers hovering in the air. "Welcome to the twenty-sixth annual Fuller Investments Gathering. Elizabeth and I are so delighted to welcome you all into our home!" There was a smattering of polite applause. Avery's mom, dressed in a black sheath with elegant cap sleeves, smiled and waved.

"Excuse me. I have to go check on someone," Calliope said softly. "I'll be back," she added, clearly for Atlas's benefit.

"What was that all about?" Avery edged forward toward the living room, a polite smile pasted on her face for the benefit of anyone who might be watching.

"It's the strangest coincidence. I met her in Africa, and now she's in New York with her mom."

"How much time did you spend together?" Avery whispered, and Atlas hesitated, clearly unwilling to answer. She bit her lip. "Why didn't you ever tell me about her?"

Avery had edged a little to the side of the crowd, and Atlas followed as their father droned on, thanking various sponsors and investors in the Dubai project.

"Because it didn't seem important," Atlas replied, almost too softly for Avery to hear. "Yes, we traveled together, but only because we were both doing the same thing: going spontaneously from place to place with no real plan."

"You never hooked up with her?" she hissed, even though she dreaded the answer.

Atlas looked directly into her eyes. "No, I didn't."

"As many of you know," their dad's voice boomed several

octaves louder—he'd obviously turned up the speakers. Avery fell silent, chastened. Had he seen them whispering, even here in this crowded room, and raised the volume in response? "Tonight is a celebration of our newest property, the crown jewel in our portfolio, opening two months from now in Dubai!"

Atlas caught her gaze and jerked his chin, to indicate that he was about to walk deeper into the party. Avery nodded in silent understanding.

As he turned, she reached out to brush a thread from the arm of his jacket. There was nothing there, but she couldn't help it. It was a final moment of privacy before she let go of him; a small, secret gesture of ownership, as if to remind herself that he was hers, and there was no letting go.

He smiled at her touch before disappearing into the crowd. With a monumental effort, Avery turned her attention back to her father.

"It is my great joy to present to you, The Mirrors!" Pierson gestured toward the ceiling. Gone was the holographic snowy sky, replaced by the blueprints of the new tower, which were projected in a tangle of lines and angles and curves. The schematic glowed like a living thing.

"The Mirrors derives its name from the fact that it is, in fact, two separate towers, one light and one dark. Polar opposites, like night and day. Neither of which has meaning without the other, like so many things in our world."

He went on to explain the tower, how the original vision for it had come from chess pieces, but Avery wasn't listening. She was looking up at her father's schematics. Light and dark. Good and evil. Truth and lies. She knew plenty about contradictions right now, with her seemingly perfect life that was riddled with dark secrets.

She heard everyone in the room whispering about the Tower,

calling it gorgeous, a dreamscape. They couldn't wait to see it. Most of them were going to the black-and-white ball in honor of its launch, their private charters all booked months ago; just like they'd all gone to Rio four years ago, or Hong Kong a decade ago. For some reason, Avery didn't want to go anymore.

Atlas's name sliced through her consciousness, and there was more applause. Avery blinked, startled. Across the room, Atlas looked just as confused as she was.

"My son, Atlas, has been working with me for several months now," her father was saying, though he wasn't quite looking at Atlas. "I am so proud to say that he'll be moving to Dubai, to take over the operations of The Mirrors when it opens to the public. I hope you'll all join me in raising a glass to the new tower, and to Atlas!"

"To Atlas!" the room cried out.

Avery couldn't think. Her mind was spinning wildly. Atlas, moving to Dubai?

She looked over, suddenly frantic to make eye contact with him, but he was smiling and accepting congratulations, playing the role of the dutiful son. A tray passed, and Avery deposited her empty champagne glass on it with such force that the stem snapped in two.

A few party guests looked her way, curious as to what set off the always-composed Avery Fuller; but the hovertray was already speeding off with the evidence, and Avery didn't really care. The only thing that mattered was Atlas, and the fact that he might leave.

Her tablet buzzed with an incoming message. *Don't worry, I'm not going.*

Everything restless and questioning and anxious in Avery stilled a little. Atlas said he wasn't going, and he wouldn't lie.

And yet there had been an undercurrent to her dad's tone that still pricked uneasily at her. *I am so proud*, Pierson had said. But he didn't sound proud; he'd been staring at Atlas with a puzzled look on his face, as if he'd woken up to discover that a stranger had been living in his house for thirteen years. As if he had no idea who her brother even was.

Feeling her gaze across the room, Atlas looked up, and for a single brief instant met Avery's eyes. She gave her head an imperceptible shake, willing him to understand. The problem wasn't Atlas. It was their dad.

Pierson knew, on some level, what was between them—or at the very least, he suspected, even if he wasn't yet able to admit it to himself.

She and Atlas had cut it close one too many times. And now their father was doing what he always did with a business problem: isolating it until he could figure out a solution.

Avery recognized her dad's announcement for what it really was. Atlas was being sent away.

LEDA

ACROSS THE ROOM, Leda's eyes darted from Avery to Atlas, missing nothing.

Well, well. It looked like the Fuller siblings had been caught off guard by that little announcement. Maybe there was trouble in paradise after all. This called for a toast, Leda decided, her feet moving automatically toward the bar.

"Leda." Her mom's hand clamped over her elbow. Leda sighed and turned around, impressed as always by Ilara's ability to pack a world of emotions—reproach, disappointment, warning—into a single word. "Why don't you come greet the hostess with me," she insisted, steering her daughter firmly in the opposite direction.

"I was going to get a soda water," Leda lied.

"Elizabeth." Ilara stepped forward to give Mrs. Fuller a stiff, formal hug. "What an evening! You've outdone yourself, as always."

"Oh, it was all Todd. He's the best event planner I've ever worked with. A creative *genius*," Mrs. Fuller gushed, and lowered her voice as if imparting an earth-shattering secret. "Wait until you ladies see what he's planned for the Hudson Conservancy Ball. It's just *beyond*! You're both coming, of course?" she added, almost an afterthought.

"We wouldn't miss it," Ilara said with a smile. Leda knew her mom was secretly dying for someone to ask her to help plan benefits like that, but no one ever did. Five years upTower and they still thought of her as new money.

Mrs. Fuller turned to Leda. "And, Leda, how are you doing? I'm sure you're looking for Avery, though I have to say I'm not sure where she is . . ."

With your son, Leda thought viciously, though she just nodded.

"Oh, she's right there! Avery!" Mrs. Fuller snapped, in a tone that brooked no argument. Leda remembered how Avery had always called it her general's voice. "I found Leda for you. We were just talking about the Hudson Conservancy Ball."

Leda watched as Avery forced a smile and walked over from where she'd been talking to some of their parents' friends. "Leda, you look amazing. Are you having fun?" she asked, her tone betraying none of what she must be feeling. But Mrs. Fuller wasn't even paying attention anymore; she'd drifted off with Leda's mom to another group, leaving the two former best friends alone.

"Oh, I'm having just the *best* time," Leda said caustically.

Avery sank into one of the chairs at the edge of the room, the ethereal tulle of her skirt fluffing around her like a little gold cloud. It was as if her entire being were deflating, now that their audience was gone. "I'm not in the mood right now, Leda."

For some strange reason, Leda found herself sitting in the chair next to Avery's.

"What are you doing?" Avery asked, evidently as surprised as Leda was by her actions.

Leda wasn't sure. Maybe she just wanted a break from the party, too. "Old habits die hard, I guess," she replied, but it didn't have quite the bite she'd intended.

They sat there in silence for a while, watching the swirl of false laughter and deal-making and schmoozing, all of it softened by the gentle glow of the lanterns.

"I'm surprised you're even here."

Avery's words startled Leda, but she quickly rallied an appropriate response. "And miss that Dubai announcement? I wouldn't dream of it!"

She wasn't sure what kind of reaction she'd hoped to get—some sort of dramatic lashing out, in sadness or even anger—but whatever it was, she didn't get it. She didn't get any reaction at all, really. Avery just sat there in complete stillness, her hands clasped in her lap, her long legs crossed. Was she even breathing? She looked like she was carved from stone. *Tragic Beauty*, a sculptor would have named her, and called it his finest work.

Leda felt suddenly grieved for the both of them, that they were sitting here in pale, pained silence, surrounded by the broken fragments of their friendship. And at a *party*. It was pathetic. She plucked a sangria off a passing tray. *Just try stopping me now, Mom.*

"You're right, I'm sorry I came. It was a mistake." It was so much easier to focus all her anger on Avery when they were both at school; when Avery was her usual cool, perfect self. Seeing how fragile she was beneath the veneer, it was a lot harder to hate her.

Avery looked up, and the girls stared quietly at each other, the air thick and heavy between them, almost stifling. For some reason, Leda refused to be the one to turn away. She just held Avery's gaze, daring her to react.

Avery was the first to break. "Enjoy the party, Leda," she said, and walked off.

Leda drained the sangria and abandoned the empty glass on a side table. She thought about what Avery's mom had said, about the Hudson Conservancy Ball. She hadn't been planning on going, but now she wanted to, to prove a point. She wanted Avery to know that it didn't bother her—seeing her like this, in the context in which they used to be best friends.

She wondered if Avery would bring anyone as a date. Probably not. After all, what was she going to do, come to the party with her brother? The last person Avery had brought to anything was Watt, and look how that had turned out.

Leda was struck by a sudden idea. What if *she* brought Watt to the gala? He might prove useful, with that computer of his— maybe he even had a way to communicate with it remotely, dig up intel for her in real time, on Avery and Rylin and anyone else dumb enough to get in Leda's way.

And as an added bonus, it would look like she'd stolen Watt from Avery. Everyone remembered meeting him at the University Club party with Avery, and now they would see him on Leda's arm, paying attention to *her*. For once, it would seem like a boy had chosen Leda Cole over the flawless and untouchable Avery Fuller.

She smiled, pleased with the notion, even as a dark, hateful part of her whispered to herself that it wouldn't be real. After all, Watt wasn't actually choosing her. Leda would have to force him into coming, blackmail him the way she blackmailed everyone in her life lately.

But then, who had ever truly chosen Leda?

AVERY

AVERY HAD ALWAYS loved her bedroom, which she'd decorated herself: with its enormous four-poster princess bed, its
scrollwork wallpaper deftly hiding all the touch screens, its two-
dimensional paintings in their antique gilt mirrors. But now it
felt like nothing so much as an ornate, blue-and-cream prison.

Atlas was still in the study with their dad, discussing the
Dubai news that Pierson had dropped on them like a bomb.
Avery knew that Atlas would flicker her as soon as he could.
She just hoped he'd be able to convince their dad to abandon
the whole plan.

She paced back and forth, still wearing her shimmering party
dress, her hair twisted up in an elaborate knot and decorated
with little gold beads that had apparently been the party planner's idea. She'd sat still for almost an hour while the hairdresser
painstakingly wove them into her hair, because while the styler
did have a few settings for updos, everyone recognized those a

mile away. Avery and her mom always had their hair done by a human professional before big events.

It all felt impossibly, dangerously heavy, as if every pin and bead—every stone around her neck, the diamonds in her ears—was dragging Avery inexorably down.

She hurried to her vanity in a sudden panic, her breath coming quick and shallow. Her hands fumbled as she tore at the pins, yanking them out violently, not caring that it hurt.

Eventually the pins and beads were scattered over the counter, her hair a tangled mess around her shoulders. Avery's heart was still racing. She fell back on her bed to stare up at the ceiling, which was modeled after one she'd admired in Florence, though hers was rendered in a moving hologram—complete with live-action brushstrokes. She thought back over every little gesture that she and Atlas might have made in front of their parents, to give them away. No matter which path her thoughts led her down, she kept arriving at the same terrible sense of foreboding.

A flicker finally came through. *Aves. I talked to him.*

She started upright. *And?!*

There was a pause, and then, *He's pretty set on the move. But we're going to talk more later. Don't worry.*

That didn't sound good. Avery slid off the bed. She'd waited long enough—she needed to see Atlas, hold him in her arms; actually talk to him, not through flickers or stolen whispers but for real.

"Do Not Disturb mode," she whispered as she stepped into the hallway. The words filtered through her contacts, alerting the various room comps that they shouldn't automatically turn on the lights or heated floors as she moved through the apartment. It was a function that Avery and her friends used to employ all the time for sneaking out late at night.

She tried to walk carefully, but her feet were betraying her, tripping over each other in her eagerness. Avery practically had to remind herself to breathe.

"Avery? Is that you?"

Her dad was sitting in a leather armchair in the living room—which wasn't his usual spot at all; usually he sat at the ponderous wooden desk in his study—in near total darkness. He held a tumbler of scotch casually in his left hand. It felt somehow like he'd been lying in wait, trying to *catch* Avery, like he'd been expecting her to sneak this way.

Avery stopped in her tracks, calling up what she hoped was a smile, but it was coming out all funny and distorted. Her chest tightened in panic. "What are you still doing up?" she asked, using Atlas's technique. Answer a question with another question.

"Just thinking things over."

"I was getting a drink of water." She sidestepped toward the kitchen as if it had been her destination all along. She knew it was suspicious that she'd been creeping around in Do Not Disturb mode, barefoot and still in her party dress, but it couldn't be helped.

"You do know that your room comp can get that for you," her dad said, almost challenging. His gaze was glittering and watchful in the darkness, as if he could see through the layers of her many lies to the harsh truth underneath.

"I couldn't fall asleep, and I thought walking around might help. It's been a long night, you know."

Even though her heart was pounding, Avery moved breezily into the kitchen and reached into the cupboard for a temp-controlled cup. She knew that even a hint of hesitation would give her away. Her dad's silhouette was just barely visible, a shadow starkly drawn against the darker shadows of the room beyond.

Avery filled the cup from the tap, then pushed the temp

setting on the cup's handle to chill the water within. The silence stretched out so painfully, she imagined she could hear tiny screams inside it. She took a small sip, fighting a growing sense of nausea. Why did it feel like her dad was weighing her every move?

"Avery. I know you're upset about Atlas moving to Dubai," he surprised her by saying.

Avery wandered toward him and took the opposite armchair. Her dad gestured impatiently with his wrist, and the lights in the room flickered on to dim.

"I was caught off guard by the announcement," she said truthfully. "But it sounds like a cool job. Atlas will be good at it."

"I know you're going to miss him, but trust me when I say that this is the best thing for the family." Pierson was speaking very slowly and deliberately. Avery wondered if he was drunk, or upset, or both.

The best thing for the family. There was something ominous about that phrasing. "And for Atlas, too," Avery pressed, suddenly determined to argue his case. "It'll be great for his career, right? To run that big a project at such a young age?" She was watching her dad carefully, and even in the shadows she could see the way he flinched a little at her brother's name.

"Yes. For Atlas too," Pierson repeated, and from the tone of his voice Avery knew he hadn't been thinking about Atlas at all.

"It's amazing of you to give him that opportunity. I'm glad." Avery suddenly felt anxious to leave. The longer she stayed here, talking to her dad, the greater the chance she might give something away.

"Anyway, I'm exhausted." She reached for the water and stood up, smoothing the front of her dress with a slightly nervous gesture. "Good night, Dad. I love you," she added, and as she said the phrase—words she'd spoken so many times before—she saw something in her father harden, as if the reminder made him even more furiously protective of her. Her heart sank at the thought.

It took all of Avery's considerable self-possession not to hurry; to walk down the hall to her room with slow, shuffling footsteps, as if she really were tired and couldn't wait to collapse into bed.

"Atlas," she hissed when she'd finally shut the door behind her, saying the words aloud to send them as a flicker. "I really think Dad knows. What are we going to do?"

There was silence for a while, but this time the silence didn't bother Avery, because she knew Atlas was composing his response carefully. He wasn't the type to give an answer that wasn't thoughtful or measured.

We'll figure it out, he said at last. *Don't worry. I love you.*

Even though she couldn't see his face, she could feel his smile, as if the warmth of it reached across their vast apartment, through all the various doors and walls separating them.

Avery fell back on the bed and let out a helpless sigh. "I love you too," she whispered in response.

She just hoped their love was enough to keep them safe.

RYLIN

IT WAS LATE Friday night, and Rylin couldn't fall asleep. She kept flipping restlessly back and forth, trying not to wake Chrissa, who was barely a meter away in the other twin bed. But Chrissa had always been able to sleep through anything.

Rylin's friends were all out at some big party tonight; Lux had pinged her about it earlier, but Rylin hadn't paid attention to the details. "I'm too exhausted," she'd said truthfully. After an interminable week at school—seeing Cord in the hallways and, worse, right there in front of her in holography class; not to mention dealing with the aftermath of her ill-planned impulse to partner with Leda on the project—Rylin hadn't felt up for a party. She knew it would be too loud and too bright, and she wouldn't even be able to hear her own thoughts over the clamor of the music. She'd stayed home instead with Chrissa, and the two of them had eaten frozen lasagna and watched a few episodes of some old holo about a girl in love with a boy, except that their families were enemies. Chrissa had sighed over their relationship, but something about it—maybe the forbidden, impossible love thing—had irritated Rylin.

She grabbed her tablet from where it lay on the floor and idly checked her messages. There were a few new ones to her school account: an announcement about tryouts for the school play, and a reminder that homeroom started at eight a.m. sharp. Her eyes caught on a message from Professor Radimajdi. Rylin opened it, curious, only to flush with anger when she saw the contents.

She'd gotten a C– on her first holography homework, a sunset vid that she'd taken from a lower-floor observation deck last week.

What the hell, she thought in outrage, tapping angrily down to read the director's comments. Hadn't he said that he *liked* sunset vids, that his own Oscar-winning film had featured one?

Rylin, this video is very soft and pretty—as well as trite, boring, and uninspired. I have to say, I'm disappointed. Next time, show me how you see the world, not what you think I want to see.

Rylin leaned back, incensed and more than a little confused. What right did he have to feel disappointment in her, anyway?

She wasn't sure why she was so angry, except that this was her first grade from Berkeley and it sucked. But what had she really expected? She was a seventeen-year-old high school dropout who, through some miracle of fate, had ended up at the most expensive, most academically challenging school in the country. Of course she wouldn't succeed there. She'd been stupid to think otherwise.

Rylin pushed back the covers. She felt shivery and anxious, and suddenly stuffy with cabin fever. What the hell was wrong with her? She shouldn't be home alone, looking at grades on a Friday night. The old Rylin would have been out right now. Well, it wasn't too late to salvage the evening.

Are you out? she sent to Lux, who replied instantly.

Yes!! We're at the public pool on 80. Come!

That sounded strange to Rylin, but she didn't even question it, just peeled off her T-shirt and pajama pants to change into a bikini. She dropped a shoe and paused, hoping she hadn't woken Chrissa; but she heard nothing except the steady rise and fall of her sister's breath, the quiet rustling of her blankets as she shifted to one side. Rylin stood a moment just watching her sleep. A fierce wave of protectiveness rose up in her. Then she pulled a dress on over her swimsuit and slipped into sandals.

On her way out the door, her gaze caught on the gleaming silver vid-cam, sitting on her desk like some kind of ominous, watchful eye. Without another thought, she tossed the camera into her bag and headed out the front door.

––––––––

Rylin had been to the public pool before. She used to come with Chrissa and her mom many years ago, when she and her sister wore matching swimsuits, and competed to hold their breath underwater the longest; and she'd come dozens of times with Lux, on summer afternoons, to fight for a spot on the deck and catch the slanting afternoon rays of the sun. But she hadn't seen anything like the pool now, at midnight, taken over by an illegal rave.

Teenagers were pressed close together inside, all wearing various combinations of swimsuits and denim. It smelled of chlorine and sweat and potshots. Someone had turned off the pool lights to keep them from getting caught; but moonlight streamed in from the windows, dancing across the shadowed forms that splashed through the water like sleek dark seals. An electric beat pulsed through the space. Rylin could make out the silhouettes of a few couples on the outdoor patio.

She peeled off her maxi dress and tossed it in a corner; but as she set down her bag, the vid-cam clunked against the ground.

Rylin found herself reaching for it. It felt warm in her palm. She lifted it up and it floated lazily overhead, following as if pulled by an invisible tether.

Tying her hair up in a loose ponytail, Rylin climbed the ladder that led to the suspended diving board. She'd heard there was a fancy half-grav one at the Berkeley indoor pool, so that the diving team could better practice their triple flips, but this had always been just fine for her. She raised her arms overhead and dove in headfirst, her thin body slicing through the water like a knife.

It was so nice underwater, dark and cool and blissfully quiet. Rylin stayed under as long as she could, until each capillary in her lungs was stretching for air, before kicking up to the surface. She gasped a little in delight and started toward the shallow end.

"Myers. It's been too long."

"Great to see you, as always, V," Rylin snapped in reply. V was leaning back with his arms behind his head, on an inflatable raft shaped like something vaguely inappropriate. He was a friend of Rylin's ex-boyfriend, Hiral, and she'd despised him ever since Hiral had forced her to sell V his drugs.

"I hope you're enjoying my little shindig," V drawled.

"Breaking into a public space, wreaking havoc; I should have known you were behind all this." She tried to keep moving through the crowds of people, but V slid off his float to block her path.

"I'll take that as a compliment. Though I guess this is far from what you're used to now, at your new highlier school," he replied. "What are you doing down here, anyway, when you could be at a party up there?"

Rylin found her footing on the bottom of the pool and managed to rise up on tiptoe, looking V squarely in the eyes. "I actually think of most of these people as my friends. Present company excluded, of course."

"I'm glad to hear that you think of me at all."

"Don't flatter yourself."

V glanced at her curiously. "Hiral's trial is coming up in a few weeks," he said, his tone deceptively matter-of-fact. "Are you going?"

"I don't know." Rylin fought the wave of emotion that rose up at the mention of Hiral. He'd been home on bail for a month now, but she hadn't seen him—things between them hadn't exactly ended on great terms, after he found out she'd hooked up with Cord. That was how the leg of their kitchen table had ended up broken. Among other things.

"Guess it depends on whether or not you're going," she finished, but her heart wasn't in it. V didn't bother challenging her.

The glow-lights above the pool changed color, from a lambent neon green to an eerie yellow. V glanced up, watching them shift, and his eyes caught on the vid-cam still floating cheerfully along after Rylin. "I see you have a new toy," he remarked—and in a sudden, shocking movement, lurched forward to grab the cam, dunking it all the way underwater.

"What the hell?" Rylin cried out, attracting a few stares in their direction. V laughed at her reaction. He opened his palm and the vid-cam floated back up, as easy as ever.

"These things are waterproof. No one told you that?" he said lazily.

Rylin was done being baited by him. "Have you seen Lux? I'm looking for her."

"She's off with Reed Hopkins." *What?* Rylin thought, trying to hide the surprise that lit up her face at that statement, but V didn't miss it; he never missed anything. "Ah," he said smugly. "You didn't know about that, did you?"

"Rylin!" As if on cue, Lux splashed over and pulled Rylin into a hug. Her hair was a dark blond again, which was always Rylin's favorite among Lux's kaleidoscope of constantly changing shades. It was almost her natural color; which made her seem younger, smoothed out the sharp angles of her nose and her pointed chin. "Isn't this incredible? V did a great job," Lux exclaimed, turning to V, but he'd already disappeared.

"You aren't worried about getting caught?"

"That new school is a bad influence on you," Lux teased. "When have you, of all people, worried about getting caught?"

"When did you start hooking up with Reed?"

Lux grew quiet, chastened. "I was going to tell you. It's really new, and I'm just . . . still figuring it out."

Rylin smiled, though she felt sad that her best friend was keeping things from her. Then again, she hadn't exactly been around much since she'd started at Berkeley; or even before that, when she was working for Cord. And she herself had been keeping something from Lux—she'd never told her about her secret relationship with Cord. "If you're happy, then I'm happy for you," Rylin said, because she was, and she really missed her friend right now. "Where is Reed, anyway?"

Lux tipped her head toward an enormous chair that someone had set up on the side of the pool, stacked precariously atop a table. Reed was sitting there, looking inordinately pleased with himself as he clinked shot glasses with a group of his friends.

"He's on lifeguard duty for the hour. Like people used to do in ancient times! We had to turn the safety bots off, you know, to keep the police away." Lux giggled. "He's not taking it that seriously, though."

Rylin had a feeling that human lifeguards were more recent than ancient times. She also had a feeling that Reed was in no shape to keep drunk teenagers from hurting themselves, but she smiled and held her tongue. "Let's dance," she said instead.

Lux nodded, and together they began to weave through the hot, crowded press of people. The vid-cam bobbed cheerfully above them, a tiny silver planet lost in a universe of glow lights.

WATT

THE FOLLOWING AFTERNOON, Watt waited for Cynthia at the corner of Madison Square Park in midTower. *I still think this is a bad idea*, he told Nadia, watching the flow of people on the carbonite sidewalk that lined the hover path. Tourists wandered around in their awful tourist clothes, jeans and fanny packs and those T-shirts that said I ♥ NY with the iconic image of the Tower emblazoned on the ♥. A group of girls across the street bought ice cream from an enormous cone-shaped snack bot, while periodically shooting glances at Watt and giggling.

"Did you have a better idea?" Nadia whispered into his ear-tennas.

I'm just curious, how many scenarios did you run for this? What likelihood of success did you calculate?

"My calculations are incomplete, given how much I'm lacking on the input variables."

So, basically null.

"Watt! I can't believe you agreed to come with me." Cynthia turned the corner with a smile.

"Of course. I wouldn't miss it," Watt said quickly.

Cynthia shot him a sidelong glance. "Really. You're telling me you're as excited as I am for the Whitney's new exhibit on post-modern sound-wave art?"

"To be honest, I'm just here because you wanted to go," Watt admitted, which elicited an even broader smile. Cynthia had been asking Watt and Derrick to come to this art thing with her for weeks—and now that Watt wanted to butter her up and ask a favor, he'd finally agreed.

That part had been Nadia's idea. Actually, Nadia was the one who'd suggested he ask for Cynthia's help in the first place.

Ever since Leda came over, Watt had been thinking about Nadia's idea. If Leda trusted him—if she thought that he was her friend, that he was *on her side*—maybe, just maybe, she would say the truth aloud. All Watt needed was one mention, one reference to that night, to get out from under her thumb.

He'd kept asking Nadia how to approach Leda, but she'd referred him to Cynthia. *There are some human behaviors that are impossible to predict*, she'd said frankly. *Studies have proven that asking a friend for advice is the most effective way to tackle trust-related issues in interpersonal dynamics.*

Sometimes I think you make these so-called studies up, Watt had replied, skeptical. Nadia sent him thousands of pages of research in silent response.

He and Cynthia headed through the museum's automatic doors into a stark, austere lobby. Watt nodded twice as he passed the payment machine, which scanned his retinas and charged him for the two tickets. "You didn't need to get mine," Cynthia said, sounding confused.

Watt cleared his throat. "Actually, I did," he said slowly. "To tell you the truth, I have an ulterior motive for coming here today."

"Yeah?" Cynthia asked. Watt wondered why Nadia was uncharacteristically silent, but then, she often shut up when he was talking to Cynthia.

"I need advice," he said bluntly.

"Oh. Okay," Cynthia breathed as they turned into the start of the exhibit, and fell silent.

It was a vast, dimly lit space filled entirely with metal pipes— the kind that still carried water and sewage throughout the Tower, like the ones that Watt's dad worked with as a mechanic. But the artist had painted them in a spectrum of discordantly cheerful colors, yellow and candy-apple green and watermelon pink. As they progressed through the space, lines of music whispered into Watt's ear before quickly changing to a new song, a new refrain. Watt realized the pipes were just for show. Miniature speakers were projecting the sound waves toward him in rapid iteration.

"What kind of advice?"

Cynthia's words echoed strangely over the sounds in the exhibit, as if coming from very far away. Watt shook his head, disoriented, and grabbed her wrist to pull her back into the hallway. Lost-sounding snatches of music drifted through the open door toward him, echoing strangely in his mind, or maybe the thought of Leda was literally driving him insane.

"I'm completely stuck. This girl—" He shook his head, immediately regretting the choice of wording; that made it sound like he *liked* Leda. Although maybe it wasn't the worst thing, he realized, if Cynthia thought he needed romantic advice. It was better than letting her guess the truth.

Cynthia stared at him in that piercing way of hers. For some reason Watt held his breath, trying not to even blink.

"Who is this girl?" she asked at last.

"Her name is Leda Cole." Watt tried not to let his irritation creep through, but he could hear it in his own voice.

"And your typical . . . techniques aren't working with her?"

Don't lie, Nadia urged him. "She's not a typical girl." That definitely wasn't a lie.

Cynthia turned back toward the stairs. "Come on," she said, sounding resigned.

"Wait, but your exhibit—don't you want to go through it first?"

"I'll come back another time, without you. Your life sounds like a mess," Cynthia proclaimed. Watt didn't argue, because she was right.

A few minutes later they were seated on one of the rotating hexagonal benches in the sculpture garden outside. "Okay. Tell me about Leda. What's she like?" Cynthia commanded.

"She lives upTower, goes to a highlier school. She has one brother. She plays field hockey, I think, and—"

"Watt. I don't want her résumé. What is she *like*? Introverted? Optimistic? Judgmental? Does she watch cartoons on Saturday mornings? Does she get along with her brother?"

"She's cute," he began carefully, "and smart." Dangerously so. Nadia was feeding him more, but Watt couldn't keep up this charade. The words began to pour from him like venom. "She's also shallow and petty, and insecure. Self-centered and manipulative."

Nice going.

You're the one who told me to tell the truth!

Cynthia shifted on the bench to face him. "I don't understand. I thought you liked her?"

Watt let his gaze drift to the trees nearby, genetically engineered to grow dozens of fruits on the same branch. An oversized lemon hung next to bunches of cherries, alongside a row of pinecones. "Actually, I don't like Leda at all," Watt confessed. "And she doesn't like me. She might even hate me. Normally I wouldn't care that I'm at the top of her shit list, except that she has something on me."

"What do you mean, she 'has something on you'?" Cynthia narrowed her eyes. "This is about your hacking jobs, isn't it?"

Watt looked up sharply. "How do you know about those?"

"I'm not stupid, Watt. The amount of money you've got is more than you could make as an 'IT consultant.'" She lifted her hands to make air quotes around the phrase. "Besides, you always seem to know just a little too much about people."

Watt could feel Nadia's uneasiness like a hand on his wrist. *We can trust her*, he thought silently.

If you say so, Nadia conceded.

"You're not wrong about the hacking," he told Cynthia, and part of him was relieved to finally admit at least this much of the truth to his friend.

"So what's happened that you're now asking me advice about Leda?"

"Like I said, Leda isn't my biggest fan. And with what she knows . . ." He shifted uncomfortably, and swallowed. "I really need her to not tell anyone. If she trusted me—or at least, if she stopped despising me—maybe she wouldn't tell."

Cynthia waited, but he didn't continue. "What would happen, if she told what she knows?" she prodded.

"It would be very, *very* bad."

Cynthia let out a deep breath. "For the record, I don't like this at *all*."

"The record has been duly noted," Watt assured her, smiling in relief. "So you'll help?"

"I'll try my best. I can't make any promises," Cynthia warned. Watt nodded, but the weight pressing down on his chest already felt lighter, just from the knowledge that Cynthia was here, and willing to try.

"First things first," she declared. "When are you going to see her again?"

"I don't know."

"You should probably ask her to hang out, so that you can take charge of the situation, reset the dynamic," Cynthia suggested.

The thought of voluntarily hanging out with Leda was so strange to Watt that he visibly flinched. Cynthia caught the expression and rolled her eyes. "Watt, this girl won't stop hating you if she doesn't ever spend time with you. Now, what are you going to say when you see her?"

"Hi, Leda," he tried.

"Wow," Cynthia deadpanned. "You overwhelm me with your incredible wit and conversational skills."

"What am I *supposed* to say?" he burst out, exasperated. "All I want is not to go to jail!"

Cynthia went very quiet and still. Watt realized with a sinking feeling that he'd said too much.

"*Jail*, Watt?" she asked. He nodded miserably.

Cynthia closed her eyes. When she opened them again, they shone with a new resolve. "You're going to have to be convincing as hell." She stood up and walked a few steps toward the museum, then turned around. "Pretend I'm Leda and I just arrived. Say something nice to me. Not just 'Hi, Leda.'"

Compliment her, Nadia offered. "Leda," Watt began, suppressing a smile in spite of everything at the silliness of the role-play. "It's great to see you."

"That's a start. This time, try it without sounding like you're getting a full-body exam from a med-bot."

Watt blinked at her in surprise.

"Come on," Cynthia urged. "You're going to have to be a better liar to make this highlier girl believe you. Think of someone else when you say the words, if it helps, but say it like you mean it."

Nadia automatically projected a series of images onto his contacts—some holo-celebrities that Watt had always found cute; and a picture of Avery, from the one night they actually went out, when she was wearing that slinky mirrored gown and his incandescent behind her ear. *Not helping, Nadia*, he thought angrily, and she backed off, chastened. He wasn't in the mood to think about Avery. He wasn't sure he ever would be.

Watt looked up again at Cynthia, who was still standing there, hand on hip. He cleared his throat self-consciously. "Hey there, Leda." He stood and moved aside as if to offer her a nonexistent chair. He managed to brush her arm as she maneuvered past him, his touch so slight that it could have been an accident. "You look fantastic tonight," he whispered into her ear, as if imparting some delicious secret.

Cynthia was absolutely still, her mouth a silent *O*. Watt was quite certain that he saw her shiver a little. He smiled, pleased with himself. *Nice to know I've still got it, right?* he thought to Nadia, who sent him a sarcastic thumbs-up in response.

"Watt . . ." Cynthia said slowly, shaking her head a little. "Cut the seduction crap. I thought you wanted this girl to *trust* you, not jump into bed with you."

That sounded like a trick question, so Watt didn't answer it.

"Girls have feelings, Watt." Cynthia looked down, toying with her purse, running its metal chain idly back and forth through her palms. "Feelings that can be easily hurt. You should remember that."

"I'm sorry," Watt said, not quite sure why he was apologizing, but feeling that it was needed. He sensed that there was some meaning behind her words, yet he couldn't suss it out, and Nadia wasn't offering anything.

Cynthia shook her head, and the moment passed. "I'm the one who should feel sorry for you. From everything you've told me, this isn't going to be easy."

She muttered a command to summon a waiter-bot from the museum's indoor café, and one of them floated over, a menu projected on its holo-screen. Cynthia typed a few keystrokes.

"We're gonna be here awhile," she said, gesturing for Watt to lean forward and pay. "The least you can do is buy me some freaking cake."

An hour and a half later, Watt felt as physically drained as if he'd been hacking all day. His very brain felt sore. But he had to admit, Nadia had been right to suggest that he ask Cynthia for advice. He wondered why he hadn't ever asked for her help before.

She was sitting cross-legged on the bench, a few crumbs of red velvet cake on the plate between them. "Okay," she said again, coaching him through the lines they'd practiced. "And what do you say next?"

Watt looked Cynthia straight in the eyes—intently, as if he could see into her very soul. "Leda. I hope you know you can trust me. After everything we've been through, you can tell me anything," he said solemnly.

Cynthia was quiet for a moment, and Watt thought he'd screwed it up yet again, but then she was laughing. The "after everything we've been through" line had been her idea, and though Watt wasn't quite sure about it, it did have a nice flourish. "God, I'm good," Cynthia boasted. "My work here is done."

"You're not going to believe this," Watt said as his contacts lit up with an incoming flicker. Now he was the one laughing, "Leda just beat me to the punch."

"Read me the message!" Cynthia demanded.

"'Watt. I need you to be my date to the Hudson Conservancy Ball next weekend. Don't bother giving me any excuses, we both know you already have the tux. You can pick me up at eight. The theme is Under the Sea.'"

"Wow. How romantic," Cynthia said sarcastically.

"Why did it have to be another formal event?" Watt groaned, standing up and offering his friend a hand. "These people can't be for real."

"Please, Watt," Cynthia said, her hand still in his, and the fear in her eyes was unmistakable. "Be careful with this girl."

He nodded, knowing that she was right. Spending time with Leda was a dangerous gamble.

He might set himself free—or he might destroy life as he knew it.

RYLIN

RYLIN BIT BACK a curse as she turned another corner, only to end up exactly where she'd started. *What the hell?* she thought wildly. Why did all the halls in this school have to look completely identical?

She spun a slow circle, trying yet again to remember the map she'd seen on her school-issued tablet before it died. She'd forgotten to charge it, which was especially embarrassing given all the ways it could possibly charge—jacked into the wall, sitting out in the sun, even next to her skin, charging off the thermal energy of her own body heat. The school's location-holos kept popping up before her at every corner and doorway, but they didn't help; they just listed the names of each room, which had all been gifted by wealthy donors. Rylin didn't care about the Fernandez Room, or the Mill-Vehra Dance Studio. She just needed to find the fencing piste, whatever the hell that was, because she was supposed to meet Leda there to film something for their holography project.

A group of boys appeared at the end of the hallway ahead, all of them sweaty and wearing shoulder pads. Rylin realized with a start that they were coming from hockey practice, and that one of them was Cord.

She started to backtrack, but it was too late—Cord had already looked up. He murmured something to the other boys and came to walk next to her.

"You okay?" he asked, amused. "You look a little lost."

"I know exactly where I'm going, thank you very much," Rylin replied neatly. She picked a random door on the right and started to push it open. "Now if you'll excuse me—"

The door swung inward, right into the middle of a small mat-lined room, where two guys were grappling with each other on the floor. They looked up at her, startled, and Rylin quickly stumbled back.

"Of course, you know exactly where you're going," Cord agreed, "which is to JV wrestling practice."

Rylin threw her hands up. "Fine. I have no idea how to get to fencing. Can you tell me where it is?"

Cord started walking. "I'll do you one better. I'll take you there."

"It's okay, just tell me," she insisted, but he'd already left her behind.

"You coming?" he called out over his shoulder. Rylin cursed and trotted to catch up.

They walked silently down a hallway, its walls lined with brass plaques commemorating the school's athletic records. Light danced on the silver and bronze statues arranged in careful rows behind the flexiglass cases. Rylin kept her head fixed on the awards, reading the names inscribed there without processing them, trying desperately to look anywhere but at Cord. She found herself absurdly grateful that, for once, her hair hung straight and shining to her shoulders, instead of being in its usual low ponytail.

"So, fencing." Cord's voice seemed to echo in the empty hall. "You *do* know that you can't actually hurt people with the épées, right? They're lined with magnetic fields that make them impact-resistant."

Rylin rolled her eyes. "I'm not trying to impale anyone today, I promise."

"Could've fooled me," he said lightly. "Why are you going to fencing, then?"

"To film something for holography." *The class where you sit right in front of me, close enough for me to touch you, and we both refuse to acknowledge each other's existence.*

"That's a good idea. It'll be interesting, visually," Cord said, and beneath his typical insouciance, Rylin could tell that he meant it. The realization warmed her.

"It would be better if I could make the team wear pirate clothes, but Leda refused," she ventured, and was rewarded with the corner of a smile.

"I'd forgotten Leda was your partner." Cord glanced at her. "The thing you should know about Leda is that she's a lot of bark but no bite. And once you're her friend, she'll fight for you to the death."

"Thanks," Rylin said, puzzled. As if she and Leda Cole would ever be friends.

He shrugged and led her down another hallway. "I just want to make sure things are going okay for you. If I can help . . ." He trailed off, not quite making an offer, but Rylin's breath had already caught in her throat. What was he trying to tell her? She felt tangled in a state of painful, sweet, unbearable confusion.

"You are helping," she said. "I had no idea how absurdly big this athletic complex is. I almost expect to see stables here, with those fences that people jump horses over."

"We passed the stables. They're on the middle level," Cord answered.

For a moment Rylin was struck speechless, until she looked at his face and saw the telltale smirk.

"Nice to see you're still messing with me."

"Nice to see you can still tell when I'm bullshitting you," Cord replied.

They stepped up to an enormous set of double doors, beyond which Rylin could hear the sounds of swooshing metallic sword-play. She felt a pang of regret that the walk hadn't been longer. It was nice, talking to Cord again. She wondered what he'd meant by the gesture, if he'd even meant anything at all.

"See you around, Myers," he said, but Rylin called him back. "Cord—"

He turned and looked at her, expectant. She swallowed.

"You don't hate me anymore?" she asked, and her voice was very small.

Cord looked at her with a funny expression. "I never hated you."

Rylin stood there quietly, watching his retreating footsteps. She couldn't help admiring the length of him, the easy, confident way he moved, the way his head sat upon his broad shoulders. She wanted to run forward and take his hand, the way she used to, but managed to hold herself back. *You can't have him anymore*, she reminded herself. *He's no longer yours.*

A buzzer sounded in the fencing arena. With great effort, Rylin pushed the door open and started inside.

It was a wide oval room, with nondescript white flooring marked by colored squares that must be the piste. Two fencers from the varsity team slashed at each other, both of them dressed in white jackets and helmets, scuttling back and forth like drunken crabs. Their impact-resistant épées whipped through the air in thin, quick motions. It would look incredible on camera, Rylin thought approvingly.

Leda stood at the edge of the piste. Her silver vid-cam already floated above them, near the overhead lights. "There you are," she hissed, not even glancing up as Rylin approached.

"Sorry. I got lost."

"Looked to me like you were busy flirting with Cord, but what do I know," Leda retorted.

Rylin gave a jerky nod. She didn't owe Leda any sort of explanation, she reminded herself.

Finally, Leda lifted her eyes to look squarely at Rylin. "What is it between you two, anyway?" she asked bluntly.

Rylin felt somehow both angered and amused by Leda's complete lack of tact. "Not that it's any of your business, but I used to work for him, and now I don't."

Leda pursed her lips, as if she knew there was more to the story, but was willing to accept Rylin's explanation for now.

They fell into silence, watching the fencing for a while, one or the other of them occasionally waving to change the position or angle of the vid-cam. Finally, something occurred to Rylin.

"Leda," she decided to ask. The other girl looked over in irritation. "Last week, you said something about how the class is only open to seniors, that you got in because of an application essay. But I'm a junior, and I'm in—"

"I told you, you're a fluke," Leda said impatiently. "Think of it as a mid-semester exception, for the sole purpose of pissing me off."

"And Cord is a junior, too," Rylin went on determinedly, an eyebrow lifted.

Leda made an exasperated motion. "It's different for Cord. After all, he has a *building* named after him. So, yes, he gets into any class he wants."

Rylin felt a strange lurch in her stomach. "What building?" She thought she'd seen the names of all the buildings, especially after getting lost so much the past few weeks.

"Maybe I should have said buildings, plural," Leda pronounced meaningfully. "The whole high school is named after Cord's family. You wouldn't have noticed, since you haven't gone downstairs to the lower and middle schools, but everything on this floor—the entire high school—is technically the Anderton campus."

The brief moment of closeness Rylin had shared with Cord seemed to dissolve into the air like smoke. Once again she was reminded of the vast distance between them, and how foolish she was to think that she could bridge it. How many times did the universe have to teach her the same stupid lesson? Here she was, at the same school as Cord, and yet she felt further from him than ever.

Rylin wanted to blame the difference in their circumstances: the fact that Cord's family had endowed the entire upper school, while she was only here because a girl had died. But she knew that only explained part of what was keeping her from Cord.

The rest of it was her doing. She'd broken something in their relationship when she violated his trust.

She wondered if someday, maybe, she might be able to fix it—or if some things you couldn't fix, no matter how much you wanted to.

CALLIOPE

CALLIOPE STRETCHED THE entire length of the lounge chair, pulling her arms overhead in a deliberately lazy gesture, though her body thrummed with alertness. How long till Atlas showed up? She knew he would be here; he was meeting with one of the hotel executives about some business negotiation or other. She took a distracted sip of her water, its non-melting cold cubes clinking together, and fiddled with the strap of her new crocheted one-piece.

Calliope should have been accustomed to waiting by now; she'd certainly done plenty of it the past few years. But she'd never been especially patient, and didn't intend to start today.

Her stacked jade bracelets slid down her arm as she propped herself on one elbow to glance around. The Nuage sundeck had one of the best views in the Tower, with its sparkling infinity-edge pool seeming to stretch all the way to the horizon. Yellow-and-white umbrellas dotted the space, solely for ambiance: the soaring blue ceiling overhead was lined with solar lamps that projected an even, UV-free sunlight. Calliope remembered that once, when she and her mom had been at a pool in Thailand, it had actually *rained* on them, because the local government didn't even bother to control the weather. Calliope and Elise had loved it—it felt like some glorious adventure out of a romance novel, as if the sky were breaking open, and suddenly anything was possible.

She heard a door open overhead and risked a glance up. Sure enough, there was Atlas, walking from the executive offices onto the hotel's famous suspended bridge, which looped over the pool and the surrounding interior vineyards. Like the umbrellas, the vineyards were mostly just for show, barely producing enough wine to make a few barrels a year.

Calliope had chosen her seat with excessive care. She waited until Atlas was directly above her. "Atlas? Is that you?" she called out, a hand raised as if to shade her eyes. She hadn't seen him or heard from him since that party as his parents' apartment last weekend, so here she was, resorting to a staged run-in. It was a little bit desperate, but every great con has to start somewhere.

"Calliope. What are you doing here?" Atlas stepped onto one of the edges of the bridge. "Down, please," he added. Calliope's mouth twitched a little as his segment of bridge detached itself to float down. Only Atlas would say *please* and *thank you* to a robotic control system.

She debated standing up to greet him but decided against it. It gave Atlas too much power, and besides, she looked better from this angle.

"I live here. What's your excuse?" she said archly, with a glance at his suit and tie. "All work and no play?"

"Something like that." He ran a hand through his hair in that absentminded way of his.

Calliope gestured to the chair next to her. "Care to join me, or do you have to hurry back?"

Atlas paused, probably checking the time. It was almost evening. "You know, why not," he decided, shrugging off his jacket and sinking gratefully onto the chaise.

Calliope lowered her eyes to hide her excitement, letting her long lashes cast shadows over her face. She lifted one shoulder toward the windows, where the sun was dipping behind the jagged man-made mountains that crowded the horizon. "It's almost time for sundowners. Champagne or beer?" she asked, and tapped the side of her chair to call up the menu.

As she'd hoped, her words elicited a reluctant smile. Sundowners had been a tradition back in Africa—the staff at the safari lodge would all climb a hill to watch the sunset, bringing salted crackers and beers in zippered backpacks. The moment the sun disappeared into the horizon, they would break open the bottles, raising them in a toast as the sky erupted in a fiery blaze of color.

"Beer," he concluded. "There's actually a local Joburg brew on the menu, if you can—"

"Done."

Their eyes met, and maybe it was Calliope's imagination, but it felt like something leapt in the air between them.

"So. How did your meeting go?"

"Not that well," Atlas admitted, "but let's not talk about work right now."

With any other boy, Calliope would have followed the cue and changed the subject to something else—probably herself—but she'd learned the hard way that Atlas wasn't like any other boy. Instead she forced herself to look into his bottomless brown eyes. "I hope the hotel wasn't demanding a renegotiation of their lease terms. You shouldn't give them one, not right now."

It was always risky, choosing not to play dumb. Calliope's heartbeat echoed around her rib cage. "And why shouldn't I?" Atlas asked, clearly intrigued.

"Their occupancy rates should be higher. It's the holidays, and they aren't even at eighty percent. Besides," she added, lifting one long leg and pointing her toes, "their customer service is woefully inadequate. You know I slipped on a drink and sprained my ankle when we checked in here?"

Atlas's eyes followed her motion for an instant, then looked away. So at least he found her attractive. She'd almost started to think she'd imagined it. She lowered her leg and leaned forward. "All I'm saying is, I'd think carefully before renewing their lease at the same terms. Especially given current interest rates."

"You're not wrong," Atlas admitted. They went back and forth for a while about discounted cash flows, and even though Calliope was talking the whole time, she was also watching Atlas's body, the way his pupils danced when he talked about certain things, the way his hands gestured to make a point. All summer she'd expected to feel those hands on her, yet Atlas had never touched her, not once.

Why hadn't he wanted her, she thought frantically. Why was he the only boy who hadn't tried to make a move on her—the one boy she'd failed to trick?

A waiter carried their beers over on a silver tray. The glass was pleasantly cold in Calliope's fingers as she lifted it to her mouth and took an enormous sip. She still hated beer—always had—but she'd gone to far greater lengths for a con before.

"What have you been up to lately?" Atlas asked. "You're not in school, right?"

For an instant Calliope wondered if she'd made a mistake, turning down her mom's offer to enroll her in school. It would have given her more time with Atlas's sister—but then she reminded herself that girls gave unpredictable assistance at best, and besides, it was always better going directly to the mark. She knew that if she stayed around Atlas long enough, she could figure out a way to get something from him.

"I'm not in school. But I assure you that I'm quite capable of entertaining myself," she answered, with what she hoped was the right amount of naughtiness.

"Atlas! What are you doing here? And who is this?" There was something familiar about the boy who approached their chairs, Calliope thought. He was tall and classically good-looking, with high cheekbones and piercing blue eyes.

"Cord! How are you?" Atlas grinned and stepped up to greet the other boy. "Have you met my friend Calliope Brown?"

Friend, really? Calliope considered that an opening bid in negotiations. Luckily she was one hell of a negotiator.

She swung her legs over the side of the chair and drew herself up slowly. "It's a pleasure," she murmured—just as another boy walked into the pool area, and she realized with a sinking feeling why Cord felt so familiar.

"Fuller! We were about to grab dinner. Want to come?"

Calliope's chest constricted. The newcomer was an older version of Cord, a little hardened by age, his smile a little more cynical. She prayed he wouldn't remember her, but her hopes crumbled when he glanced her way and frowned in puzzled recognition. "Do I know you?"

"Unfortunately, I think not," Calliope said lightly.

He shook his head. "No, we've met, in Singapore. You dated my friend Tomisen, and we went to that moonlight party on the beach?"

Calliope had never been recognized before. The world was becoming too small for people like her, she thought, trying not to reveal any trace of her fear. She just hoped that Brice didn't know the rest of the story—that a week after the beach party, she'd asked Tomisen for a loan, closed her fake bitbanc account the moment his funds cleared, and skipped town.

She glanced at the door, its EXIT holo illuminated in glowing letters. *Always know your way out*, as her mom constantly reminded her. Just looking at the holo made Calliope feel calmer.

She sharpened her features into a smile and held out her hand. "Calliope Brown," she said tartly. "I'm afraid you have me confused with someone else. Though she sounds quite fun, so I'll take it as a compliment."

"Brice Anderton. Sorry, my mistake." His grip was too firm on her hand, his voice tight with an unspoken threat.

"Please ignore my brother. He obviously has trouble remembering all the women he meets in his travels," Cord joked, oblivious to the tension.

Brice still hadn't let go of her hand. Calliope gently tugged at it, and he released it with obvious reluctance. "Why haven't I met you before, Calliope Brown?" He said her name as if there were quotation marks around it, as if he wasn't convinced it was hers.

"I don't live in New York."

"And where did you say you're visiting from?"

She refrained from pointing out that she hadn't, in fact, said. "London."

The older boy's expression shifted for a moment. "Interesting. You have a very *unique* accent."

Calliope glanced at Atlas, but he was making some remark to Cord, ignoring her conversation with Brice. Her blood quickened a little.

"Since you aren't from New York, I'm guessing you need a date to the Under the Sea ball," Brice went on.

Calliope quickly lifted her gaze. "Under the Sea ball?" she repeated, like a moron, and caught herself. "That sounds fun," she went on, raising her voice for Atlas's benefit.

As if he'd seen and understood her intentions, Brice turned toward Atlas. "Fuller, your mom is chairing that Under the Sea party, right?"

"The Hudson Conservancy thing? I think so," Atlas replied, puzzled.

So Atlas would be there.

Brice smiled, and Calliope couldn't help thinking that there was something wicked in it. She wondered with a little thrill that was half panic, half excitement whether he'd seen through all her lies. It felt like he'd made that comment to Atlas specifically to bait her.

"So, Calliope," Brice went on intently. "You'll come to the party with me, right?"

She kept track of Atlas in her peripheral vision, even as her gaze remained on Brice. This was Atlas's cue—he was supposed to interject and offer to take her himself. But he wasn't saying anything.

Fine, then. Some part of Calliope knew it was a terrible idea for her to go out with the boy who had just almost recognized her, but wasn't there an old saying about keeping your enemies close? And after all, a party was a party. She'd never been one to turn down an invite, no matter the occasion.

"I'd love to," Calliope said to Brice, and held eye contact with him to link their contacts. His gaze was steady and unblinking.

By the time the Anderton brothers had said their good-byes, Calliope had decided that this might work to her advantage. There was no better way to get a boy's attention than showing up to a party, dressed to kill, on someone else's arm. She would make damned sure that Atlas regretted not asking her to that party first. And then she would take him for everything she could, before she and her mom skipped town.

It might just be her greatest con yet.

AVERY

THE SOUND OF bells rang clear and sweet through the cold night air. Avery nestled closer to Atlas beneath the pile of blankets, her heart pounding in excitement as their sleigh moved down the tree-lined path.

She still couldn't quite believe they'd gotten away with this. It was Saturday night, and they were in Montpelier, Vermont—together, in the open. Far away from New York, with all its restrictions and limitations and *no*s.

Atlas had planned everything. They'd both been at the breaking point lately: walking around the apartment constantly tense and on eggshells, acutely aware of each other's every move yet trying desperately to pretend they didn't care at all. Avery felt like she'd been holding her breath since the Dubai announcement. When Atlas suggested that they get out of the city for a night, it had seemed too good to be true.

"I'm so glad we were able to sneak away." Her breath came

in puffs of crystallized cloud against the chill. She looked over at Atlas's profile, his straight nose and the full line of his mouth, the light dusting of freckles across the pale peach skin of his cheekbones. By now his features were more familiar to her than her own. She could draw every line of his body blindfolded, she'd memorized him so thoroughly.

"Me too, Aves." He reached an arm around her to pull her closer.

"You don't think Mom and Dad will suspect anything?" She still felt nervous that they were both gone from home on the same night. It felt like an enormous red flag.

"Didn't you tell them you're at Leda's?"

"Yeah," Avery said shortly, though she'd actually told them Risha's, on the off chance they pinged to check on her. She couldn't trust Leda to cover for her, not anymore.

"And I told them that I'm going to the Rangers-Kings game in LA, with Maxton and Joaquin. I even bought the tickets to prove it. Don't worry."

Avery nodded, but she couldn't help fidgeting a little, trying to quiet the nervousness that kept pricking at her. She was reminded of when she'd tried to steal a bag of sugar chips from the kitchen, once, when she was little. She'd pulled it off without a hitch, only to find that when she got the chips back to her room, she was too wrung out with anxiety to enjoy them.

Atlas noticed the movement and sighed. "Aves, I know that whole scene with Dad made you nervous, but I promise we're safe here. And we only get this one night together, away from it all. Can't we make the most of it?"

Avery silently cursed her own stubborn fear. She knew how much effort Atlas had put into planning this; trying to find somewhere they wouldn't be recognized, something he knew she would love. And here she was, apparently doing her best to ruin it. She shifted beneath their temperature-controlled blanket so that her head was on his shoulder.

"You're right," she murmured.

Atlas laced his fingers in hers, bringing her hand lightly to his mouth and kissing it. It was a tender, almost courtly gesture, and it melted Avery's lingering anxieties.

She glanced at the darkness swishing past, thick and layered and beautiful. It felt like there could be ghosts out there in the woods—or nymphs maybe, some kind of ancient spirit. The Tower felt worlds away.

They were on their way to see the Northern Lights. Because of the shifting movement of the tear in the ozone layer, the aurora was visible this far south only once a year. Avery had always longed to see it, had watched it in VR countless times, yet for some reason she'd never come in person before.

They pulled into a clearing where a dozen other self-driving sleighs were already parked, separated by discreet distances, like some enchanted version of old-fashioned drive-in movies. A hushed spell had fallen over the gathering. Steaming mugs of cocoa, topped with fluffy dollops of whipped cream, were passed on floating hovertrays. Their seat began to recline until they were lying flat, blinking up into the darkness. It seemed to Avery that there was nothing in the world at all except the cold outside and the warmth of Atlas's body next to her, and the velvety vault of the sky stretching endlessly above her.

An array of colors burst suddenly into life: streaks of blue and green, of blush and apricot, arcing and twisting around one another. For a brief moment Avery felt almost afraid, as though the earth were careening toward a distant galaxy. She held tight to Atlas's hand.

"Are you listening to anything?" she asked quietly. There were dozens of soundtracks recommended to accompany the lights, everything from violin concertos to oboe solos to rock music. She'd shut them all off. She imagined that she could hear the lights swishing in the silence, whispering to her against the curtain of the sky.

"No," Atlas murmured.

"Me neither."

Avery snuggled closer to him. Tears pricked at her eyes, and the tears fragmented the light even further, splintering it into a million beautiful shards.

She must have dozed off at some point, because when she opened her eyes, the sun's rosy fingers were appearing on the horizon.

"We're here, Sleeping Beauty." Atlas tucked her hair behind her ears and kissed her tenderly on the forehead.

Avery looked up at him, no longer tired at all; her whole being suddenly and painfully alert to how close he was. "I like waking up to you," she said, and was rewarded with one of Atlas's dazzling smiles.

"I want to wake up with you every morning, always," he agreed as the sleigh pulled up to their hotel with a jolt. They were staying at the famous Snow Palace, where everything was made of nonmelting ice, even the fireplaces. Around them, other couples were rising sleepily from their blankets, starting toward the massive double doors carved like icicles. Avery bounded lightly from the sleigh as Atlas stepped out the other side.

"Avery?" Boots crunched on the snow behind her.

Avery tensed at the sound of her name. She didn't dare glance over at Atlas; but in her peripheral vision she saw him crouch, pulling his hat lower over his brow and pushing quickly through the hotel's doors. A strange pang clutched her chest as she watched him walk away from her without a backward glance. It felt like a terrible portent of things to come.

She turned around slowly, calling up a fair approximation of a smile. "Miles. What a surprise," she exclaimed, and gave the newcomer a hug. Miles Dillion had been in Atlas's high school class. She wondered in a wild panic if he'd seen him.

"I know!" Miles laughed, and his companion stepped forward, a tall young man with smooth, handsome features. "This is my boyfriend, Clemmon. Are you here alone?"

"Unfortunately, yes." Avery didn't dare step forward in case her knees gave out. She pulled her coat tighter around her, trying to pin her mind down to some kind of focus. "My dad might acquire this hotel, and he wanted me to come check it out for him. So far, I like it. What do you think?" It was a good enough lie, given the short notice.

"We love it," Clemmon exclaimed. "So romantic. It really is too bad you're here alone," he added, in the same puzzled tone that people always adopted when Avery told them she was single.

"Do you want to come get breakfast with us?" Miles offered, but Avery shook her head, that smile still pasted on her face.

"I think I'm going to take a nap. Thanks, though."

She waited until the two boys had walked hand in hand toward the dining room, with its soaring ice ceiling and stalagmites dotting the floor, before hurrying down the hallway toward her room.

When she stepped inside, Atlas was already there, gazing into the fire from one of the slouching armchairs. On a side table gleamed a silver tray laden with Avery's favorite things: croissants and fresh berries and a carafe of hot coffee. She smiled, touched as always by Atlas's thoughtfulness.

"I'm so sorry about that," she said slowly. "What an awful coincidence. I mean, what are the chances?"

"Evidently not as low as we thought." Atlas's jaw was strong and hard in the flickering light of the fire. He looked up at her.

"This isn't a coincidence, Aves, this is our reality. We can't be together in New York, but look what happens when we try to leave."

Avery walked slowly around to sit in the other chair, kicking her legs close to the fire. "I don't . . ."

Atlas leaned forward, his hands on his knees, a frightening new urgency in his tone. "We have to run away, like we always planned, before it's too late."

For a moment Avery let herself sink blissfully into the fantasy: walking with Atlas along a sun-drenched beach, shopping in a colorful fish market, holding him in a hammock under the stars. Actually getting to *be* together, without fear of being caught. It was a beautiful dream.

And an impossible dream, at least right now. Her stomach dropped at the thought of Leda: who knew the truth about them, and wouldn't hesitate to blast it out if they ran away together. Avery couldn't imagine putting her parents through all that. What would happen to them, if news of Avery and Atlas's relationship became public?

Although by now her father might already suspect the truth.

"There's nothing I want more than to run away with you," Avery said, and she meant it, with every fiber of her being. "But I can't, not yet." If only she had a better explanation.

"Why not?"

"It's complicated."

"Whatever it is, Avery, you can—"

"I just *can't*, okay?"

Atlas looked down, his features wounded and closed off.

"I'm sorry. I didn't mean to snap. I'm just on edge," she said quickly, and reached across the space between them for his hand.

Atlas gave her hand a little tug, prompting Avery to cross to his chair and sit in his lap. She circled her arms around his neck and leaned her face into his chest, closing her eyes. The steady beat of his heart reassured her, made her breath come a little easier.

"It's okay. Seeing Miles put me on edge too," Atlas said, tracing a small circle on her back.

Avery nodded. She wanted so desperately to tell Atlas the truth—about that terrible night on the roof, what really happened to Eris, and the lie she'd told. The real reason that they couldn't run away.

But Atlas would look at her differently once he knew what she'd done. Avery wasn't sure she could bear that.

He sighed. "It's Mom and Dad, isn't it? They'll be all right without us. Certainly better than if we stay and get found out." His arms tightened a little around her. "Although . . . as much as I want to go now, maybe we *shouldn't* leave right away. It might be better if I go work for Dad in Dubai for a year, and then we head out after you graduate. We wouldn't even have to go at the same time. There would be fewer questions that way." He smiled. "Plus, you deserve to finish high school with your friends."

"Dubai is so far," Avery said instinctively, hating the idea of their living separate lives, half a planet away from each other.

"I know, but, Aves, we can't live like this either—both of us in New York, in constant terror of being caught."

Avery didn't have an answer. Dubai felt like a terrible option, but she knew Atlas was right; they couldn't go on this way. "I'm sorry. I just need more time," she whispered helplessly, because she had no idea what she was going to do.

"I get it. I'm being as patient as I can." The trust in Atlas's smile nearly broke her. "And of course you're worth the wait. I would wait a lifetime for you."

Avery couldn't listen anymore, so she silenced his words with her lips.

Later, when Atlas had fallen asleep under the pile of bear-skin blankets, Avery glanced around the beautiful ice bedroom, its walls smooth and unyielding. She kept thinking of Miles and Clemmon, of her parents, of Eris and Leda and everything else digging little tears into the fabric of her relationship with Atlas.

Even here, far outside New York, she and Atlas couldn't escape the cold hard truth of who they were. There was nowhere for them to hide. Her heart constricted in panic. What if it was like this forever? The world was so small now—how could she and Atlas ever be free?

She tried to push that thought aside, but it felt like the ice-cold walls were slowly closing in on her, crushing the air from her lungs, and she couldn't escape.

RYLIN

RYLIN LEANED FORWARD on the counter of the holography edit lab, so deeply absorbed by the work that she'd almost forgotten where she was.

She'd met up with Leda after school to edit their fencing footage, which Rylin had to admit had turned out pretty awesome. But Leda had left a while ago. On a whim, Rylin had loaded the rest of the footage from her vid-cam—and was now submerged in something else entirely.

She kept rewatching what she'd filmed at the pool party last weekend, scrolling back and forth through it, her eyes glittering with excitement. Because even as she sat in this room, on a black velvet chair, Rylin felt transported back in time.

The party ebbed and flowed around her, light dancing on the walls like candlelight flickering on a primordial cave. The blue-green pool seemed to ripple up to Rylin's waist. Next to her, Lux surfaced from underwater and gave her head a shake—Rylin instinctively threw up an arm, recoiling from the droplets that flung from Lux's close-cropped blond hair, before lowering it self-consciously, because of course Lux wasn't there.

This was even more intense than halluci-lighters, she thought, searching eagerly for a clip to show her friends.

"Rylin? What are you doing in here?" Xiayne stepped inside, and the door shut automatically behind him to block the light. He was wearing a white T-shirt again, the inktats on his chest almost visible through the thin material.

She slammed her console's central button, and the holo went dark. "Just working on something."

"Wait—pull that back up, will you?" Xiayne's voice was eager, curious.

Rylin crossed her arms. For some reason she felt defensive. "Do you need me to leave? Last I checked, this room wasn't reserved."

"No, by all means, stay. I'm not here to kick you out." Xiayne sounded amused by her reaction. "I'm glad that someone is finally using this space. God knows the school spent enough money on it, and it's always empty."

"Professor—" Rylin began, but he interrupted her.

"Xiayne," he corrected.

"Xiayne," she forged on, a little exasperated. "What was wrong with my video of the sunset?"

"Nothing. It was a beautiful video," he said evenly.

"Then why did you give it a bad grade?"

Xiayne gestured to the chair next to her as if to say, *May I?* When Rylin didn't shake her head, he sat down. "I marked your video down because I know you can do better."

You don't even know *me*, Rylin wanted to protest, but it sounded petulant, and she didn't feel as angry anymore.

"I'm sorry if I was hard on you," Xiayne went on, studying

her. "I know firsthand that it isn't an easy transition, coming to a place like this from downTower."

Rylin let out a sigh. "I just don't think I fit in up here." It was nice to say this out loud.

"Of course you don't," Xiayne agreed, which shocked her into momentary silence. He grinned. "But I don't think you really want to fit in, do you?"

"I guess not," Rylin admitted.

"Now, can I please see what you were working on?"

She hesitated before pushing PLAY.

The pool flared to life around them, glimmering with a wild, almost frantic energy. The neon lights of the glow-lamps danced against the darkness. Music and gossip echoed sharply over the water, mingled with the sounds of laughter and drunken splashing. A couple was pressed up against the corner, another curled beneath the diving board. Rylin could see it all in perfect detail, as if she were diving into her own memory except better, everything brighter and more starkly drawn than her flawed human recollections. She could practically taste the chilled shots of atomic, could smell the chlorine and sweat.

She risked a glance at Xiayne. He was watching, his eyes wide open, as if he didn't even want to blink for fear of missing something.

When V grabbed the camera and dunked it beneath the surface of the pool, the room seemed to spin wildly, the entire world turning to water. Rylin let out a gasp of panic and shut off the holo.

"No! Don't stop!" Xiayne cried out.

"You aren't angry about the camera?" Let alone the fact that she'd recorded an illegal party in a public space, with underage drinking.

"No, it's fine, the camera's waterproof! *Rylin*"—he scooted closer and put his hand on top of hers, lacing their fingers and waving, so that she waved along with him to continue the playback—"this is incredible."

Rylin blinked, startled by the physical contact, but Xiayne had already let go; he didn't even seem fully aware that he'd touched her. He was walking in a circle, the light from the holo falling in startling patterns across his features. "You did it."

"Did what?"

"I asked you to show me how you see the world, and you did it. This footage—it's visually arresting, it's narratively compelling, it's colorful and vibrant. It's . . ." He shook his head. "It's fucking great, okay?"

"All I did was bring the camera to a party that was already happening," Rylin protested, uncertain.

Xiayne waved his arms so the holo shut off. "Lights on!" he croaked, and blinked at her in the sudden brightness. "That's the whole point of this class—to be a careful observer, to re-learn how to *see* the world. What I see from this"—he threw out his arms to encompass the room, which now felt strangely empty without all the chaos of the party—"is that you have a natural eye."

She was still confused. "You didn't even *like* my sunset vid. And that's when I was actually trying."

"You were trying to be something that wasn't you. But this is!"

"How? This isn't even edited!"

She thought Xiayne might take offense at her tone, but he just leaned back and laced his fingers behind his head, as carelessly as if he had all the time in the world. "So let's fix that."

"Right now?" Surely she hadn't heard him correctly.

"Did you have other plans?"

Something in his tone, in the challenging set of his shoulders, broke through Rylin's irritation. "Didn't you?"

"Oh, I did, but this will be more fun," Xiayne said easily, and Rylin couldn't help but smile.

Three hours later, the holo glimmered around them in glowing tatters. Snatches of different images had been spliced apart and pulled into various groupings, overlapping in the air like a chorus of ghosts. "Thank you for spending so long with me. I didn't realize how late it is," Rylin said, feeling a little guilty that she'd taken so much of Xiayne's evening.

"You'd be surprised how quickly time disappears in here. Especially since there are no windows, no natural light." He paused at the doorway to let the edit bay's lights flicker out. Rylin hurried to follow—and tripped forward, barely catching herself from sprawling headfirst in the empty hallway.

"Whoa, you okay?" Xiayne put out a hand to steady her. "Where are you headed? Let me walk you out; it's so late."

Rylin blinked, a million voices shouting in her head at once. She felt a pang of embarrassment at her clumsiness, mingled with a surprised, not-unpleasant warmth. Xiayne hadn't let go of her elbow, his hand steady on her bare skin although she was no longer in danger of falling.

Someone turned the corner at the end of the hall. Of course, Rylin thought wildly, it just had to be Cord.

Rylin saw the entire scene on his face as he walked forward: Rylin and a young, attractive teacher, alone, late in the evening, walking out of the dark edit bay together; the teacher's hand on her arm in an unmistakably intimate gesture. She saw Cord weighing it all, adding it up, and she knew he would be drawing conclusions about what was going on.

She told herself she didn't care, but as they grew closer in the empty hallway, her body strummed with a sharp and familiar longing. She kept her head high, unblinking, determined not to reveal to Cord how much it was costing her.

And then it was over: he had walked past, and the moment was gone.

WATT

THE NEXT WEEKEND, Watt took a steadying breath as he marched up to Leda's front door, a bouquet of flowers clutched firmly in his hand. He was wearing the tux that he'd bought for the party with Avery—just a few months earlier, though it felt like a lifetime ago.

He waited for Leda to buzz him in, glancing curiously up the street, which was lined with vertical residences inspired by old Upper East Side town houses. A young girl skipped down the sidewalk, pulling her golden Lab puppy on a wireless proxi-leash.

Any last words of wisdom? he asked Nadia, surprised at how nervous he felt, given that he didn't even like Leda. Then again, he'd never really been one for going on dates.

Just be your usual charming self.

We both know my usual self is far from charming, he replied as the door flung open before him.

Leda's hair fell past her shoulders in elaborate curls, and she wore a voluminous purple gown; the sort of deep purple that royalty used to wear, back when they had official portraits painted on two-dimensional squares of canvas. Come to think of it, she looked like one of those portraits come to life, with her enormous diamond earrings and cool, impatient expression. The only thing missing was a tiara. She'd dressed to look not beautiful, Watt realized, but intimidating. He refused to fall for it.

"Watt? I messaged you to meet me at the party."

He bit back a sarcastic reply. "I wanted to pick you up," he said, with as genuine a smile as he could manage.

The flowers, Watt! Nadia prodded.

"Oh, um, these are for you," he added, awkwardly thrusting out his arm to hand Leda the bouquet.

"Whatever. Let's just go." She tossed the flowers on an entry hall table, where they would no doubt be scooped up and deposited in a vase somewhere, and pulled Watt forcefully forward.

Conversation has been known to ease social awkwardness, Nadia reminded him as they settled stiffly into the hover's interior. Watt would have laughed if this weren't already such a disaster.

"So, who's throwing this Hudson Conservancy party anyway?" he attempted.

Leda shot him an irritated glance. "The Hudson River Conservancy," she said curtly.

"No, really?"

They spent the rest of the ride downTower in silence.

But when they got off on the ground floor and walked out onto Pier Four, Watt couldn't hide his surprise. The entire space—normally crowded with children clutching snack-pops, or tourists watching the trained schools of flying fish—was empty. *Nadia, where's the party?*

Down there. She directed his gaze to a set of stairs that led straight into the water.

"Wait a minute," Watt said aloud. "Is this is an Under the Sea–themed party that's *actually* under the sea?"

"And here I thought you knew everything," Leda snapped, and let out a breath. "Yes, the party is at the bottom of the Hudson. Haven't you heard they're growing crops down there?"

Watt knew that. Apparently all the junk that people had tossed into the river for centuries somehow made the soil on the river's floor incredibly fertile. The New York Department of Urban Affairs had started farming potatoes down there, illuminated by tiny solar-lamp submarines that floated back and forth over the rows of crops. But Watt had never thought that *people* would actually go down there—certainly not for a party.

Then again, he'd spent enough time watching the upper floors that he shouldn't be surprised by anything they did anymore.

The murky river water lapped around the covered staircase, protected by a cylindrical tunnel made of some elastic hydrocarbon. Watt ran his hand lightly along the wall as he walked down the stairs; the material gave way easily, leaving an indentation where he'd traced his fingers as if it were iridescent cake frosting. The steps shimmered and changed color beneath his dress shoes, like something out of that old Disney holo about the mermaid.

Then they reached the bottom and Watt saw the party, right there on the floor of the river, eighty meters below the surface.

The ceiling arced overhead like an enormous crystal fishbowl. Instead of its usual muddy brown, the water outside looked a deep marine blue. Watt wondered if they'd tinted the flexiglass to give it that color. Clusters of well-dressed men and women swirled around in effortlessly coordinated motions, like groupings of tropical fish.

Leda started instantly toward the bar, which was draped in silk-spun netting, nodding at a few other guests as she passed.

Watt trotted to keep up. "Are you planning on talking to me at all tonight, or am I just here as arm candy?" His campaign to make her like him was hardly off to a great start.

Leda flashed him a look. "'Arm candy' would imply that you're a male model. I believe the term you're looking for is 'meat puppet.'"

He started to protest, then realized that a smile curled at the edges of her lips. So, Leda Cole had a sense of humor, and a bit of a dark one at that. Maybe he would manage to have some fun tonight after all.

They had paused near an array of oversized fake seashells, a strip of sand along one side to approximate a beach. Nadia projected the script that he and Cynthia had rehearsed onto his contacts, but Watt figured he should go with a compliment first. "You look beautiful tonight, Leda," he said, gaining confidence as he spoke the familiar line.

She rolled her eyes. "Cut the crap, Watt."

This is why I gave you the script, so that you could read it, Nadia chided him.

Watt shifted his weight uncomfortably. "I just . . ."

She cursed. You should too, according to psychological studies about mirroring, Nadia offered.

"Why the hell did you bring me here?" he said abruptly.

Not quite what I had in mind.

Leda tossed her head in that careful way of hers, as if the motion were practiced. Which, Watt realized, it probably was. "Because when you aren't being stupid, Watt, you're quite useful. I was thinking that you and Nadia could help me keep an eye on people. If you're able to communicate with her remotely, that is."

If only you knew. "What people?" he asked, deliberately avoiding the question about Nadia.

"Just anyone who could cause me trouble," Leda declared.

"Mainly Avery and Rylin. And you, of course," she added, with some amusement.

In other words, everyone who knew her darkest secret. Something about Leda's flippant nervousness made Watt almost sad. He might have pitied her, if he didn't resent her so much.

"Leda, everyone isn't always out to get you," he said, not really expecting her to respond.

"Of course they are. This is all a zero-sum game."

Nadia had to translate that one for Watt. It meant a competition, where there was only one clear prize and one clear winner. He lifted his eyes to Leda in evident shock. "This is a *party*," he said slowly, as if he were speaking another language and she needed time for her contacts to translate. "Not a fight to the death."

"No, that's exactly what it is. And I refuse to lose just because I didn't grow up like the rest of them." Leda's voice was like steel. "You wouldn't understand, Watt, but it's a shitty feeling, always worrying that you're not good enough."

He tensed in sudden anger. "Leda, my parents moved here from Iran and took underpaid jobs wiping old people's asses, for *my* sake. If I don't get into MIT, it will crush them. And did I mention that MIT takes at most one student a year from my high school, and I'm up against my best friends?" He leaned toward her, his heartbeat surprisingly erratic. "So I would say that I know *exactly* how shitty it feels, worrying that you're not good enough."

The space between them pulsed with anger and something else that Watt couldn't identify. "I don't care what you think of me," she said at last. "But I'm done letting other people *use* me. Especially the ones I care about."

Watt knew she was thinking of Atlas, who had halfheartedly attempted to date Leda earlier this year in an attempt to hide—or overcome—his feelings for Avery.

"Come on." He held out a hand. "We're at a party. I refuse to let you sulk like this."

"I'm not sulking," Leda argued, but she moved toward the dance floor with more alacrity than he would have guessed.

They swayed there for a while, neither of them speaking. Watt was surprised at how little resistance Leda offered as he led her through the dance, how easily she fit into his arms. It felt like the tension was seeping slowly from her like poison from a wound. She curled her arms around his back and leaned her head on his chest, closing her eyes as if to momentarily shut out the world.

Watt wondered how many of Leda's issues were a direct result of everything that had happened with the Fullers—the combined pain of losing her best friend, and of finding out that Atlas had never actually cared about her—and how much was her own innate restlessness. Clearly, she'd suffered a lot, and at the hands of people she trusted. Yet Watt suspected that no matter how perfect her life was, part of Leda would always be stirring up trouble, searching for something without quite knowing what it was.

He had a terrifying suspicion that if it weren't for Nadia's voice in his head, he might be the same.

"There are other schools besides MIT, you know," Leda said after a moment, interrupting his thoughts.

"Not for what I want to study."

Leda tipped her face up to his, her hands clasped behind his head. "I'm shocked at your lack of confidence in yourself. You can build Nadia, yet you're worried about something as prosaic as college applications?"

You're just going to let her talk about me? Nadia asked huffily.

"As you're well aware, I can't exactly write about Nadia in my essays."

"I'm surprised you aren't having Nadia write the essays *for* you," Leda countered, and now she was unmistakably smiling.

Watt felt himself smiling back, for the sake of the mirroring effect Nadia always talked about.

"Oh, I've tried to have her write them, but they always come out too perfect."

"Too perfect. Now *there's* an underused phrase if I've ever heard one. If only more things in the world were too perfect." Leda's dark eyes glimmered.

"I know, I don't expect you to feel sorry for me."

The music changed, and Leda stepped back, breaking their strange truce. "I'm thirsty," she declared.

Watt recognized that cue from all his years of hitting on girls at bars. "Let me get you a drink," he offered quickly.

The bartender was a Hispanic girl who looked about their age, with bangs and sharp eyes. Watt asked her for two whiskey sodas. She raised an eyebrow at the double order, but didn't question it.

When he found Leda, she was leaning forward on a high-top table, one foot tucked behind the other. Watt stopped in his tracks, hesitating at the sight of something in her expression—something frail, and tentatively hopeful. It was as shocking and unexpected as seeing her in her underwear.

He'd thought he knew her so well, but he was starting to wonder if he understood Leda Cole at all.

When he handed her the drink, Leda gave it a slow stir, holding up the glass for inspection as if to check the amber liquid's color. "How much alcohol do you think it would take to make us forget all the things we've done that we regret?" she said darkly.

Watt wondered what had prompted this change of mood. "I typically drink to make new, fun memories, not erase the ones I already have. You should try it—you might enjoy it," he said lightly.

He'd hoped to shift the tone, make her laugh a little, but Leda just looked at him sidelong. "What about the night I came over to your place? You were definitely drinking to forget something then."

Watt reddened at the thought of that night. He'd been drinking to forget something, all right—the fact that Avery was in love with her brother. A fact that Leda had wormed out of him when she showed up at his apartment, still in her school uniform, only to drug him and seduce him into telling her everything. "I don't remember," he mumbled, suddenly unable to stop replaying that moment in his head, when Leda had planted herself on his lap and kissed him.

This might be a good time, Watt, Nadia prompted.

She was right. If Leda was dwelling on the past, maybe she could be tricked into referencing Eris's death.

He stepped forward a little so Nadia could get perfect footage, in case this worked. "I've been thinking lately about the roof," he said.

Leda looked at him in sudden horror. "Why would you bring that up?" she asked, her voice a whisper.

"I just wanted to—"

"Back the hell off, Watt," Leda snapped. She stormed away, her shoulders drawn up defensively, her movements injured and angry.

I give up, he told Nadia. *How can I ever make that girl trust me? I don't even like her!*

You don't like most people, Nadia pointed out ruthlessly.

Watt sighed and turned around, only to see that he was standing quite close to Avery Fuller.

She was as resplendent as always in a draped strapless gown. Her hair was combed back into a low twist, showing off the perfect symmetry of her face, which was currently creased in puzzlement as if she couldn't fathom why Watt would be here, or couldn't even remember who he was. Watt realized with a start that Avery probably hadn't thought about him a single time since that night. God knows he hadn't been sitting around pining after her, either—he didn't want her anymore, now that he knew she was with her brother—but he'd at least wondered what had happened to her, whether she was okay. Yet here she was, blinking at him as if she'd forgotten his very existence.

Watt suddenly understood what Leda had meant earlier, about feeling used by the people she cared about. Had he ever meant anything to Avery, or was he just another attempt at distracting her from her feelings about her brother?

"Hi, Watt. You look great," she said, with a smile toward his tux: which she had helped him pick out, and which he'd bought in a pathetic, misguided attempt at impressing her.

For some reason, Watt was irritated with her for bringing up the afternoon they'd gone tux shopping together. How did she expect him to reply, anyway—was he supposed to tell Avery that she looked great too? As if she didn't already know that.

"Thanks, I guess," he said wearily.

"What brings you here tonight?" Avery pressed, evidently still confused.

"Leda brought me."

Avery sighed. "I'm sorry. It's my fault. She's trying to get back at me."

"What's that supposed to mean?" Watt was getting really sick of these highliers and their oblique statements.

Avery glanced down, fiddling with a bracelet to avoid looking at him. "She brought you here as a dig at me—because everyone remembers that I asked you to the University Club party, and now when they see you with Leda they'll think she stole you from me," she said miserably.

Watt was stunned. Part of him felt appalled by Avery in that moment, at how utterly self-centered her view of the world was, even as another part of him recognized that she was probably right.

"I'm sure you're not here alone tonight either, are you?" he heard himself ask, wondering who her next victim was.

Avery looked back up at him. "I came with Cord, but we're just friends."

"You should probably double-check that Cord knows that," he shot back, surprisingly angered. "Because I happened to miss that particular memo, about the real reason Avery Fuller asks a boy as her date to anything."

She looked like she'd been slapped across the face. "Watt—"

"Forget it," Watt said, and walked away from her. He needed a drink if he was going to keep getting further tangled in the Gordian knot of these highliers' screwed-up lives.

AVERY

AVERY STOOD THERE in bewilderment as Watt turned angrily away. It pained her that he clearly thought so little of her. Her intentions toward Watt had always been genuine: she'd never intended to hurt him, never set out to use him, or trick him. Yet he obviously resented her for what had happened. And that last thing he'd said, about "the real reason" she asked anyone to be her date . . . it made her wonder if he knew the truth about her and Atlas. But how could he, unless Leda had told him?

The band struck up a new song, one of Avery's favorites. Suddenly she wanted nothing more than to dance. She glanced around in search of a partner, and her eyes lit almost instantly on Cord. It had been Atlas's idea that they each ask dates to this party—it might soothe their parents' suspicions—and besides, it would help keep Avery and Atlas from talking to each other too much.

Cord had always been Avery's go-to for events like this. Atlas, meanwhile, was here with Sania Malik, a girl he'd known for years. Not the most believable fake date, but it was all Atlas could come up with on short notice.

Avery walked over to where Cord was standing next to Brice, along the edge of the flexiglass bubble. On the other side grew rows of potatoes, their fronds swaying back and forth in the water, lit by cheerful solar subs.

The radzimir skirt of her deep blue gown swished pleasantly as she approached. "Cord, will you dance with me?" she asked without preamble.

"Of course." He held out a hand and led her onto the dance floor. "Can I hold your bag?" he added, with a nod to her tiny silver micro-clutch, barely large enough for a single paintstick.

Avery nodded as he slipped the bag into a pocket of his tux jacket. She was struck by a sudden memory of Cord's mom, back before she died, shepherding them both to cotillion when they were in fifth grade. "When you take a girl to a party, Cord, you should always offer to hold her drink or her purse, ask her to dance, make sure she gets home safe, and—"

"I get it, Mom," Cord had groaned, and Avery had stifled a giggle, exchanging a knowing look with Cord.

Cord didn't speak as they moved expertly around the dance floor. The space between them felt relaxed, uncomplicated. Avery remembered the way Watt had danced—his steps correct but so painstaking, his brow furrowed in nervous concentration—and felt another pang of regret for the way she'd treated him.

She saw her parents across the dance floor and gave them a little wave. *Happy now?* Her father nodded, his eyes lifting in evident approval. He'd always liked the idea of her and Cord; after all, her parents had been good friends with the Andertons before they passed away six years ago. Avery was glad now that Atlas had insisted on their both asking dates. It might relieve the pressure cooker they all found themselves in.

The song ended, and Cord took a small step back, grabbing a champagne for her off a passing tray. That was when Avery saw Atlas and Calliope.

They were standing on the far side of the bar, their faces too close together. Atlas was leaning back on his elbows with a relaxed, casual smile—a smile that Avery didn't see very often, except when he was with her. She realized with a start that he *trusted* this Calliope girl. And Atlas didn't easily give his trust.

Calliope was talking animatedly, making little flourishing gestures with her wrists as if to show off the jeweled bracelets she wore on both arms. Her vermilion gown skimmed shockingly low over her cleavage. She'd kicked one foot behind the other, and Avery saw that she was wearing carved bamboo heels, which were way too casual for black tie, but which she seemed to have gotten away with since they were on theme. It was the sort of shoe Avery's mom would never let her wear, and for some reason that irritated her.

She gazed into her champagne without taking a sip, watching its bubbles dance merrily upward, and attempted to make sense of her own feelings.

It might be foolish and juvenile, but Avery couldn't help instinctively disliking Calliope, given what she now knew about her travels with Atlas. The truth was, she still resented Atlas for just leaving her like that; taking off on a spree of adventures without saying good-bye, making all those memories that Avery wasn't a part of. It hurt more than she cared to admit, learning that those memories had included a languid, leggy mystery girl.

She and Atlas had agreed not to talk to each other tonight, but maybe if she went over there and said hi—just for a minute, to reassure herself that nothing was happening between him and Calliope—she would feel better.

Avery took a deep breath and pushed her way through to where they were standing.

"Hey, guys!" Her tone sounded perky and overbright to her ears. She didn't miss the flicker of low-lying resentment that darted across Calliope's face at the interruption, or the weary resignation that Atlas turned on her. He was obviously disappointed with her for barging in like this, after all their promises to ignore each other. But what was she supposed to do, when she saw another girl circling him like some kind of jungle animal closing in on her prey?

"Hi, Avery," Calliope said, after a beat. "You look fantastic. I love that dress."

Avery didn't return the compliment. "Who did you come here with tonight, Calliope?" *Maybe you should go pay attention to your own date*, she thought, though to be fair she hadn't done the best job of that either.

"It's funny—he's actually your date's older brother! I'm not sure where he is," Calliope exclaimed, smiling.

"What a funny coincidence," Avery said, in a tone that made it clear she didn't find it funny at all. Atlas was looking back and forth between them, clearly at a loss as to what he should say.

"Avery, are you and Cord dating? He's really cute," Calliope went on, seemingly unconcerned by the hostility in Avery's voice.

Avery almost choked on her sip of champagne. "No, we're not," she finally managed. "Actually, he's single, if you're interested."

"Aves," Atlas interrupted, "do you know where Mom and Dad are?"

She knew he was just saying something, anything, in an attempt to halt her attack on Calliope. But his comment sparked something in Avery.

"Actually, that's why I came over here. Mom and Dad sent

me to find you. Sorry, Calliope, do you mind?" she added half-heartedly.

"Of course not." Calliope shrugged and headed off into the crowd, lifting the sheer tulle skirts of her gown to keep from tripping. Her toenails were painted a deep purple. Avery thought she saw a flashing silver inktat on one ankle, but she couldn't be sure.

"Aves. What the hell?" Atlas asked, but Avery didn't answer, just reached for his arm and began dragging him through the crowds. She led him toward one of the small setup stations along the back of the party, where a few tired-looking caterers were depositing plates for bots to stack.

"Can you give us a minute? We have a family emergency," Avery requested, wielding her smile like a knife. The caterers shrugged and stepped aside. Avery pulled Atlas into the tiny setup station and yanked the door shut.

He took a step back, and even though the room was tiny, it felt like a vast distance suddenly loomed between them. "We weren't supposed to even *talk* tonight, and now you brought me here alone? What the hell, Aves?" he demanded.

"I'm sorry," she said resentfully. "I just couldn't watch that girl hit on you anymore. God, did you not realize that she was literally throwing herself at you?"

"Of course I realized," Atlas said, and the matter-of-factness in his tone made her even angrier. "That's the whole *point*. I thought we were trying to distract Mom and Dad—bringing dates, not talking? And now you've gone and dragged me into a room, in front of all the waitstaff."

Avery felt her anger dissipate. "It just sucks," she said miserably. She hadn't realized how much it would hurt, seeing Atlas with other girls. She didn't want it to be like this. Except this was the only way it *could* be.

Atlas leaned against the sturdy prefab wall and looked at her, his brown eyes steady. "It absolutely sucks," he agreed. "But what else do you want me to do? If we're going to keep sneaking around like this without Mom and Dad suspecting something—which they might already—then occasionally we'll have to talk to other people. Maybe flirt with them."

Avery didn't answer right away. She stared around the tiny space filled with half-eaten appetizer platters and a small bot that kept UV-sanitizing silverware before depositing it in a neat stack.

"You don't know how difficult it is for me, seeing you with her," Avery said at last.

"Trust me, I do."

She resented that. Atlas had done far worse to her than she had done to him, and they both knew it. "No, I don't think you do," Avery replied tersely. "Just because you saw me at a party with Watt, once? That hardly counts. Look at our track record, Atlas—which of us *slept* with someone else?"

He opened his mouth, then shut it again. "I'm sorry, Aves, but I can't help what I did before you."

"Yes, you could have helped it! You could have decided not to hook up with my best friend—you could have *waited* for me, like I did for you!"

Avery's vision was getting blurry. She was a little surprised with herself for bringing that up, but maybe she shouldn't have been. It was always there, a small hurt that she stubbornly kept nursing deep inside her: the knowledge that Atlas had been with Leda, probably even with other girls, while she'd only ever been with him. It made Avery feel wounded, and inadequate.

"It's just hard, seeing you with other girls after that," she finished, her voice small.

"That's not fair. I can't change the past." Atlas started to reach for Avery, only to think better of it, and let his hands fall helplessly to his side. "There's one easy way to fix everything, Aves, and it's to *leave*. But you're the one who won't run away, and won't tell me why."

Avery shook her head. "I want to, I just need—"

"Time, yeah, I *get* it," Atlas snapped, interrupting her. "I've tried to be understanding about it all. But how much longer am I supposed to wait?"

"I'm sorry," she started to say, but she didn't have an answer, and he knew it.

"Are we ever going to run away together? Aves"—Atlas seemed to falter a little—"do you even *want* to run away with me anymore?"

She blinked in shock. "Of course I do," she insisted. "It's just complicated. I can't explain."

"What can't you explain? What aren't you telling me?"

Avery shook her head, hating herself for keeping secrets. She swallowed against the hard, vicious sobs that rose up in her throat.

"I'm going to leave now. You should probably wait, so that we aren't seen walking out together. You know, for appearances' sake," Atlas added, with just a touch of acid, and then he was gone.

Avery wrapped her arms around herself. She realized that a few tears had escaped, probably running in dark rivulets over her makeup. She reached up brusquely to wipe at her face. The part of her that was seventeen and in love felt utterly snubbed, and bruised, and a little bit eager to lash out.

Atlas didn't get it. He couldn't understand all the pressure she was under. And aside from that one date with Watt, which anyway had ended with Avery confessing her love for *Atlas*, Atlas had never really seen her with another boy. He didn't understand how it was, knowing he'd been with other people, torturing herself with mental images of them together—

Maybe Atlas should find out what it was like, she thought

spitefully, storming back into the party with new purpose. He deserved to see how it felt, watching Avery laugh and flirt and drink and dance with someone else.

Her eyes lit on Cord, standing alone near the bar, looking as aloof and handsome as ever. He was her date, after all. And he was always game for a little fun.

"I want a drink," she announced, leaning her elbows forward on the bar in a way that her mother would have scolded her for. But she couldn't find it in her to care about much of anything right now, except her new determination to let Atlas see how it felt, just a little.

Cord smiled at her abrupt greeting. "Champagne, please," he told the bartender, but Avery shook her head.

"No, I want a *drink* drink."

"Okay," Cord said slowly, studying her a little to gauge her mood. "Vodka? Atomic? Whiskey?" he guessed, but Avery didn't care what she drank as long as it was something strong.

"Whatever you're having. But make it a double."

Cord raised an eyebrow. "Two scotches on the rocks, double," he told the bartender, then glanced at Avery. "Not that I don't love when you get all reckless, but can I ask what happened to prompt this?"

"You can ask, but I won't tell you." Avery felt a few curious sets of eyes on them, but for once she didn't care who saw, didn't care whether they all posted snaps of her directly to the feeds. Let them.

"Well, then," Cord said equitably, as if this was exactly what he'd expected her to say. "How can I help?"

"Easy. You can help me get as stupidly drunk as possible."

"My pleasure." Cord's ice-blue eyes danced with mischief, and Avery felt a slight uptick in her angry mood. If nothing else, she reflected, Cord was a good partner in crime.

She clinked her glass to Cord's and tossed back the drink, draining it in a single gulp. It was bitter on her throat, but she didn't care. For the rest of tonight she would be the most sparkling, unattainably gorgeous version of herself, nothing but smiles and flashing eyes—and no one would ever see how hurt she was, beneath it all.

CALLIOPE

CALLIOPE WAS QUITE pleased with her decision to come to the Hudson Conservancy Ball with Brice Anderton.

She and her mom had always loved making an entrance: the way all eyes in a room inevitably circled toward them when they arrived at a party; especially in new cities, where people wondered in hushed whispers who they were and where they'd come from. Every now and then Elise made a halfhearted attempt at keeping a lower profile—"We don't want to be too notorious, it isn't safe," she would remind Calliope. As if she didn't love the attention even more than her daughter did.

By now, Calliope thought she was used to attracting that sort of attention. But she hadn't been prepared for the reaction to her and Brice walking into the underwater ballroom together.

She hoped at least some of the glances were because they looked so striking together, both of them tall and lithe and dark-haired, with haughty smiles. But she admitted to herself, with some reluctance, that Brice was the more intriguing of the pair. Everyone's eyes kept darting toward him with undisguised interest. They all clearly knew who he was, followed his various misadventures, wondered about the new girl on his arm.

And it definitely caused Atlas to take notice. Calliope had made sure to flirt with him—no thanks to Avery's inept attempts at joining the conversation, and her weird insistence on dragging Atlas away. Calliope had dealt with protective siblings and parents before, especially when she tried to con sheltered private school kids. But she had to say that Avery was one of the worst she'd ever encountered.

She lifted her head with proud purpose and surveyed the underwater domain, glittering with money and status and connections. Her mom was here too, with Nadav and his daughter, Livya. Calliope had chatted with them for a few minutes earlier. Elise kept glancing at her with raised eyebrows, clearly hoping that Calliope would take Livya off her hands so she could focus better on Nadav, but Calliope hadn't been in the mood to play nice. As far as she could tell, Livya was a pale, insipid bore, and babysitting her was a waste of Calliope's talents.

She stood now with Brice and a group of his friends. They were telling a story about an old prank, where they'd graffitied a bunch of hovers in writing you could see only on a certain contacts setting. It sounded lame, but Calliope joined in their laughter anyway. She glanced over at Brice, who was laughing too, but standing a little apart from the rest of them, with the sleek self-assurance that comes from being wealthy and drunk in a bubble at the bottom of a river.

The music changed, and Brice stepped forward to take her hand. "Dance with me," he asked, more a demand than a request. Calliope set down the drink she'd been holding for show—she was trying to keep a level head tonight—and followed.

Why not flirt with Brice a little? She definitely couldn't con him; it was too risky, given that he'd almost recognized her. Of course, Atlas was risky too, since he'd already rejected her once. But he wasn't about to blow her cover.

And now that she knew how rich he was, part of Calliope was determined to steal something from him, just to say she'd conned the boy on the thousandth floor. God, what a story it would be. Not that she could ever brag about it to anyone, except her mom.

When they reached the dance floor, Brice turned around, moving his hands confidently around her waist. Overhead, holographic jellyfish glowed like floating candles, chased by the occasional neon shark. The dappled blue light played over Brice's features, his aristocratic nose and sharply carved cheekbones. It wasn't a face that had been made for gentle expressions.

"Calliope." Brice pronounced it with that same laughing irreverence, and she wondered again how much of the truth he really knew. "Tell me about London."

"Why?" she challenged. "You've probably been to London dozens of times. There's nothing I could add that would change your opinion of it."

"Maybe it's not my opinion of London I'm looking to revise, but my opinion of you."

She gave a little spin to gain herself some time, letting the folds of her dress fly out around her body and then fall sculpturally behind her. "Well, now I'm curious about your opinion so far."

"Please. I know better than to walk into a trap like that."

Brice pulled her nearer as the music picked up speed. Calliope wanted to retreat a step—this was too close, she could feel his heartbeat through the layers of his tux, could smell his cologne, light and just a little bit astringent—but his hand was playing idly with the zipper on the back of her dress, and her breath seemed stuck in her throat.

"Since you're so curious, I went to St. Margaret's. An all-girls boarding school in SoTo," she volunteered, hoping to redirect Brice's attention.

"I have to say I'm surprised. I wouldn't have pegged you as the boarding school type."

Calliope's thoughts turned inexplicably to Justine Houghton. She'd probably spent her teenage years at a boarding school, being disciplined and monitored—while Calliope had traveled the whole world. And now she was here, spinning on an underwater dance floor, surrounded by sumptuous gowns and laughter and the unmistakable flash of diamonds.

It was clear to Calliope which of them had come out on top.

"I'm not really the *type* to do anything," she answered Brice.

He smiled slowly, his hand skating lower down her dress. "I'm aware. You're nothing like the girls I usually meet."

"I remember, all the mysterious girls you meet on your travels." As they turned slowly about the dance floor, Calliope felt the gazes of other couples brushing over them like a hand tracing down her cheek. She gave her head a vain toss, letting her hair spill over one shoulder, and bared her teeth in a smile.

But then she felt Brice's eyes on her again, and it seemed that he could read straight through every movement of her body. Her smile became less fierce. "Where do you go all the time, anyway?" she challenged. She doubted he'd traveled anywhere she hadn't also been. She *was* a professional.

"Everywhere. I'm a walking cliché. The boy who inherits lots of money, then promptly attempts to spend it all on expensive trips and gifts to himself."

He'd delivered the line with styled indifference, yet for some reason it seemed melancholy to Calliope. She wondered what he would say if he knew that she did the same thing, just with other people's money. "Why is that?"

Brice shrugged. "I guess it's what happens when you lose both parents at age sixteen."

Calliope's breath caught. "Oh," she managed, a little stupidly. Why hadn't she caught that on the feeds when she'd stalked him earlier? She was losing her edge, she thought; but everything to do with Brice was making her feel muddled and uncertain. She had a panicked sense that she'd missed a lot about him. She needed to be careful.

Just then, Atlas stormed past. Calliope wavered. This was her chance—Atlas was here and alone, no Avery to interfere. It would be the work of a moment to go strike up a conversation with him, pick up their flirtation from earlier tonight.

Brice hadn't missed the way her eyes darted instantly toward the other boy. "Really? You and Fuller? I wouldn't have guessed." He shook his head disappointedly. "I just don't understand what all you girls see in him."

Calliope summoned her most imperious look, the one she'd learned from Justine all those years ago. "I have no idea what you're talking about," she declared. And what did he mean by "all you girls"? Just how many had Atlas been involved with, exactly?

"He's too boring for you," Brice went on, as if she hadn't spoken. "Don't get me wrong, I like the guy. He's just plain vanilla, and you're so . . . complicated."

This was exactly why she shouldn't be spending time around Brice. He was too insightful, too careful and calculating; nowhere near emotional or naïve enough to fall for a con. If anything, he was so observant that he might have already realized what she was up to.

She needed to get away, before it was too late.

"I don't know what you mean. Now, if you'll excuse me," Calliope said stiffly, and beelined in the direction she had last seen Atlas.

He was standing alone at a high-top table, nursing a drink, hunched over as if to ward off anyone who might consider approaching. Calliope squared her shoulders and took a deep breath.

"Hey there," she murmured, sidling over.

Atlas seemed momentarily bewildered, as if he'd forgotten where he was. Then his face broke out into that familiar off-kilter smile, a little wider than usual. "Calliope. How's your night been?"

"Informative," she said mysteriously. "What about yours?"

"Not what I expected." He was still glancing down into his drink. He wasn't even *looking* at her, she thought in mounting frustration, and if he didn't ever look at her, how would he notice how gorgeous and alone she was, right now when he seemed to need someone most?

There was only one thing to do. Calliope reached across the table for Atlas's drink and drained it in a single sip, lifting her head so that he could admire the arcing curve of her neck, letting her eyes flutter sensually closed. The drink was very strong.

She set the empty glass down on the table with more force than was necessary. Atlas startled at the sound. Well, at least something had finally gotten his attention.

"Sorry, I was thirsty."

"Clearly," Atlas replied, though he didn't sound particularly angry. He lifted a shoulder toward the bar. "Want a refill?"

Calliope followed as he ordered them another round of drinks, a little surprised at how quickly he worked through his second glass. She didn't remember him drinking like this in Africa. *It is a party*, she told herself, and yet she couldn't help wondering what was bothering him. He'd seemed so much happier over the summer. She had a feeling that something—his family, probably—was holding him in New York, keeping him from ever really leaving for good, when this wasn't where he truly belonged.

She shook off the sudden and uncharacteristic burst of introspection. Atlas was here now, which was all that mattered to her.

"Want to dance?" she suggested.

Atlas looked back up at her, and Calliope knew at once that something had changed; her instincts could sense it in the air between them like a shift in the weather, like when they'd been sitting on the ridge back in Tanzania and night began to settle its folds around them.

He didn't say anything as Calliope led him purposefully onto the dance floor.

When she moved his hands onto her hips, he responded by pulling her closer, circling her back. His grip was warm on her bare skin.

After a while she whispered, "Take me home?" in Atlas's ear. He nodded, slowly. She took his hand and led him up the stairs—he stumbled a little; he might be drunker than she realized—and crossed the pier to hail a waiting hover. Perfect. Now she would be able to scope out their apartment, start planning what she could take from them. Maybe even take something now, without anyone noticing.

She typed in the Fullers' address, watching for a reaction from Atlas. When he didn't protest, she lowered her mouth to his and reached for the buttons of his jacket in the semidarkness, unfastening each one with a brutal, determined energy.

It made her feel surprisingly vindicated, proving that the only boy who'd ever rejected her wanted her after all. Finally. It was about damn time.

LEDA

IT WAS LATE—late enough that Leda wasn't even sure whether Watt was still here. She circled the fringes of the party, clutching a pineapple cocktail so tightly that her fingers had hardened into claws around it. She hadn't even wanted this drink, but some passing waiter had handed it to her, and Leda quickly learned that there were even *more* waiters walking around with pitchers, refilling her fluted glass every time she took a couple of sips. She'd begun to revise her opinion of the stuff. It might be sickeningly sweet, but at least it was never empty.

She reached up and touched her hair, which was falling in sweaty curls down the back of her neck. The old familiar fear was prickling at her again, the panic that no matter what she did, she would never be pretty enough, clever enough, *enough* enough. And on top of it was the newer, even sharper fear that someone would learn what she'd done on the roof and her life would come crashing down in a million fiery pieces.

She wasn't sure why she'd gotten so upset earlier, except that Watt had been acting genuinely nice to her, and she knew it all must be an act because he hated her. How could he not? After everything she'd done to him, drugging him and tricking him and blackmailing him into attending this stupid party, he must wish he'd never met her in the first place.

Like always, the thought of that night—of Eris—made Leda feel cold all over. *It's not my fault*, she reminded herself, but she knew deep down that the words were a lie. It *was* her fault. She'd pushed Eris; and now she was at a party, alone and unwanted, and maybe that was what she deserved anyway.

"There you are," she exclaimed. Watt was standing alone, hands behind his back as he studied one of the weird modern art installations near the exit.

"You told me to back the hell off. So I did," Watt pointed out logically.

Leda bristled a little at the reminder of her earlier words. "I noticed you didn't leave Avery alone," she said snidely.

The dig didn't elicit the reaction she'd hoped for. Watt just shrugged and offered her his arm, not angry at all. "Can I take you home?"

Leda glanced around. The party was beginning to slow down: most people still here were either too old or too young for Leda to care about, including several freshmen from school who were clearly thrilled to be at a bar without an age-scanner. Her parents and Jamie had left over an hour ago. Leda tilted her head at Watt, still inexplicably determined to piss him off.

"You can take me home. But don't get any ideas," she warned.

Watt chuckled, not answering.

When they finally pulled up to her apartment, he walked around the hover and chivalrously opened the door for her. Leda brushed past him and stormed up the stairs without a backward glance. She felt like the flexiglass from that damned fishbowl they'd been partying in, holding back an endless muddy torrent and about to burst from the pressure.

"Good night, Leda." Watt started toward the hover. Before she'd even thought about it, Leda was calling him back.

"I'm sorry, where do you think you're going?"

Watt turned around. "Home?" he asked, as if it was a trick question.

"You don't leave until I say you can leave."

She watched in delight as the last vestiges of Watt's self-control snapped and he stormed up the steps to her, his hands clenched in anger. "Seriously, Leda, you need to *stop*. What more do you want from me?"

What she wanted was an outburst, a reaction—something that she could push against. Watt was the only person in the world who knew what she'd done and would actually call her out on it, and she was sick of him playing nice when they both knew he would rather play dirty. She put her hands on his shoulders and shoved him.

Watt stumbled backward, clearly shocked by the physical contact. Finally. It felt good to *do* something.

The silence roared in her ears. Watt stared at her without blinking. "You're despicable, you know that, right?" he said slowly.

Leda didn't care. She was suddenly so sick of pretending, of making her whole life one massive charade where she went to school and to parties as if nothing at all was wrong. No one even *knew* her anymore.

Except Watt. He knew the unfathomable things she'd done, had seen the gaping black hole inside her, and for some reason that knowledge didn't bother her.

"Congratulations, Watt, you know all my deepest, darkest

secrets." Her voice was low and throaty. "But guess what? I know yours too. Because we're *the same*, Watt, you and me."

"You and I are nothing alike." He stepped close, his face right up next to hers, his breath ragged. "Go to hell, Leda."

The entire world was spinning, and then it was still; and without Leda knowing how it had happened, Watt's lips were on hers.

She pulled him forward, his hands tangled in her hair. Leda felt like her whole body was one exposed nerve ending. She tried not to make any noise as they stumbled into the hallway, but it didn't matter; her parents' master was on the third floor, and they wouldn't expect her to bring home a boy anyway. She'd never done it before.

When they fell backward onto her bed, Watt hesitated. "I still can't stand you," he told her. His dark eyes danced with something she couldn't read. She reached behind her back to unfasten her dress, feeling like a primordial, vengeful goddess.

"Like I said before, I can't stand you, either. Now shut up," she told him, and put her mouth over his.

Watt's skin felt warm and oddly reassuring against hers. Leda clung wordlessly to him. It was glorious and dangerous and utterly without compassion. Watt could never find out how much she needed him right now, she promised herself: the strong clean lines of his body, the strong solidity of him, the bitter press of his anger pulling her back from the edge of the vortex. Holding her demons at bay, for just a little longer.

AVERY

AVERY STOOD AT the center of a group of people—Risha and Ming and a few others, their faces all seeming to float against the raucous backdrop of the dance floor. The world seemed to be tilting violently, as if the planet had spun wildly off course, and the sky was beneath her feet.

She had no idea how late it was. She'd been so studiously determined to ignore Atlas that she hadn't seen him leave. Instead she'd focused all her energies on laughing and flirting, and drinking. She'd had so much to drink that her laughter eventually stopped feeling forced, and started feeling genuine.

"Hey there." Cord's hands were on her shoulders. Avery closed her eyes against the dizzying riot of color. "I think it's time we got you home," Cord said, and Avery managed an abbreviated nod.

Somehow she walked with him through the tattered remnants of the party, a smile fixed on her face. Cord held tight to her forearm as they went all the way up those steps and across the pier—whose stupid idea had it been to have an underwater party, anyway?—and back into the Tower, where Cord helped her into a waiting hover.

"Here." He shrugged off the jacket of his tux and quickly placed it over her shoulders. Avery leaned her head back and closed her eyes. She listened to the familiar tapping as Cord entered an address on the hover's internal view screen.

A frantic instinct forced her eyes open, and sure enough, there was her address on the thousandth floor, illuminated in bright white letters as their destination. "No," she said automatically. "I don't want to go home."

Cord nodded, as if it were the most normal thing in the world for Avery to refuse to go back to her own apartment. He didn't ask another question, and Avery didn't answer. She just pulled his jacket tighter around her shoulders. She felt like she might vomit.

When they reached the 969th floor, Avery followed Cord into his massive living room. Her whole body was still shaking with shock, or maybe regret. Her skin felt hot and stretched tight over her body, as if her very flesh were expanding. She sank wordlessly onto the couch, her head in her hands.

"Do you want a T-shirt or anything?" Cord asked, with a nod toward her heavy dress.

His words broke through the stupor suffocating Avery, and she glanced around, truly seeing her surroundings for the first time. What was she doing at Cord's apartment late at night? She stood up abruptly. "I'm sorry, I should go," she said—only to stop in defeat.

There was a reason she hadn't gone home. She didn't want to see Atlas. She couldn't face him, not yet.

Cord stood there watching it all. "Avery. What's going on?" he asked carefully.

"I can't go home. It's—I'm—" she fumbled to speak, but there were no words to express her feelings. "I just can't," she finished, helplessly.

Cord was too understanding, or too polite, to press her. "Do you want to stay here?" he offered. "You know we have plenty of guest rooms."

"Actually, yeah." Avery was surprised to hear her voice crack. She swallowed anxiously and rubbed her hands over her arms. "And I'd love a T-shirt, if the offer still stands."

"Of course." Cord disappeared down the hallway.

Avery glanced curiously around the living room. She hadn't been to Cord's in a while, except for parties, when the space was packed with people. Of course, there was a time when she and Eris and Leda had been here constantly, with Cord and his friends—it was easiest here, with no adults to watch over them. Except for Brice, she supposed, but he didn't really count. She remembered all the stupid things they'd done: like the time Cord pulled their gelatin shots from the rapid-freezer too early, and one of them exploded up onto the ceiling in a firework of gloppy green. Or the time that they'd set up a slip-and-slide down Cord's enormous staircase, and they all ricocheted down from the second floor screaming and laughing. That had been Eris's idea, Avery remembered; she'd seen it on some holo and wanted to re-create it, and of course they all joined in, caught up in her ineffable enthusiasm.

It all seemed childish and giddy, and very long ago.

"Here," Cord said, returning with a neatly folded stack of clothes. Avery quickly ducked into the bathroom to change. It was funny, she thought; the shirt smelled like the normal UV-wand fresh scent but also somehow like Cord.

Moments later she emerged from the bathroom in an old school shirt and mesh shorts, her bare feet padding on the heated kitchen tiles; her hair still set in its elaborate twist, diamond studs in each ear. She knew she looked absurd, but she couldn't find it in her to care.

"I got you all set up in the blue room, the one at the base of the stairs," Cord told her as she returned. "Let me know if you need anything."

"Wait," Avery blurted out as he started toward his room. Cord turned to look at her. She glanced hopefully at the couch. "Any chance you want to stay up for a while?" Just until her mind stopped whirling so frantically, until she could wipe her stupid fight with Atlas—all the pettiness between them—from her brain.

"Sure, yeah," he said, still watching her.

Avery nestled into her old favorite corner of the couch and pulled her knees up to her chest. Cord sank down next to her, an arm's length of space between them. His bow tie was loosened, his vest unbuttoned, his sleeves rolled up to his elbows. It all cast his profile in a slightly rakish air.

"Do you want to talk about what's going on," he asked, "or should we watch a loud, dumb holo instead?"

"Loud, dumb holo. The more explosions, the better," Avery said, with an attempt at a smile.

She couldn't believe Atlas hadn't pinged her or flickered her even once. What was he doing? And why couldn't she stop thinking about him, since it hurt her so damned much?

"Loud, dumb holo it is." Cord waved his hands in the air to call up the on-demand menu, then turned to her, his clear blue eyes lit up with a quiet intensity. The full weight of it was almost too much for Avery to bear. "Whatever's going on, Avery, you know I'm always here if you want to talk about it."

"Thanks." For some reason she had to look away from Cord or she might cry. The holoscreen lit up with a hoverchase scene, and she stared at it gratefully, trying to lose herself in the mindless glowing action sequence. Maybe if she focused on the confusion on the screen, she could ignore the tangled, tender mess that her life had become.

Avery realized that the last time she'd been alone with Cord was months ago, when he'd told her that he and Eris had broken up—and she'd figured out that he liked someone new.

"Hey," she said, eager to think about something else, "what ended up happening with you and that girl?"

Cord blinked, clearly startled. "You mean Rylin? It didn't work out."

"Wait—Rylin Myers, who now goes to our school? You were dating *her*?" The girl from the roof? How had she become so entwined in all of their lives?

"I was, until she lied to me." Cord looked as if he wanted to be angry, but all he could call up was a wounded sort of regret. Avery knew the feeling. "It's just hard to get past. I'm not sure how to trust her again, you know?"

"I do know." She looked away.

"Hang on." Cord vanished down the hallway, only to return holding a tapered gold candle, covered in flecks of glitter that caught and refracted the light.

"Is that an IntoxiCandle?" Avery had never burned one before. They were just normal candles, with air-transported endorphins and serotonin baked into the wax. But all candles were illegal in the Tower, due to the fire hazard—especially this high up, where the air was pumped with extra oxygen to compensate for the altitude.

"I thought you could use it. It used to help me, when I was drunk and moody."

"I'm not moody!" Avery cried out, and Cord laughed at her. "Though I am pretty drunk," she admitted. The room had stopped its slow spin, but she still felt a bizarre sense of unreality, as though none of this was quite believable.

"I can say with firsthand experience that you're moody as hell, and unquestionably drunk," Cord declared. She knew he was trying to be lighthearted, but his phrasing only heightened Avery's sadness. "The candle was Eris's, actually," Cord went on. "She bought it for—"

He broke off awkwardly.

"No, it's okay." For some reason it felt good talking about Eris, as if by turning to the older, more aching hurt, Avery could ignore the new one that burned in her chest. "I like the idea of using something that was hers. She would want us to burn it." Avery watched as Cord hunted for an old-fashioned lighter, since no bot would burn anything, not inside.

"I miss her a lot," she added softly, as he clicked a small flame to life and held it to the candle's taper.

"I miss her too." Cord glanced down. The light of the candle cast small shadows under his eyes.

"You know, if I met Eris now, I think I would be intimidated by her. She was so unapologetically original," Avery mused aloud, fumbling for the words. "But we'd been friends for so long that I took her for granted." *I can't take anyone for granted ever again*, she promised herself, except that she was already losing the people she cared about. Leda hated her, Watt obviously resented her, she and Atlas were fighting, and her parents were watching her like a pair of hawks. When had all of Avery's relationships started falling apart?

"Eris's funeral didn't do her justice," Cord was saying. "It was too generic for her. She needed something spectacular, like confetti bombs. Or bubbles."

"Eris would have loved that." Avery smiled and took a deep breath, letting the scent of the candle travel from her lungs all the way to the farthest corners of her body, seeping into her hair, to the tips of her fingers. It smelled like honey and toast and camp-fires.

The holo switched to a commercial for a new karaoke game. A silence stretched between her and Cord—the sort of easy, companionable silence that falls between two people who've known each other a long time.

She nodded at the commercial. "Why don't we ever play games like that anymore?"

"Because you're a terrible singer. Which I've never understood, given the whole genetic engineering thing."

"Not fair!" Avery protested, though she secretly liked it when Cord brought up the fact that she was a custom-order baby. No one else ever dared to.

"It's okay. There are more important things," Cord said, and there was a strange note in his voice that made her look up. At some point—she wasn't sure when—he'd shifted nearer to her, or maybe she'd been the one to move. Either way, here they were.

Time seemed to stretch out like a liquid. Avery's face was so close to Cord's, and he was looking at her with that unfamiliar blue-eyed intensity, none of his usual nonchalance or sarcasm, his gaze focused and resolute. Avery couldn't breathe over the pounding of her heart. She knew she should pull away, but she didn't, she couldn't move, it was all too sudden and unexpected. She'd stepped into some strange universe where Cord Anderton might lean in and kiss her.

Then suddenly Cord was sitting back, making another teasing comment about how her singing sucked, and Avery wasn't sure what had happened, or if anything had even happened at all.

Her eyes lit on the candle, which still flickered there on the table. Little pockets of happiness melted out to drift blissfully upward, beads of wax sliding down the sides to gather in golden pools at the bottom.

Maybe she'd imagined the whole thing.

———————

Avery's eyes fluttered open and she shut them again, shifting in her bed. Except that she wasn't in her bed at all. She was lying on the Andertons' couch.

She sat up quickly, reaching up to touch the matted knot of her hair. Her eyes frantically skimmed the room. The candle was still on the table, its flame long since guttered out. Early morning light streamed through Cord's enormous floor-to-ceiling windows.

She couldn't even remember falling asleep. She and Cord had been talking about Eris, and he'd lit the candle to help her relax . . . that must have been when she drifted off.

Her gown was right where she'd left it, draped over the back of a chair. Avery stumbled to the hallway closet where the Andertons kept self-steaming garment bags; she quickly grabbed one and tossed her dress in it, then slipped on her satin heels and muttered under her breath for a hover, already halfway out the door. At the last minute, an unbidden impulse caused her to turn back and grab the melted remains of the candle. There was still a good hour left to burn, and she had a feeling she might need it.

Safe inside the hover, Avery leaned back and closed her eyes, struggling to sort through the events of the last twelve hours. She still felt hurt by her stupid fight with Atlas; but also ashamed of her immature reaction, setting out to flirt with another boy in order to irritate him. No wonder he hadn't flickered her. He must have seen her laughing and dancing, taking all those shots with Cord, then stumbling home with him at the end of the night.

Her cheeks colored. What did Atlas think of her? For all she knew he might assume that something had actually *happened* between her and Cord.

Had it, almost?

Avery kept replaying that moment, trying to parse out what it was and what it meant. Had Cord almost kissed her, or was it just the product of her alcohol-soaked, IntoxiCandled mind? *Well*, she thought firmly, *thank god nothing had happened in the end.*

The hover raced upstairs, getting ever closer to the thousandth floor. Avery leaned forward, her head in her hands, trying to shut out the world. What would she do when she saw Atlas—storm past him, ignore him, talk to him?

Kiss him and tell him it'll be okay, no matter what, her mind whispered to her, and she knew that it was true. She'd hated seeing him flirt with Calliope, but in the cold light of day, she knew he was right: it didn't mean anything, and if it helped divert their parents' suspicions, then so be it. She loved Atlas, and nothing else really mattered. They would figure it out, she told herself, like they always did.

The hover pulled up to their front door and Avery walked inside, the dress floating alongside her in the garment bag. She started to turn left toward Atlas's room, but she heard the sound of clanging of pans, and broke into an involuntary smile. She knew she looked like the definition of a walk of shame, wearing a boy's clothes and holding her silver micro-clutch, but she would explain everything the moment she saw him.

"Atlas?" she called out, walking into the kitchen. "I hope you're making chili eggs—"

Avery's words cut off abruptly when she saw who was there, because it wasn't Atlas at all.

Calliope stood at the stovetop, wearing Atlas's boxers and T-shirt—a shirt Avery had *bought* for him, she realized, stunned. Her feet were bare, and her riotous dark waves were piled atop her head, pinned with one of Avery's favorite clips.

Calliope caught sight of Avery in the refrigerator's reflective surface and grinned. "Good morning, sunshine. Sorry it's not Atlas's chili eggs, but I'm making toast and bacon if you want some."

Avery couldn't speak. The world was spinning again and the pain was back; far, far worse than before.

Calliope turned around, holding her hands beneath the UV-cleanser. Her eyes traveled up and down Avery's attire, and she winked. "Nice outfit. Makes me feel a little less shameful, knowing I'm not the only one."

"Is that my hair clip?" Avery heard herself ask. She started to walk toward Calliope. Was she really going to *pull* it out of her hair? she thought wildly, watching her actions as if another person were performing them. Calliope beat her to the punch, tossing the clip on the counter.

"Sorry," Calliope said carefully, clearly aware she'd done something wrong. "I knocked on your door, but you weren't there, so I just grabbed it from your counter. I didn't have any hair bands in my purse."

Avery grabbed the clip. She had become an enormous well of grief, as if someone had shaved off the edges of her nerve endings and they were dripping raw, liquid pain into her body. Somehow—though it took every last shred of her self-control, though she knew she would pay for it all day long—she managed a tight smile, and nodded at the sizzling bacon.

"It's fine. And thank you for the offer, but I'm not really hungry."

RYLIN

THE FOLLOWING WEEK at school, Rylin sat perched on a bench at lunch, her tray balanced precariously on her lap as she took a bite of her truffled chicken sandwich.

Sometimes Rylin ate with a couple of other girls from her English class. They'd asked her once, a few weeks ago, and she'd come to enjoy their company; they spoke in soft voices, and didn't make any demands of her outside the cafeteria. But today she'd wanted a moment to herself. She picked idly at her sandwich's orange citrus loaf, letting her mind wander.

School had definitely gotten better. There were still awful parts, of course: Rylin didn't think she would ever enjoy calculus, with its convoluted equations and funny-looking Greek letters; and she kept getting odd looks on the morning express lift, when she stepped on board in her preppy pleated uniform. Still, she'd grown accustomed to her routine, and at least now she could find her way around campus without help from Cord.

Friday afternoon had quickly become the highlight of Rylin's week—not because of the weekend, but because of holography class. She was now that student that she and Lux used to make fun of, the one who constantly raised her hand, eager to volunteer information or ask questions. Rylin couldn't help it; she loved the class. It wasn't just Xiayne, though he was part of it, full of constant praise and encouragement, and giving her straight As ever since their long editing session after school that day. She'd watched all his films by now—some of them multiple times.

Rylin had found to her surprise that she loved holography. She loved that she could see the direct result of every lesson, how each new technique or idea made her work immediately cleaner and sharper and more impactful. She'd never paid so much attention in a class before. Not even the sight of Cord, shifting restively in the seat in front of her, could ruin it.

And she couldn't stop thinking that maybe someday, if she got good enough, she could make a holo that would explain her feelings to Cord. Her words had clearly failed her, but wasn't that what holography was for—to convey the things that words failed to?

Rylin stretched out her legs, curling her toes in the new black flats she'd splurged on, which were a little girly for her taste, but she couldn't handle the blisters from Chrissa's shoes. She glanced around at the other kids in the courtyard. A few meters away, some boys were playing a game she'd never seen, where they kicked around a small beanbag with their feet and tried to keep it from hitting the ground. A group of freshman girls—the popular ones, Rylin could tell by their shining hair and unimpressed attitudes—lounged in the nearby grass, pretending not to notice the boys but clearly preening for their benefit.

Across the way, she saw a familiar figure bobbing through the crowd. Rylin immediately sat up straighter and tossed back her head, acting just like those stupid freshman girls. Would she ever be able to see Cord Anderton without feeling a nervous twist in her stomach?

He glanced up and caught her staring. *Crap.* She tried to look down, to pretend to be reading something on her tablet, anything; but he was coming over—

"Rylin. Thank god I found you, I've been looking everywhere."

She startled to attention as Xiayne slid onto the bench next to her. Cord had halted in his tracks and turned away.

"Hi," she said cautiously. "Is everything okay?" It wasn't even a Friday. What was Xiayne doing on campus—and looking for *her*?

Xiayne grimaced. He was sitting very close, close enough for Rylin to see the stubble breaking through his swarthy skin; the way his lashes fanned out, long and damp around his sage-green eyes.

"My film is a nightmare. The DP just quit, so I've had to bump up his assistant, who I'm not sure is ready, but then I don't have much of a choice. I've got barely a week before my star leaves to shoot her next holo," he complained. "Long story short, I'm in the market for a new filming assistant."

"That all sounds like a mess. I'm sorry," Rylin replied.

"I'm not," he said evenly. "Because now it means I can offer the job to you. What do you say—will you come to LA with me?"

"What?"

Xiayne leaned forward a little, his words spilling over one another, fast and intense. "Rylin, you're an incredibly promising holography student. Sure, I could hire someone out in LA, if all I wanted was to get the film done. But I'd also love to help start your career." He smiled. "You've got a lot of natural talent, but there's still so much for you to learn. Which is why you'd benefit from some practical experience."

"You want me to quit school to come work for you?" *What about my scholarship?* her dazed mind thought, but Xiayne was already answering her unasked question.

"Berkeley has a system for things like this. Hell, last year one of your classmates took a month off to go scuba in the Everglades, study the underwater biologics or something. It's a quick shoot; I've already filed it as a weeklong internship. And don't worry, all your travel costs are covered by the arts department," he added.

"But what would I be doing, exactly?"

"Can I have one of those?" Xiayne gestured to her package of choco-berry cookies. Rylin held it out, confused, and he grabbed one, taking an enormous bite. Then he wiped the gooey chocolate onto his jeans and spoke again. "Don't get me wrong, Rylin, being an assistant is hard work. A lot of fetching and carrying, helping set the lighting, managing the talent. They can be . . . difficult." He gave a little eye roll to emphasize just how difficult. "But it's also rewarding. I started just like this, back in the day. I promise it all feels worth it when you see your name in lights at the end of the film."

Rylin felt a sudden flutter in her chest. "You'd put my name in the credits?"

"Of course I would. I do that for all my assistants."

Rylin thought guiltily of Chrissa, who would be alone for an entire week; but Chrissa was self-sufficient enough to handle things on her own. And Chrissa would want her to go. She was so proud that Rylin was back in school, and actually enjoying it.

Why not? She owed herself the opportunity to at least try. "What do I need to do?"

Xiayne grinned. "I already sent the paperwork to you. Just have one of your parents sign it, and we're good to go."

"Actually, I don't have any parents at home. I'm a legal adult," Rylin declared. She pulled up her tablet, quickly located the file, and held her thumb to the bright blue circle to stamp the document. A moment later, the screen flashed green in approval.

"You don't have any parents at home?" Xiayne repeated, puzzled.

"My mom died a couple of years ago. Since then, it's just been me and my sister. I was working the last few years. That's why I'm a little behind on academics." For once, Rylin didn't feel embarrassed admitting that. Of all people, Xiayne would understand—hadn't he just said he'd worked his way up from nothing?

Xiayne nodded. "You continue to impress me, Rylin," he said, and stood up with a smile. He looked so young when he smiled, barely older than Rylin, with his soft features and shaggy dark curls. "If you're a legal adult, I guess I have to pay you."

"Oh, you don't—"

"It's only minimum wage, but if you have a problem, take it up with the union," he went on, and Rylin laughed.

"Thank you," she told him.

He nodded, his eyes dancing. "We leave tomorrow morning on the 'loop. I'll send you your ticket."

The last time she'd been on one of the Hyperloop trains was with Cord, to Paris, but Rylin reminded herself not to think about that.

———

Later that afternoon, Rylin walked into the front office for her mandatory meeting with the upper-school dean. Apparently the dean needed to personally approve every request for academic absence, even for a school-sponsored internship.

"Take a seat," the front-desk attendant intoned, bored. Rylin sank onto the couch and pulled up a map of LA on her tablet, then began to zoom over various parts, trying to familiarize herself with the city. Not that she would probably see any of it except the film lot, she thought eagerly.

She felt worlds different from the girl who'd walked in here on her first day, all anxiety and uncertainty. Now she just felt excited, and curious about the week ahead.

"We can't keep running into each other like this." Cord took the seat next to her.

"You can't keep stalking me like this," Rylin retorted, her mood buoyed by her good news.

Cord grinned. "If I wanted to stalk you, trust me, I could do better than the school's front office."

They both fell silent. Rylin willed herself not to look at him, to look down at her tablet, at the stupid posters on the wall with inspirational quotes and images of mountains, anything but at Cord. She lasted a full eight seconds.

When she couldn't take it anymore and turned in his direction, she caught Cord staring at her, with an expression of mingled wariness and curiosity and—she hoped—a glimmer of attraction. For a moment it seemed to Rylin that no time had passed, that it was the olden days again, back when he was deciding whether or not to trust her the first time. Back when Cord hadn't been a wealthy, arrogant boy set to inherit billions and she hadn't been the girl who cleaned his bathrooms—but instead, somehow, they were just a boy and a girl, talking in quiet tones about the losses they had both suffered.

She wondered if they would ever be that way again.

"How did your fencing match go?" Cord asked.

"Oh, you know, I'm ruthless when it comes to fighting," Rylin teased.

She'd meant it as a joke, but Cord didn't laugh, and Rylin wondered if she'd hit too close to home. After all, the things she'd said to him the night Eris died had been cruel, and ruthless.

"What are you here for, anyway?" he went on, after a moment.

"I'm here to meet with the dean." She couldn't keep the pride from her voice. "I'm missing a week of school for a work-study program with Xiayne. I'll be a filming assistant on his new holo."

"I thought you were here on *scholarship*. Shouldn't you be studying, not jetting off to LA?"

Rylin recoiled at the harsh phrasing. "This is a great opportunity. It's rare that students our age get to actually work on set, get hands-on experience."

"Or maybe it's a chance for Xiayne to get some free labor. He's not paying you, is he?" Cord said, and she was surprised by the venom in his tone.

"Actually, he is." She hated how defensive she sounded.

"Well, I'm glad he's taken such a *special* interest in you."

"Cord—" Rylin broke off, not quite certain what she was about to say, but the dean's door swung open before she could answer.

"Rylin Myers, sorry for the wait! Come on in," his voice boomed.

Rylin looked searchingly at Cord, feeling both saddened and hurt. But he was shaking his head. "Whatever, Rylin. God knows you don't owe me an explanation. Have fun taking teacher's pet to a whole new level."

Suddenly Rylin's mind was able to form sentences again. "Not everyone is as cynical as you are, Cord. You should try being happy for me sometime."

She squared her shoulders and walked away before he could reply.

CALLIOPE

CALLIOPE WALKED EAGERLY through the Nuage lobby, which on this sunny afternoon was all soaring white and blue, making the hotel live up to its name. She felt like she was floating through the center of a cloud, maybe of Mount Olympus.

In the nick of time she remembered her fake limp, for the benefit of the front-desk managers. The last thing she and Elise needed was to start being charged for the room they had no intention of paying for. But Calliope could hardly think straight; she was heading to afternoon tea with her mom, and her stomach was bubbling with a pleasant sense of anticipation. For Calliope and her mom, afternoon tea always meant something.

She turned into the hotel's formal dining room, which was lined with gilded paneling, its delicate tables covered in wisp-thin linens and set with antique Francis I sterling. Young girls in bright pink bows squirmed in their seats, accompanied by harried moms; groups of women clinked champagne glasses; there were even a few tourists, eyeing the society crowd with trepidation and a degree of envy. Calliope found her mom at a table in the middle of the room. *Of course,* Calliope thought, unsurprised and amused. *All the better for being admired.*

"What's the occasion?" she asked, settling into the opposite seat.

"The occasion is, I'm taking my daughter out for tea." Elise smiled, looking cool and careless in a printed sheath.

Calliope leaned back. "Every time we do this, it reminds me of Princess Day," she said, her tone reflective, but not quite wistful.

Calliope had been obsessed with tea ever since she was a little girl, when she and her friend Daera would put on Justine's hand-me-down clothes and serve each other water in plain white mugs, calling each other made-up names like Lady Thistledown and Lady Pennyfeather. Elise had picked up on the fixation and started an annual tradition, just her and Calliope, called Princess Day. It instantly became Calliope's favorite day of the year.

On Princess Day, Elise and Calliope would dress up—sometimes even carrying Mrs. Houghton's purses, or wearing her scarves or jewelry. It was the only occasion when Elise would let them do so—and go to the Savoy Hotel for its expensive afternoon tea. Even at that age, Calliope had known that it was willfully stupid of them to do something so extravagant, something they clearly couldn't afford. But they *needed* Princess Day. It was a chance for the two of them to escape their routines and step into someone else's life, just for a moment. And Calliope could tell that her mother loved it as much as she did: being the one catered to, for once, rather than the other way around. She loved being presented with a silver tray of delicate little sweets and being asked which she would like, and she would lift her ring-crusted finger and say in an imperious tone, *that one and that one, and also that.* Commanding someone else, the way that Mrs. Houghton constantly commanded her.

Calliope would never forget the way her mom had turned to her, that first morning on the train to Russia, when their old life was long gone, and their new one just unfolding. "It's Princess Day, sweetheart," she'd said.

Calliope shook her head in confusion. "But we had one a few months ago."

"Every day is Princess Day now," Elise had said with a smile. Not the pinched, forced smile she'd worn for so long, but a genuine, easy smile; and Calliope saw that her mother was shedding some terrible skin she'd been forced into, and becoming someone new. As the years went on, she would realize that Elise had never been happy in London. It wasn't until their life on the road that she'd seemed to find her true calling.

Even now, tea was still their tradition, as cherished and as sacred as any church. Calliope loved the ceremony of it being poured, hot and steaming, into a shape-shifting china cup, the beautiful array of fluffy scones and clotted cream and fancifully cut sandwiches. There was something soothing about the ritual of high tea. No matter where you went in the world, it was always stuffy and traditional and comfortingly British.

Whenever they had a big decision to make, Calliope and Elise would do so at afternoon tea, at whatever five-star hotel they'd conned their way into. It was how they chose when to move locations, how much cash Elise should try to swindle from her latest boyfriend or girlfriend, when they should next get their retinas replaced. It was how they made every important choice, Calliope realized . . . except her decision to get involved with Atlas. That was the only real choice she'd made on her own.

Just then, a waitress with a turned-up nose and jaunty ponytail approached their table. She looked younger than Calliope. Actually, Calliope thought, she seemed familiar, though she couldn't have said why.

"Good afternoon, ladies. Are you familiar with our tea menu?" she asked smoothly.

A holographic scroll shimmered in the air before them both, with the menu written in calligraphy. Calliope could see the edge of each droplet of ink, the glitter that seemed dusted over it all.

"We'll have the classic tea tower and lemon water, no tea," Elise said briskly, waving her arm through the scroll so that its refracted pixels dissolved into nothing.

The waitress smiled. "Tea is complimentary with your tower. We have teas from every nation on earth, and several off-planet as—"

"Whatever is your favorite," Calliope said quickly, then lifted an eyebrow at her mom as the girl scurried away. "Come on, I know we're celebrating something. What did this Nadav guy give you?"

Elise shrugged. "Show tickets, a funny little invention of his that tracks your heartbeat and muscle movements, nothing of any real value. But he's asked for a family dinner soon," she added, her tone lowering several octaves.

Calliope understood in a flash what today's tea was about. She was being scolded—very lightly, with a lot of sugar and fanfare, but a scolding nonetheless.

"You want me to be friendlier with Livya."

"I'm not asking for much. But it would have meant a lot to me, if you'd put in just a *teensy* bit of effort with her at the ball." Elise sighed. "I thought you were going to play backup for me, but you went off, focused on your own thing."

"I was with a date, Mom," Calliope pointed out.

Elise threw her hands up in a conciliatory gesture. "I get it, I get it. I know you like running your own little side cons." *They aren't* little, Calliope thought, slightly peeved. "And I never tell you no, do I? I think I've been more than fair," her mom went on.

Calliope shrugged. "Of course I'll do a family dinner," she promised, as if she hadn't done a million of them in the past— some ending with a wedding ring, others not. She wondered how quickly her mom would wrangle a proposal out of this relationship.

But Elise wasn't finished. "I was hoping that you could play a little less . . . loose, when we're at dinner," she suggested. "Act more like Livya."

"You mean act boring," Calliope pointed out.

"Exactly!" Elise laughed.

The waitress deposited an opulent display of treats on their table. It tapered upward like the real Tower, complete with a miniature sugar spire. "This is lunar tea," she said, pouring a steaming mug of tea that smelled vaguely like aloe. "My favorite. It's grown on the moon's surface. The plants see a much weaker sun, so their growing season is twice as long."

Calliope took a tentative sip from the mug, which, sensing the tea inside, had shifted into a golden half-moon shape. She immediately spit it back, disgusted by the bitter taste. The waitress pursed her lips at her reaction, as if holding back a smile; and Calliope suddenly wondered whether the younger girl hadn't recommended the revolting tea on purpose, just to screw with what she likely thought was a pair of entitled, rude women.

It was the kind of thing Calliope would have done, if she'd been in that girl's shoes. She glanced down at her chic printed skirt and the fuchsia Senreve bag perched next to her chair. Did this girl think of her the way Calliope used to think about Justine Houghton? But she was *nothing* like Justine Houghton.

"Does that waitress remind you of someone?" she blurted out, after the girl had walked away.

"I don't think so." Elise was reaching around the offending tea for her water glass, with a cheerful slice of lemon floating on top. "Now tell me more about *your* progress. It's clearly going well, since you didn't even come home until Sunday morning."

"I'm not so sure," Calliope said, her usual confidence faltering. She didn't know what to make of the situation with Atlas. She'd tried to scout around the Fullers' apartment a little, later that night, but almost all the rooms had no-guest settings on their doorways. And she hadn't really been in the mood to steal a random antique off a tabletop. She wanted something bigger. She wanted jewelry, but she had a feeling she might never get any from Atlas.

He'd been perfectly nice the morning after that party, sitting and eating breakfast with her, even calling her a hover home. But Calliope could see that his mind was elsewhere. Maybe he regretted letting her come over the night before. Not that anything had even happened between them; Atlas had been so drunk that he promptly passed out, leaving Calliope to sneak around their apartment uninhibited. Eventually she'd come back to his room and found a T-shirt of his before drifting off on the other side of the bed, alone.

"I can see why. That boy is almost too gorgeous to con."

It was a moment before Calliope realized her mom meant Brice Anderton. "Oh, I just used Brice for an invite to the party. He's not connable," she said quickly, knowing that Elise wouldn't push it. "No, I'm targeting a different boy. He's the one I went home with." She looked down at her hands, nervously slicing a cucumber sandwich into tiny triangles. Her mom always seemed to understand what other people were thinking, what they wanted. Maybe she would have some insight into Atlas. "Actually, I could use your advice," Calliope admitted.

Elise leaned forward eagerly. "What else are moms for?"

Calliope told her everything. About how she'd recognized Atlas at the Fullers' cocktail party and staged a run-in with him at the Nuage pool, then accepted Brice's invitation to the Hudson Conservancy Ball knowing that Atlas would be at the same party. How she'd gone home with Atlas—proving, once and for all, her conviction that he did want her—only to realize that maybe she'd been wrong.

"Let me get this straight," Elise said, reaching for a bite of scone. Tiny sugar-flecked pieces crumbled down, sparkling like scattered gems against the china plate. "You met this boy in Africa?"

Calliope nodded. "But then he left me one day, with no explanation. I never told you, because—"

"It's all right," Elise said quickly. They didn't talk much about that con in India, the worst one they'd ever done. Elise had gotten involved with an older gentleman who worked in the government, and solicited a donation to a fake charity organization, but then the old man had died, all of a sudden, under mysterious circumstances. Suddenly the country's entire police force had been after them. It had been so terrifying that Calliope and Elise had split up as they fled the country. Just in case.

"I just didn't realize you ran a con in Africa," her mom went on, sounding a little hurt.

"It doesn't matter, because it didn't work."

"Yet. It didn't work *yet*," Elise corrected. She gave a narrow smile, her eyes glinting like a cat's. "It's a longer con than you'd expected, but who cares? You can afford to play a long game."

"Not too long. He's moving away soon." It was less than a month before Atlas went to Dubai, to run his dad's tower there. She had to get something from him before that happened.

"Well, don't worry if it doesn't work out. I'll get enough for the both of us," Elise promised, and sighed. "You did say this boy comes from money, right?"

"He's Atlas *Fuller*." Hadn't Calliope said that already? "That cocktail party was at his family's apartment."

Elise froze like a character in a holo game, an iced cake lifted halfway to her lips. The only movement was the slow, stunned blink of her gold-shadowed eyes. For a moment Calliope worried she'd gone too far—that maybe it wasn't such a good idea, trying to con the boy whose family literally lived on top of the world.

But then Elise was laughing, so hard that tears gathered at the corners of her eyes. Seeing it made Calliope laugh too. "The thousandth floor! Let it never be said that you don't aim high. Cheers to *that*." Elise clinked their water glasses with renewed purpose.

"What can I say, I have expensive taste," Calliope conceded with a smile.

Her mom was right; Calliope was a pro, and she always landed her mark in the end. She would land Atlas too, no matter how long it took.

The waitress came over to collect their tea tray, scattered with smears of butter and half-eaten tarts. In a flash of insight Calliope knew who the waitress had reminded her of: Daera, her childhood friend. She had the same chestnut hair and wide-set eyes.

She wondered what Daera was up to now, all these years later.

"Do you want to get the check this time, or should I?" Elise asked.

"We can't pay with the bitbanc money? I thought our last payout was a big one." Surely they hadn't spent all that money so fast. The thought of doing one of their tricks right now felt strangely wearying.

Elise shrugged. "We blew through most of that money on our girls' week in Monaco." Calliope cringed at the thought of that extravagant trip, with shopping sprees and decadent hotels and a boat they'd rented on a whim. Maybe they should have been a *little* more responsible. "I'm trying to save the rest for our tickets out of here," her mom added. "But don't worry, I'll get our tea."

She glanced around, then reached over to yank out a few of Calliope's hairs.

"Hey—*ow!*" Calliope cursed. She wanted to clap a hand to her head, but she knew it would ruin the con. "You didn't bring anything with you?" she hissed, under her breath.

"Sorry. I'd use mine, but they aren't nearly dark enough to pass for the waitress's." Elise started to place the hairs on a plate, then thought better of it, and curled them in the bottom of the teacup. She leaned back, draping a pale arm carelessly over the back of the chair as she took a sip of the previously untouched tea.

An instant later she let out an affected shriek, a hand lifted to her chest. Heads swiveled automatically in their direction. The waitress who looked like a grown-up version of Daera hurried over.

"Oh my god. There's *hair* in my tea!" Elise cried out, her tone dripping with revulsion. Her eyes lifted accusatorily to the waitress. "You *shed* into my tea!"

More glances kept shooting their way. New Yorkers did love drama, Calliope reflected, as long as they weren't the ones causing a scene.

"I'm so s-sorry," the waitress stammered, reaching up hesitantly toward the crown of her head as if to confirm that her hair was up in a slick, high ponytail. Her expression was one of unmasked fear.

During the ensuing familiar hubbub of calling a manager, complaining, getting their meal comped, Calliope said nothing. She found herself wondering what would happen to the waitress when this was all over. Probably she would have her wages docked for the amount of their tea, Calliope thought, shifting a little in her chair. Surely she wouldn't be fired, right?

"You okay?" Elise asked when it was all over and they stepped into the elevator back up to their suite. "You look pale."

"I think I ate too much sugar." Calliope put a hand on her stomach, which was, in fact, aching. "I'll be fine."

But as the doors closed, revealing the gleaming mirrored interior of the Nuage's elevator, Calliope looked down at her hands clasped tight around the handle of her purse. For once, she didn't really feel like admiring her own reflection.

AVERY

AVERY LAY ON her bed, staring up at the delicate clouds that floated across her ceiling without seeing them. It had been several days since she'd come home to find Calliope in the kitchen, wearing Atlas's boxers, though she wouldn't ever forget the image. It was burned into her mind with such searing clarity.

She and Atlas hadn't spoken since that morning. She hadn't even seen him in the apartment: they'd both made themselves scarce lately, as if they'd agreed to some mutual, temporary cease-fire.

Somehow Avery had managed to hold it together at school. But every night she'd collapsed into her champagne-colored lace pillows and let herself erupt in hot, bitter tears.

"Avery?"

She shouldn't have been surprised that he was knocking on her door, but still, it took a moment for Avery to process what was happening. She'd been longing for this conversation, yet she'd been dreading it too.

"Unlock," she muttered, standing up as the room comp released the magnetic block-field from over her door.

Atlas stood there. He looked different; there were circles around his eyes and a pallor to his skin, but it was more than that. Something had fundamentally changed about him, as if he was no longer the boy Avery thought he was.

"Hey," she said simply. Let him give the next syllable; that was all she had to offer right now.

"Hey," Atlas echoed. His eyes searched hers, but she just returned his stare, cool and level. "Look, can I come in?" he asked.

Avery stepped aside and he walked past her, shutting the door. "Took you long enough," she muttered.

"I had a lot to think about."

But Avery wasn't finished. "I assume so. You really screwed up this time, Atlas."

"I'm sorry, *I* screwed up? Don't you hear yourself? You came back that morning from Cord's! Who are you to talk?"

"You know full well that Cord and I are just friends." Avery felt oddly pleased to have made him shout.

"I don't know anything anymore," Atlas replied, with a bitterness that surprised her.

They were standing beneath an enormous crystal chandelier, utterly still. It was as if the act of finally having this conversation had anchored them to the ground, and neither of them could move until they resolved things one way or another.

Avery bit her lip, wishing she'd rehearsed some kind of speech. "Look, I'm sorry about how I reacted when I saw you flirting with Calliope. It was stupid and immature. I came back that morning wanting to tell you I was sorry—but then I found *her*, prancing around in your underwear!" She blinked back a fresh onslaught of tears. "Atlas, I know we fought, but you didn't have to *sleep* with her that same night!"

"Nothing happened between me and Calliope," Atlas insisted. "Not that you'll believe me, since you seem determined to think exactly what you want."

Avery sighed. "Even if you didn't sleep with her, you shouldn't have brought her home. Don't you see? When something bad happened, you went straight to *her*. You ran away." *To someone easier. Someone you could actually* be *with, in public*, she wanted to add.

"It wasn't just me. We *both* ran away to someone else."

"Like I said, nothing happened between me and Cord." Avery wasn't quite sure why she wanted to make the point, but it didn't matter; Atlas was shaking his head.

"I believe you. But what about next time, Aves? Maybe something will happen then, for either of us. Don't you see what a huge problem it is that when we fought, we both turned to someone else, someone more . . ."

"Easy. Uncomplicated. Which is exactly what you and I are not," she finished for him.

Atlas looked up at her. "Is that why you love me?" he asked, very quietly.

At first she didn't understand. "What?"

"Did you fall in love with me because it was complicated, and forbidden—because I was the only thing in the entire world that you were ever denied? The only thing you ever wanted that you were told 'no,' instead of 'yes'?"

Avery felt the blood drain from her face. "That's cruel, Atlas. You don't mean that."

At the hurt in her voice, something of the old Atlas came back to his features, and he let out a breath. "I had to ask," he replied, sounding more defeated than upset. It scared Avery, because she knew it meant he was shutting himself away from her, forcing himself not to feel, not to care.

"You know I love you," she insisted.

"And you know *I* love *you*. After all this, though . . ."

Avery heard the note of finality in his voice. And she realized, with a terrifying sense of clarity, that it was the beginning of the end.

"It isn't working, is it?" she said quietly, because the words were so very painful, and Atlas shouldn't have to be the one to say them.

"It can't *ever* work. It's impossible. Aves, it might be best for us to just . . . stop."

Atlas spoke hollowly, almost formally, as though Avery were a client to whom he was proposing a new construction plan. But Avery knew his mind better, almost, than she knew her own— she could see what this was doing to him, the excruciating effort he was making to keep from breaking down in front of her.

I love you, and nothing else matters, she wanted to say, but she held the words back, because in the end they weren't useful. *Everything* else mattered. She loved Atlas, and Atlas loved her, and yet it would never work between them.

She knew the events of last Saturday were her fault. She'd picked at their relationship, peeling off little pieces of it like a destructive child, until it all inevitably came to a head. But their problem was bigger than that one evening. Atlas was right, what had happened was just a symptom of the larger issue: the sheer impossibility of them being together.

There was nowhere they could go that was safe; nowhere that the truth of who they were, the forbiddenness of their love, wouldn't come chasing them.

Maybe love wasn't enough after all. Not when every last obstacle was arrayed against you, all the odds stacked to make you fail. When the entire world was keeping you apart.

"Okay," Avery said, as the universe quietly rent itself in two. "Let's just . . . I mean . . ."

She couldn't finish the sentence. Let's just go back to the way things were before? Go back to being brother and sister, after everything they had shared?

Atlas seemed to understand her, the way he always did. "I'm going to take the Dubai job. I'll be halfway around the world soon. That should make it easier on you. I'm sorry," he added.

She wasn't sure how long she stood there after he left, her eyes still closed. A single tear ran down her cheek.

It felt to Avery as if someone had died. And in some sense there *had* been a death, she thought: of her relationship with Atlas. It had been a living, breathing thing, full of sound and color, until the two of them just dealt it the final blow.

Atlas was leaving, and he wasn't coming back.

LEDA

LEDA SAT IN bed, trying to catch up on her reading for English class, but her mind was racing too fast to focus on the words. She couldn't stop thinking about Watt, and what had happened on Saturday night.

She'd woken the next morning to find nothing but rumpled bedcovers, Watt already gone. Then she'd remembered everything—the press of his mouth on hers, the strong, certain way his hands had traveled over her body—and she'd rolled over to bury her face in her pillow, stifling a groan. Thank god she hadn't let it go too far. What had she been thinking, bringing home Watt Bakradi? She didn't even *like* him. Might, in fact, detest him.

Well, she decided crisply, at least not liking him meant that it would be easy to erase this whole incident. No need to bring it up ever again.

Except that even now, she couldn't hold back the memories

flashing hot and bright through her mind, faster and faster. She closed her eyes against them, but that just made them come more quickly—

"Leda," her mom said, pushing open her bedroom door.

"I thought we agreed that you were going to start knocking." Leda couldn't help being immediately on the defensive. She hoped the flush on her cheeks didn't somehow betray what she'd just been thinking about.

Her mom wandered over to her closet, tapping angrily through the clothing display on Leda's touch screen. She'd always found a strange comfort in clothes, as if by organizing the single perfect outfit she could ward off all the unpleasantness of life.

"I'm worried about you," Ilara said, still looking at the screen. She was wearing silk pajamas that were covered in printed chickens, which for some reason struck Leda as absurdly comical. "I've been worried since before Eris died. Which is why we're going to your check-in at Silver Cove next weekend, just you and me."

Leda jumped out of bed, startled. "What? No!" Leda didn't want to go back there—especially not with her mom.

"Leda, the four-month follow-up is a recommended part of your treatment. I think it would be good for you, given everything that's been going on. Dr. Vanderstein agrees with me."

"God, Mom, you have *got* to stop discussing me with him! It is *completely* unethical!" Leda cried out. She took a deep breath and tried to regain a measure of calm. "I don't need to go. I promise."

Leda couldn't bear the thought of returning to Silver Cove. It was crowded with too many memories. If she went back, she would be forced to confront everything that had happened in the past few months—would have to remember the Leda Cole who'd first shown up there; young and wounded and still in love with

Atlas. That girl may have been stupid, but at least she was better than this new Leda, who had killed someone, then blackmailed others into lying about it.

Leda was afraid, she realized, of the ghost of her former self.

Her mom sighed, and this time her tone was firm. "I know you've been lying to me."

Leda's heart raced. The mirrors in her closet made it seem as though there were three of Ilara, all of them reprimanding her daughter in the same disappointed tone. "You tell me that you're going to Avery's all the time, but then I hear from Elizabeth Fuller that you haven't stopped by in weeks! What's going on that you aren't telling me?" her mom went on, defeated.

Leda stepped forward and pulled her mom into a hug. Her poor, sweet, trusting mom, who still didn't know that Leda's dad had cheated on her, who just wanted the best for her children. "I'm sorry," Leda murmured, trying desperately to buy time. "I love you." Ilara was so thin that Leda could feel each bone in her spine, all stacked on one another like curved puzzle pieces.

"Please, Leda. Whatever it is, I promise I want to help. I of all people have no room to judge," Ilara said softly, and now she sounded close to tears. "After all, it's my fault you got into this mess to begin with."

Leda blinked, momentarily startled by her own insensitivity. She'd never considered that her mom might blame herself for Leda's addiction. It had been Ilara's xenperheidren that Leda had started popping back in seventh grade, when she first realized what they were. Her mom's were legal, of course, prescribed for anxiety by none other than Dr. Vanderstein. But still.

If there was no way out of this rehab check-in, then at the very least Leda needed to go without her mom. It would be too emotionally taxing for Ilara. Leda couldn't ask that of her.

"I'll go by myself," she offered, but her mom shook her head.

"You need an accountability partner there with you. What about Dad?"

Leda's heart leapt in wild panic. Absolutely not. There was no way in hell she was spending an entire weekend alone with her dad. All those lectures and sharing circles—he might try to talk to her about Eris again, make some bizarre confession to relieve his own conscience, all under the guise of "healing."

And then Leda realized exactly who she should ask. Someone who couldn't make any demands of her, who would let her go to yoga and holo screenings instead of all the actual rehab activities. Someone who couldn't tell her no.

"You were right, Mom. I have been keeping something from you." Here it was, the gamble. Nothing ventured, nothing gained, right? "I have a new boyfriend."

Sure enough, Ilara gave a sharp intake of breath, pleased to be proven right. "Boyfriend? Who is he?"

"Watt Bakradi. I brought him to the Hudson Conservancy Ball. He lives downTower, so I thought . . ." She purposefully let the silence drag out.

"What? That I wouldn't approve?"

Leda shrugged, letting her mom take that as a yes.

"Come on, Leda. I hope you think better of me than that. I came from nothing too." Ilara reached for Leda's hands and gave her a firm, well-meaning squeeze.

"Thank you." Leda exhaled in relief. "So, I was hoping Watt could come to the rehab check-in with me instead."

Her mom still frowned. "I'm happy that you've found Watt, but I'm not sure he's the right person to bring to Silver Cove. You haven't been dating him that long; he's not equipped to talk about your history. I would feel much better if your father went instead."

Leda looked down as if embarrassed; digging herself further

in, burying herself under more lies. "Watt does know my history. And he's known me for a while, actually. It's just a sensitive subject, because of how I met him."

"What do you mean?"

"His older sister went to Silver Cove. She went through something similar." Leda's stomach twisted at the lie, but then she thought again of going back there—of seeing the old familiar places, and worse, what it might do to her mom—and her resolve hardened.

"Watt's been my accountability partner recently. After everything that happened with his sister, it's important to him to be part of my healing process. And it would mean a lot to me to have him there."

Ilara was silent for a moment, studying Leda as if she wasn't quite sure what to make of this new development. "Let me discuss this with your father. But I guess it's all right." She paused at the doorway. "You should bring Watt over for dinner sometime soon. And his sister," she added warmly. "I'd love to meet them both."

Leda held her mom's gaze as she stretched her web of lies even further. "I can bring Watt. But his sister died last year."

"Oh, Leda. I'm sorry." Her mom's face paled, and she swallowed. And Leda knew she had won.

"I love you, Mom."

"Love you too. I'm proud of you," Ilara said softly, shutting the door behind her.

Leda fell back onto her bed and began composing a message to Watt. *Clear your plans for next weekend and pack your bags,* she wrote. *You're coming with me to Nevada.*

RYLIN

RYLIN FOLLOWED XIAYNE out of the LA train station, which was shaped like an enormous seashell and gleamed a blinding white in the morning sun. She raised her hand automatically to her eyes to shade them, glancing at her new black suitcase, which whirled automatically behind her. Chrissa had given it to her as a congratulations-on-your-internship present. Rylin was so excited that she couldn't even argue at the extravagance.

"You okay if we head straight to the set? Filming starts in an hour," Xiayne asked, with a glance at Rylin. He was wearing jeans and a black T-shirt with a single white word on it, though the word was constantly shifting, in alphabetical order. So far this morning Rylin had seen everything from *parallel* to *toast*. She wondered how long it took the shirt to cycle through completely and start over again.

The two of them had left early that morning, on the eight a.m. train from New York. But since the cross-country trip was only two hours, it was now just seven a.m. in LA, giving Rylin the curious sensation of having traveled back in time.

"Of course," she said quickly. She'd barely been able to sleep all night from anticipation. She still couldn't quite believe she was going to work on an actual holo set.

As they got into a hover and started off, Rylin glued her eyes to the window, desperate with curiosity about this unfamiliar city. Streets fanned out in various directions, the buildings illuminated and softly curved. Rylin had never seen anywhere like it. It seemed so unnecessarily spread out, with people living and working and going to school in all those different buildings. Rylin expected as much from the suburbs, but wasn't this supposed to be a *city*? The whole thing struck her as absurdly inefficient.

They passed a luxury apartment complex, shiny and new-looking, with glamorous terraces on each level. It was barely twenty floors, yet clearly had been designed for rich people. Rylin didn't know a single wealthy New Yorker who would pay for something this low—what kind of views could it possibly have? Her apartment was on 32, and she guaranteed it was cheaper than anything in this entire neighborhood.

"Welcome to LA, the city of dreamers. Beautiful, yet hopelessly illogical," Xiayne said, as if reading her thoughts. He sounded both sarcastic and oddly proud. "I'm glad you came, Rylin," he added, and the words traveled pleasantly throughout her body. She smiled.

"Me too." Suddenly, she thought of Cord's cruel insinuation, the way he'd said that she was taking teacher's pet to a new level. She shifted a little farther from Xiayne in the tiny space. He didn't seem to notice the movement.

"How do people here get around?" she asked, curious.

"Medusa." At Rylin's confused look, Xiayne gestured up, so that the hover's ceiling turned suddenly transparent. "It's an acronym. The Metropolitan Department of Under-Sphere Air-trams."

The sky overhead was cluttered with an incredibly complicated, tangled system of monorails. They were all colored bright neon, like a glowing nest of snakes. Far above them she saw the blue arc of the sky.

A cartoon clown face appeared against the azure blue, projected with the words MCBURGER KING! 2 FOR 1 BURGERS ON MONDAYS! Rylin gasped.

"Oh, have the morning ads already started?" Xiayne peered up and shrugged. "They project those on the Bubble."

Rylin had heard about the Bubble. Back before rain was controllable by hydropods, when global warming was still a concern, Los Angeles had worried about their city growing too hot. So they'd "bubble-wrapped" it—built an enormous supercarbon dome that surrounded the entire city. Years later, once the dome was no longer needed, they refused to take it down. Maybe they'd become too addicted to the ad money, Rylin thought. She pictured the strong clean lines of the Tower, so unlike this cluttered, flashing, chaotic city, and found herself oddly missing it.

"Here we are," Xiayne said when their hover pulled up to a series of squat interlocking buildings that could only be the studios.

The cavernous soundstage was silent, and empty of people. Rylin stole a quick glance at the set: an enormous throne room with marble pillars and a heavy gold dais. Of course: *Salve Regina* was a historical film, about England's final monarch before Britain voted to abolish the whole institution. The lights dimmed, then brightened, then dimmed again as someone, probably the head of photography, tried to perfect the way the light fell on some specific detail. Rylin tried to drink it all in again before Xiayne turned left and walked through a wall—

Her eyes widened, and then she realized that it wasn't a wall at all but an opaque light-divider, to keep all the messiness out of sight of the cameras. She quickly followed into the backstage world of cheerful, disordered chaos.

Carts whirled past, laden with sleek metal stylers and brightly colored makeup tubes, funny-looking sketches of noses and eyes and mouths scattered like abandoned limbs. Cameras of various sizes and shapes floated, forgotten, in corners. And into every tiny slice of space were crammed an assortment of people—stage managers and assistants talking frantically into their contacts, a full team of costumers checking every detail of the historic attire, and, of course, the actors and actresses in their full makeuped glory.

"Seagren." Xiayne grabbed the arm of a passing young woman, who had ebony skin and a wispy bun. "This is Rylin, your new assistant. Rylin, Seagren is your boss for the week. Good luck, you two."

"Okay, thanks. How will I—" *find you later?*, Rylin started to ask, but Xiayne was already gone, vanished into the horde of clamoring, demanding people. *Right, he's in charge of this whole production*, she reminded herself. She didn't have first claim on his attention—didn't have any claim at all, really. But she suddenly found herself longing for the last few hours, when it had been only the two of them on the Hyperloop and they'd chatted so easily.

"*You're* my new filming assistant? How old are you?" Seagren wrinkled her nose dubiously.

Rylin decided to skirt the truth. "I'm one of Xiayne's students. He asked me to come help out," she said, deliberately leaving out the part where she was seventeen. "It's really nice to meet you," she added, and held out a hand. She'd hoped that calling him by his first name would help her sound more professional, but Seagren just rolled her eyes, exasperated.

"One of the high schoolers. Great."

The whole crew actually looked quite young to Rylin; barely anyone here seemed older than thirty. Maybe that was an organic result of Xiayne's own youth, or maybe he thought having a young crew was crucial to producing a film that was edgy and cool. "What should I get started on?" she asked Seagren, ignoring the dig.

The assistant director rolled her eyes. "Why don't you organize this?" she said curtly, and flung open the door to a massive closet along one wall.

It was crammed with what looked like generations of accumulated film paraphernalia: old pieces of cameras, lightboxes, discarded props. Rylin was pretty sure she saw an old box of soda pods in there, with one of the dispenser machines. A fine layer of dust covered every surface.

This wasn't at all what she'd had in mind when she'd agreed to come work as a filming assistant. She'd thought she would at least be on set—holding lights in place, maybe; or fetching coffee, but standing there, watching the action. Rylin looked up at Seagren's face and saw that she was smirking a little, daring Rylin to challenge her.

I worked my way up from the bottom, Xiayne had said. Well, Rylin could do it too. She'd been the maid for the Andertons, after all; she wasn't afraid of rolling up her sleeves.

"Sounds perfect," she said, and walked into the dim closet to get started.

––––––––––

Hours later, Rylin was neck-deep in that impossible closet when she realized with a start that the set had grown quiet. It was later than she'd realized; when had everyone else gone home? She grabbed her suitcase, which was still tucked into a corner, and started toward the doorway, thinking she would head back to her assigned room at the crew hotel.

It had been a long day, filled with grunt work for Seagren: organizing that damn closet and picking up lunch from the craft cart and hunting down missing actors in the various break rooms. But Rylin hadn't minded it all, especially not hanging out with the actors. She loved watching them, helping them go over their lines, asking them questions about the filming. She'd realized quickly that the actors were the most talkative of anyone, at least once you got them talking about themselves.

A light was still on in one of the edit bays. Rylin hesitated, curious, then walked over to knock boldly at the door.

"What do you *want*?" came Xiayne's irritated voice.

"Never mind," Rylin said quickly, stepping back. "I'll just—"

"Rylin? Is that you?" The door swung open and Xiayne stood there, looking more agitated than Rylin had ever seen him. He was barefoot, and his hair was sticking out wildly every which way. There was a ketchup stain on his T-shirt, which had frozen on the word *yesterday*.

"I'm sorry, I thought you were someone else. I didn't mean to snap like that." He kept reaching up to push back his hair, which fell forward over his eyes.

"Is everything okay?" Rylin asked, and Xiayne sighed.

"Not really. I'm just reviewing the dailies, and to be honest . . ." He gave an embarrassed shrug. "They suck."

"Is there anything I can do to help?"

Xiayne seemed surprised by her offer. "Sure. Come check them out. You'll see what I mean," he warned. When she'd pulled up the chair next to him, he flicked his wrist, and the footage resumed playing.

They watched for a while in silence. The footage wasn't all that bad, Rylin decided, though it wasn't as good as Xiayne's other films. She tried to focus on certain scenes and images, reminding herself that this was just the raw material, not the finished product. She kept stealing glances at Xiayne's profile. His eyes gleamed in the dimness; the flickering light of the holo picking out his strong nose, his firm jaw. Occasionally his lips moved as he murmured lines of dialogue alongside the actors.

"Okay, look at the prime minister here," Xiayne said abruptly. "She should seem more important—she's about to denounce the queen in the next scene. But she just disappears in this shot. It's that stupid navy suit we dressed her in." He lifted a hand to his chin, his eyes narrowed. "I kept upping the lighting, but that navy suit absorbs photons like a black hole. It has no *texture*. I'd reshoot it, but we only have her for two more days, and I still need to get through act three . . ."

Rylin stood up and walked a slow circle around the room. "What about the queen's gown?" she asked after a moment. "After she walks in, it throws off a lot of light."

Xiayne went silent. For a moment Rylin feared she'd overstepped her bounds, but then he twirled his finger, skipping forward to the queen's grand entrance in her elaborate court gown.

Rylin watched his face as he watched the scene. When he saw what she meant, his eyes lit up with an almost fanatical fervor. "You're right," he said wonderingly. "That skirt casts light like a mirror. Look how it brightens the prime minister's face and hands."

"Can you use it?" Rylin pressed.

"I'll grab a few of these stills, track all the beams around the PM and then copy them into the earlier shots. It'll be a bitch to do, but yeah, it'll work." Xiayne stood up and stretched his arms overhead, then took a sudden step toward her. "Rylin, that was a fantastic idea. Thank you."

For a panicked moment, Rylin thought he was about to kiss her. Her stomach constricted in a wild, fluttering nervousness—because he was her teacher and she knew it was wrong, and yet some tiny part of her wanted him to.

"I knew you were a natural." Xiayne grinned, then reached for his tablet from the counter behind her and returned to his seat. "I'm ordering coffee. Want anything?"

Rylin blinked, startled. "No, thanks," she stammered, to hide her relief. Being around all these self-centered actors was clearly messing with her head.

"You should get one. We're going to be here half the night fixing this. Unless you don't want to stay," Xiayne quickly backtracked. "You've already worked way more than union hours. But if you don't mind, I could use the help."

"Of course I'm staying," Rylin said firmly, and sat up straighter. "And actually, yeah, a coffee would be great."

"Awesome." Xiayne clicked on the tablet a few times to place their orders, then smiled at Rylin as the footage began again.

AVERY

AVERY WAS TAPPING her stylus on her tablet, frowning down at a physics problem, when a knock sounded at her door. For a glorious, terrible instant she thought it might be Atlas, before she remembered that they weren't speaking, and besides, Atlas's knock had always been louder and more self-assured.

"Yeah?" She turned around, one leg crossed over the other in her chair.

Her mom paused in the doorway. She was wearing a red-and-black day dress with tights and a cropped black jacket. "I just wanted to make sure you knew about dinner," she said, smiling. "Sarah is cooking short ribs."

Avery's eyes widened. "What are we celebrating? Did Dad already figure out his next project?" Genuine short ribs—the kind that weren't grown in labs—were hard to come by and, even for the Fullers, implied a special occasion. Usually a new real estate acquisition.

"Atlas is officially taking the Dubai job! He and your father negotiated all the details," Elizabeth exclaimed. She gave a little laugh, as if the idea of Atlas negotiating his salary with his own father was too amusing. So, Avery thought, that explained why both her parents' spirits had visibly lifted these past few days.

She'd known this was coming, yet the news still stung her, more than it should. "I wish I could," she said immediately, "but it's actually Risha's birthday, and we're all going out to dinner." No way was she staying here with her parents and Atlas, pretending to toast to the news that threatened to shatter her already-broken heart into even smaller pieces.

"Really? Do you have to?" Elizabeth pressed, but Avery held firm.

"It's her birthday, Mom! I'm sorry." Her mom finally nodded and shut the door.

Avery wandered mechanically into her bathroom to splash water on her face, then grabbed a towel from the UV sanitizer to pat it dry. The touch-activated floor was warm on her bare feet. Her counter was enormous, lined in pristine white marble, not a fingerprint or smudge in sight. And all around her were mirrors: curved mirrors, flat mirrors, even an antique hand mirror that her grandmother had given her on her first birthday. They were positioned at all angles, as if Avery might need to constantly check herself from new and unexpected perspectives.

Normally Avery switched the mirrors to project an ocean view—she hated the way her mom had decorated this bathroom, made Avery the focus of it, just as she was the centerpiece of the rest of their lives. But now she leaned forward on her palms and studied her reflection. A ghostlike self, pale and hollow-eyed, looked back at her.

She watched the ghost tap a series of commands into her makeup diffuser, making Avery beautiful, it seemed, without any help from her actual self. She closed her eyes as a fine mist sprayed over her face, instantly brightening the shadows around her eyes, darkening her lashes, highlighting the sweeping architecture of her cheekbones. When she looked up, she felt almost like Avery Fuller again.

She reached for the jasmine lotion in its crystal dispenser and rubbed it over her bare arms. It had been a gift from Eris, who used to order it from a tiny boutique in the Philippines, and always smelled like it. The scent was soothing, and so painfully familiar that it made Avery want to cry.

Eris would have understood this feeling, Avery thought: the sensation that there was a terrifying emptiness inside her, where something sharp and brittle rattled hollowly. Probably the broken pieces of her heart. Eris would have hugged Avery, and assured her that she was better than the rest of them combined. She would have sat with her eating cookie bites and hiding from the world until Avery felt ready to face it again.

But Eris wasn't here, and Avery had to get out of this apartment if she wanted to avoid seeing Atlas tonight.

"Compose flicker. To Risha, Jess"—she hesitated a moment—"and Ming." Avery still resented Ming for the way she'd embarrassed Eris at her birthday party, but she wanted a lot of people around her right now, and Ming was the type of person you needed on nights like this, loud and game for anything, with a flair for the dramatic. If nothing else, Ming would help keep Avery from thinking about Atlas.

"We're going out tonight. Dress up. Meet at Ichi at eight."

———

"What's going on?" Jess asked when they were seated at Ichi a few hours later. Despite the late notice, all three girls had shown up, as Avery knew they would.

Avery tugged nervously at her laser-cut black dress and

reached for the platter of lobster tempura on the table before them. Ichi was a trendy sushi restaurant, an old favorite of Eris's, nestled like an opulent gem in the center of the 941st floor. It had no exterior windows, but that worked perfectly with the clubby atmosphere: dim lighting, techno music, and especially the low-slung tables that forced everyone to sit on the ground, amid piles of red silk cushions.

"I just wanted to have a fun girls' night," she said, flashing a smile.

"It's a Wednesday," Risha pointed out.

"I'm avoiding my parents," Avery decided to admit. "They wanted to have a big family dinner at home, but I'm upset with them and not in the mood. I don't want to get into it," she added, and Ming—who'd already opened her mouth to ask a question—reluctantly stayed silent.

A waiter swooped over with the rest of their order: eel sashimi, tartare tacos, an enormous baked miso soufflé. When he started to deposit bright purple drinks at the corner of each place setting, Avery looked up in surprise. "We didn't order lychee martinis."

"I did," Ming announced, and turned to Avery with a challenging smile. "Come on, you know you want one."

Avery started to protest; she wasn't in the mood to drink, at *all*. But then she thought of Atlas, sitting there with her parents, toasting to the job she'd never wanted him to take. One drink wouldn't hurt.

The girls were all looking at Avery, awaiting her judgment. "Okay," she said, lifting the martini to her lips.

"Let's take a snap!" Jess squealed.

Avery started to shift aside like she normally did. She'd always hated being in snaps: she couldn't control how the images made their way through the feeds, never knew who saw them, and despite all that effort there were far more pics out there than she wanted. But tonight, something stopped her. Maybe it wouldn't be such a bad thing, if Atlas saw her out right now with her friends. Maybe it would start making things normal between them.

"Here, take one with me in it," she said, her voice ringing strange even to her own ears. She felt slippery with anxiety.

"Of course." Ming pulled her lips into a tight, angular smile as the other girls turned and posed with practiced ease. "But, Avery, you *never* want to be in snaps. Who are you trying to make jealous?" Ming demanded, suspicious.

"Everyone," Avery said easily, and they all laughed, even Ming.

Avery leaned back and glanced around the room. Everyone here was young and well-dressed, their skin bright with the elusive glow of wealth. A few boys at other tables glanced their way, clearly wondering about the young women in their short dresses and long glittery earrings, but no one had yet ventured over to talk to them.

"Risha. Tell me more about you and Scott," Avery commanded, just to hear someone talk.

Risha dutifully recounted the latest development in her on-again-off-again romance with Scott Bandier, who was a senior at Berkeley. Avery forced herself to laugh so that no one would notice her strange mood. If she laughed and smiled and nodded enough, nothing would really be wrong.

But inside, her mind was roiling erratically, fluttering from one topic to the next without any resolution. She couldn't focus on anything, couldn't think—just kept picking at the cold remains of the miso soufflé. The kaleidoscope of light and sound washed over her, dulling the persistent ache in her heart. She kept taking sips of her martini, which Ming must have refilled at some point, though she hadn't noticed.

Eventually their group began to swell. First it was a couple of other girls from their class, Anandra and Danika; they'd seen the snaps and wanted to join. And then more Berkeley kids showed up, clustering around the bar, ordering that signature purple martini and posting snaps to the feeds, bringing even *more* people. Soon Avery felt like half the Berkeley student body was there, spilling onto the dark wooden dance floor in sticky clumps. She thought she saw Leda at one point, but before she could be sure, a trio of guys—Rick, Maxton, Zay Wagner—bore down on their table.

"Zay dumped Daniela, you know," Ming whispered, with a meddlesome wink.

Avery didn't react to that news at first. She'd been sitting in the same place all night, a little like a queen presiding over her subjects; not that she'd meant it that way. She just hadn't cared enough about anything to bother moving.

But Ming had a point. Why *shouldn't* she talk to Zay? What was left to hold her back? She didn't have Atlas anymore, no matter what she did.

Avery suddenly remembered how whenever Eris felt heartbroken after a relationship, she would throw herself violently and wholeheartedly into a flirtation with someone new. Avery had asked her about it once. "There's no forgetting like *that* kind of forgetting," Eris had replied, with an arch smile and a knowing flash of her eyes.

"Zay!" Avery exclaimed after a beat, standing up slowly, the way Eris would have. "How've you been?"

Zay seemed startled by her attention; after all, she'd soundly rejected him several months earlier. "Great, thanks," he said cautiously.

But Avery was determined not to be ignored. She turned her flirtation on full wattage, flashing her brightest smile. Poor Zay didn't stand a chance.

She was just about to lead him onto the dimly lit dance floor when someone tapped at Zay's elbow.

"Mind if I cut in?" Cord took Avery's arm and smoothly led her away. Zay stood there about to protest, his mouth half open like a gutted fish.

"That line was a bit clichéd, even for you," Avery accused, though she didn't really mind. She hadn't actually cared about Zay. She'd just felt strangely loose and unmoored, and needed to do something—anything—to feel anchored.

And if Atlas saw her on the feeds, bright and glittering and careless, that wouldn't have bothered her either.

"Here I thought you were going to thank me for the rescue."

"Zay isn't that bad," Avery protested unconvincingly.

Cord laughed. "I wasn't talking about *you*. I was rescuing Zay from another broken heart. You're a little cruel sometimes, you know, Avery," he said lightly.

Avery glanced up at him. They hadn't spoken since the party the weekend before. "I didn't know you were coming out tonight."

"I wasn't, until I saw all the snaps."

"Cord," she said, not quite certain what she wanted to tell him. That he shouldn't read anything into that moment on his couch, that she was raw and hurting and that he should stay away from her. But before she could formulate a coherent thought, she let out a hiccup.

Cord laughed. Avery had always loved the way Cord laughed—*really* laughed, not his cynical dark laugh but the genuine one. He laughed with his whole body, the way he used to when they were kids.

Before she'd quite realized it, they were dancing, his hands at her waist. "You're still not going to tell me what's going on, are you," he said at last.

"I'm *fine*." Avery gave her head an emphatic shake.

"Look, I don't know who this guy is, but if you really want to make him jealous, you need to do better than Wagner."

"How did you know it's a guy?" she asked quickly, wondering what had given her away.

Cord gave a triumphant grin. "I didn't, until just now. Thank you for confirming my suspicions."

Now it was Avery's turn to laugh. It made her feel surprisingly good; almost normal again, for a fleeting second, if there could be such a thing as normal in a world without Atlas.

"Come on, you'll have to get closer to really sell it," Cord told her, his voice husky. Avery hesitated before stepping in to loop her arms around Cord's shoulders. He really was very tall. A terrible, sinful part of her hoped that someone was snapping it and uploading it to the feeds. It would serve Atlas right.

But then she thought of Atlas actually looking at the snap, wondered what he would think of her for going straight to Cord—again—and her arms fell back down. Cord didn't miss a beat, just began twirling her in an easy, friendly way.

"Besides," he added, "I've been your friend since we were in preschool. I know you wouldn't command our whole class out on a weeknight without good reason."

"I didn't command them, they just showed up!" Avery protested, realizing a beat later that he'd used the word *friend*. A sense of relief flooded through her. They swayed back and forth for a while, the electric lights above them flashing drunkenly from one color to another.

Avery felt suddenly exhausted. Too much had happened lately—her world falling apart, all the tears she'd shed, the knowledge that Atlas really was leaving, going halfway across the world. She closed her eyes and allowed herself the luxury of resting her head on Cord's chest.

"Thank you, Cord. For all of it," she murmured, knowing he would understand.

He didn't say anything, but she felt him nod.

And so it begins, Avery thought, as if she were squaring her shoulders to pick up an impossibly heavy load. She needed to start putting herself back together, piece by piece, because this was the start of her life without Atlas in it.

WATT

"WAKE UP, WATT," Nadia whispered into his ear as their hydrogen-fueled jet began its descent.

Watt stirred and rubbed his eyes, a little annoyed with himself for falling asleep on this flight. It was his first time on a plane— first time leaving New York, really, unless you counted the one time his science class went to the space museum in Washington, before the latest round of budget cuts eliminated things like out-of-state field trips. Watt glanced out the window on his left and gave an involuntary intake of breath. He was looking out over Nevada, which stretched stark and pigmentless all the way to the horizon. It was like seeing the surface of some desert planet. How surreal to think that normally he was that far down, chained to the earth's surface by the restraints of gravity.

Next to him, Leda crossed one skinny leg over the other and closed her eyes, glossy and cool and indifferent.

Nadia, what should I say to break the ice?

I don't know, Watt, I haven't found much precedent for a couple that's blackmailing each other, hooked up, and are now headed to a rehab check-in, Nadia replied. *I did find one on a holo show, but removed it from the data set as unrealistic.*

Watt ignored the sarcasm, though Nadia's conclusions weren't far off his own. He had no idea what to make of the situation with Leda. That night with her had been dark and bitter and reckless and honestly, the most electric hookup of his life.

He hadn't expected to hear from Leda after that—or at least, hadn't expected anything but more surveillance requests. He'd been shocked when she messaged him demanding that he come to Nevada with her, for some meeting with her old rehab counselor. She'd offered no further explanation than a link to his airline ticket.

There's no way she'll ever trust me enough to confess the truth about Eris. Is there? Watt asked Nadia, not really expecting an answer.

I'd say you're not off to a great start, given that you both said you can't stand each other, Nadia pointed out drily.

When he remembered the exchange that Nadia was talking about—how they'd been half-dressed, in Leda's bed—Watt felt suddenly uncomfortable. *I thought I told you to always shut off when I'm in, um,* intimate *situations*, he reminded her. He'd made that command a long time ago. There was something he couldn't handle about having a third presence in the bed, even if it was just a computer.

Yes, but you also directly commanded that I never turn off when Leda is around, Nadia reminded him.

Please reinstate the block on romantic situations, he thought firmly.

We should revisit your definition of romantic, *because whatever is going on right now, I don't think it qualifies.*

You know what I mean, he thought, and stretched out a little farther in his plush first-class seat. *Honestly, Nadia, I'm losing track of all the commands I've given you.*

I'm happy to make you a list, with time stamps. Snarky as usual.

Watt knew he just had to get through the weekend and get on with his life—and try to have some fun pushing Leda's buttons in the process. It was the best outcome he could hope for, at this point.

The plane touched down with a thud, steam rising from the hydrogen-fuel system like liquid smoke, a few droplets scattering onto the scorched runway below. Watt remembered that once upon a time planes had been powered with carbon-based fuels, not water. How shortsighted, and wasteful.

He and Leda still didn't speak as they made their way into the waiting area, where floating hover-bots brought over their luggage. Leda tilted her head for a moment, receiving an incoming message. "Our car is here," she said shortly, and headed into the glaring outdoors. She moved like a ballet dancer: her carriage erect, her shoulders back, her steps light and quick as if the ground were on fire and she couldn't bear to touch it for any length of time.

Something unfamiliar danced along the periphery of Watt's vision. It took him a moment to realize that it was his shadow. The solar lighting in the Tower was perfectly even from all angles—unlike the real sun, a single, focused source of light that actually moved throughout the day—so he never saw his shadow within the Tower itself. He suppressed the urge to stop and study it.

He and Leda maintained their chilly silence as they slid into a car, its polymer exterior set to a bright silver-blue, and turned onto the speedway. The dusty horizon line glimmered in the distance. Watt closed his eyes and played mental chess with Nadia. She felt such pity for him that she let him win, for once.

Suddenly they were turning down a side road into a lush profusion of green. A village of sandstone buildings was centered on an enormous pool, with a waterfall that flowed upward—a cleverly constructed illusion, Watt realized. Flowers cascaded over the red tile roofs, and palm trees stretched their fronds up into the sky.

Girls walked throughout the space. Like Leda, they all had an aura of wealth and privilege, yet a hollow, haunted look about their eyes. Next to him, Watt felt Leda tensing up. No wonder she didn't want to come here, he thought. Despite looking like a high-end spa, it probably brought back some memories that were complete shit.

He didn't speak until they'd arrived at their rooms, each a self-contained cottage on wooden stilts, in a far corner near the pool. "Separate rooms? I thought I was supposed to be your boyfriend," he said, raising an eyebrow.

What little composure Leda had left seemed to snap at his remark. She unlocked Watt's door and grabbed his shirt by the collar, pulling him roughly inside. She was suddenly very close, so close that he could feel her pulse leaping through her wrist. There was a microscopic fleck of green in one of her dark eyes. Watt had never noticed it before. He found himself staring at it, wondering which of her parents it had come from.

"Let's get this straight. You are here for one thing only," Leda told him. "To get my mom off my back by helping me pass this stupid rehab check-in, preferably with as little actual rehab as possible. I only told them you're my boyfriend so that you could be here as my accountability partner instead of my mom."

Watt wondered why Leda was so against bringing her mom here, but decided it was too complicated a question. He'd rather keep rattling her composure. "You're sure this isn't a cross-country booty call?"

"What happened last weekend was a drunken mistake that we will never repeat and never speak of. You are *working* this weekend, got it? This is not your damn vacation." Leda's voice crackled with tension.

Watt smiled. "Of course this is my vacation. It's not every day that I'm coerced into flying to Nevada."

Nadia directed his attention to a schedule projected on the cottage wall. *She loves yoga*, Nadia reminded him, probably attempting to be helpful. But Watt knew exactly how Leda would react if he hijacked her beloved yoga class.

"Now if you'll excuse me, I'd like to make afternoon yoga," he said, with a nod at the schedule.

"No. You are *not* coming to yoga with me," Leda threatened, but the more she protested, the more Watt was determined to be there.

The fun was just beginning.

———

Later, after an hour of yoga in the meditation tepee—which Watt had mostly spent sitting cross-legged, watching Leda flow effortlessly through the poses despite Watt's attempts to make distracting noises—they were both in the waiting room of the main building. Watt crossed an ankle over the opposite knee and jangled his foot impatiently. Leda kept shooting him glances, clearly piqued, so of course he didn't stop.

"I'll do all the talking," she volunteered at last. "You don't have to say anything. Just smile and nod, and answer any direct questions as quickly as possible. All you have to remember is that you're my supportive, helpful boyfriend. Oh, and that your older sister died tragically of addiction," she added, almost as an after-thought.

Watt pretended to gasp in horror. "You invented a big sister for me and then *killed* her? How could you?"

Leda rolled her eyes. "Don't make me regret bringing you here, Watt."

"Don't worry, I already regret it enough for the both of us," he replied cheerfully, just as the door opened to reveal a slender, red-haired woman in a doctor's coat.

"Leda, nice to see you again." The doctor held out a hand. She wasn't wearing a nametag, but it didn't slow Watt down, because he already knew everything about her.

Game time, Nadia, he thought, and stepped forward. "Dr. Reasoner, Watt Bakradi. I'm Leda's boyfriend." He gave a charming smile and shook her hand as they all sat down.

"Watt's here as my accountability partner," Leda hurried to explain.

Dr. Reasoner's brow furrowed. "Leda, I don't have any mention of a boyfriend in your file . . ."

"We only started dating this fall, after Leda came back." Watt reached out to put a hand on Leda's, where it sat on the arm of her chair, and laced his fingers in hers. She shot him a dark look.

Dr. Reasoner leaned forward, regarding them both curiously. "And how did you two meet?"

"Watt was actually interested in a friend of mine first, but once he met me, he realized that we were *much* more similar," Leda said tersely. She dug her fingernails into his palm. He turned his grimace into a smile.

"Yes, I regret to say that like Leda, I'm entirely self-absorbed and insecure. It's something I'm working on," Watt declared, so matter-of-factly that Dr. Reasoner blinked, unsure how to react. He could feel Leda seething next to him, her anger radiating in small swirling waves.

"And, Watt, you understand what it means to be an

accountability partner?" the doctor said after a moment, clearly deciding to ignore that last comment. "That your job is to enable Leda to keep making good choices?"

"Of course I understand, Dr. Reasoner," he said quietly. "Although Leda is really the one who helped me. I can't tell you what an inspiration she was to my sister. You see, my sister suffered from crippling addictions for years—"

"Yes, poor *Nadia*—" Leda said meaningfully, but Watt ignored the veiled threat.

"—she was addicted to xenperheidren, alcohol, attention, you name it. Leda was an incredible role model for her because, of course, Leda has been addicted to *all* those things at some point."

"And how is your sister now?" Dr. Reasoner asked, her face lined with well-bred concern.

"Oh, she died," Watt said flippantly, and shot Leda a satisfied look, as if she should be proud of him for remembering. She looked like she wanted to strangle him with her bare hands.

"I'm so sorry to hear that. I wish we could have treated her here," the doctor managed, clearly taken aback. She cleared her throat uncomfortably and turned to Leda. "Leda, have you felt any addictive tendencies in the last few months?"

"No," Leda said quickly.

"Not for drugs or alcohol, at any rate," Watt interrupted, with an exaggerated wink.

"Well. I'd like to go over our recommended follow-up for treatment." The doctor faltered, her eyes rapidly dilating and contracting as she looked at two different versions of something. "I guess we'll use the partner's plan, instead of the parent—though, Leda, I still think your mom will want to see—"

"Of course we should use the partner's plan. I'm not going anywhere," Watt promised, watching in unabashed delight as Leda gritted her teeth and nodded.

Later that night, Watt lay in the oversized king bed in his Mexican-inspired casita, a superfluity of pillows piled around him like whipped frosting. He was, honestly, confused to be in bed alone. Not that he really wanted to hook up with Leda, he told himself. But why didn't she want to hook up with *him*?

He'd been so sure that they would end up together tonight. After that hilarious farce of a check-in, which Leda had accused him of sabotaging—"Are you kidding? I *saved* it," he'd boasted—they'd declined the optional-but-clearly-encouraged share circle and eaten dinner in the cafeteria. Then they'd gone to Watt's room to watch a silly kids' holo about a cartoon donkey. They'd been sitting on the couch, not the bed, with plenty of distance between them; yet they'd been laughing with such ease that for once, Leda had seemed genuinely relaxed.

He'd been shocked when the holo ended and Leda said good night, then stood up and just walked out the door. Now here he was, alone in the most luxurious bedroom he'd ever set foot in, utterly bewildered.

"Nadia. What do you think Leda really wanted, bringing me all the way here?" he mused aloud.

"I would have called this a statistical anomaly, except there are no statistics," Nadia replied. "I'm glad, at least, that you seemed to have fun." She said that last bit a little huffily, as if this weren't an appropriate time for fun.

A bloodcurdling scream sounded through the wall, from Leda's room.

"Nadia, is she okay?" Watt cried out, sliding out of bed and stumbling forward.

"There isn't a feed in her room," Nadia replied, but Watt had already run barefoot onto Leda's front step and started pounding at the door. An instant later the bolt slid open as Nadia infiltrated the rehab center's system and granted Watt access.

Leda was twisted in a knot of sheets, her eyes closed, her mouth contorted in a grimace. She was screaming—a primal, otherworldly cry that made Watt want to cover his ears and back away. Instead he hurried forward to grab Leda's hands, which were clawing frantically at the covers.

"Leda, it's okay, you're safe. I'm here," he kept saying, rubbing his thumbs over the backs of her wrists.

Eventually the screams became moans, and died down, and then Leda grew still. Her eyes fluttered slowly, her lashes thick and damp against her cheeks. "Watt?" she asked drowsily, as if she didn't understand why he was there.

Watt wasn't sure either. He quickly let go of her hands.

"You were screaming," he said helplessly. "It sounded terrible, like you were being tortured. I just—I wanted to make sure you were okay."

"Yeah, right. You would rejoice if I was tortured," Leda croaked. She sat up and tucked her hair behind her ears with a quick gesture. Watt saw that she was wearing a white silk nightgown. It would have been almost girlish, except that it clung so suggestively to the contours of her body. He averted his eyes.

"Normally, yeah, but I need to make that flight home tomorrow, and I'm not sure I can return without you." Watt realized he was babbling. There was a strange pressure on his chest. He took another step back. "Sorry, I'll let you get some sleep."

"Please don't go," Leda said quickly, her eyes wide. She swallowed. "The nightmares . . . Please, just stay until I fall asleep."

In that moment she didn't look anything like Watt's enemy, like the bitter, hard-edged girl who had threatened and coerced him. The girl in this bed was a stranger, who looked young and lost and achingly lonely.

Watt started to pull up a chair next to the bed, then hesitated. Sitting in a chair next to Leda's bed felt somehow strange, as if she were sick in a hospital. Which, he realized, might have been how she'd ended up in this place to begin with.

His eyes met Leda's, and she inclined her head ever so slightly in understanding, wordlessly shifting to create space for him.

Leda was very still, and very small, as Watt slid into the bed and curled around her. He listened to the ragged rise and fall of her breath. There was an excited nervousness spiking up and down her body, and Watt knew that he was the cause of it, and he realized he was glad.

She turned around to face him, so they were both lying on their sides, twin silhouettes in the darkness. The only thing that separated them was a shaft of moonlight slicing through the open window. Still, Watt waited. He refused to do this unless the first move came from her, no matter how crazy it was, no matter how crazy *he* was for wanting it.

Leda lifted her chin and planted a kiss on his lips, tentative, feather light.

Then she pulled back. "This still doesn't mean anything, okay?" she whispered, and even though he couldn't make out her expression, Watt could picture it—her brow furrowed in stubborn determination, and fierce pride.

"Of course. It means nothing," Watt agreed, knowing full well that they were trading lies.

CALLIOPE

CALLIOPE STOOD AT the base of the Tower's famous climbing wall, an enormous vertical structure that began on the 620th floor and spanned almost thirty floors upward, along the Tower's north interior. She glanced at the clock that glowed constantly in the top left corner of her vision: she never turned it off, preferring to give a minimum of verbal commands to her contacts. There was nothing romantic about muttering "clock" during a flirtation.

Almost five p.m. Calliope tried to resign herself to the fact that Atlas wasn't coming. When she'd casually flickered him this afternoon to let him know that she was climbing, she'd thought it was a brilliant plan. She remembered how much Atlas loved rock climbing—or at least, he used to. But she was starting to realize that New York Atlas had less in common with Tanzania "Travis" than she'd expected.

She adjusted her aeroharness and brushed her hands together

before reaching for the first handhold, then the second. It might clear her head, climbing alone for a while.

"Starting without me, Callie?"

Calliope closed her eyes, allowing herself a brief self-satisfied grin. She stayed clasped where she was on the wall, only a few meters above Atlas, arching her back just so as she looked down at him. "I'm glad you made it," she called out.

Atlas smiled in that lopsided way of his, lifting only one corner of his mouth, as if he hadn't fully committed to the decision to smile. He stepped into an aeroharness and lifted a strap over one broad shoulder. "Sorry, it wasn't easy for me to escape work."

Calliope let go of the wall and the aeroharness caught her just a few centimeters into the fall, suspending her in midair. She pushed the soles of her shoes against the wall and spun lazily about, her black artech pants showing off her long, lithe form. "Your boss sounds unnecessarily strict, given that he's your dad," she pointed out.

Atlas gave an appreciative laugh. He yanked on a pair of gloves, fastening the second one with his teeth even though there was an auto-fasten setting. "Piece of advice, don't ever take a job for your mom. Because it really sucks, working for a parent."

You'd be surprised. Calliope wondered what Atlas would say if he knew the deadly efficiency with which Calliope and Elise worked together.

Atlas pushed a few buttons on a screen, setting his handholds to orange—Calliope's were already colored her signature bright fuchsia—and started up. She waited until he was close before spinning around to regain her handholds and join him.

The wall was almost empty right now. There was a trio of climbers in the distance, but Calliope could barely hear them, let alone see them. It felt like she and Atlas were alone on some remote desert peak. The sun streamed in through the massive windows behind them.

There was something so soothing about climbing, Calliope thought as they crept beetle-like up the sheer, exposed face. Find handhold, find new foothold, pull yourself up, repeat. The motions were clean and uncomplicated, but they required focus, leaving no room for her mind to wander. She loved the rush of adrenaline in her stomach as she climbed ever higher, her body contracting a little in instinctive fear that she might fall; though of course the aeroharness wouldn't let that happen. Her shoulders began to ache with a pleasant soreness. She would definitely need to use a massage pillow in the hotel tonight.

Next to her Atlas was swinging wildly, like a creature let out of hell. He took huge, leaping jumps, missing hand- and footholds, scrabbling desperately for purchase. More than once Calliope saw him fall, only to be caught in midair. Then he would grit his teeth and start the furious climb again.

"You know that aeroharness is a safety device, not a toy. This isn't a race." Her tone was deceptively lighthearted. What was Atlas so worked up about?

"You're only saying that because you're losing," Atlas called out from several meters above.

Calliope stifled a smile and tried to move faster, her footholds slightly less sure, her hands burning beneath the high-tech super-grip gloves. This high up, the rock face was covered in tiny ice crystals, to simulate climbing Kilimanjaro or Everest. Against it, Calliope's pink handholds stood out as particularly ludicrous. She marveled at how the light turned the ice almost blue, little swirls of color sparking off it each time she brushed it.

When she reached the summit, Atlas held out a hand to pull her up and over the top. She kept her palm in his for a moment, absorbing the unfamiliar but pleasant feel of it clasped around her own. When he let go, she felt a surprising pang of disappointment.

The ceiling soared overhead, its solar panels a robin's-egg

blue, with little wisps of cloud darting across them. Despite the ice crystals, it was comfortably warm up here. Calliope plopped down on the gravelly surface and took a sip of water from her pack, her legs stretched out before her.

"So," Atlas asked, "what do you think of our man-made mountain?"

"A better climb than the one in the Singapore Tower, and definitely a better view than Rio," she replied, just to remind him how worldly and well-traveled she was. "But not as nice as the real thing. After all, it's not Africa."

Atlas was leaning back on his elbows, his heather-gray shirt damp with sweat. Expressions darted across his face too quickly for Calliope to make sense of them all. She wished she could snatch his thoughts from the air with her hands and take them to some lab to analyze. How did he really think of her—as a stranger, a travel buddy, a mistake? Or as someone he wanted to get to know?

He's just a mark, she chided herself. It didn't matter what he thought of her, as long as she could figure out how to get something of value from him.

"No, it's not Africa," Atlas agreed, with a note of something like defeat. "But nothing ever is."

"Don't you want to go back?"

"Do you?"

Calliope hesitated. A month ago she would have said "maybe someday," the way she always spoke about the places she'd already been. The problem was simply that there were so *many* places in the world, so many corners she hadn't yet seen, and Calliope felt a deep, primal hunger to taste them all. Which was why she always spoke about the familiar with a touch of impatience.

But there was something different about New York. Perhaps it was the energy that beat just below the surface, like a pulse, or a drumbeat. Especially now, with the city suffused in a golden pre-holiday glow, there was a tangible magic in the air.

Calliope found that lately, she'd viewed the people she passed on her way to the lift—the people she normally pitied, whose lives seemed so routine and dull—with an uncharacteristic fondness. Like the girl who worked at the flower stand outside the Nuage, where Calliope always stopped to smell the freesia; or the wizened old man at Poilâne bakery, where she got a croissant almost every morning, because unlike other girls her age she'd never bothered to count calories. Even those wild-haired people who belted out songs on the lift had become strangely dear to her.

New York called to something in Calliope's soul. She felt a kinship with the city, she thought, both of them dramatically remade from their previous incarnations, gleaming and exquisite and one of a kind.

Against that, she weighed the siren song of all the new places she still had yet to explore, the adventures still lying in wait for her.

"I'm not sure," she admitted.

Atlas nodded. "Listen," he said after a beat. "I've been wanting to tell you, I'm sorry about last weekend."

"There's nothing to be sorry about," Calliope protested, attempting to sound flirtatious, though it came out a little high-strung. This afternoon wasn't playing out the way she'd hoped.

"Honestly, I was a mess that night. I guess I'm trying to give a blanket apology, in case there's anything I *do* need to be sorry for," Atlas explained.

So he didn't remember anything. He'd been so drunk that he probably hadn't even intended to bring her home with him. Calliope had been so proud of herself for finally getting somewhere with Atlas, when it hadn't really meant anything at all.

Still, there was one question she did want to ask, while she and Atlas were companionable and easy in the afternoon light.

"Atlas, I'm curious . . . Why did you go to Africa?" It was a question she'd never posed him, in all their months together. And if he answered it honestly, it might offer her some insight into why he didn't seem to want her.

He weighed her question carefully. "I got myself in a bit of a mess," he said at last. "It's complicated. There were other people involved."

Other people sounded like a girl. That explained a lot.

"You act differently here," she said quietly, knowing it was a risk, but wanting to say it anyway. "I miss the old you."

Atlas shot Calliope a curious glance, but he didn't seem angered by the remark. "What about you? Why did you go to Tanzania?" he asked.

Never ask a question that you yourself don't want to answer: that was another of Elise's cardinal rules, and Calliope knew she should have had a careful, flippant response ready. But for some reason all she could think about was India: that family torn apart and the old man on his deathbed and Calliope standing there, a useless witness to it all, unable to do anything. She felt suddenly like the truth was beading on her skin like sweat, running in ugly rivulets down her body for Atlas to see.

"I had a bad breakup," Calliope said. It was a lame excuse, but it was the best she could think of.

They were quiet for a while. The sun fell ever lower in the artificial sky. Atlas's hand was right there on the ground next to her, drawing all of Calliope's awareness like a magnet. She wanted to feel it in hers again.

Feeling reckless, she reached out and put her hand on top of his. He started at the movement, but didn't pull away. She took that as a good sign.

"When do you leave for Dubai?" she asked. She needed to know how much time she had left on this con. It was a ticking clock.

"I'll probably stay full-time after the party. At least, that's what my dad wants." Atlas didn't sound that excited. Calliope wondered if going to Dubai hadn't been his idea at all.

"Atlas. Do you even *want* to go to Dubai?"

He lifted one shoulder in a shrug. "Does anyone ever really know what they want? Do you?"

"Yes," Calliope said automatically.

Atlas's eyes were sharp on hers. "What?"

She opened her mouth to give another empty, flippant answer—something like, *how could I want for anything, my life is perfect*—but found that the words crumbled to ash in her mouth. She was tired of telling people exactly what she thought they needed to hear. "To be loved," she said simply. They might have been the truest words she'd ever spoken aloud.

"You *are* loved."

Calliope let out a breath. "By my mom, sure."

"And all your friends, back home," Atlas said urgently.

Calliope thought again of Daera, the only real friend she'd ever had, whom she'd left without even saying good-bye. "I don't actually have that many friends," she confessed. "I just . . . I don't make friends easily, I guess."

"You have me." Atlas flipped his palm over so that it was touching hers, their fingers interlaced. His hand felt very warm and steady.

Calliope looked over at him, but Atlas was staring at the window, to where the sun was setting below the jagged horizon of rooftops and spires, a blaze of crimson and fire. *Friends*, he'd said, but friends that held hands.

He felt her gaze and turned to her, his face lifting into a smile. It was good enough for now, Calliope thought, even if it didn't quite reach his eyes.

AVERY

AVERY LEANED AGAINST her heavy bedroom door, bracing herself for the walk down the hallway. Over the past week, that walk—sixteen steps; she'd counted them the other day—had become its own distinct sort of agony. Here in her room she was safe, but the moment she opened that door, she risked seeing Atlas.

Losing someone you loved was harrowing enough already, Avery reflected, without the added cruelty of constantly running into that person.

Part of her still refused to believe that this wasn't all some terrible dream, that she wouldn't wake up and everything would be normal again, Eris still alive and Atlas still hers and Calliope Brown off in Africa where she belonged. She would have given anything to go back to that awful night, except this time she would keep the trapdoor to the roof firmly shut.

But that wasn't the world she lived in, and Avery could ignore the real world for only so long. Slinging her red gym bag over one shoulder, she stepped out into the hallway—just as Atlas turned the corner from his room, headed the same direction, several boxes rolling along behind him.

It seemed that Avery's body was suddenly frozen in nitrocryo. She couldn't move a single cell, couldn't even breathe.

"You're leaving," she said into the fractured silence. For some reason she hadn't thought that Atlas would be leaving yet, at least not until next weekend's party. The sight of him standing in the entry hall—surrounded by all his things, his eyes shadowed, wearing the soft brown sweater she'd always loved—struck Avery with a terrible finality. This was really it, she thought dazedly. Atlas was leaving, and he hadn't even been planning to tell her good-bye.

"Actually, this is just stuff I'm sending ahead," Atlas explained, and the panic in her chest relaxed a little. "Dad let me pick out an apartment in the new tower. I wanted to have some of my things waiting for me, you know?" His voice was stiff and mechanical.

"That makes sense." She didn't know what else to say. When would it stop hurting, seeing Atlas? Maybe it never would. She would become like those amputees from before they could regrow body parts; her relationship with Atlas like a ghost limb that she kept trying to use, even though it was no longer there.

Whether it was tomorrow or a month from now, he was still ultimately leaving. Avery stood there looking at him, thinking of all the things they had been to each other—all the jokes they'd shared as children, the secrets exchanged; the way Atlas had been the cool older brother, helping her navigate high school. And then, of course, all the secret kisses and whispered *I love you*s of the past year.

Now here they were, with nothing left to say to each other.

"Sorry, I'm late to aquaspin." Avery hiked her bag higher up on her shoulder and moved to the elevator. The tension in the air was so thick she imagined she could see it, like water droplets hanging there, distorting her vision.

When she finally got to the aquaspin studio at Altitude, she peeled off her clothes with an audible sigh of relief. Wearing her old one-piece from swim team, she quickly slid into the pool, which was full of freshly imported Himalayan salt water.

It looked like an almost-full class today, though there was still an empty bike in the corner of the front row. Avery waded through the waist-deep water toward it, then lifted the seat to fit her long legs. Her eyes were adjusting to the dimness of the studio, which was illuminated by nothing except the floating fairy lights that danced above the water's surface. Serene spa-like music emanated from all the speakers, creating the feel that they were in a mermaid's cave.

None of it could relax Avery today. She kept mentally replaying her conversation with Atlas, wishing she'd said something more to him than "that makes sense." She almost wished that she'd screamed at him instead, or punched him—anything to relieve the press of emotions roiling through her. It felt like her blood had turned to jet fuel and was bubbling hot near the surface of her skin, burning her from the inside.

A gong sounded to indicate the start of class, and a holo of a thin, tanned woman on a bike appeared on the opposite brick wall. A few of the surrounding men and women in class muttered to their contacts as they logged into the competition board. Avery had never done it before, but why not? "Pedal Board," she said aloud. A silver icon labeled with her bike number immediately appeared on the wall next to the dozen other bikes, all of them moving in a holographic race to the finish line. The studio echoed with a deep electronic beat.

Avery picked up speed, her legs sloshing the pedals as she pushed endlessly against the heavy resistance of the salt water. She tried to lose herself in the movement, to work so hard that she would cut off the oxygen to her damn brain, so that for at least a few blissful minutes she wouldn't torture herself with thoughts of Atlas.

Sweat poured down her back. Calluses were forming on her hands where they gripped the handlebars. Avery realized that she was neck and neck for first place with someone on bike eighteen, in the back row. She didn't know who it was and it wouldn't have mattered if she did; she just felt a sudden, primal resolve to win. It was as if all the mistakes and problems in her life had crystallized into this single race, and if she didn't win, Avery was doomed to be this miserable forever. She raced as if the act of doing so could change things—as if happiness was right there ahead of her, and if she went fast enough, she might be able to catch it. She tasted salt, and wasn't sure whether it was the water, or her sweat, or maybe her tears.

And then it was over and she looked up and almost cried from relief because she'd won; she'd beaten bike eighteen, just barely. She slipped off her bike and ducked her head under the water, not caring that her hair would get crunchy from the salt. She felt a strange and bizarre urge to weep. *I'm a mess*, she thought bleakly, and finally pushed herself out of the pool.

"I had a feeling that was you. On bike seven?" Leda was standing at the slatted wooden bench that lined the room, hands on her narrow hips.

"You were bike eighteen?" *Of course it was Leda,* Avery thought, somehow unsurprised.

Leda nodded.

They both stood there, immobile as statues, as the rest of the class streamed past into the golden light of the hallway. Neither of them seemed willing to make the first move. Leda wrapped a towel around her waist, tucking its corner into a makeshift sarong, and suddenly Avery registered the bright blue print along the edge of the towel. "That's from Maine," she heard herself say.

Leda looked down and shrugged. "I guess it is." She traced the pattern for a moment before looking up at Avery, her eyes glinting in the dim light. "Remember that time we went hunting for colored sea glass because we thought we could give it to your grandmother? And that huge wave knocked me over?"

"I ran in after you," Avery recalled.

"Wearing your new white sundress." Leda exhaled a breath that was almost a laugh. "Your mom was so pissed."

Avery nodded, torn between confusion and a mingled pang of gratefulness for the memory. She'd lost so many people in her life lately—Eris, Leda, now Atlas. Suddenly, all she wanted was for the cycle to end.

"Any chance you want to get a smoothie?" Leda asked, very quietly, as if reading her mind.

The silence in the aqua studio was suddenly deafening. Everyone had gone, leaving nothing but the quiet lapping of the saltwater pool, the intermittent flashing of the fairy lights. The holo on the brick wall before them flickered out.

"Can we make it tacos instead?" Avery's blood was still pounding from class, her face flushed with exertion. She realized that for the first time in a week, she felt something other than howling grief—or worse, that terrible aching numbness. She wanted desperately to preserve this fragile sense of warmth before she clattered inevitably back to reality.

Leda smiled in response. "Cantina?"

"Where else?"

Avery wasn't sure whether this was a good idea. She wasn't sure how to treat Leda anymore, given everything that had happened between them. Were they best friends, or enemies, or strangers?

She slid her feet into her flower-printed sandals, determined to find out.

LEDA

CANTINA WAS THE same as always, slick and intimidating, its blazing white surfaces so pristine that Leda almost felt nervous to touch them. She remembered how wide-eyed she'd been the first time she came here, in eighth grade, with Avery and her parents. Everyone was so thin and expensively dressed that to Leda's thirteen-year-old mind they'd all looked like models. Then again, some of them actually were.

Now she and Avery walked up the bold white staircase with spiky blue agave plants lining each step and settled into a cozy two-person booth upstairs. They'd both showered and used the stylers at Altitude before coming here; and now that they were no longer in the surreal quiet of the aqua studio—now that they looked like their normal, immaculate selves—Leda was questioning whether this was a good idea.

Avery saved her by speaking first. "How are you, Leda?" she asked, and for some reason the absurd formality of the question made Leda want to burst out laughing. All the countless hours they'd spent together at this very restaurant, and yet here they were, acting like a couple on the worst first date of all time. Suddenly she knew exactly what to say.

"I'm sorry," she began, the words coming out awkwardly; she'd never been very good at apologies. "For everything I did, and said, that night on the roof. You know I didn't mean for it to happen." No need to clarify what *it* was; they both knew. "I swear it was an accident. I would never—"

"I know," Avery said tersely, her hands clenching just a little under the table. "But you didn't need to act all wild and threatening about it afterward, Leda. It would have been all right, if you'd come forward and told the truth."

Leda stared at her blankly. Sometimes it shocked her how delusional Avery was. Sure, if it had been Avery Fuller who pushed Eris off the Tower, no one would give her more than a slap on the wrist. But Leda's family was nowhere near as powerful or established as the Fullers, even though they did have money now. If Leda came forward, there would have been an investigation, probably even a trial. And Leda knew how the evidence looked.

A jury would have very happily convicted Leda for manslaughter. Unlike Avery, who was inherently unpunishable. No one would ever even consider sending her to prison. She was simply too beautiful for it.

"Maybe," she said cautiously, hoping that would be enough. "I'm sorry for that too, though. I'm sorry for everything I said that night."

Avery nodded, slowly, but didn't answer.

Leda swallowed. "Eris did some stuff that really hurt me, some seriously messed-up stuff. I didn't even want to *talk* to her, but she kept coming at me, even though I told her to back off—but still, I never meant—"

"What did Eris do?" Avery asked.

Leda nervously tucked her hair behind her ears. "She was sleeping with my dad," she whispered.

"What?"

"I know it sounds crazy, but I saw them together—I saw them *kissing*!" Leda's voice pitched wildly, she was so desperate to be believed. She took a deep breath and began the whole sordid story: How her dad had been acting funny, as if he was hiding something. The Calvadour scarf that Leda had found, which she then saw her dad give to Eris. How he'd lied and said he was at a client dinner, but instead she'd found him at dinner with Eris, holding hands and kissing across the table.

Avery was silent with shock. "Are you sure?" she asked finally.

"I know. I didn't want to believe it of Eris either. Let alone my dad." Leda couldn't even look at Avery's face right now, couldn't face the shock, the disgust, that was surely written there, or she might burst into tears. She busied herself tapping on the surface of the table to place their order. "Medium or spicy guacamole?"

"Spicy. Plus queso," Avery added. "God, Leda . . . I'm so sorry. Does your mom know?"

Leda shook her head. "I never told her." Avery of all people would understand how painful it had been, keeping something that big from her family—how Leda had felt stretched thin by the secret, which pressed slowly and inexorably down on her, never relenting even for a minute.

"I'm sorry. That's terrible." Avery traced a circle on the pristine table. She didn't seem able to make eye contact either. "How can I help?" she asked finally, looking up. Her eyes were brimming with tears.

Typical Avery, thinking she could take on all the problems of the world. "You can't solve everything, you know," Leda said, as a hovertray whirled over to deposit the guacamole on their table. It was chunky and fresh, made with real avocados, not the infused algae-protein cubes that they mashed up in midTower and called guacamole.

"I know. That was always your job." Avery wiped at her eyes and sighed. "God. I wish we'd never fought in the first place."

"Me neither!" Leda agreed. "Atlas wasn't worth it. I mean, not to me, he wasn't," she fumbled to explain.

Across the table, Avery's eyes were very blue and very serious.

"I never loved him. I realize that now," Leda went on, bravely. She knew this wasn't what Avery wanted to talk about—that it would be safer to avoid it altogether. But talking was the only way to make things right. Leda imagined her words spanning the space between her and Avery, like the etherium bridges that built themselves molecule by painstaking molecule.

"I thought I loved him, but it was just . . . infatuation. I loved the idea of him. Or maybe I should say that I wanted to love him, but I never succeeded in it." That night in the Andes felt so long ago now, when Leda thought she'd fallen hopelessly for Atlas. But all it had really been was hormones and excitement.

Like what you feel for Watt? a voice in her whispered, a voice she tried desperately to silence. She hadn't told anyone that she and Watt were hooking up. God, she and *Watt* didn't even speak about it. But in the few days since they'd come back from Nevada, he'd come over to her place every night. She never even asked him—he just showed up the first evening and she let him wordlessly in the back door, and then they collapsed together onto her bed in a tangle of silent, crushing need.

Still, Leda hadn't let Watt get too far. She'd learned that lesson the hard way. She kept holding something back, out of self-preservation.

Because she was developing feelings for him, and that was the one outcome she had never expected.

Next to Watt, what she'd felt for Atlas felt long-ago, and childish. She realized that she no longer even cared whether Avery dated him. Hell, why not? It wasn't any more fucked-up than anything else in this crazy, fucked-up world.

"*You* love him, though, don't you?" she asked, already knowing the answer.

"Yes," Avery said, with more pause than Leda had expected. She let out a great breath. "But he's really hurt me."

"By hooking up with *me*?" Leda demanded, and immediately winced at the baldness of her words. "That was so long ago, it's ancient history," she added, more tactfully.

Avery seemed almost not to have registered her outburst. "No, it's not that . . . he's been with someone else. More recently." Her eyes flicked downward. "I'm pretty sure we're over, for good."

"You don't mean that girl from the gala, with the tacky dress and the British accent? What was her name, Catastrophe?"

"Calliope," Avery corrected, with a ghost of a smile. "They met while Atlas was traveling, in Africa. She and her mom just moved here."

"Really. She met Atlas halfway across the world and now she's in New York. How awfully convenient." Leda's instincts pricked to life. "What's this girl's story? Where is she from?"

"I don't know. She went to boarding school in England, I think."

"What does her page on the feeds say?"

"I haven't really looked at it," Avery said reflexively. Leda knew what that meant: Avery didn't want to look at it, because the moment she did, Calliope became real.

Thank god Avery was so pretty, Leda thought, because otherwise this world would destroy her with its unforgiving ruthlessness. And thank god that Avery had Leda, to protect her.

"Here, *I'll* look her up," she offered, and muttered to her contacts. "Calliope Brown, feeds search." When she found the right account, way down the page, she gasped.

"What is it?" Avery asked.

"Send link to Avery," Leda said, and watched as the page appeared on Avery's contacts too.

Calliope's page only dated back a couple of months. There were pictures of New York, a few from Africa, and before that—nothing.

"Maybe she's new to the whole feeds thing," Avery said, but even she sounded dubious.

Leda rolled her eyes. "Every ten-year-old on the planet has an account. This is seriously bizarre. It's like she never existed at all until she met Atlas this summer."

No way was this a coincidence. Something was going on, and whatever it was, Leda was determined to find out.

The decision sent a wave of energy snapping through her, a renewal of confidence in herself—and a fierce determination to fix this for Avery. They were friends again, and therefore any enemy of Avery's was now an enemy of hers. She was still Leda Cole, damn it, and no one hurt the people she cared about.

Avery's voice was shaky. "Can we talk about something else, please?"

Leda nodded, temporarily setting aside her quest for retribution. "Like what?"

"Like what's made you all happy and easygoing. Is it a boy?"

"Maybe." Leda's face flushed at the thought of Watt.

Their queso arrived, a skillet of melted cheese topped with shaved green onions, and Leda used the opportunity to change the subject. "You go first, though. What else have I missed?"

Avery scooped queso onto her plate with a quinoa chip. "Everything. This Dubai party is kind of a mess, to be honest.

You should see how worked up my mom has gotten . . ."

Leda sat there, listening as Avery poured her heart out, feeling like her own heart was expanding within her chest. She had her best friend back. And there was a new boy in her life—a confusing, dangerously addictive one.

Everything was finally starting to right itself in her world.

RYLIN

RYLIN MOVED THROUGH the *Salve Regina* wrap party after the final day of shooting, feeling glamorous in her slinky red dress and studded heels, grinning so hard she thought her face might break.

They'd rented out a penthouse bar for the occasion, on the top floor of a skyscraper—well, the LA version of a skyscraper, which had a measly 104 floors. But since none of the buildings here were very high, it still had sweeping views over the city, and of the glowing Hollywood sign in the distance. Lush plants dotted the dimly lit space, which was all curves and gilded surfaces and scattered mirrors.

Rylin wandered contentedly through the crowds. Crewmembers nodded and greeted her as she passed, which made her smile even brighter. She'd been pleasantly surprised by how readily the cast and crew had drawn her into their fold. She hadn't realized what an instant bond it would create: working such long hours in such close quarters, the whole group striving to build something together.

It had been an incredible week, she reflected, as she slid into a banquette next to Seagren and some of the other film crew. She'd worked hard during the filming hours, and still spent a lot of time with Xiayne in the edit bay late at night: cropping out the bits of holo that they wanted, folding the slices over one another like layers of soft, transparent lace. They'd pulled all-nighters twice, resorting to caffeine patches and four a.m. Tater Tots to keep them going; returning to the hotel at dawn to shower and then hurrying straight back to set, where it started all over again. But it had been worth it. Rylin knew she'd learned more from this week of work than from a year of lectures at school.

Around her the laughter was growing wilder, as the night wore on and everyone kept drinking the fresh-squeezed cocktails. Rylin saw one of the minor actors, the queen's cousin, making out with the prime minister in the corner. The tiara worn by Perrie, the actress who played the queen, had been passed around all night as various people put it on to take drunken snaps— even Rylin had sent Chrissa a snap of herself in it, just for fun. Perrie now stood in the center of the room, still resolutely wearing the bodice from her costume, though she'd paired it with black leather pants. She was attempting to lead the crowd in a drinking game, where she read snippets of dialogue and they all guessed which of the cast or crew she was impersonating, but everyone was shouting too loudly for much of anything to be heard.

Rylin leaned back in the banquette, laughing, as Xiayne approached their table.

"Slide over, you two." He was wearing a navy shirt and jeans, and his usual infectious smile. His hair looked tousled, as if he'd been standing outside, though they were too high up for that.

Rylin and Seagren obediently scooted over to create space. Xiayne took two grapefruit cocktails from a passing tray and handed one to Rylin. She didn't even think twice about the fact that her teacher was handing her a drink.

"Okay, spill. Which of you hated the other one more?" Xiayne's voice was light and teasing.

Seagren snorted into her cocktail. It wasn't her first of the night, and she was obviously loosening up. "Rylin *hated* me."

"Not at all! You were a great boss!" Rylin protested, which made Seagren laugh even harder.

"I was terrible," she slurred cheerfully, "But that's the way my first boss treated me, so it's only fair. Circle of life, and all that."

One of the stage managers came over and held out a hand to Seagren. "Wanna dance?" he asked, nodding to the center of the room, which was devolving into a loose, drunken dance floor.

"Why not?" Seagren took the guy's hand.

Rylin glanced at Xiayne. His eyes danced as he looked over the crowd, clearly pleased by the roiling chaos on the dance floor. She felt suddenly like he was a high school boy who was proud that everyone had shown up to his party.

"So, Rylin. Are you still glad you came out here?" he finally asked, turning back to her. A tiny curl of his inktat had escaped the collar of his shirt to snake up onto his neck, like the tongue of a flame. Rylin forced herself to look up at his face.

"It's been incredible. Thank you for making it possible," she told him.

"Thank *you* for all your help in the edit bay. You have an incredible natural eye."

There was a sudden collective squeal from the other side of the room. Everyone had huddled around the windows, excited about something. "What's going on?" Rylin asked, but Xiayne had already stood up.

"The first display ad, on the Bubble, for *Salve Regina*. I didn't think it would go up for another week! Come on!" Xiayne grabbed her hand, sending a shiver up Rylin's arm. She stumbled after him, around the corner to a side room. It was suddenly very quiet, and private.

"Look." Xiayne pointed to where Perrie's face was projected on the Bubble, tossing her long dark hair, glamorous and beautiful. *Royalty comes with a price*, the tagline read, in calligraphied script above her tiara. Rylin was stunned to think that she'd worn that very tiara just half an hour ago—that she'd helped edit that image of Perrie, and now there it was, projected over an entire city full of people.

"It's amazing," she breathed.

Xiayne tried to shrug off the compliment, but Rylin could tell he was excited. "It's just a few production stills, nothing fancy," he demurred, and stepped closer to the window.

Rylin followed, moving so close to the flexiglass that her nose was almost pressed up against it. To think that each glowing pinprick was a person, all of them caught up in their own lives within this funny bubble-wrapped world. How many of them were looking up right now, seeing the ad for a holo that Rylin had helped make?

She and Xiayne were both reflected in the flexiglass, their silhouettes dim outlines against the glare. They were like forgotten spirits gazing over the star-flecked city below.

"You like the view?" Xiayne asked. Rylin nodded, not quite trusting herself to speak, and he grinned. "I thought you might. This is the highest point in LA, you know."

"I didn't know." Rylin's heart was pounding in her chest. She suddenly wanted to go back to the sensory overload of the party, but she felt strangely immobile.

"Rylin," Xiayne said softly, and placed his hands tentatively on her shoulders. She watched as if from a great distance as he leaned in and pressed his lips to hers.

Rylin hadn't been kissed by anyone since Cord—hadn't, in fact, been kissed by anyone at all except for Cord and her ex-boyfriend, Hiral—so at first, she tentatively returned the kiss, out of some combination of curiosity and flattery. She'd liked spending time with Xiayne. And she'd seen how all those senior girls looked at him, sending him doe-eyed glances heavy with meaning. Part of her felt oddly pleased to know that of all the girls at Berkeley, he'd chosen her, Rylin Myers, the talented scholarship student from the 32nd floor.

And then she remembered what Cord had said, what he'd implied about Xiayne's interest in her, and suddenly it felt wrong, all wrong. Maybe Cord was right, and all Xiayne had ever wanted was this—to get her alone in the dark.

She broke away and took an unsteady step back.

Xiayne's face was a mask of bewildered shock. "Rylin," he stammered, "I'm sorry. I never—"

"Do you think I'm talented at all?" she interrupted.

He blinked, startled. "Of course you're talented," he assured her, but she wasn't sure she believed him anymore.

"So this wasn't just a game to you," she said slowly. "Bringing me to LA, letting me help in the edit bay, this wasn't all just because of . . . this?"

Xiayne ran a hand through his hair. "Shit, Rylin. You think I'm in the business of hiring filming assistants because I think they're pretty? Not that you're not pretty," he added quickly, "because you are. I mean—shit," he stammered again, and looked at her with something like panic. "I'm sorry I crossed a line. I just thought . . . you're a legal adult, and . . ."

Rylin took a halting step back. Some part of her registered what Xiayne was saying, but Cord's words kept replaying in her head. She couldn't help feeling used, and wounded. Looking at Xiayne now, all Rylin could think was that he seemed like an immature teenager—a very talented teenager; but at the end of the day, he had a teenager's desire that everything be a big party, with himself at the center of it.

In that moment, Rylin lost all respect for Xiayne. And for herself, too, for letting it all happen the way that it had.

"I'm sorry," Xiayne said again, but Rylin was already stumbling backward. She felt her face burning from shame. She needed to get out.

She pushed blindly toward a crowd near the door. Seagren and a few of the other crew were standing with Perrie, who looked like a modern goddess in her leather pants and heels and the enormous fake tiara.

"Rylin!" Seagren called out, but Rylin ignored her.

"Poor thing," she heard Perrie coo softly, when she was almost around the corner. "She looked like she was about to be sick. Do you think she drank too much?"

Rylin hurried away before she could hear anything more.

CALLIOPE

CALLIOPE HAD BEEN to more holiday markets than she could count, in Brussels and Copenhagen and even Mumbai, but none of them quite compared to this one, at Elon Park on the 853rd floor. Though she had to admit, a huge part of the appeal was simply being here with Atlas.

She kept glancing over at him, wondering why exactly he'd asked her to come with him today: whether this was a date, or just Atlas calling in backup for his holiday shopping. Calliope had no idea how things stood between them after that moment last week, when they'd held hands at the top of the climbing wall, and Atlas had declared with such conviction that he was her friend.

All week long they'd been exchanging warm, yet decidedly not flirtatious, flickers. Then this morning Calliope had woken to Atlas's message: *Callie, I have so many presents to buy, and you're the greatest shopping expert I know. Can you help?*

Of course she would help. She had less than two weeks left

to wrap up this con before Atlas moved to Dubai—unless she planned on following him there, which she wasn't especially interested in.

Calliope had suggested they head to the upper-floor boutiques, but Atlas insisted they come here instead. She had to admit, it was certainly more festive. Red and green lights floated above them like dancing fireflies. The entire park was crisscrossed with vendors, their stalls filled with everything from cheap gimmicky nutcrackers and low-tech toys to expensive jewelry and Senreve purses, the latest models that shrank and expanded depending on what you needed the bag to hold. Calliope held her own fuchsia Senreve bag close to her chest. Her boots crunched on the snow underfoot, which was made with frozen velerio fluid instead of water so that it never melted or even looked dirty. In several corners, the snow attempted to form itself into small snowmen, self-generating into little round stacks, complete with buttons.

She and Atlas had both accumulated heaps of gifts, which floated before them on carrier bots: this market was upscale, but not quite nice enough to offer charge-send like the boutiques did. Calliope found that she didn't mind. There was something delightful about watching her purchases bob along ahead of her, as if her own unabashed materialism were pulling her forward on an invisible cord like those children on proxi-leashes.

"I think I've discovered the way to make Callie Brown go any-where. Just send a bot covered with shopping bags ahead of you, and you'll inevitably follow," Atlas said, as if reading her mind. Calliope laughed at being so blatantly caught out.

"I'm glad you dragged me here," she replied, rewarding him with the full force of her smile.

"Me too," Atlas said softly.

They turned a corner, and were surrounded by an enormous crowd pushing toward one of the stalls. Calliope took a step forward, curious—she never could resist being in the center of the action—but the animal yelps and squeals of the children gave it away before she'd seen the holo-sign.

The booth was full of tousling, barking puppies, all wearing festive red and green collars. They were forever-puppies, dogs whose DNA had been tweaked so that they never aged. There were always protests surrounding them—some people claimed they were unnatural, that it was cruel to deprive any living thing of a normal, full existence. Calliope didn't think it sounded all that bad, being young and adorable your whole life.

Her eyes were immediately drawn toward one of the dogs, a sleek terrier puppy with a bright pink tongue. For a moment she let herself imagine taking him home. She would name him Gatsby, after that book she'd read at the boarding school in Singapore, the only school reading she'd ever finished. She would carry him in her purse and feed him treats and—

She let out an involuntary gasp. A little girl was reaching for Gatsby and handing him to her father. Calliope had a bizarre urge to cry out at them to stop, to let go of her puppy, but she stifled the impulse. There was no room for a puppy in her glamorous, nomadic life.

"You okay?" Atlas asked, watching her face.

"Of course. Let's keep moving." She hoped he wouldn't notice the quaver in her voice.

Atlas nodded. "I don't know about you, but I need a sugar break," he declared, casting his eyes toward the blustery gray ceiling overhead. "And it's scheduled to snow soon. What about hot chocolate?"

"Hot chocolate sounds fantastic," Calliope agreed, still surprised by her unfamiliar pang of longing.

They walked to the cocoa stand beneath the frozen ice rink— the park's famous centerpiece, which was suspended ten meters in the air. The area beneath the ice rink was packed, shoppers and tourists gathered close together, their boots all tracking snow on the enormous silver-threaded carpet beneath them. Red poinsettias dotted the bar every few meters.

"Two large hot chocolates, with extra marshmallows and whipped cream," Atlas told the serving-bot, then leaned back on his heels with a contented sigh. The light from above was soft and muted, filtered by the enormous burden of the hovering ice rink and the bodies of the skaters.

Calliope gave an appreciative laugh. "You don't do anything halfway, do you?"

Their hot chocolates arrived, and they both poured peppermint flakes over the top. "Thanks again for shopping with me today. I don't know what I would have done without your help." Atlas took a sip of the cocoa, leaving a goofy whipped cream mustache over his upper lip. Calliope decided not to tell him. She wanted to see how long it would take before he noticed.

"You would have bought decidedly worse gifts," she declared, then lifted a hand to her mouth as she realized that they'd forgotten someone crucial. "Atlas! We didn't get anything for Avery!" She'd helped purchase gifts for Atlas's various family and friends: beautiful stitched sweaters and perfumed hand creams and a fantastic new laser brightener for his aunt in California. How on earth had they left out his sister, especially given that Avery was Calliope's best chance to show off? She racked her brain, sorting through various ideas, trying to determine which of them was rare and fine enough to impress the girl who literally had everything.

"It's okay. I already have something for Avery." If she hadn't known better, Calliope would have thought that a brief embarrassment flickered over Atlas's face.

"What is it?" she asked, curious. You could tell a lot about a boy by the presents he bought for his family.

"An old historical print, of New York three hundred years ago."

"A print?" Calliope wrinkled her nose in confusion.

Atlas tried to explain. "Ink on paper. You hang it on the wall. It's like an instaphoto that doesn't move."

Paper, Calliope thought, rapidly losing interest. Honestly. If Avery Fuller weren't so rich and beautiful, no one would want to be around her, because she was kind of a bore.

A group on the other side of the cocoa stand broke out into cheers. Calliope realized that they were all wearing obnoxious yellow jerseys. They must be football fans, watching the game on their contacts, and their team had probably just scored a goal.

"You're coming to the Dubai launch, right?" Atlas asked as the sound died down.

Calliope took a sip of her hot chocolate to stall for time. It was hot and creamy and exploded in tiny pockets of sugar at the back of her tongue.

She so desperately wanted to go. Events like that were a great staging ground for cons, because they were crowded and full of strangers, and everyone dropped their guard when they were drinking.

Besides, it sounded like one hell of a party.

"I wasn't invited," she admitted, watching his reaction.

"Really? Then you should come with me."

Calliope's chest tightened in anticipation. What did he mean by that? Was he asking her as a friend, or as a date? But Atlas's dark brown eyes were as inscrutable as ever.

"I'd love to," she told him.

As they stepped out from beneath the ice rink, Calliope found that tiny flakes of silver were falling from above, catching in Atlas's hair, settling on the dark sleeves of his sweater. The machine-made snow. She stuck out her tongue and let the flakes settle there, cold and crisp, the way she used to do in London as a child.

Atlas looked over and saw her. "You know that's made of velerio. You shouldn't actually eat it," he said with a strangled laugh.

"I'm not worried," Calliope decided. After Atlas's invitation, she felt invincible. As if a little velerio could harm her, when her life was so evidently charmed.

"Calliope Brown, you're nothing like the other girls I know," Atlas said, still shaking his head in amusement. Calliope decided to take it as a compliment.

———————

When she got home that evening, Calliope heard a series of thuds coming from her mom's room across the suite. She ducked in to see Elise sitting cross-legged on the floor, folding a stack of flimsy silk dresses into an airtight bag.

"You're back! Where were you?" Elise glanced up and asked, but Calliope could tell that her mind was elsewhere.

"With Atlas. Actually, he invited me to that launch party in Dubai." Calliope's gaze was still trained on the clothes scattered all over the floor. "What are you doing?"

"Just reorganizing my things. We're leaving soon," Elise announced, as casually as if she were commenting on the weather.

"How soon?"

Her mom shot her a knowing look. "Things are moving more quickly than I expected. I think I'm going to get a proposal from Nadav. Can you believe, another engagement ring—and a big one!"

"Oh." Calliope thought of Atlas, and the party, and didn't know how to respond.

Elise was staring at her curiously. "You don't seem excited. Come on, darling!" She laughed a bit, standing up and reaching for Calliope's hand to give her a little spin. Calliope didn't join the laughter. "You're the one who's always so eager to move on!

I'll even let you pick our next spot. What about Goa? Or the Mediterranean? I could use a beach, this time of year."

"I don't know." Calliope managed a lackluster shrug. "What if we didn't leave right away?"

Elise took a step back, her movements—and her voice—suddenly much heavier. "You of all people know we can't do that, sweetie. We can't afford the life we're leading. The hotel is about to kick us out, we're running through our credit at all the boutiques, and you know how much is left in our bitbanc."

Calliope did know. She'd checked all the global bitbancs just yesterday. It consistently shocked her, how little cash they seemed to have. Of course, it was all wrapped up in clothes and jewels and accessories, she thought, her eyes narrowing at her mom's overflowing closet.

"A few days from now and we're done here, whether Nadav has proposed or not," Elise finished.

They'd lived this way for years, and yet it had never really bothered Calliope till now. "I just wish that for once, we could stay somewhere. Just for a while," she said, almost plaintively.

"Staying means getting attached to people, and we can't afford that even more than we can't afford this hotel."

Calliope didn't answer. Her mom's voice lowered. "This is about Atlas, isn't it? Look, it's okay if you can't get anything of value from him. You tried hard, that's what counts—"

"Oh my god, *stop*!" Calliope cried out.

Elise shut up. Her smile had frozen funnily, falling off her face in shaky little pieces, almost as if it were melting.

"Just back off, okay? You're the world's greatest expert on *lying*, but you've never even seen a relationship through." It came out harsher than Calliope intended.

She thought of Atlas—the way he smiled, the earnest warmth in his brown eyes, the sad wistfulness that seemed to haunt him, no matter what she said—and felt an odd protectiveness of their relationship, or friendship, whatever it was. She found that the thought of stealing from him wasn't as appealing as it used to be. *He probably won't even notice*, she reminded herself, but that wasn't the point.

"I don't want to talk about this con with you anymore," she added quietly.

Elise took a step back, a stricken expression on her face. The same oval face as Calliope's, same high forehead and strong cheekbones; only softened by age, and all the surges. Calliope had a curious sensation of looking through a fun-house mirror, through a tear in the fabric of the universe at a vision of herself in twenty years. She didn't like what she saw.

"I'm sorry. I won't bring it up again," Elise said after a moment, her voice strained.

Calliope tried to nod. She couldn't remember ever speaking like that to her mom—couldn't remember disagreeing with her about anything before. "I just don't want to leave yet, right when things here are getting fun. I want to go to this Dubai party with Atlas. He's staying in Dubai after that, anyway. It's my last chance to get something really big from him."

"Of course," Elise conceded. "If that's what you want, we'll stay through the party. Hey," she ventured, as if getting the idea, "maybe I'll come too. It could be fun!"

"That's a great idea." Calliope turned to walk across the suite to her stiff, impersonal room, with its cold windows and heavily stitched pillows and the frothy white comforter that looked like something out of a magazine.

She was Calliope Brown, she reminded herself, and once again she was getting what she wanted. But for the first time, it didn't feel like such a victory.

RYLIN

"**THE ENTIRE FARM** was designed as one enormous Fibonacci spiral. When you stand at the pinnacle, you can look down over all the levels and see the breathtaking symmetry of the plans . . ." the tour guide droned on.

It was Monday morning. Rylin had completely forgotten that she had a field trip for biology class today—she'd only realized it when she showed up to school and her tablet immediately prompted her to board the waiting shuttle. Rylin had never really minded being in biology before, but standing here now, surrounded by the entire freshman class, she felt an overwhelming sense of injustice. These kids were Chrissa's age. Why couldn't the school have let her get away with skipping biology altogether?

After the weekend she'd just had, a field trip was the last place she wanted to be. She'd gotten back from LA early yesterday morning—she'd rebooked herself onto the five a.m. train home, not even bothering to tell Xiayne her new plan. She knew he would receive an automated message notifying him of the ticket change, and he would obviously know what had prompted Rylin's early departure.

She still hadn't told Chrissa what happened. Chrissa, who believed in her so fervently, who'd handed her a new suitcase they couldn't afford and told her to go follow her dreams. How could she confess to her little sister that her faith was missplaced—that her teacher was thoughtless and shortsighted, and it had all been a farce?

Just thinking about it made Rylin want to melt into a vicious black hole. She should have called in sick, curled up in bed all day, and shut out the world.

Instead she was here, standing at the main entrance to the Farm on the 700th floor. Like the Tower itself, the Farm was a one-word kind of place; there was only one farm in Manhattan, because there wasn't space for more than one. It took up a massive chunk of the Tower, spiraling up through the center of the building from the 700th to almost the 970th floor. Each of the Farm's three thousand agricultural plots was lined with solar panels and smart mirrors, which shifted from reflective to opaque depending on the season or the time of day, controlling how much light each plant received down to the very photon. And it was a constant-harvest operation, which meant that no matter the month, at least some crops were always ready to pick. Rylin half listened as the tour guide explained that the crops closer to the top of the building were currently experiencing fall, while farther down the conditions shifted to those of spring and wheelbarrow bots moved up and down the rows to plant new seeds. It was the greatest example of indoor farming in the world, the guide stated proudly.

"Not as good as the ones in Japan, of course, but no one will ever admit that," said a voice next to her, and Rylin instinctively stood up a little straighter, her heart racing. Cord was one person she hadn't expected to see right now.

"Felt like crashing the freshman field trip?" she deadpanned. She wasn't sure why, but the sight of Cord irritated her, as if he'd come here for the express purpose of ruining her day.

"Seems like you had the same brilliant idea." Cord rocked back on his heels, the corner of his mouth lifting as if to resist a smile. Rylin didn't smile back.

"Unfortunately for me, I'm actually *in* this class. I never took biology at my old school. What's your excuse?"

"I'm a TA, of course. For Professor Norris's section. Too bad I didn't get yours—I would have had fun grading your essays."

"You, a TA?" she repeated in surprise. Her section of the class had a TA, but it was a quiet girl whose name Rylin couldn't even remember. She would never in a million years have guessed that the other TA was Cord.

"I know, I'm so devastatingly good-looking that no one ever suspects me of actually being smart. But I got a perfect score on the AP exam." Cord grinned. "Besides, Rylin, you of all people should know that I'm an expert in biology."

Rylin rolled her eyes and edged away from Cord, as if listening to the tour guide. She had no desire to be teased right now.

"Whoa, you okay?" Cord asked, stepping in front of her.

At the concern in his voice, Rylin felt herself crumble. "Not really. It's been a long week, and kind of a rough one."

"Want to get out of here?" he offered.

"Can we?" The thought of escaping was so painfully attractive that Rylin didn't even stop to think about what it meant for her to leave with Cord, alone.

"As long as we stay inside the Farm, I don't see why not. Come on."

Rylin followed him through the soil cultivation tunnels, past fields of spirulina and hydroponic ponds of leafy spinach, until they reached a bank of plain gray elevators. The doors opened easily for them. When they stepped inside, Cord pushed a button marked 880 AND ABOVE: RESIDENTS AND MAINTENANCE ONLY. He looked up and held his eyes open toward the retinal scanner. After a moment, the doors clicked shut with approval, and the elevator started up. Rylin lifted an eyebrow at all this, but didn't comment.

"There's a private park on my floor that's part of the Farm. All the residents have access," Cord explained haltingly.

Of course you do, Rylin thought. She just nodded. Her tablet vibrated with an incoming ping from Lux, and she quickly pushed a button to decline it.

The park that they stepped into at first looked overwhelmingly formal and French; all close-cut emerald grass and trimmed parterres sweeping toward a narrow landscaped canal. Then Cord led them past a brick wall with an old-fashioned iron gate, into an area of the garden that was clearly much younger, and less orderly. Rylin wasn't sure what she'd expected, but it wasn't this.

"Here," he said, and sat abruptly on the ground beneath an enormous tree with spreading branches. After a moment, Rylin lowered herself to sit opposite him, leaning back on her palms. She thought she heard frogs croaking somewhere nearby, but she couldn't see any water. Overhead, the ceiling was a beautiful false blue.

It was easy to forget you were inside a steel Tower in places like this, full of life and oxygen and growing things.

"Okay, Myers. What's going on?"

"Um . . ." She wasn't sure she wanted to get into it, not with Cord. She ran her hands over her arms, feeling suddenly cold at the memory.

He shrugged wordlessly out of his school blazer and held it out to her. Rylin accepted it gratefully. She remembered the last time she'd worn a jacket of Cord's—when they'd been in Paris and he'd draped it chivalrously around her, his hands brushing her bare shoulders. That felt like so long ago.

"Thank you," she said, sliding her hands into the sleeves. There was a loose button in the front pocket. She played with it idly, the plastic cool on her fingers. It was nice to know that even Cord's buttons fell off.

"I'm sorry I was an ass to you about going to LA," he said, trying again. "You asked me to be happy for you, and I really am. Not to mention, really proud of you."

Rylin looked down. "Don't be. I'm not sure I even deserved it."

"What are you talking about?"

"Just that you were right." Feeling a flush of shame rise to her cheeks, Rylin told him how Xiayne had kissed her at the cast party the final evening.

"What the hell, Rylin? Are you serious? He should be fired for that." Cord started to stand up, as if to go confront Xiayne this very minute. Rylin put a hand on his to still him.

Cord's eyes darted to hers at the touch, and she quickly pulled her hand away, scalded.

"No," she said slowly. "I don't want to get him fired. It was wrong of him, but he wasn't aggressive or . . . forceful about it. He was just being stupid."

Cord watched her closely. "It's still not okay," he said at last.

"Of course it's not." Rylin fumbled for a way to explain it to him, that she wasn't angry about the kiss so much as hurt by its implications. She wanted to go back to being the star holography student, the prodigy whose Oscar-winning professor had invited her cross-country to help because she was so talented—instead of what she was now: the assistant whose director had hit on her.

Even *she* knew that that was a tired Hollywood cliché, and she'd only spent one week there.

"I just thought he wanted me there for real. But in the end, you were right," she said wearily.

Cord flinched at the reminder of what he'd said. "I'm really sorry that I was."

"It doesn't matter. I'm going to drop the class."

"You can't quit!" Cord exclaimed. "Don't you see that if you do, you've let Xiayne win?"

"But how can I face him again after what happened?"

Cord gave a strange sigh, as if he wanted to be frustrated with her, but wasn't. "There's another holography class—intro level, taught by a professor who's been here forever. The class is mostly freshmen, and it'll probably be too slow for you, but it's better than nothing. If you have to, you should at least switch to that."

Rylin murmured her thanks and reached for a blade of grass, rubbing it thoughtfully between a thumb and forefinger. "I just wonder, sometimes, if my being at Berkeley wasn't some huge mistake. In case you haven't noticed, I don't exactly fit in here." She laughed, a laugh that was as dry as the leaves whispering above them.

"It wasn't a mistake. You're talented. Don't ever let anyone make you think otherwise," Cord declared, with a conviction that startled her.

"Why do you care, anyway?" Rylin heard herself ask. *After what I did to you*, she thought, but didn't have to say.

Cord took a moment to answer. "I never stopped caring what happened to you, Rylin. Even after everything that happened between us."

I never stopped caring what happened to you. That meant that he still cared even now, didn't it? But did he care as a friend . . . or something more?

Cord brushed off his navy uniform pants and stood up, and Rylin knew the moment was over. "We should be getting back. I can't afford to lose my job as TA. It's the only extracurricular on my college applications," he said lightly. He held out a hand to pull her to her feet. Where their skin touched it sent electric vortices down Rylin's nerve endings, all the way to her toes.

"What, street racing old driver-cars out in the Hamptons doesn't count?" Rylin teased, and was rewarded with a smile at the shared memory.

The whole walk back, some new feeling was pressing at Rylin, subdued and insistent and joyful and terrifying, and she didn't dare look at it too closely in case she was mistaken.

But as the tour guide droned on, she kept sneaking glances at Cord's profile, wondering what it all meant.

AVERY

MONDAY AFTERNOON, AVERY stepped off the monorail in New Jersey and pulled her navy coat tighter around her shoulders. She began the walk up to Cifleur Cemetery, ignoring the lone hover that detected her movements and began to float alongside her, flashing a hopeful green to indicate that it was free. Avery needed the walk right now. She'd woken up this morning feeling listless and hollow, her pillow soaked with tears. No matter how hard she worked at it during the day, every night she forgot that she and Atlas were over, and then she had to wake up and remember the cold harsh truth all over again.

She felt isolated and lonely, and worst of all, she couldn't even *talk* to anyone about it. She'd thought fleetingly of Leda, but although they were making peace, the whole Atlas thing was still too raw for Avery to discuss it with her. She really missed Eris.

Which was how she'd ended up here, at the cemetery, wearing her heaviest coat and cowboy boots—the brown ones with white detail that Eris had always begged to borrow. It seemed somehow fitting. She passed the main front gates, nodding at the security cam installed there, and turned left toward where Eris was buried, in the middle of the Radsons' family plot. Despite everything that had happened with Eris's father in life, he'd ended up claiming her in death, after all.

Avery hadn't been back since Eris's interment, after the funeral service and the seemingly endless visitation—which they'd held in an impersonal rented event space, since Eris's mom was still living downTower, and Eris's dad at the Nuage. By that point, the only people left had been Eris's parents and grandmother, and the Fullers . . . and Leda. Avery remembered standing in the blistering wind, watching the priest lower the tiny urn containing Eris's ashes into the ground, thinking that this couldn't be all that remained of her expansive, vibrant friend.

She picked her way down the gravel path until she found Eris's headstone. It was smooth, with nothing inscribed on it but her name: until you tapped the top, and a hologram materialized before you, of Eris smiling and waving. Avery thought it was a bit absurd, but then, Caroline Dodd-Radson had always insisted on the newest and trendiest in all things. Even funeral accessories.

Tears pricked at Avery's eyes as she stood there, wishing more than anything that she could talk to her friend.

So talk, she thought. There was no one around to hear, and what did it matter anyway? She shook out her scarf, spread it over the cut grass, then sat down and cleared her throat. She felt a little foolish.

"Eris. It's me, Avery." She imagined her friend sitting there, her flecked amber eyes wide with amusement. "I brought you a few things," she went on clumsily, pulling the items from her bag one by one. "A gold sequin, from that dress you let me borrow for the holiday party one year." She set it carefully by the headstone, letting it catch the light of the sun in a way Eris would love. "Your favorite perfume." She spritzed the jasmine scent Eris always used to wear. "Your favorite raspberry bonbons from Seraphina's," she added, unwrapping one of the smooth dark chocolates and then holding it uncertainly, wondering why she'd even brought it. She hesitated before popping it into her mouth. Eris would want Avery to enjoy it here, with her.

She started to lean back, but felt a lump in her bag.

"Oh, and the candle!" Avery fumbled in her bag for a beauty wand, flicked the setting to HEAT, and held it determinedly to the stumpy remain of the IntoxiCandle she'd stolen from Cord's. It took a while, but eventually a flame guttered to life on the tiny gold wick, dancing wildly in the wind.

Avery propped herself on her elbows and stared at the candle through lowered lids, remembering what Cord had said, that Eris had been the one to buy the IntoxiCandle in the first place. She wasn't surprised at all. Eris had a magpie-like obsession with anything bright or sparkling, not to mention anything just slightly forbidden—and the fire-hazard IntoxiCandle was a perfect example of both. Even now its movement was quick and capricious, just like Eris.

Little pockets of serotonin drifted upward as the candle melted down. Avery felt her awareness melting slowly away.

And suddenly she saw Eris, sitting there on her own headstone as easy as you please. She was wearing a fluffy pink dress—like something a little girl would wear, playing dress-up—and her bright, fresh face was devoid of makeup. "Avery?" she asked, swinging her bare feet. Her toes were painted a glittering silver.

Avery wanted to hug her friend, but somehow she knew she wasn't permitted to touch her. "Eris! I miss you so much," she said fervently. "Everything is really falling apart without you."

"I know, I'm the best. What else is new?" Eris said airily, with one of those smiles that seemed to dance about her expressive features. Her perfectly arched brows lowered as she caught sight of the flame. "You brought the IntoxiCandle? I love that thing!"

Avery wordlessly held it out, and Eris reached for it, their hands almost brushing as she did. She inhaled deeply, her eyes closing in rapture. "You got this from Cord, didn't you?"

"He said I needed it more than he did." Avery looked down, overwhelmed by a sudden flash of guilt at the thought of that night. It had been a mistake, going over to Cord's. Maybe if she hadn't made such a point of obviously flirting with him, Atlas would never have gone home with Calliope—wouldn't have questioned everything about their relationship—and they never would be in the torturous mess they were in now.

"So what's going on, then?" Eris asked. "Is it Leda?"

"Things with Leda are actually getting better," Avery said, faltering. "Even though she did, I mean—"

"It's okay. We both know she didn't mean to push me," Eris said gently. Her hair fell loose over her shoulders, red and gold as liquid fire in the slanting afternoon sun.

"She didn't mean to," Avery repeated. "And she feels terrible about it," she added, knowing that it wasn't useful, that it was nowhere near enough.

Eris winced, a pained expression on her face. "There are a lot of things I should have done differently that night. It's not Leda's fault. But enough about that," she said briskly. "What's bothering you, Avery?"

"Atlas, actually," Avery confessed. Her tone was full of meaning, and a look of comprehension crossed her dead friend's face.

"Wait. You and Atlas? Really?"

Avery nodded, and Eris let out a low whistle.

"I thought my life was messy," she finally said, with a mix of sympathy and respect. "But it turns out yours is even more of a disaster."

"That's not particularly helpful," Avery pointed out, with a smile. Eris was the same as always.

"Okay, so it's a little bit complicated . . ."

"A *lot* bit complicated," Avery corrected, and Eris smiled at the silliness of the phrase.

"Who cares? Life is always complicated. Don't let other people get in the way of you and Atlas, if it's what you really want. I learned that one the hard way," Eris added, her voice small.

"Oh, Eris." Avery felt a million things at once, guilt and loss and a fluttering regret for what might have been. "I'm so sorry. I just—"

"I mean, you're not *actually* related," Eris went on, with the stubbornness that used to get her into so much trouble. "Screw all the haters, and go be with Atlas, and let that be the end of it."

"Except that Atlas and I ended things. It was for the best," Avery said unconvincingly.

"Was it? Because you seem pretty damned miserable to me. Here." Eris held out the candle. "Cord was right. You need it more than I do."

Avery realized that she was crying, great fat tears sliding down her cheeks to plop like rain on her sweater. "I'm so sorry," she whispered. "For all of it. I'm sorry I wasn't there for you, when everything happened with your family. And I'm sorry about that night—"

"Like I said, it's no one's fault, Avery," Eris insisted.

"It was *my* fault! I opened that trapdoor—I let everyone up on the roof! If it hadn't been for me, none of this would've happened!"

"Or maybe it wouldn't have happened if I hadn't gone up to talk to Rylin, or fought with my girlfriend, or tried to explain things to Leda, or flirted with Cord, or worn my tallest heels. We'll never know."

"I just wish . . ." That things had been different that night, that she'd seen the warning signs with Leda, that she hadn't thrown that party in the first place.

"You really want to do something for me?" Eris said suddenly, her lovely face turned up to the sun. She closed her eyes. Her lashes fell in thick brushstrokes across her cheeks. "*Live*, Avery. With or without Atlas, here in New York or on the damned moon, I don't care. Just live, and be happy, since I can't. Promise me that."

"Of course I will. I love you, Eris," Avery vowed, her heart constricting. It came out a whisper.

"Love you too."

———

"Avery?"

She woke to someone shaking her shoulder. "Are you okay?"

"Cord?" She sat up blearily, rubbing at her eyes. The candle was burned out, pink-wrapped chocolates scattered over the grass before her. She shivered and wrapped her arms tighter around herself. The air was biting out here in the real outside, where temperature wasn't regulated by a mechanical system.

"What are you doing here? Did you come to visit Eris too?" she asked him.

"My parents," Cord corrected. Of course, she thought clumsily, she should have known. "Did I just catch you *napping*, here in the cemetery?"

"I didn't mean to! I was talking to Eris," Avery said, and felt an immediate pang of embarrassment; she hadn't meant to admit that—it was too intimate. To her relief Cord just nodded, as if he understood exactly what she meant. "I guess I drifted off," she added, pushing herself to her feet and starting to collect her things.

She should have been bothered, she thought, that Cord seemed to catch her at all her weakest moments—close to tears at the Hudson Conservancy Ball, making a fool of herself with Zay, and just now, sleeping at the grave of her dead best friend. But maybe because she'd known him so long, because she knew he wasn't perfect either, Avery didn't mind.

She thought of how Eris had reacted to the news about her and Atlas, as if it wasn't all that terrible. It had only been a dream, but still . . . for the first time, Avery let herself wonder what it would be like to share her secret with someone else. What would Cord say, if she told him? Would he be disgusted, or would he somehow understand?

Footsteps sounded on the path behind them, and they both turned around, startled. A girl about their age stood there, her dark hair cut into bangs. She was wearing a heavy puffy jacket and jeans, and holding a single white rose. Belatedly, Avery realized that she wasn't moving past—that she'd paused at this entrance, as if she meant to come into the Radsons' plot, but the sight of Avery and Cord had stopped her.

Before Avery could say anything, the girl had turned and sprinted away, vanishing into the air like smoke.

Avery tried to dismiss it as a coincidence, but the whole walk back to the monorail stop, she couldn't shake the prickly feeling that someone was watching her.

WATT

THAT SAME EVENING, Watt was finishing up his first math club meeting. At Nadia's suggestion, he'd tried to join a few clubs to improve his transcript, though the only one willing to accept him at this late date was the math club—and then only because Cynthia was co-president. He wished he'd done more of this stuff earlier in high school, instead of devoting all his efforts to hacking jobs.

But unlike after-school clubs, hacking jobs *paid*, and in his family, money was pretty impossible to turn down.

"Thanks again for letting me join," he said to Cynthia as they walked out the school's main doors.

"You should have been in the club ages ago. I knew you were good at differential equations, but I didn't realize how good," Cynthia replied, sounding impressed.

You're welcome, Nadia said archly. She'd been the one to calculate those equations at record speed—though Watt shouldn't have needed her to. They'd both been a little surprised, actually, when he had to ask for help.

Sorry I needed the save, Watt told her now.

You were thinking about Leda, weren't you?

Just making plans, Watt answered vaguely, though he never could hide anything from Nadia for very long. And she was right.

Even while he'd been in that math session, a part of his mind—a part that was dangerously close to the whole—had been thinking about Leda, alternating between fantasies of her demise and fantasies of a decidedly different nature. He didn't understand his fixation with her. How could he resent her, want to make her to pay for everything she'd done, and yet still want her as much as he did?

He wished he could be more like Nadia. More rational, less reckless.

Speak of the devil, Nadia flashed before his eyes. Watt looked up, and was struck speechless at the sight of Leda herself, lounging casually against a brick wall at the edge of his school's tech-net, seven hundred floors below her own. She was wearing black yoga pants that left little to the imagination, and her face was glowing from exertion. Her hair was swept up into a loose knot, though a few damp curls escaped at her ears.

"Watt. There you are," she greeted him, with a note of possessiveness that simultaneously thrilled him and pissed him off. He wanted to kiss her, roughly, right there. But he didn't.

"Leda," he said slowly, to cover his strange mix of feelings. "To what do I owe the pleasure?"

Next to him he felt Cynthia tense at the name, glancing back and forth between them. He knew what she was thinking: so this was the infamous Leda, the girl who knew far too many of Watt's secrets.

"I need to talk to you about something. In private." Leda's

eyes darted to Cynthia. "Sorry, I don't think we've met. I'm Leda Cole. Cynthia, right?" she asked, holding out a hand. Cynthia didn't take it.

How did Leda even know who Cynthia *was*? He must have mentioned her, Watt thought—or else Leda had been trolling through his page on the feeds. He found the notion strangely pleasing.

"Hi, Leda," Cynthia said, without moving forward. It was clear from her tone what she thought of the other girl. After a moment, Leda lowered her outstretched hand and turned to Watt.

"Watt? Let's go," she commanded, and started off, clearly assuming he would follow.

Watt looked back at Cynthia. "Sorry, I have to—"

"Whatever, the queen bitch summons," Cynthia said tartly, too low for Leda to overhear. "Go ahead."

Watt didn't hesitate. Cynthia would forgive him later, but Leda never would. He hurried to catch up with her. "You didn't need to make that scene," he said, though for some reason he'd found it a little entertaining. Maybe he was getting too accustomed to being with Leda Cole.

"Sorry if I made things difficult with your girlfriend," Leda said briskly.

"I've told you before, she's not my girlfriend."

"I've told *you* before, I don't care." She didn't even glance his way as she turned onto his street. Watt was a little surprised that she wanted to go to his place tonight, and even more surprised that she knew her way around down here.

"Look, if you wanted me to come over, you could have just messaged me," he said, his mind already racing ahead to what his parents would say when they walked in together. Though they'd met Leda before; they thought she was a classmate, after all.

Leda laughed. "I'm not here for *that*," she said, and he loved the way she said "that," as if she wanted to be dismissive of the notion but couldn't quite manage it.

"There's someone I need you to look into," Leda went on. "I keep meaning to ask you about her, but, you know . . ." She broke off awkwardly.

"But I keep distracting you." He grinned at her discomposure.

"Don't flatter yourself."

They stepped up to his front door. Watt hesitated and glanced over at Leda. "Could you just tell my parents that you're here for a school project, and—"

"Relax, Watt. This isn't my first rodeo."

"I don't even know what that means," he replied as he opened the front door. "What the hell is a rodeo?"

Leda shrugged. "It's an old saying," she said dismissively, and followed him down the hallway, her expression transforming from exasperated sarcasm into a brilliant smile. "Mrs. Bakradi!" she exclaimed, going to give Watt's mom a hug. "How are you? I've been meaning to bring this over for Zahra. I found it when I was cleaning out some of my old things." To Watt's astonishment, Leda reached into her purse and produced a tiny horse figurine. She pushed a button and the horse began running across the floor.

Damn, she was good, he thought with grudging respect.

When they were finally in Watt's bedroom with the door shut, Watt stared at Leda. She'd already claimed a seat on his bed, crossing her legs beneath her with proprietary ease. "How did you know that Zahra's in a horse phase?" he asked suspiciously.

"Your mom *told* me the last time I was here." Leda rolled her eyes. "Seriously, Watt, that quant of yours has made you unforgivably lazy. Do you ever *listen* to people?"

"I listen to you," he replied, caught off guard by the insight.

"I don't think so," Leda said lightly. "Is Nadia on?" For a

moment Watt thought he was dreaming; it was still surreal hearing anyone talk about Nadia.

"I'm always on," Nadia replied, projecting from the speakers. She sounded slightly offended.

Leda nodded as if unsurprised. "Nadia," she said, with a respectful tone she never used with Watt, "would you please research someone for me? Her name is Calliope Brown. She's around our age."

"Searching now," Nadia replied.

Watt felt increasingly annoyed. *You're making it too easy on her. She asked nicely. Unlike you.*

"Just what are we looking for, exactly?" Watt sank into his desk chair and stretched his arms overhead, trying not to think of how close Leda was, the fact that she was so casually sitting there on his bedsheets.

"I'm not sure," Leda admitted. "But something is off about this girl, I know it."

"So we're basing this on a hunch of yours?"

"Laugh all you want, but my hunches are spot-on. After all, I had a hunch that there was something off about you, and I was right, wasn't I?"

Watt had nothing to say to that.

Leda leaned forward as Nadia's search results populated the monitor. There was a Calliope Brown registered in the Tower, on floor 473—an older woman with a narrow smile. "No, that's not her," Leda said, disappointed.

Watt frowned. "Nadia, can you widen the search to the United States?" They scrolled through dozens of faces, then expanded the search internationally, but Leda just shook her head impatiently at every image that appeared.

"She's staying at the Nuage! Can we find her that way?" Leda impatiently yanked out her ponytail to redo it.

"I'll show you the cams at high-speed, pulling out the faces. Tell me which one she is," Nadia offered, using snapshots of the video feed to create an instant database of all the guests. Watt could feel Nadia getting into the search a little, despite herself. There was nothing she loved more than a good puzzle.

After a few minutes of scrolling, Leda leapt off the bed, pointing to a figure in the top right. "There, you see! That's her!"

"Nadia, can you grab her retinal scans?" Watt asked. Moments later Nadia had pulled up the information. The girl's retinas were registered to Haroi Haniko, a woman from Kyoto who'd died seven months ago.

"Okay. She's got a stolen retina pattern," Leda said, clearly stunned. "She must be a criminal, right?"

Now even Watt was getting curious. "Nadia, what about facial-reg? Full international scope." She could change her eyeballs, he thought logically, but it was much harder to drastically change her face.

The screen came up blank. "No matches."

"Try again," Leda asked, but Watt shook his head.

"Leda, that search included every government—national, state, province, municipal—in the entire world. If this girl existed, we would have found her."

"What are you saying, that I made her up? She's right there on camera, you can see for yourself!" Leda burst out, exasperated.

"I'm saying this is really weird. If she'd ever lived anywhere, she would have gotten registered, for an ID ring or a tax card or whatever."

"Well, there's your answer," Leda declared. "She's never actually *lived* anywhere—only visited. She never got an adult ID."

Watt wouldn't have thought of that, but it made sense. "Why would anyone live that way?"

"Because she's *up to something*, obviously." Leda delivered the phrase with a dramatic flair, as if she were an actress performing in an old tragic play. She frowned. "But why hasn't anyone figured out that her retinas are wrong?"

"No one actually verifies retinal scans in public places, just cross-checks them with the criminal list. I'm guessing you haven't seen her in any private homes," he pointed out.

"Just Avery's, but it was for a party," Leda said, and Watt nodded.

"Whatever she's *up to*," he said the phrase the way Leda had, which elicited a smile, "she's clearly an expert at it."

They both grew quiet at the notion.

Then Leda looked up with a new idea. "What about schools? Could you run her facial-reg on school networks, not government ones? Or are they hard to crack?"

It was a good idea. Watt wished he'd thought of it first. "Nothing is too hard for Nadia," he boasted, which wasn't totally true, but sounded badass. "Nadia?" he prompted, but she'd already found a hit. Clare Dawson, who attended St. Mary's boarding school in England for a single year.

"*Yes!* That's her!" Leda cried out in excitement.

Another match popped up. Cicely Stone, at an American school in Hong Kong. Aliénor LeFavre, in Provence. Sophia Gonzalez, at a school in Brazil. And on and on, until Nadia's screen was covered in at least forty aliases—all clearly linked to images of the so-called Calliope.

"Wow," Watt said at last. This was way more intense than what he normally dealt with on H@cker Haus, which was usually just student grade-wipes and cheating spouses, the occasional ID search.

"This proves it. She's a criminal," Leda said triumphantly. Her dark eyes were dancing with the thrill of the chase.

"Or a sociopath, or a secret agent, or maybe her family is crazy. We can't jump to conclusions."

Leda moved closer to the screen and bent down. He found himself distracted by her presence. "Nadia," he added, clearing his throat, "can you find records of any incidents at these schools? Expulsions, misdemeanors, anything unusual in her files?"

"And cross-reference all her classmates at these schools, see which of them were her friends? Maybe we can find something through them," Leda added. Without warning she sat on Watt's lap, laced her fingers up in his hair, pulled his head down to hers. Her mouth on his was warm and insistent.

Watt was the one to pull away first. "I thought you said that wasn't why you came here," he teased, though he wasn't complaining.

"It wasn't the *only* reason," Leda corrected.

"You don't want me to go up to your—"

"Shut up," Leda said impatiently, and kissed him again, her arms over his shoulders. It was easy to stand, to carry Leda to the bed—she was so light—and lay her gently down, never breaking the kiss. Then his hands were on her back, the curve of her hip, and her skin was so soft, and Watt didn't know anymore whether he liked her or detested her. Maybe he felt both, at the same time, which would explain why all his nerve endings were going haywire, like his whole body might explode at any moment.

He started to ask Nadia to turn off the lights, but the room was already dark, a deadbolt sliding firmly across the door.

LEDA

LEDA BLINKED UP into the darkness.

She was wrapped around Watt's sleeping form, the two of them cocooned in the warmth beneath his blanket, tangled so closely that even their breath had subconsciously aligned: their inhales and exhales occurring together like in that old medieval poem about the star-crossed lovers. "Clock," Leda whispered, as quietly as she could.

The blinking numbers in the top left corner of her vision told her it was 1:11 a.m. *Crap.* She hadn't meant to stay so late—had only come over on a sudden impulse, when she saw Calliope at antigrav yoga with Risha and remembered her conversation with Avery. She'd hoped, desperately, to find something on Calliope— as if she could give it to Avery as a peace offering, and undo all the wrongs she'd inflicted on her friend.

And, she admitted, she'd wanted an excuse to see Watt.

She shifted over in the narrow bed, not especially surprised that she'd fallen asleep there. She felt so . . . at ease with Watt, her sleep finally free of the nightmares that normally chased her down long, endless hallways and grasped at her with phantom fingers.

Thank god she'd at least had the presence of mind to tell her parents she was studying late with friends. Hopefully they wouldn't notice her tiptoeing upstairs at this hour. Then again, they hadn't noticed her sneaking Watt into her room all week, either.

Leda propped herself on one elbow to glance down at Watt's sleeping form, tawny and lean and dangerous. He was like a flame, drawing her in, and she couldn't stop even though she knew it might hurt her.

She let her gaze trace over his features in a way she never would while he was awake, studying his strong nose; his full, sensuous mouth; the shadowed lids over those glowing hazel eyes. His eyes were twitching a little, as if he was dreaming. What did that mind of his dream about? Maybe he dreamed of her.

She reached her hands up into his thick dark hair, playing with its curls, feeling the ridged smoothness of his skull beneath. So much intelligence in that whirling, humming, genius brain of his, she thought, so much that she didn't understand. Watt fascinated her, and scared her a little too, because he was so unlike anyone she'd ever met.

Her fingers traced a bump under his right ear, and her breath caught. His skin was raised in a perfect circle, far too regular to be natural. It was firm to the touch, as though something had been surgically embedded there. She tried to lift his hair to get a glance at his scalp, but she couldn't see even a trace of a scar.

A cold shiver of foreboding traveled up her spine, and her hand darted quickly back. *Surely not*, Leda thought, in answer to the bizarre thought that had traveled up from some place deep within her. Surely Watt's computer wasn't embedded in his brain. It seemed impossible.

Yet it explained so many things about him—the way he moved through the world more effortlessly than other people, without ever mumbling to his contacts. All those times he seemed to communicate with Nadia in complete silence. The fact that Leda had never been able to locate Nadia, no matter how diligently she'd searched through his room.

It seemed impossible, yet if Leda had learned anything in her seventeen years, it was that the impossible was very often true.

Watt stirred, his eyes fluttering open. "What time is it?"

"Shh, it's late. Go back to sleep." Her mind was still frantic, trying to sort out the implications of what she'd found.

"Don't leave yet," Watt said drowsily, reaching up to run a hand down her bare arm. His touch sent tiny explosions along her skin. Leda wanted more than anything to lie back down, press herself into him, unlearn the truth that she'd inadvertently discovered. She wanted to ask Watt about the strange bump in his skull. How had he gotten Nadia in the first place, and did it hurt? Did he regret it, being part computer?

Watt started to sit up. Leda cast her gaze wildly around the room so that he wouldn't catch her staring, and her eyes caught on something she hadn't noticed before, a virtual reality headset on his bedside table. It looked like a half-completed prototype; even Leda could tell that huge chunks were missing. Only really hardcore gamers still wore headsets, since the rendering on them was still better than even the most powerful contacts. "Did you build this?" Leda asked, picking it up, hoping to distract him from her rapidly beating heart.

Watt shrugged. "That's just a side project. I was trying to see if I could improve the motion-tracking features, using Nadia's computing abilities."

She pulled the headset on, but nothing happened. "It doesn't actually work yet," Watt pointed out, though he seemed amused by her efforts.

Leda left the headset on for a moment. She liked having the safety of the lens between herself and the world, liked hiding her features from Watt's incisive gaze. She wondered what Nadia was thinking right now, hiding there in Watt's brain, watching her. Oh, *god*—had Nadia been watching them through Watt's eyes this whole time? Something about it creeped Leda out, as if there had been a ghost in bed with them.

She pulled the headset off and stood up to hunt for her clothes, which were scattered in the textured darkness. "I should go."

"Okay," Watt said. He sounded disappointed, but maybe she was imagining it.

Leda paused in the doorway to look back at him. He'd kicked off the sheets and lay back in bed like a sketched shadow. The soft light from the hallway picked out his unruly hair, his disarming smile. He suddenly looked very young and boyish and not scary at all. Leda's heart slowed a little.

She remembered that she was going to Dubai for the weekend. It would be her first night without Watt since before the rehab check-in.

"Hey," she whispered. Watt looked up at her, expectant. "Do you want to come with me to Dubai, for the Mirrors launch party?"

Watt smiled. "Yeah. I'd like to come."

Later, as she walked home from the lift stop, Leda looked around, startled, at the familiar yet somehow alien streets. Her block seemed simpler, cleaner; the lights from the lamps falling in beautiful pools against the darkness. It was the same and yet utterly different from normal, and Leda realized that maybe *she* was what had changed. There was a great gulf between the Leda of yesterday and the Leda of today.

She knew that Watt had a computer inside him. But so what? It wasn't any weirder than anything else that had happened lately. He was still Watt, she reasoned, and he was still going to Dubai with her. Coming for real; not coerced, or blackmailed, but because he actually wanted to be there as her date.

For the first time in her life, Leda Cole had dirt on someone—serious dirt, come to think of it—and had absolutely no intention of putting it to use.

RYLIN

"PLEASE, MRS. LANE. I really need to switch to the intro-level holography class," Rylin pleaded, standing at the registrar's desk yet again.

It was Friday morning, and she was repeating the same plea she'd been making all week long to no avail, begging the registrar to switch her from Xiayne's holography class to the Intro to Holography section that Cord had mentioned. *That* class was taught by a woman named Elaine Blyson—who had white hair and bright red lipstick and seemed like a perfectly safe choice for a professor.

So far Mrs. Lane had been no help, but Rylin refused to give up. She couldn't bear the thought of walking into the classroom that afternoon and seeing Xiayne. She wanted to put the whole damn mess behind her and move on.

"I'll do anything," she said urgently, leaning her forearms onto the woman's desk. "I'll take double arts next year. I'll do another independent study. I just cannot stay enrolled in that class."

"Miss Myers, as I've reminded you all week, the course selection period has long since ended. It's too late for you to drop a class now. It was already too late when you were added to the class—you only got in at all because you were a mid-semester addition." Mrs. Lane sniffed and turned back to her tablet. "Frankly, I don't understand your desire to drop the class. You know it's our most popular elective. And after that fabulous independent study you just participated in . . . I'm a bit shocked."

"Is there a problem here?"

Rylin was stunned to see Leda Cole in the doorway of Mrs. Lane's office. "Forgive me for interrupting," Leda went on, with a charming smile, "I was just on my way back from a student government meeting and had a question for Mrs. Lane."

Rylin tried to make eye contact with her, baffled, but Leda was staring determinedly at the administrator.

"Miss Cole! Maybe you can talk some sense into Miss Myers here," Mrs. Lane exclaimed. "She's trying to drop down to the intro-level holography class, and I've been telling her all week that it's simply impossible."

"Intro to Holography? Really?" Leda glanced at Rylin with a questioning expression. Rylin stayed silent. She had no desire to piss off Leda.

Leda seemed to read something in Rylin's demeanor, and turned back to the older woman. "But you know, Mrs. Lane, our class is *incredibly* oversubscribed. Perhaps it wouldn't be the worst thing if Rylin were to drop it."

"I forgot that you're in that class as well!" Mrs. Lane exclaimed. "So you understand how important it is to maintain the classroom balance—"

"Mrs. Lane," Leda cut in smoothly, "Rylin is an incredible

student, but she might benefit from the intro class. You should see the holos she took at Hotel Burroughs last Thursday—the material is *scintillating*, but the lighting is far too bright. You can see every last *dirty* little detail in the shots." She slightly emphasized the last few sentences. Mrs. Lane colored, but said nothing.

"Of course, I'm aware of the school policies," Leda went on, an eyebrow raised meaningfully. "But I'm not sure Rylin is yet. Perhaps it would help to have Dean Moreland explain them to her, so she can understand the *implications*? I know he has just the right *touch* when it comes to sensitive matters, like this."

Mrs. Lane's mouth was hanging open, utterly speechless. Rylin looked back and forth from Leda to the registrar in bewilderment. She wasn't sure whether or not to speak. "Mrs. Lane—" she finally began, but the woman cut her off.

"Yes, Miss Cole, I see your point," she said, nodding vigorously. Her expression was strangely pinched. "Miss Myers, I'm dropping you down to the base-level course. It meets on Tuesdays and Thursdays in the arts pavilion."

"Um, thank you," Rylin stammered, but Leda was already dragging her out into the hallway, a satisfied smirk on her face.

"You're welcome," Leda declared, and turned away.

"Wait! What the hell just happened? How did you do that?" *And why?*

Leda shrugged. "Mrs. Lane is having an affair with Dean Moreland, who, as you may know, is married. They meet at the Hotel Burroughs every Thursday."

Rylin hadn't heard anything about an affair. "Does everyone know about that?" she asked, surprised.

"No. Just me," Leda answered mysteriously.

"Oh." Rylin stood there, overwhelmed by a curious sense of relief, and resentment that she was now indebted to Leda Cole. "Well, thank you."

"Don't worry, you can owe me one."

"Leda—" she called out, and the other girl turned back expectantly. Rylin gulped. "Why did you just help me? I thought you hated me."

A brief flash of something, guilt or indecision or maybe even regret, crossed Leda's face. "Maybe I'm just sick of everyone thinking I'm a coldhearted bitch," she said matter-of-factly.

Rylin couldn't think of an appropriate answer to that.

"Can I ask, though," Leda went on, "why *did* you want to drop the class?"

Rylin briefly considered lying, but after what had just happened, she felt she owed Leda the real story. "During my independent study last week, Xiayne kissed me. I don't want to see him again, for obvious reasons."

"Xiayne came on to you?" Leda repeated. Rylin nodded, and Leda rolled her eyes. "God, what an ass. I'm sorry. And here I thought he might actually be one of the decent ones."

"Do those exist?" Rylin said drily, and to her surprise, Leda laughed.

"You make a good point. Hey," she said, as if a sudden idea was striking her, "are you going to the Dubai launch party this weekend?"

Rylin had heard the other kids talking about it all week—scheduling their private hydrojets and discussing the gowns they'd ordered, since the theme was a black-and-white ball. She'd told herself it was all ridiculous. Partying in New York was no longer good enough for these highliers—they had to fly halfway around the world to get drunk with the same people as always?

Still, some absurd part of her wanted to go, if only to see it all.

"I wasn't planning on it," she said now, to Leda.

"You should," Leda urged. "It'll help take your mind off things like self-centered holography professors."

"I wasn't invited," Rylin protested.

Leda waved a hand in careless dismissal. "It's Avery's dad's party; of course you can come. That's not an issue."

Rylin blinked at her, stunned. Was this some kind of trap? And since when were Leda and Avery best friends again? Rylin wasn't exactly clued in to the social scene, but even she knew that those two hadn't been speaking since the night on the roof.

"Thanks. I'll think about it," she said cautiously, suspicious of Leda's motives.

"Well, I have to go. One of us is about to be late to our favorite arts class," Leda said with a smile, as if they now shared a private joke. She paused, seeming to think of one last thing. "By the way, the Andertons are big investors in Fuller Enterprises, which means that Cord is probably going. If that changes your mind at all."

"How did you—" What secret weapon did Leda have, that she seemed to know everything about everyone?

The bell rang, leaving Rylin standing there alone and bewildered, wondering what exactly had just happened.

When school was out that afternoon, Rylin walked directly to the edge of the tech-net and pinged Lux. No answer. Well, Rylin decided, she would just go and see her—and make a quick pit stop first.

When she knocked at the Briars' door, Lux answered, wearing an old sweatshirt and shorts with a hole in them. Her hair was jet-black today, chopped off in terrible uneven bangs. "Wow," Lux said, her voice flat. Her eyes traveled from Rylin's uniform to her preppy ballet flats and the pink-and-white-striped shopping bag in her hands. "You look like a moron."

"And you look like a disaster," Rylin replied. When Lux didn't say anything, didn't open the door farther, Rylin faltered. "Can we talk? Is now not a good time?"

"I don't know, Rylin. I tried to talk to you all week and you were completely MIA. I called you several times, but you never tried me back, not even once." Animosity, and pain, flashed in Lux's eyes.

Rylin crumpled with shame. She remembered receiving the ping when she'd been with Cord on Monday, and a few others on Tuesday, too, but she'd completely forgotten to try Lux back. "I'm so sorry," she apologized. "What's going on?"

"For starters, Reed dumped me."

"Oh, Lux." Rylin stepped forward to give her friend a hug. The other girl was stiff for a moment, but allowed it. "It's his loss, you know," Rylin murmured.

"Thanks. But that wasn't why I pinged you."

"What was it?"

Lux stepped back to look at her, and now the accusation was clear in her expression. "Hiral's trial was the other day. I pinged to see if you were planning on going." She shrugged casually, but Rylin could see that she was bothered—for Hiral's sake as much as her own. "I ended up going with Indigo and Andrés."

Rylin had totally forgotten that the trial was this week. She hadn't exactly been counting down the days on her calendar, but she still felt guilty for not at least thinking about it. "What happened?"

"You don't even *know*? You dated him for three years and you couldn't be bothered to look up whether he went to *prison*?"

"I was in LA," Rylin started to say, but Lux was talking over her.

"Not that you give a shit, but he got off."

Rylin felt a pang of relief at the news. Even though she still resented Hiral, for everything he'd put her through, she'd never hoped that his life would end at age eighteen.

She realized suddenly how Lux had seen her recently—absent,

careless, too involved in her new highlier school to pay attention to her friends. It wasn't a very flattering picture.

But Lux didn't know the whole story, and that was Rylin's fault for not telling her.

She exhaled slowly. "Would you please come talk with me?"

Lux opened her mouth, and Rylin saw at once that she was going to say no; there was something cold and distant about her, as if she weren't actually here, like an insubstantial character in a holo. She reached for Lux's hand. It was reassuringly solid.

Recognition flickered in Lux's eyes, and she nodded. "Fine."

Rylin kept holding tight to her friend's hand, the way they used to when they were kids. She led her down the street and around the corner, to a tiny ViewBox that lay tucked away between two of the apartments.

ViewBoxes were like tiny, half-forgotten parks: little slices of real estate with metallic benches and imitation-window view screens, which only existed in spots where the Tower's architects hadn't known what else to do with the square footage. This particular one had its view screen set to depict a dramatic sunrise over the New York skyline, though of course they were much closer to the center of the Tower; real windows, with real views, were far away. Technically, ViewBoxes were public spaces, though they were too small to be of much use to anyone. Most of the time they were just spots for teenagers to go smoke up or stick their hands up each other's shirts.

Rylin and Lux sat on the empty bench, staring at the funny, fake-looking sunrise in bright Technicolor. "Oh, I almost forgot this," Rylin said, passing over the shopping bag she'd been holding.

Lux broke out in a reluctant smile when she saw the contents. "You got every flavor?"

Inside was a dazzling array of Popper Chips—xtra cheddar,

salted caramel, cilantro lime, even spicy plantain. She and Lux used to always walk past the gourmet snack store and wonder what it would be like to try them, but they'd never been able to afford even a single bag.

"All twelve. A well-balanced dinner, right?" Rylin said, and sighed. "I'm sorry I've been a terrible friend lately."

"I've just *missed* you," Lux said, with less resentment than before. She opened the bag of salted caramel chips. "I feel like I've been losing you ever since you started working for that high-lier kid."

Because Rylin had been hooking up with him, and hadn't told anyone, she thought guiltily. "There's something I kept from you, about Cord," Rylin admitted, her heart hammering. "I didn't want you to judge me—it's not exactly my proudest moment."

Lux silently passed the enormous bag of chips, and Rylin took a handful of the xtra cheddar. The chips crumbled deliciously on her tongue. She felt suddenly very far away from the shifting holos and MarsAqua and gourmet fruits of the upper-floor cafeteria. This was so much more real.

She started at the beginning, telling Lux how she fell for Cord while she was working for him; how she'd tried to break up with Hiral, but he got arrested, then forced her to sell his drugs so that he could get out on bail. How she'd been with Cord while Hiral was still technically her boyfriend, even though she wished he wasn't. How Cord's older brother had found out and forced her to break up with Cord, to tell him that she'd been using him the whole time just for the money.

By the time Rylin had finished, they'd worked their way through almost every bag of chips. "Sorry. I didn't mean to keep you here so long," Rylin said.

"I had no idea, Ry." Lux leaned forward, her uneven bangs sweeping across her brow. The light from the view screen gleamed in her eyes, making her pupils seem impossibly dark. "I mean, especially about Hiral and V. They're in way deeper than I realized. And the way they treated you was not okay." She shook her head angrily and brushed her hands on her sweatpants, leaving little half-moons of pink-orange-blue powder on them. "Show me a picture of this Anderton kid," she commanded, changing tack.

Rylin pulled up the link to Cord's profile on the feeds and passed her tablet to Lux, who gave a sharp intake of breath.

"Damn, Ry. He's hot! Is he hiring another maid? Maybe *I'll* apply," she declared, and Rylin gave her a playful shove. Lux giggled, the air between them clear now. Rylin's whole body felt worlds lighter, as if she were one of those rain balloons they tethered to the earth, then cut loose.

"So what's the update? Now that you're a highlier, hasn't he realized he wants you back?"

"I'm not a highlier," Rylin protested, and Lux laughed.

"That's true. No self-respecting highlier would be caught dead in a dirty makeout ViewBox, eating a week's worth of Popper Chips," she agreed. But she wasn't done asking about Cord. "Seriously, though, Ry. You'll never learn the truth if you don't ask. Why haven't you?"

Lux had a point, Rylin realized. She needed to stop guessing at Cord's feelings and just *act*. She thought of what Leda had said this afternoon, about the party, and gave a reluctant smile. "You're right," she admitted, and got out her tablet, pronouncing a phrase she never thought she would say.

"Ping to Leda Cole."

WATT

"TAKE NOTES. AND be careful. We're so proud of you," said Watt's dad, Rashid, giving Watt a rough slap on the back.

"Ping us if there's anything you need." Watt's mom, Shirin, tightened the scarf she'd insisted he wear; a silly gesture since the Tower was temperature controlled, but Watt knew she was just trying to keep from crying. Then she gave up and pulled Watt into a hug, her voice breaking. "We love you so much."

Watt tried to ignore the guilt that bubbled up at this elaborate farewell. His parents thought he was heading to a college weekend at the University of Albany. He'd considered telling them he was at Derrick's house, the excuse he'd used when he went to Leda's rehab check-in, but felt like he'd barely gotten away with it last time and didn't want to tempt fate.

The Bakradis had been overjoyed at his "news." They were so worried about his obsession with MIT—they feared he might not get in, that he would be devastated and, worse, have no backup schools—and since Albany was a state school, he would pay in-state tuition. They were too excited to even question his announcement, or ask for any kind of proof. Watt felt awful, but what choice did he really have? They certainly wouldn't be thrilled at the idea of his jetting off to Dubai with a highlier girl. Especially since he'd already told them that Leda was a classmate, and would have to explain why he'd lied about that.

Honestly, if he didn't have Nadia, Watt wasn't sure how he would keep track of all the secrets and half-truths and lies anymore.

Zahra and Amir came barreling down the hall, all squeals and high-pitched laughter, ponytails and shirttails flying. Watt leaned down to hug them both. Then with a final murmured farewell he was out the door, pulling his dad's low-tech suitcase—the same one he'd had to borrow for the rehab weekend—behind him.

He rounded the corner onto the main avenue only to nearly collide with Cynthia, who'd been turning onto Watt's street, her enormous school tote over one arm. Watt remembered with a sudden, sinking feeling that he'd had plans to study with Cynthia and Derrick today.

"Cyn, I completely forgot." *Nadia, why didn't you remind me?* The whole point of having a quantum computer in your brain was to be one step ahead of other people, not behind.

I'm sorry, Nadia said, but she didn't seem very sorry. Watt couldn't help but wonder if she was purposefully interfering. She hadn't been enthusiastic about this Dubai trip, though Watt wasn't sure why.

He gave Cynthia his best, most charming smile—the one that had gotten him out of detentions and homework assignments and his mom's anger. But it had never really worked on Cyn. "I'm actually leaving town," he told her, forging ahead. "I'm so sorry I forgot to tell you."

"Leaving town?" Cynthia repeated, a sarcastic emphasis on the phrase, and Watt winced at his choice of words. He and Cynthia weren't the type of people to be casually "leaving town," and they both knew it. "Where are you going?" she asked slowly.

Unlike his parents, Cynthia wasn't someone Watt dared lie to. "Dubai," he admitted.

"With Leda." It wasn't a question.

He nodded.

A crowd of younger kids streamed past, loud and rowdy. Cynthia grabbed Watt by the shoulders and pulled him aside, to a little retail corner that was half McBurger King and half a small pharmacy. Watt could hear the fast-food takeout-bot asking one of the customers whether he wanted fries with that.

"What the hell, Watt?" Cynthia snapped. Anger crackled over her skin like lightning, breaking through her normally cool demeanor. Her eyes were wide, her cheeks flushed. Watt was startled to realize, for the first time in his life, that Cynthia was quite pretty. Why hadn't he ever seen it before?

"Look, it's a long story," he began, but Cynthia cut him off.

"You've been acting strange for weeks, you let her drag you away from school yesterday, and now this? What's going on between you two?"

"I told you, she's got something on me," Watt said impatiently. But he knew that it had become more than that. He thought of Leda in his bed earlier that morning—propped up on one elbow, looking down at him, her hair long and loose around her shoulders. *Whatever's going on between us, it's just physical*, he told himself firmly. He still wanted what he'd always wanted: to make her trust him enough to confess the truth to him, about what had happened on the roof, so he could get out from under her thumb once and for all.

And now he was actually getting close. Soon enough it would

all be over, and he wouldn't have to spend any more time with Leda—could send her to jail, if he wanted.

For some reason he thought of the way she'd sounded this morning, the hopeful twang in her voice when she'd asked him to Dubai. He shook the memory away, unbidden.

"What does she have on you? It can't be *this* bad," Cynthia demanded.

"It's complicated."

"Whatever it is, I'll help. Come on, we're two of the smartest people I know! Don't you think that together, we could beat Leda Cole?"

"Cynthia, it's not that, it's just—I don't want to get you involved."

Cynthia let out a sigh. Little holographic Happy Meal ads kept popping up behind her head, making Watt strangely want to laugh.

"Don't you see that I'm already involved, whether you like it or not? Watt, I can't help you if you won't let me!" she exclaimed. "And I'm sick of this. I never get to see you anymore. You're with Leda all the time."

"I told you, it's complicated," Watt said again, feeling like a broken record.

Cynthia took a small step forward—and Watt knew, suddenly, that they had come to a crossroads in their friendship. "You like her, don't you?" Cynthia asked.

"No," he said quickly.

"If you don't like her, then don't go to Dubai." Cynthia's whole body was taut, as if she were a drawn bowstring. "Stay away from her. Stay with me." The last sentence was uttered almost under her breath, but there was no mistaking its meaning.

On some level, Watt had known this was coming for a while now. What he hadn't known was what he would say.

He stood there, looking at his friend—a brilliant, fascinating, remarkable girl, who lived in his world and knew where he came from, the type of girl his parents would love for him to date—and he still didn't know.

"Cynthia . . ." he faltered.

Maybe because she was sick of waiting, or maybe because she didn't want to hear what he had to say next, she rose up on tiptoe to kiss him.

Watt was surprised into kissing her back. He was surprised by this new version of Cynthia, who held him tighter and kissed him more fiercely than he'd expected.

"So?" she asked when she finally stepped away, looking vulnerable and afraid and familiar and like a stranger.

Watt shook his head. There were a million things he wanted to say, but he didn't know which of them was right. He felt that he didn't know anything anymore. "I'm sorry. I have to go."

"You don't *have* to do anything," she told him. "If you leave now, you're choosing her."

"That's not fair. I don't have a choice," he snapped, and turned away like a coward, before he had to see the hurt in Cynthia's eyes.

But he couldn't help wondering if she was right.

CALLIOPE

CALLIOPE LEANED FORWARD on the vanity, which was littered with gleaming silver beauty wands and spray powders and a fresh manicolor mitt—all of it arrayed carefully before her, like weapons polished and laid out for battle. Her own lethal tools, which had always made her so dangerously beautiful.

"You ready?" her mom called out from the other room of their suite.

Calliope had been unsurprised that her mom had decided to come to the Mirrors launch party after all. Like her daughter, she had an incurable weakness for anything bright and glittering and extravagant—and tonight promised to be all those things. She and Calliope had been acting chipper and normal all week, but Calliope sensed that something was unresolved beneath the surface. Things had been weird between them ever since their fight.

Still, here they were, in a suite that Nadav had booked for them at the Fanaa, the gorgeous luxury hotel in the dark half of

The Mirrors. The Fullers' rooms were in the other tower, but Calliope had insisted on staying here; there was something seductive, almost forbidden, about saying one was on the dark side. She glanced around at the walls, which were lined entirely with mirrored screens. Calliope could have switched them to opaque, of course; but she left them on, enjoying the sight of her reflected selves swishing pleasantly about the room.

"I'm ready. Atlas should be here any minute now," Calliope replied. He would need to head down early, as the host.

The entire day had been one long tribute to excess and indulgence. Calliope had ridden over with the Fullers on their private jet, which wasn't exactly private, given that dozens of other people had been invited to catch a ride on it, all of them walking around the plane and chatting and clutching glasses of champagne as if the flight itself was just one big cocktail party, a logical prelude to the night to come. Maybe that had been the intent all along.

Elise leaned in the doorway, showing off her delicate white dress, which made her look intentionally bridal. "What do you think?"

"Amazing. What about me?" Calliope turned back and forth in a model-esque pose. Her long hair was gathered into a low bun, emphasizing the glamorous length of her neck; and her sparkling black gown clung to her with an almost shocking closeness. She relished the way the silk faille felt against her bare skin—like a seductive whisper in her ear, assuring her that she was young and beautiful and rare.

Elise came forward and took her daughter's hands. "You know that you look stunning. Have an incredible time tonight, darling. You deserve it." Her voice rang with an unusual sentimentality, and she was smiling at Calliope in an odd way, as if she was trying to make up her mind about something. "You like this boy, don't you? Not just to con, but for real?"

Calliope was caught off guard. "I like him fine," she answered, fighting the twist of guilt she felt at the thought of stealing from Atlas tonight. He was a good person, though admittedly a little tortured and confusing. "Don't worry, I'm not about to go elope with him anytime soon," she added jokingly.

Elise didn't laugh. "And you like New York?"

Calliope turned toward the mirror, pretending to retouch her lips so she wouldn't have to look directly into her mom's eyes. It was easier to lie to people when you didn't have to see them face-to-face.

"New York has been fun, but it's time we moved on. I'm glad we're going out with a bang," Calliope said firmly, ignoring the way her chest constricted at the thought of leaving. Her mom met her eyes in the mirror, and Calliope smiled at her reflection.

A knock sounded at the front door. "That's probably Atlas," Calliope said.

"Have fun. Don't do anything I wouldn't do!"

"In other words, go crazy?" Calliope called out, and pulled the door open.

Atlas stood there in a simple black tux, looking more elegant and grown-up than Calliope had ever seen him. He'd cut his hair, she realized, but left the slightest shadow of stubble along his jawline.

"You look amazing." Atlas held out an arm to lead her down the hall.

"You clean up okay yourself," she told him.

He smiled, revealing that small dimple on one corner of his mouth. "Thanks for coming with me tonight, Callie."

They turned down a hallway that dead-ended into a window, looking directly across at the light tower. The waters of the canal churned far below them. "Do you mind if we stop by my parents' first?" he asked. "They wanted us to meet there and all head to the party together."

"Of course." Atlas's parents hadn't been on the plane earlier—they'd flown over a few days earlier, to help set everything up. And Calliope had to admit that she was curious to finally meet the famous Fullers.

She expected Atlas to turn toward an elevator, but instead he stepped forward to the window and traced a circle on it. The flexiglass immediately shifted, shooting a clear tunnel across the empty sky as easily as if it were a beam of light.

Calliope was shocked into silence. She briefly wondered if the tunnel was a hologram—if this was some kind of virtual reality game, to test her willingness of disbelief—but a glance at Atlas's proud face confirmed that it was, in fact, real.

"Etherium," he explained. Calliope had heard about the programmable material, which used linear induction and carbon mesh to quickly build and un-build structures for the military, usually on-demand bridges needed for only a few minutes at a time.

"I see," she replied, in an almost careless tone, as if she'd seen instant-construction bridges dozens of times and could hardly be called upon to seem impressed now.

"We got the first civilian license for it. Let me tell you, it wasn't easy." Atlas sounded proud. Calliope realized with a start that he'd actually done this himself, had been the one to ping and persuade and make it happen.

"And here I was wondering what you did at your desk all day," she teased, though she felt uncharacteristically proud of him too. She took a bold step forward, her stiletto landing emphatically on the bridge, and willed herself not to look down at the thin, flimsy layer of material separating her designer shoe from the vast distance below.

"You're not afraid of it," Atlas remarked approvingly.

Calliope turned to glance back at him over one arched

shoulder. Her expression was almost a dare. "I'm not afraid of anything."

As they emerged on the other side and the tunnel blinked back out of existence, Calliope felt a little shiver of adrenaline. There was something about crossing the sky in a temporary tunnel that felt like a good omen, like everything that happened tonight would go her way.

They reached the Fullers' penthouse and the door swung open. Atlas's dad stood on the other side. "You're Calliope, right? Pierson Fuller," he said with a charismatic smile, and shook her hand.

"Nice to meet you." Calliope wondered what exactly Atlas had told them about her. If she was meeting his parents, did it count as a date?

It probably depended on where she spent the night tonight.

She followed Mr. Fuller into the living room, its gleaming touch screens carefully hidden behind carved furniture and plush cushions. The crystal chandelier overhead bathed them in a soft halo of light. Everything was decorated in shades of white and cream, against which the touches of black—Atlas's and his father's tuxes, and of course Calliope's midnight-black gown— stood out like stark exclamation points.

A woman who must be Atlas's mom glided in from the bed- room, glittering in alabaster tulle covered with Swarovski crystals. "Which earrings should I wear?"

She posed the question to all of them, holding out her hands, in each of which lay a dark velvet box. One contained a set of pear-shaped colorless diamonds, the other a pair of perfectly matched pink diamonds. The jewels seemed to burn against the contrasting velvet, light kindling within them to flash in a thou- sand small sparkles.

Calliope's breath caught, and she tried to take a few snaps

without being conspicuous. What her mom wouldn't give to see these earrings. It was hardly Calliope's first time around excessive wealth, yet everything she'd seen over the last few years suddenly felt garish next to this. These people practically *breathed* money. Their every gesture was painted with it, glazed with it.

She wondered what they would do to her, if they ever found out why she and her mom were really here. Her grip on her purse tightened until her knuckles cracked. She knew the answer: they would destroy her with the same ruthless elegance that made up the rest of their lives.

Mrs. Fuller glanced belatedly around the room, then set the boxes down as she registered Calliope's presence. "Calliope, my dear! Elizabeth Fuller. How lovely to meet you."

"Thank you so much for having me," Calliope said.

Mrs. Fuller just smiled and nodded. "Where's Avery?" she asked her husband and son.

Mr. Fuller moved to the couch and leaned back, one ankle crossed over the other knee. "Who knows?" he mused, seeming unconcerned. Atlas stayed oddly silent.

"Well, then, which do *you* think that I should wear?" Mrs. Fuller went on, returning to the gleaming white side table where she'd placed the two velvet boxes with their priceless contents. After a moment, Calliope realized that the question had been directed at her.

Her mouth felt suddenly dry; her eyes flicking back and forth between the showstopping gems, both sets of which probably belonged in a museum, rather than on a wealthy socialite's earlobes. "The clear ones," she decided, finally. "The pink are a little heavy with your dress."

Mrs. Fuller turned her plain but expertly made-up face back and forth, studying her reflection in an insta-mirror that had materialized out of nowhere.

"You're right," she concurred. "But someone should wear the pink ones. It would be a waste not to."

Calliope could never in her wildest imaginings have anticipated what happened next. To her complete and utter shock, Mrs. Fuller held out the earrings—toward *her*. "Do you want to try them, Calliope?" she offered.

Calliope opened her mouth, but no sound came out. "Oh, I don't know," she finally stammered, though she could practically hear her mom's voice in her ears, hissing at her to stop stalling and take the damned earrings. She'd just been too surprised to react properly.

Mrs. Fuller smiled. "They would look striking against your hair. Stones this color have to be worn by us brunettes, you know." She gave a little wink, as if she and Calliope were allies against an army of diamond-stealing blondes, and dropped the earrings onto Calliope's bare palm as easily as if they'd been a couple of chocolate candies.

This couldn't be real. People didn't act this way on their own, unbidden. Calliope thought of all the times she'd been given expensive things in her life, always by boys who were trying to get into her pants, and then only after a great deal of persuasion and manipulation, of dropped hints and innuendos and excruciatingly thoughtful conning. Yet here was Atlas's mom, offering up the most expensive, exquisite items Calliope had ever laid eyes on, without any sort of prompting at all.

Calliope didn't understand. She'd only met the woman five minutes ago. Maybe Atlas's judgment of her character was good enough for Mrs. Fuller, she thought uneasily. Or maybe the Fullers were genuinely nice people.

Her mind flashed to that waitress at the Nuage; to the old man in India; to poor adoring Tomisen, Brice's friend, whom she'd taken a "loan" from and left without a backward glance. They had all trusted her, and she'd cheerfully turned around and violated that trust. Maybe they had been genuinely nice people too.

Calliope wouldn't know, because she'd never stuck around long enough to find out.

She felt shame rise up in her throat as if it were a physical thing, horrible and blocky, like that time she'd tried to swallow one of Mrs. Houghton's rings and almost choked on it. *What on earth have you been doing?* her mom had screamed, giving her six-year-old shoulders a little shake.

What on earth *had* she been doing all these years? Calliope thought, as some core part of her worldview began to crumble. She felt like she was looking at herself from the outside in, as if she were seeing herself through someone else's contacts. It made her dizzy.

Somehow, mechanically, she unscrewed her own small drops and fastened the spectacular pink diamonds into her ears. "They're beautiful. Thank you," she whispered, leaning toward the insta-mirror. The stones were radiant against the smooth curve of her cheek. She wanted them and she hated herself for taking them and she couldn't look away from them.

The doorbell rang, and everyone momentarily forgot Calliope as a sudden influx of people poured into the room. The hum of voices grew louder, all of them laughing and complimenting and greeting one another.

"Flicker to Mom," she whispered, turning aside, and closed her eyes against the dizziness as she began to compose under her breath. "Mom, you'll never guess what I'm wearing." Forget Nadav; they would have to leave in the middle of the party, catch a flight down to South America. These earrings would set them up for several years, at least.

She couldn't finish the sentence. Calliope knew this was her chance, the kind of opportunity that would come along only once in a lifetime, and yet here she was, freezing up like a complete newbie.

"Callie," Atlas said as he pushed his way toward her, and Calliope let out a strange sigh of relief. She would finish the message later. "A few of my friends are here. I'd love for you to meet them." He nodded toward the entry hall, which was becoming even more packed, filled with teenagers and adults in their perfectly creased tuxes and elegant black or white gowns.

Calliope had always loved moments like this; glamorous and expensive, money softening the edges of it all. But looking at all the people gathered at the Fullers', she felt strangely bereft. These weren't her friends, this wasn't her laughter and gossip, and this certainly wasn't her boyfriend standing next to her. She was just borrowing the whole scene the way she was borrowing the pink diamond earrings.

And this time, she knew, the eventual moment of reckoning was going to hurt.

"Of course," she said to Atlas with a forced smile. "Lead the way." She gave her head a little toss as she followed him, feeling the heavy weight of the earrings that she no longer wanted to steal.

She would let herself indulge this fantasy—would pretend that she was a normal girl, at a party with a cute boy in a tux— for just a little bit longer.

WATT

WATT STUDIED THE party, which swirled and flowed wildly around him, with unabashed astonishment.

A black-and-white parquet dance floor sprawled on each side of the canal, reminding Watt of a shining chessboard. A hundred languages fell discordantly on his ears, too many people speaking at once for Nadia to even bother translating. Above him soared the two massive towers of The Mirrors, rising up into the darkness to new dazzling heights.

For the first time, Watt felt like he finally understood the name; this was like a dream city, full of mirrors and reflections. Every last detail on one of the towers—every archway, every glittering square of glass, every curve in the railing of a balcony—had been cunningly doubled on the other side, in alabaster carbonite or smooth dark nyostone. Even the movements of the serving staff seemed choreographed to echo one another across the expanse of the canal.

Everywhere Watt looked were women in black or white

gowns, men in designer tuxes. There wasn't a single stitch of color in the whole evening, not even the bright red of a cherry at the bar. The effect was striking, like a work of art—as if Watt had stepped into one of those old two-dimensional holos where everything was rendered in shades of gray.

Nadia, what do you think Cynthia meant by all that, earlier? He hadn't been able to stop thinking about the way she'd asked him to stay—and kissed him. What would he do when he saw her again? He felt a feverish anxiety at the thought, guilt and confusion roiling through him all at once.

"You know what it meant, Watt," Nadia replied, whispering the words into his eartennas.

Watt was startled into alertness. Nadia sounded accusatory. *Did I do something wrong?*

"All I know is that the situation has changed, and that it's becoming increasingly difficult for me to anticipate the outcome."

Girls are always complicated, he thought, a bit resentfully.

"People aren't like tech, Watt. They aren't predictable, and they malfunction far more readily."

That's for damn sure.

Cynthia had told him that actions spoke louder than words, but what did that mean when Watt's actions were reactive instead of proactive? He hadn't felt in control for a very long time, and he wondered, suddenly, if it was his own fault.

He'd met Leda at the airport earlier, fully prepared to find her angry and scheming—they were flying over on Avery's family's plane, and Watt assumed that would make her tense. But Leda had been so relaxed, she didn't even comment on his lateness. She just turned to Watt when he arrived and told him it was a five-hour flight, and what movie did he want to watch together? When her hand kept brushing his on the armrest, Watt hadn't said anything, but he hadn't moved his hand either.

They'd barely seen Avery, or anyone else, the entire flight, but Watt had found that he didn't really care.

Nadia, he decided to ask, *do you think Leda trusts me yet?*

"It's hard for me to estimate emotional states, except for yours," Nadia replied. "Anything I said about Leda's feelings would be pure speculation. It's easier for me to track *your* state of mind, since I have years of data on you. Which is how I know, for instance, that you like Leda."

It was the last thing he'd expected her to say.

No I don't! Leda had drugged him and manipulated him and blackmailed him, and just because she'd made him laugh a few times—just because she was fun to kiss—didn't mean that Watt *liked* her.

"Evidence points to the contrary. When you're with her, you exhibit all the typical physical signs of attraction: your heart rate speeds up, your voice deepens, and then, of course, there's—"

That doesn't count, he thought furiously, interrupting. Pinwheels of sparks flew from an enormous fire sculpture out into the night. *Like you said, it's just data, and besides, physical attraction has nothing to do with liking.*

"You've mimicked her motions and gestures. Your blood rushes to the surface when you're near her, which, in over half of studies, has been linked to formation of emotional bonds," Nadia continued relentlessly, "and you keep asking me about her, which—"

You don't get it, okay? he snapped. *How can you understand something you don't even feel?*

Nadia fell silent at that.

"Watt!" Leda appeared at his side, looking stunning in a white Grecian-style gown. "I've been looking for you. Calliope is here."

Watt's eyes flicked in the direction Leda was pointing. Atlas stood there with the girl from the photos. She looked lean and tan and ruthless; her dark hair spilling over her golden shoulders, her black dress skimming lightly over her form. And it all clicked ruthlessly into place.

"Are you spying on Calliope because she's with Atlas?" Watt asked slowly. Was this Atlas and Avery all over again? Was Watt just the filler, the time killer—a meaningless distraction, while Leda tried all the while to get the guy she actually wanted?

"Yes, of course," she said impatiently.

Watt was stunned at how angry he felt. Well, Leda hadn't meant anything to him either, he reminded himself.

"It's killing Avery," Leda went on, and there was a strange note in her voice—a fierce protectiveness, folded in with concern for Avery—that silenced the high-pitched buzzing in Watt's brain.

"Hold on," he said slowly. "Let me get this straight. You're spying on Calliope because she's with Atlas, because you want Atlas to be with *Avery*?"

Leda flinched. "I know it all must seem weird to you, but I can't bear to see Avery hurt. Besides, if this Calliope girl really is hiding something big, then Atlas has a right to the truth."

Watt still didn't understand. "I thought you and Avery weren't speaking." He felt like an ass, inserting himself into girl drama. But he needed to know.

Leda made an impatient, dismissive gesture. "That's old news, we're fine now." She grinned. "Nadia isn't on her A game, if you didn't already know that."

"But we avoided Avery on the plane today— I thought—"

Leda laughed, making him feel even more foolish. "Avery was avoiding *you*, Watt. Because for some reason she thinks you're upset with her. Besides, I thought it might be more fun, sitting just us," she added, in a slightly less certain tone.

"Oh," was all he could think to say. He was still trying to

understand this new world where Calliope was competing with Avery for Atlas; where Leda was okay with Avery and Atlas dating, and was being considerate of *his* feelings. He wondered where it left them.

Leda's arm tightened on his. "Who is that, with her?"

Watt lifted his gaze back to Calliope. She'd left Atlas, almost furtively, and walked to where another woman stood at the edge of the terrace.

Next to him, Leda was muttering at her contacts to zoom in. Watt didn't need to say anything because Nadia had already focused in on the woman. She looked like a slightly older version of Calliope, her features similar but more deeply etched by time and cynicism.

"Avery told me Calliope lives with her mom," Leda offered. "That must be her, right?"

They glanced at each other, clearly getting the same idea at the same moment. "Watt—could Nadia do facial-reg on the mom?" Leda asked.

Already running it, Nadia replied, still huffy. She'd switched from voice to text, layering the words over Watt's vision as if they were an incoming flicker.

I really am sorry.

It's okay. As you so aptly put it, I don't have any feelings for you to hurt.

Watt knew what she said was true, and yet for some reason, it made him inexplicably sad.

He watched as Calliope and her mom kept talking. At first their expressions were clearly tense; their gestures rigid and tight, loaded with significance. Then Calliope's mom said something, and Calliope smiled uncertainly. *Nadia, are you picking up what they're saying?*

Nadia sent him a transcript of their conversation, without

any commentary of her own. When he read it, Watt's eyebrows shot up in surprise.

"Leda," he started to say, but she shushed him impatiently.

"I'm listening! LipRead," she added, in answer to his questioning look.

LipRead was an application designed for the hearing impaired. Watt wondered why he'd never thought to use it to eavesdrop.

He wasn't sure whether to be impressed by Leda's brilliance, or terrified.

He leaned forward again, to watch them more closely—and Nadia sent him the facial-reg results on Calliope's mother.

"Leda," he croaked, grabbing her elbow and dragging her farther away, despite her protests. "You're going to want to see this."

AVERY

AVERY STOOD IN the eye of a storm of people, laughing uproariously at every joke that was told, looking spectacular in the attention-getting—and exorbitantly expensive—bridal gown that she'd bought on a whim and chopped off at the knees. Even the alterations-bot had refused to make the drastic change, so Avery had set her beauty wand to scissors mode and sawed it off herself; watching the frothy layers of tulle, covered in hand-embroidered seed pearls and tiny crystals, fall to the floor of her closet with a surreal sense of detachment. The gown was so thick that it had taken several minutes of resolved focus to cut it all. Part of Avery had felt that she was watching herself from a distance; normal Avery would have cried out at the sacrilege of cutting a couture wedding gown like that. But then, normal Avery had retreated into a shell, and the only thing left was this irrational Avery, volatile and highly unpredictable.

She kept glancing over to where Atlas stood with Calliope,

their heads bent together, their faces easy and smiling. The sight of them hurt more than Avery dared reveal.

Risha grabbed her arm in surprise. "Oh my god." She gasped, her gaze clearly following the same direction as Avery's. "Are those your mom's pink earrings?"

Avery felt a stab of shock at the sight of her mom's iconic earrings in Calliope's ears. "Looks like they are," she said, trying to sound like the question bored her, so that Risha would drop it.

Across the way, Calliope was leaning forward to whisper something, her gown so thin it was almost nonexistent. Avery felt a darkness rising up in her—a vast empty blackness, like a pool with no bottom. She reached down to feel along the uneven hem of her gown. For some reason its frayed, flawed imperfection was reassuring.

"If your mom lent her those earrings, then she and Atlas must be getting serious," Risha pointed out.

"I don't know, and I don't care." Avery realized she was grinding her back teeth, sending a dull ache throughout her jaw, and forced a tight smile. "I'm going to get a drink."

She turned around abruptly, not inviting Risha to join her, and tried to push her way toward the bar. But of course, Avery Fuller didn't need to elbow through the crowds like a normal person. They fell back instinctively, as if she had a spotlight trained on her, just like always.

It was all the same, wasn't it? The same women moving across the terraces in a familiar click of heels, the same men murmuring to one another in low tones about the same things they always discussed, their eyebrows drawn together in the same clichéd expression of concern. It all struck Avery as futile, and purposeless. Here they were, halfway around the world, and yet everyone was stuck in their little loops—engaging in the old tired flirtations, doomed to the same disappointments.

"Avery! I've been looking all over for you!" Leda hurried toward her. Her face was flushed, her eyes shining fierce with determination.

"Here I am," Avery said uselessly. She searched within herself for the best smile she could find, but it came out shaky. Leda saw, and narrowed her gaze at Avery; a sort of knowing, you-didn't-fool-me expression.

"We need to talk. In private," Leda insisted.

She led Avery backward through the party, through the enormous gilded arch that opened into a luxury housing development within the dark tower. A few partygoers were here, milling about the empty space; everything too pristine and perfect, with that un-lived-in construction glow. Avery had been in plenty of her father's towers while they were still unoccupied, and each time she found it a little unnerving. Empty windows gazed out from the apartments' front hallways like soulless eyes.

"What's going on?" she asked when Leda finally came to a halt. They stepped too close to one of the for-sale apartments, and little ads popped up on both their contacts. They quickly edged closer to the middle of the street.

"I have news, about Calliope." Leda took a deep breath and lowered her voice dramatically. "She's a con artist."

"What?"

Leda gave a pitiless, dangerous smile as she explained.

The story she told sounded more like fiction than reality. It was a story of two women, mother and daughter, who worked together, skimming a cheated, stolen existence off the surface of the world. She told Avery how they tricked their way into expensive hotels—and meals, and clothes—always managing to vanish into thin air before actually paying. How Calliope's mom had been married over a dozen times, only to clean out the joint bank account after each wedding and disappear. How she and her daughter moved constantly from place to place, always changing their names and their fingerprints and their retinas, always finding new people to take advantage of.

"You can't be serious," Avery croaked when Leda was finally done talking.

Leda pulled out her tablet and showed Avery photographic evidence. Calliope, in dozens of school photos under different aliases. Her mother being arrested for fraud in Marrakech, then breaking out of prison under unusual circumstances. The marital records of Calliope's mom, with signed marriage certificates under all the fake names.

"I told you something was off about that girl!" Leda exclaimed, sounding decidedly proud of herself for having figured it out. "Don't you see? Atlas is her next target!"

Avery took a step back, her red heels fumbling beneath her, and the stupid real estate ads scrolled across her vision again. She shook her head angrily to dispel them. "How did you learn all this, if they're always getting their retinas replaced?" She still couldn't quite believe Leda's story. It felt too outlandish, too impossible.

"Facial recognition. It doesn't matter." Leda gave a little wave to dismiss Avery's concerns. "Don't you see? This whole thing isn't Atlas's fault—he's being *played* by a high-rolling professional con artist."

A small part of Avery marveled at the fact that Leda, of all people, was encouraging her to forgive Atlas. "You don't understand. We ended things for good."

"Why?" Leda asked baldly.

Avery scuffed her shoe back and forth on the shining new carbonite street in the perfect new community her dad had built. "I wouldn't run away with him. We went home with other people from the underwater party. It all just felt impossible. I don't know." She sighed. "I'm not sure if we even have a chance any-more."

"Well, you'll never know if you don't at least try," Leda pointed out with ruthless pragmatism. She gave Avery a curious look. "Besides, even if nothing happens between you and Atlas, you aren't really going to let that girl get away with trying to seduce him and *steal* from him, are you? We have to get rid of her!"

Avery bit her lip, a spectrum of emotions tumbling confusedly through her mind. "It's just so . . . unbelievable."

"I know." Outside, they heard the sound of a lone violin play-ing itself. "What are you going to do?" Leda asked after a moment.

"Rip my mom's earrings from her earlobes," Avery said, to which Leda responded with a strangled, choked laugh. "After that, I'm not sure."

"Whatever you're planning, let me know if I can help." Leda gave a small smile, and suddenly they'd traveled back in time, and it was just the two of them again in seventh grade; promising that they would always have each other's backs. Plotting to take over the world.

Avery pulled Leda into a brusque hug. "Thank you. I don't know how you do it, but thank you," she murmured.

"Anything for you, Avery. Always." Seeming to sense that her friend needed some time alone, Leda retreated.

Avery stayed awhile, walking slowly through the overpriced ghost town, with its expensive finishes and soaring ceilings and private gated entrances to each townhouse. She needed to make sense of everything in her bruised, disoriented mind.

Calliope was a fraud. She'd been targeting Atlas since the beginning, probably since Africa.

Avery thought back to her conversation with Atlas after the Under the Sea party—when in the cold light of day, they'd decided that it was too hard, that they should take a step back.

She tried to remember which of them had been the one to say it first. She had a sinking, sticky feeling that it had been her.

And anyway, hadn't she put the initial strain on their relationship, by telling Atlas they couldn't run away together but refusing to explain why? Looking back, Avery felt like she'd leaned unfairly on Atlas in the wake of Eris's death; that she'd taken and taken from him, without ever stopping to ask how he was feeling. Between that and the secrecy—the fact that they were constantly on edge, living in fear that their parents might catch them—it was more than any relationship could bear.

Then Calliope—or whatever the hell that girl's real name was—had come along, with her empty smile and empty words, and set her sights on Atlas. Did she actually think she could just stroll into their lives, take what she wanted, then breeze out of town again? That bitch had another thing coming.

Avery missed Atlas so fiercely that the force of it clawed at her chest. She reached up roughly to wipe at her tears. She hadn't even realized she was crying.

The day Atlas told her he loved her had been the happiest day of Avery's life. It was the first day she'd felt truly alive. As if the world up till that moment had existed only in shades of black and white, like this ridiculous party, then exploded into Technicolor.

She loved Atlas and she always would. Loving him wasn't even a choice. It was hardwired into her very DNA; and Avery knew, deep down, that it was the only love her heart would ever be capable of, for all the days of her life.

She turned resolutely back to the party. There was no time to waste.

CALLIOPE

CALLIOPE FOLLOWED HER mom dutifully across the terrace, to an empty area with a few scattered chairs and a lone figure standing at the railing. "What's going on?" she asked, trying to pull a few loose strands of her hair forward to hide her ears. Her mom didn't seem to have noticed Mrs. Fuller's earrings, which was decidedly out of character. Elise had an obsessive, almost photographic memory of everything she and Calliope owned. The fact that Calliope was wearing massive pink diamonds without Elise noticing was, more than anything else, an indicator that something big was going on.

Calliope had already said hi to her mom, barely an hour ago; they'd run into each other on one of the lower terraces and exchanged a quick check-in on their progress for the evening. Calliope hadn't expected to see her again so soon.

Then they reached the table, and the figure standing there resolved itself into Nadav Mizrahi.

"Hi, Mr. Mizrahi." Calliope shot her mom a curious glance, trying to take her lead, but Elise was just smiling, her eyes bright with unshed tears.

Calliope had never been as good as Elise at crying on demand.

"You couldn't find Livya?" Calliope heard her mom ask, and her heart sank a little, because she realized what was happening. Calliope had witnessed enough of her mom's proposals to recognize them a mile away.

Nadav shook his head. "I wanted her to be here for this, but that's all right. I can't wait any longer."

To no one's surprise, Nadav sank down on one knee. He fumbled a little as he reached into his jacket—it was endearing; he clearly loved Calliope's mother, the more fool he—and produced a small velvet box. There was a fine sheen of sweat on his brow. "Elise," he said fervently. "I've only known you a few short weeks, but it feels like a lifetime. I want it to be the rest of our lifetime. Will you marry me?"

"Yes," Elise replied, breathless as a schoolgirl, holding out her hand so that he could slip the ring on her finger.

It was quite a good proposal, Calliope thought woodenly, even if it *was* a bit uninspired, getting engaged at a party that someone else had thrown. But at least Nadav hadn't rambled on for too long, or said anything mushy. Belatedly she remembered to clap, smiling up at her mom's new fiancé—her fourteenth, if memory served. "Congratulations! I'm so happy for you both," she said, with a decent amount of surprise and enthusiasm. Here it was, she thought sadly, the end of their time in New York. And then it will begin all over again.

She leaned forward to examine the ring, and her breath caught in spite of herself. Elise's engagement rings were usually tacky and awful, because any guy foolish enough to fall for her tricks generally had bad taste. But this one was surprisingly lovely, a simple diamond solitaire surrounded by a beautiful pavé band. Calliope felt a pang of regret that they would have to strip it for parts and sell it on the resale market.

"Calliope, Livya and I are so looking forward to getting to know you better. I'm thrilled to be combining our families." Nadav launched into a description of all his utterly doomed plans. He thought that he and Elise were getting married in the Museum of Natural History, because they were both so enamored of it—Calliope almost laughed at the notion of Elise wanting to get married surrounded by dusty old stuffed taxidermied animals. And, he asked, what did they think of visiting Tel Aviv next month, so that she and Elise could meet his extended family?

"You should both move in right away. There's no need for you to live at the Nuage anymore," he added. "Of course, we'll have to start looking for a new apartment. One that's big enough for all of us."

For a brief moment, Calliope imagined what it would be like, getting a taste of normal, stable life. Living in a *home*, a place that was actually hers, with unique and personalized touches—rather than a glamorous, completely anonymous hotel. Actually being stepsisters with Livya. No longer conning innocent people and then leaving them, in a constant whirlwind of senseless extravagance.

It would have been weird, Calliope thought, actually doing what Nadav said: living with these two strangers. Yet she didn't completely hate the idea.

"Oh—it's Livya," Nadav murmured, tilting his head to receive an incoming flicker. "I'm going to find her and bring her here, to share the good news." He planted a kiss on Elise's mouth before heading off into the crowd.

"So, what do you think?" Elise asked, lowering her voice, the moment he was out of earshot.

"It's a great ring, Mom. I'm sure you'll get half a million for it at least. Nice work."

"No, I meant, what did you think of the plan, of everything Nadav said?"

Calliope's stomach gave a strange lurch. "What do you mean?"

"I mean, what do you think of staying in New York?" Elise smiled and took her daughter's hands.

Calliope couldn't answer. She felt suddenly irritable and nervous and unable to think clearly. "For how long?"

"We're *staying*, sweetie," Elise repeated. "That is, if you want to."

Calliope sank wordlessly into one of the Lucite armchairs and looked out into the night. It was so dark. The torches flickered in the rising wind, which was how Calliope knew they were real flames, not holos. Some bizarre part of her wanted to walk over and touch the flames, just to be sure.

"I've been thinking about what you said last week, that you wished we could stay somewhere, for once." There was a strange undercurrent to her mom's voice. This was unfamiliar ground for both of them. Calliope stayed very still.

"I'm worried that I haven't always been the best parent for you, the best role model." Elise looked down at her clasped hands, fidgeting with her new engagement ring. "I've been thinking a lot lately about that day when we left London."

So have I, Calliope thought, but she wasn't quite sure how to voice it.

"I thought it was the right thing at the time," Elise said haltingly. "God, when that woman hit you, the things I wanted to do . . . and after all the years of mistreatment I'd suffered at her hands. It seemed only fair that we take something from her and run."

"It's okay, Mom." Calliope could hear the angry roar of the

canal far below, echoing the roiling churning confusion of her thoughts. She'd had no idea that her mom felt conflicted like this—that she'd questioned their life too, when for so long it had seemed like she'd sailed blithely and blissfully along.

Her mom sighed. "No, it's not. I'm the one who led you down this path, with no actual plan. I got to have a normal teenage experience, with school and friends and relationships, but you . . ."

"I've experienced those things," Calliope offered, but Elise waved her words away.

"I don't know where the time went. I feel like I look at you, and it was just yesterday that we were running away from the Houghtons' house, not seven years ago. I should never have let it go on this long." She lifted her gaze, and Calliope saw that her eyes were bright with unshed tears. "I've deprived you of the chance to live your life, a *real* life, and that wasn't fair to you. Where on earth will you end up, when all of this is over?"

Far off, a chorus of shouts arose as an enormous cake floated out from the kitchens on a gleaming black platter. The buttercream icing was packed with microscopic digestible LED chips, so that the entire cake seemed to light up like a torch.

Calliope didn't answer her mom. She'd never really thought that far into the future, probably because she was afraid to.

"I was thinking," Elise went on, with a little more self-possession, "that we could make this a bit of a longer con, our longest one yet. We could get you into school, so that you spend your senior year in New York. If you hate it, of course, we can always cut bait and leave on the next 'loop out. But we might as well see how it treats us first." She ventured a smile. "It could be fun."

"You would do that?" Calliope wanted what her mom was offering—so, so very much. But she also knew what it meant: that Elise would have to give up her independence, and live with a man who, no matter how kind he was, she didn't love.

"There's nothing I wouldn't do for you," Elise said simply, as if that answered every other question. "I hope you know that."

"Look who I found!" Nadav stepped back onto the terrace, with Livya in tow.

Calliope stepped forward to give the other girl an impulsive hug. "You look beautiful tonight," she gushed, in a burst of charitable fondness. It was true; her makeup made even Livya's pale, watery features into something interesting, and her ivory cloqué gown with its full skirt gave her skinny figure some much-needed shape.

"Thanks," Livya said stiffly, quickly extricating herself from Calliope's arms. She didn't return the compliment.

"Cheers to our new family!" Nadav cried out, brandishing a cold bottle of champagne like a weapon as he popped the cork. The sound ricocheted loudly over the hum of the party, drawing a few glances their way, but Calliope didn't care.

She noticed that Livya barely took the smallest, almost imperceptible sip of the champagne before setting it down, her lips pursed. Clearly she wasn't as pleased by this turn of events as Calliope was.

Ah, well. You can't win 'em all, Calliope thought ruefully.

They were done conning. They wouldn't have to cheat or lie or betray anyone's trust; wouldn't have to put on fake names and couture dresses and start the whole vicious cycle over again. The entire world felt brighter, lighter, and full of infinite possibility.

She would live in New York, for real—actually be herself, not some character her mom had made up to play the supporting role in their latest fiction. She could go to school, and have friends, and actually *become* someone.

She couldn't wait to find out what Calliope Brown, New Yorker, was really like.

"Darling," her mom hissed, with a sidelong glance, as Nadav

handed each of them a champagne flute. "Are those new ear-rings? They look almost real."

Calliope tried desperately not to laugh, but the corners of her mouth lifted into a smile in spite of everything. "Of course they're not real. They're beautiful, though, aren't they?"

Elise's unfamiliar new diamond sparkled in the moonlight as she held her glass towards Calliope's. "Here's to this time."

"Here's to this time," Calliope repeated, and no one but her mother would have heard the hopeful, eager edge to the phrase she'd spoken so many times before.

RYLIN

FROM WHERE SHE stood on the edge of the dance floor, Rylin could see the mirroring of The Mirrors to full effect. Three stone bridges dotted with lanterns spanned the canal, each of them so thick with people that they were near impossible to move across. Overhead, etherium bridges winked into being with a burst of light and then vanished seconds later, reminding Rylin of the planes she and Chrissa used to watch from the elevated monorail station. From that far down, the planes had looked like lightning, vanishing from the sky almost the moment Rylin saw them.

What an unexpected day it had been. Just last night Rylin had pinged Leda from the ViewBox—she'd half expected Leda to ignore her, but Leda picked up right away. "What's up?" she'd asked briskly, as if it weren't at all weird for Rylin Myers to be pinging her on a Friday night.

"I want to come to Dubai," Rylin had explained, and from that instant it had all been a whirlwind. She'd bought a new dress, flown overseas on Avery's family's plane, and now here she was.

She hadn't seen Cord yet, but the night was still young. The thrill of what he'd said last week, that he never stopped caring about her, buzzed warm and pleasant in her chest. She was determined to find him—and to find out what it meant.

Her tablet buzzed with an incoming message. Curious, Rylin glanced at it—and was shocked into reading the whole thing.

From: Xiayne Radimajdi.

No subject.

Rylin, it read, *I missed you in class yesterday. And I've just received notification from the registrar that you're dropping down to the base holography section. I hope this isn't true, but if it is, I understand.*

Please let me apologize for my actions the night of the cast party. The fault is mine, for any and all lines that were crossed. Please also know how grateful I am, for all your help with Salve Regina.

You are incredibly talented, Rylin. The way you see the world is a gift. I am deeply sorry to lose you from the class. If you change your mind, I would be honored to have you back at any time.

I look forward to following your holography career.

Xiayne

Rylin felt like the wind had been knocked out of her. She would need some time to think about it, to sort through her various emotions and come to a decision. But just reading the e-mail had made her feel better. She leaned against a hammered metal table, colored in a checkered black-and-white pattern. Maybe she would add the class back after all. Maybe.

"There you are!" Leda sidled over, holding the skirts of her sweeping white gown with both hands so that she could move more easily. She smiled, and it transformed her face: softened the angularity of her features, brought out the liveliness in her eyes.

She looked nothing like the angry, drugged-out girl who'd threatened Rylin on the roof that night. Now she actually looked . . . happy.

"Hi, Leda," Rylin greeted her.

Leda came to stand with her at the railing, following Rylin's gaze over the glimmering crowds, lit by the sparks from the fire fountains. There was a live human chorus singing on one of the other terraces. Their voices unfurled like interwoven ribbons into the night.

"So," Leda asked, after a moment, "how do you like your first party?"

"It's not my first party." Rylin rolled her eyes in amused disbelief.

"You could've fooled me," Leda replied evenly. "You came all the way here to Dubai and now you're standing alone, not talking to anyone? Come on, Rylin, you go to school with a lot of these people. Surely by now you can at least say hello to some of them."

Rylin flushed. Leda was right. "Just because I go to school with them doesn't mean I like them," she said defensively.

"I don't see the problem. You can dislike someone and still have a *conversation* with them. God knows you detest me, and yet you're still talking to me."

But to Rylin's surprise, she found that she no longer hated Leda.

"I don't understand you," she said quietly. "A few months ago, you were threatening to *destroy* me. Now you're bringing me to parties, helping me get out of classes. What changed?"

"*I* changed." Leda let out a heavy breath but didn't tear her eyes from Rylin's. "And for the record, so have you. You're not the same girl I bullied at lunch that first day." A new song had started playing over the speakers, yet Rylin had heard every word.

"You're right," Rylin said, a smile creeping over her features. "Now I'm way too tough for you to boss around."

"You were always tough," Leda replied, with a funny look. "But now you're also smarter, and more observant, and—I *think*—not quite so prickly. Besides," she added, smiling now, "I don't need to bully you anymore. I've moved on to other victims lately."

Rylin couldn't tell whether the other girl was serious or joking. Maybe a little bit of both.

A memory flitted into her mind, unbidden, from one day in the edit bay, when Xiayne had told her that holography was all about perspectives. That different people saw the world in different ways. Rylin knew she had wronged so many people—and been wronged by them too: Hiral, Leda, Xiayne, and most of all Cord. But maybe she needed to look at it from another angle.

"Oh my god, Rylin. This is a party and you look like you're trying to solve the mysteries of the universe." Leda reached for a drink and handed it to her. "Relax, and try to smile, 'kay?"

Rylin took a sip of the drink from the frosted white glass. It tasted bitter on her tongue, and far too strong. "I can't drink this on an empty stomach," she protested.

"I know, I'm starving. Have you seen the risotto balls? They look incredible." Without another word, Leda was looping her arm in Rylin's and dragging her toward one of the food stations. For a moment Rylin hesitated—she still wanted to find Cord— but then she remembered that there were still hours left in this party, and she was hungry, and it was kind of nice, not hating Leda anymore.

How strangely the world worked sometimes, that Rylin Myers and Leda Cole were off to find risotto together, forming a bizarre sort of truce under the soft, glittered sky.

CALLIOPE

CALLIOPE WAS STANDING alone near an arrangement of mood-flowers, which currently glowed a soft, contented gold to match her happiness. Their so-called emotion-detection system was pretty flimsy—based on heart rate and body temp and, supposedly, pheromones—but for once Calliope thought their reading was actually spot-on.

She'd retreated to this side terrace to catch her breath and wait for Atlas to find her. Sure enough, she heard footsteps behind her this very moment. She turned around, a smile breaking over her features, only to see that it wasn't Atlas at all, but his sister.

Avery looked like a creature half-wild. She was wearing a shimmering white dress with an illusion neckline, sewn with several layers of lace and delicate pearls. The skirt cut off just above her knees, Calliope realized; not evenly, but in a jagged line, as if it had been sliced with a blade. Her hair fell loose from its pins to surround her face in a tangled blond cloud.

"I've been looking for you," Avery declared, something ominous in her tone.

"Hi, Avery." Calliope lifted an eyebrow curiously. She had to ask. "Is that a wedding dress?"

"It was, until I chopped it off and made it a party dress."

Well, it was certainly attention-getting. "What can I do for you?"

"It's simple, really. I want you to get the hell out of New York." Avery spoke with distinct spaces between her words, as if she needed Calliope to understand the full import of every last syllable.

"Excuse me?" Calliope demanded, but she had a sudden, nauseated feeling that Avery *knew*.

Avery took a menacing step forward. "I know the truth about you and your mom. So now you both are going to get the hell out of New York and never speak to Atlas again, since you were playing him this whole damn time for his *money*. Since he was just a game to you."

Fear spiraled in eddies over Calliope's skin. She took a careful breath. "It's not like that, okay?"

"What was your plan tonight, anyway? Were you about to run off with my mom's earrings?"

Calliope felt a stab of guilt at the accusation. She'd considered it, hadn't she? And she would've done it, too, not so long ago; yet tonight something had held her back. She hadn't wanted to treat the Fullers that way. She hadn't wanted to treat *anyone* that way anymore.

Maybe she was developing that thing people called a conscience.

She started to speak, but Avery was shaking her head at Calliope's silence, her perfect features twisted in disgust.

Quietly, with all the dignity she could muster, Calliope reached up to unfasten the magnificent pink diamonds still hooked in her ears. She held them out to Avery, who snatched them back.

"You have no idea what you're talking about," she maintained, watching as Avery switched out her own earrings for the pink diamonds. "You don't even *know* me."

Avery looked up, and her blue-blue eyes were nothing but cruel. "I already know far more than I ever wanted to know about you."

"How did you find out? Was it Brice?" More than anything, Calliope felt saddened by the fact that she and her mother would have to leave again. After all her mom's hard work—after her acceptance of Nadav's proposal, her decision that they could stay—they would have to turn tail and run yet again. Pick up new retinas and new identities and start tricking some poor person into giving them something. There would be no more Calliope Brown, that was for damned sure. The thought made her feel hollow inside.

Avery looked up, startled. "What does Brice have to do with this? Is he in on it?"

"Never mind."

"*Ten, nine, eight . . .*" Around them, the party broke out in a sudden countdown to midnight. The first round of fireworks was about to start—they would continue all night, on the hour, all the way until morning. Calliope felt dazed that it was still so early, when in the course of a single evening her whole world had been radically upended. Twice.

She kept her eyes on Avery, trying to interpret the dance of her emotions across her face. She'd predicted so many actions of so many people in her life, yet for the first time, her instincts seemed to have failed her.

Then Calliope thought of something her mom had said once: that if she was ever caught in a tough situation—if her lies weren't working, if all else failed—sometimes the best way out was to tell the truth.

She'd never spoken her real name aloud. *Don't tell anyone,* her mom had drilled into her ever since they'd left London. *It's too dangerous; it gives people power over you. Just give them another name, a fun name, anything you like.* It had been a game she'd played—quite skillfully—for years. She'd worn so many names, played so many cons. She'd traded herself away in tiny little pieces with each lie, and now she had no idea what was left.

"Calliope isn't my real name," she said softly, so quietly that Avery had to lean forward to hear it beneath the drunken hum of the party. "It's Beth."

Avery's rage seemed to falter, as if that tiny grain of truth had momentarily stilled it. "I wouldn't have pegged you for a Beth," she said, which was an odd thing to say. Then fireworks erupted overhead, breaking the temporary spell. "Whoever you are, I don't care. You need to be gone before we get back to New York. If I ever see you in the Tower again, there will be hell to pay. Do you understand?"

Calliope clenched her jaw and stared unblinking at Avery. A flash of the old defiance scorched through her. "Trust me, you've made yourself clear," she snapped, and Avery stormed off.

And so it was ending, yet again. Calliope allowed herself a few minutes of melancholy—of gazing out at the water, wishing things were different, that she'd played her cards with better skill. Then she turned with a defeated sigh and started back toward the party.

She intended to enjoy the rest of the night. Not with Atlas, since Avery would surely be watching him, but with anyone, or even alone; it didn't matter. None of it mattered anymore. Tomorrow morning she would tell her mom the truth, and they would have to skip town as quickly and silently as possible.

Calliope wasn't particularly worried about the details. They'd fled many places in their day, and under worse circumstances than this; she knew they would get out all right. But after her mom's announcement, she'd allowed herself to hope that this time might actually be different. Now she felt strangely adrift, as if she'd been offered something bright and wonderful, only to have it snatched away.

At the thought of going to another city—doing recon work and starting another con and stealing from another trusting, hapless person—her entire body ached. She felt tired, and saddened, and alone.

For a moment she thought she heard a sound from far off, as if someone had cried out, echoing the mournful wail of Calliope's own heart. But when she listened again, it wasn't there.

She turned slowly, the elegant fishtail of her gown swishing out behind her. For one last night she was going to be Calliope Brown, consequences be damned.

WATT

WATT'S ARMS CLOSED around Leda from behind. "Where'd you disappear to?" he murmured into her hair, which smelled of dusty roses, a smell he'd grown quite accustomed to these past few weeks.

"I was off meddling," Leda said mischievously.

"Were you?" Watt released his arms to spin her around. She looked radiant, her face lit up from within, her whole being almost floating off the terrace where they stood.

"I'm trying to get Rylin back with Cord. It might take a while, though. They're both being a little stubborn."

"A few months ago, you were threatening Rylin, and now you've gone all Emma Woodhouse on her?" Watt was amused.

Leda tilted her head at him. "Am I mistaken, or did you just make a Jane Austen reference? Will wonders never cease."

"Hey, I can read!" Watt protested, though in truth, Nadia had fed him that line. He decided to change the subject. "Anyway, what makes you think you should be the one to decide whether Cord and Rylin are together?"

"Because I know best," Leda declared, as if it were self-evident.

"Because you enjoy playing puppeteer with other people's lives."

"Oh, please. Like you don't."

"Just because I *could* spend all my time spying on other people doesn't mean that I choose to do it. I usually end up offloading my surveillance on Nadia. You'd be surprised how boring it can be."

"Except for spying on me, of course," Leda quipped.

"Right, of course." Watt stifled a grin.

Nadia prompted him toward a garden on the far side of the terrace. It looked nice, so Watt took Leda's hand and led her there, down a pathway lined with trees and enormous flowering blossoms.

Bring up Eris, Nadia urged him. *Now is the right time.*

Not right now, Nadia. Okay?

This is your chance, Nadia insisted. *Don't you want to be free of Leda?*

Leda gave him a squeeze, her hand still clasped firmly in his, and Watt was no longer sure of anything.

He glanced at Leda, taking in her elegant profile, the impulsive way she moved in her flowing white dress, everything about her—her eyes, her hands, her mouth—softened in the dimness. He thought of all the different sides of Leda he'd come to know. Her ruthless, fierce determination; her aching vulnerabilities; her nightmares; her incredible brilliance. The one thing Leda Cole wasn't, he thought, was uncertain.

"You really do think you always know best, don't you?" he mused.

"I know I do," she countered.

"Well, then. If you know best, what should I be doing differently?" He'd framed the question as a joke, but suddenly, he was curious to know.

"Where do I begin? For starters, you could get rid of that terrible Nerd Nation T-shirt you always wear."

"I won that T-shirt in a science fair—" Watt began, but Leda was talking over him, ignoring the protest—

"You could pay a little more attention to your family." A new seriousness settled over her small, passionate face. "They really care about you, Watt. I can tell. And unlike mine, they would never lie to you."

That last comment made him inexplicably sad, but before he could press on it, Leda had shaken it off. Watt decided to let the moment pass.

"As for right now, you could start by kissing me," she concluded.

There was no disobeying a direct order.

Finally, they pulled away and turned deeper into the garden. Everything was silent. It felt to Watt like they were the only two people in the world. Leda seemed content not to say anything, just to tip her face up to the sky and breathe slowly.

"I lied," she said suddenly, and her voice was very small. Watt looked at her in confusion. "I don't always know best. Especially for myself. There are so many things I should have done differently."

"Leda, we've all made mistakes," Watt began.

She retreated a step, shaking her head. Watt realized that his hand felt cold without hers in it. He was shocked to see small tears gathering thickly in her lashes, sliding down her cheeks.

"You *saw* what I did, Watt. You know my mistakes are worst of all. I just wish . . ."

Here it is, Nadia said eagerly, as Watt pulled Leda close, folding her into his arms. He felt oddly nervous, and at the same time relieved that Leda was finally talking about that night, after all this time.

"Shh, it's okay," he murmured, running his hand lightly over her back. "It'll be okay, don't worry."

"I didn't mean to. You know that," Leda said, so quietly that he couldn't be sure what he'd heard. His heart skipped a beat.

Make her clarify, Nadia urged. *This isn't enough for evidence. Make her say the whole sentence.*

"You didn't mean to what?" Watt asked, hating himself, and yet saying it anyway, because the words were written right there, prompted by Nadia, and he was too shocked right now to formulate any words of his own.

Leda looked up at him, her eyes wide and trusting, brimming with tears. "Eris," she said simply. "You know I didn't mean to push her off. I just wanted her to back away—she kept trying to hug me, and after everything she did to me—I just wanted her to leave me alone." Her hand clutched his so tight he felt like the blood was being cut off. "It was an accident. I didn't mean for her to fall. I never, *ever* meant that."

Got it, Nadia declared, in evident satisfaction.

But Watt's human mind was snagging on Leda's words. "What do you mean, after everything she did to you?"

"You didn't know?" Leda asked. Watt shook his head dumbly. "I thought you knew everything." This time her words were completely devoid of sarcasm.

"I never really paid much attention to Eris," he said, which was true. Avery had always been the one he'd focused on.

Leda nodded, as if that made sense to her. "Eris was having an affair with my dad, before she died."

"What?" *Nadia, how did we miss that?*

Watt felt a sickening sensation of being trapped in something much bigger than he was. He'd fallen too deep, and now he was at the bottom of a bottomless black hole, and he couldn't come up for air.

Most of all, he felt an overwhelming sense of self-loathing. He'd tricked Leda into opening up her most private, vulnerable self to him—all so he could destroy her.

Leda reached for his hand, taking a shuddering breath. "I don't know why I brought this up. Let's go back to the party."

"I'm sorry, I just—" Watt snatched his hand away, ignoring Leda's startled look. *Don't send that footage anywhere, Nadia. Don't you do a damn thing regarding Leda without my approval, okay?*

"Watt? What's wrong?" Leda frowned, sounding puzzled, even *worried* for him. It killed him, that she was thinking about him at all after what he'd just done to her.

He took a step back, running a hand through his hair. He couldn't think, not with Leda so close, looking at him in that wide-eyed, wounded way. He felt dazed and shaky.

What had happened to him? When had he become the type of person who tried to trick other people into revealing their darkest secrets?

"I can't right now. I need to . . . I'm sorry," he mumbled, and ran off, steeling himself to the hurt that flashed across Leda's face.

LEDA

LEDA STOOD THERE in shock as Watt's figure retreated into the cresting night.

What the hell had just happened? She'd offered him her deepest and most dangerous truths—told him all the ugliness in her family, in *herself*—and he'd turned and run away.

She sank onto a suspended bench, propelling it with her heels to rock slowly back and forth. She was far from the party now, in some sort of multilevel botanic garden. Around a corner she heard the hushed voices of couples walking along the shadowed paths, stealing furtive kisses. Colored lanterns bobbed along in their wakes. She felt very distant from them.

Did Watt leave because of what she'd done to Eris? But he'd known that already—that was the nice thing about being with Watt, she'd thought, that they understood each other for who they were, and all their secrets.

Maybe Watt hadn't fully appreciated it until now. Maybe

when she bared her soul and he realized all the darkness that lay coiled there, he had realized he wanted no part of it.

Leda bit her lip, replaying the conversation in her mind, trying to determine what she'd done wrong. She felt strangely on edge. What was it about Watt that kept nagging at her? Hadn't there been something odd in his expression, his eyes . . . ?

He hadn't blinked. The realization came to her all at once, with an animalistic certainty. He'd been watching her the entire time without blinking, as if he'd been a cat patiently waiting for a mouse.

Had Watt been *filming* their conversation? she thought wildly.

Surely not, Leda's rational brain hastened to remind her—she would have noticed, would have heard Watt say "record video"; that was how contacts *worked*, after all. She closed her eyes, slightly comforted.

Except that Nadia was in his brain.

It had been so easy for Leda to forget Nadia's presence, to get caught up in the excitement of being at the party with Watt— but of course Nadia had been there the whole time, listening and recording and transmitting and god knows what else. Leda had no idea what Watt was even capable of, with Nadia inside his mind.

She curled her hand into a fist, so tight that the nails dug painfully into the flesh of her palm, but the pain was good: it kept her focused.

She thought of all the times Watt had seemed to watch her a little too closely, whenever anyone mentioned Eris. And he'd agreed to be her date to the Under the Sea party, and to rehab, so readily. She hadn't thought anything of it at the time, but it was strange, wasn't it, that he hadn't put up any sort of a fight? Could he have actually been playing her the whole time—getting close to her in the hopes that something like this would happen, that Leda would eventually get drunk and trusting, and admit the truth?

Leda reached up to wipe away a tear. She shouldn't really be surprised. But it hurt more than she would have guessed, realizing that all time they'd spent together had been a lie.

How stupid of her, to think that Watt could care about her for real. She didn't even blame him for wanting revenge. She would have done the same, if their roles were reversed. Hadn't she said more than once that she and Watt were cut from the same cloth?

An old familiar instinct for self-preservation was stirring, urging her to fight fire with fire—to use every weapon in her arsenal to destroy Watt, before he could destroy her—but Leda found that she didn't have the heart. Besides, with that quant in his brain he'd probably already sent her confession video to the police. They might be coming for her right now.

Leda felt a heavy dullness settling over her, turning her entire body to lead. Perhaps it was resignation. Or despair. Leda Cole had never been resigned to anything before, but then, she'd never met anyone who could best her, until Watt.

To think that she'd found the one boy in the world who was her equal, and fallen for him; yet in typical Leda Cole fashion, she'd managed to make him her sworn enemy.

She got up and trudged toward the nearest bar—a lonely table set up among the lemon trees near the edge of the garden path. It was so remote from the party that it felt as if someone, maybe providence, had brought it here in her hour of need. She might be heading to prison tomorrow, after all. Might as well enjoy her last few hours as a free woman.

"Whiskey soda," Leda said automatically as she approached. "And another after that."

The bartender looked up at her, and for some reason Leda's brain sparked in recognition. "Have we met?" she asked.

The girl shrugged. "I work at Altitude. My name's Mariel." She began to mix the cocktail with quick, practiced motions.

"And now you're here?" Leda was still confused.

"The Fullers imported some of the Altitude staff to work this party. Pretty over-the-top, huh?"

"Oh." Leda hadn't heard about that, but it sounded like the Fullers.

"Are you here alone?" The other girl slid the drink across the bar with a raised eyebrow.

"At the moment, yes." Leda frowned down at the glass, which was a dark, opaque black. "This cup is seriously morbid," she pointed out. It looked like a goblet that lost souls would drink from in hell. As black as all her secrets, she thought, taking a gulp. The whiskey had an astringent bite she didn't recognize.

"Sorry. All they gave me was black and white." Mariel pulled out a white glass, but Leda shook her head; it wasn't worth the bother. "Well, Leda, no one should drink alone at a party like this," Mariel insisted, and fixed a drink for herself.

Had she told this girl her name? Leda startled, a little confused. The whiskey was hitting her faster than she thought. She felt a little like she was going to be sick, but she couldn't decide whether that was the drink, or the thought of her confession video playing on all the global newsfeeds.

For a moment, Leda thought she caught a glimpse of something eager and intent in Mariel's gaze. It puzzled her. She set down her half-empty drink to look up at the sky. It glowed with stars, scattered about like tiny pinpricks of something fervent and bright. Hope, maybe.

But Leda knew there was no hope for her. She picked up the black goblet and braced herself for another sip of the biting whiskey, hoping it would obliterate the pain of what Watt had done.

AVERY

AVERY HURRIED, BREATHLESS, toward the pulsing star in her field of vision that was leading her to Atlas. Thank god he'd never turned off location sharing, even after everything they'd said to each other. She made her way through crowds draped all in black and white; the only spots of color their paintsticked faces, a discordant blur against the darkness. Avery pushed past all of it, heading toward that pulsing light as if it were her own personal North Star leading her home.

She turned a corner and saw with relief that yes, he was right there, beneath the shining yellow star inscribed on her contacts. He was frowning slightly, deep in conversation with their father and a group of investors. Avery reached up to smooth her hair, adjust the fine lace at her neckline, before venturing over.

"Atlas. I need to talk to you." She saw her dad flinch a little at the request, but it didn't matter. None of it mattered, as long as she and Atlas had each other.

His eyes swept toward her for a moment, then away. "We're kind of busy right now."

The dismissal hurt, but she let it go. "Please."

Atlas wavered for a moment, then gave some excuse to the group and followed her a distance away. "What's going on?" he hissed, but she didn't answer, just led him determinedly downward, to lower and still lower terraces, until they were at a gateway marked NO ACCESS. She pushed it open and dragged Atlas onto the small, grim, dingy balcony behind it, crowded with machinery and jutting directly over the canal. The rush of water beneath them was loud in her ears.

"Think we're far enough yet?" Atlas demanded sarcastically.

She hated how hostile he sounded—not like Atlas at all, but some stranger inhabiting his body. Ignoring the question, Avery grabbed the collar of his shirt and pulled him roughly down to kiss him.

He was still her Atlas, she saw with relief: same mouth, same hands, same shoulders as ever. She slid her hands over those shoulders to twine up in his hair, at the back of his neck where it curled, just a little. *I love you so much, and I'm sorry.*

Atlas pulled away, shaking his head. "This isn't fair," he said, his voice only a little shaky. "You can't be furious with me for weeks and then just decide to kiss me here, at the most crowded party of our lives."

"I'm sorry," she whispered.

"What's going on with you, Avery? What happened to prompt . . . this?" Atlas made an impatient gesture, taking in her mutilated dress, her tangled hair. The kiss.

She told herself not to panic that he'd called her Avery and not Aves. "There's something you need to know about Calliope. She's not what she seems." That sounded a bit theatrical, so she tried again. "She's a fraud, Atlas—she's been lying to you this whole time, playing you. She doesn't even *like* you."

"What are you talking about?"

"She and her mom are . . ." She fumbled for the right word. *Con artists* sounded like something out of a bad holo. "Operators. They use people for their money, then move on to a new place, with a new identity."

Carefully, haltingly, Avery explained the whole thing. She told Atlas about Calliope's various aliases, her mom's arrest record; she sent him the pics that Leda had found, of all their many identities. Through it all he just nodded silently, scarcely blinking.

"Shit," Atlas muttered when she finally fell silent. He shook his head in disbelief, his brown eyes glazed over.

"I know. I'm so sorry." She wasn't really, though. She wanted Calliope gone, and Atlas back, and the world restored to its rightful order.

"How did you learn all this?"

Avery reached for his hand, lacing his fingers in hers. "I just did. I can't explain, but I promise it's all true."

A murmured cry rose up from the crowds above them as another round of fireworks began to launch. Avery didn't glance away from Atlas's face. He was very quiet, thinking everything over. He seemed lost in a world of his own making.

"Don't worry," she said softly, a little concerned by his silence. "I already told her to leave. And if she doesn't, we'll *make* her. We can do anything, together."

Atlas withdrew his hand from hers in a sudden, jerky motion. "*We* aren't going to do anything. I'll handle this on my own."

"Atlas—"

"Please don't. This is hard enough already." He was looking determinedly at the water, which unnerved her, because it meant he couldn't even bear to look her in the eyes. Fireworks erupted in great black-and-white bursts overhead, casting otherworldly shadows that danced across his face.

"I'm a little stunned, to be honest. And pissed off. Not that

386

anything has happened between me and Calliope," Atlas added, which made Avery's heart leap eagerly. "But I'm still exhausted," he went on, his words heavy. "I need to get away from this—from all of it."

"Exactly. We can get away together, you and me, like we planned!" Avery exclaimed. Now that Leda was back on her side, and wanted to help her, there was nothing keeping them apart anymore.

But Atlas shook his head. "We were right to end things when we did. We tried, but no matter how hard we try, we haven't been able to make it work." He gave Avery a look that terrified her. "Do you know what Dad named the hotel in the dark Tower?"

"Fanaa." A sudden panic was creeping over her skin.

"It means destroying yourself for the one you love." Atlas spoke urgently. "That's *us*, Avery. Don't you see? We're literally destroying each other. It's too complicated, and there are too many people who can be hurt. Especially you and me."

"So you don't love me anymore." That was the only explanation that made sense. How could he love her and not want to be with her?

"Of course I love you," Atlas insisted. "I'll always love you. But love isn't necessarily enough. You can't build a life on it."

"Yes, you can!" Avery cried out, her voice pitching wildly.

"I'm just trying to be realistic," Atlas said, and the reasonable way he spoke made her want to shake his shoulders and scream. "What do you think we're actually going to do, go live on that remote island, just the two of us?"

"Yes, exactly!"

"And what happens when you're sick of it—when walking around that small island and reading books and eating fish isn't enough for you anymore?" he asked quietly.

"I'll have *you*. And you'll be enough."

"I don't know if I am." Atlas's voice cracked, but she pretended not to hear it. "Honestly, I'm scared. I'm scared of losing you. But I'm even more scared of forcing you down a path you don't want to be on."

"You're not forcing me to do anything!" Avery protested, but it was as if he hadn't heard.

"You're incredible, Aves," Atlas said softly. "You're far too intelligent and talented, too remarkable, to spend your life shut away from the entire world. You belong *in* the world, laughing and traveling, having friends. You deserve to see everything the world has to offer, and I can't give you any of that."

"You and I can have all those things. We'll make friends, and travel," Avery started to say, but he was shaking his head.

"And be looking over our shoulder every moment in case someone recognized us, in constant fear of being caught? No, Vermont showed me that's pretty much impossible."

Avery's voice was almost a whisper. "I don't care about any of that. I would trade it all to be with you."

Atlas surprised her by taking her hands, clasping them together and wrapping his own hands tight around them. "I know you mean that when you say it now. But I'm terrified of the moment in five years when you turn to me and regret the choice you made. By then it might be too late for you to go back."

Atlas's breath was ragged. He looked close to tears. Instinctively, Avery knew that she couldn't let him cry in front of her, for his sake. She took a step back, her own eyes brimming with grief, and waited.

"Don't you see? It can't ever work for us. I'm just saving us heartache, down the road," Atlas said at last.

Here it is, Avery thought with dreadful certainty. This was really and truly the end.

She couldn't take it anymore—she flung herself into Atlas's arms and kissed him, over and over, and this time Atlas returned the kisses, returned them wildly and passionately, and it made Avery's heart break because she knew deep down that he was kissing her good-bye. She clung tighter to him, pressing her body the whole length of his, trying to hold him so close that he could never leave, as if she might anchor him here through sheer force of will. She wished she could snatch each kiss from the air and tuck it away somewhere safe, because each kiss was one kiss closer to the final kiss of all.

When they finally pulled apart, neither of them spoke. The river rushed on below them. The sounds of the party emanated down as if from another world.

"Okay then," she said at last, her voice small, because it seemed like one of them should say something.

"Okay then," Atlas repeated.

Tears gathered in Avery's eyes, but she swallowed them back. She needed to be strong right now, for Atlas's sake. So she held back the tears and nodded shakily, even though it cost her more than Atlas would ever know; even though it felt like someone was holding a razor and inflicting a million small cuts all over her skin.

Atlas started to turn away, but paused as if thinking better of it, and reached out to touch Avery one last time. He tucked a strand of hair behind her ear, traced the line of her jaw, brushed a finger lightly over her lower lip. As if he were blind, and trying to recognize her through nothing but his fingertips.

Avery closed her eyes. She concentrated on memorizing his touch, wanting to stop time and stop the world and hold on to this moment forever, because as long as her eyes were closed, she could believe that Atlas was still here. Still hers.

"I'm sorry, Aves, but I promise it's better this way," he said, and then he was gone.

Avery stood there awhile, her eyes firmly shut, just herself and her secrets and her heartbreak alone in the dark.

CALLIOPE

CALLIOPE HAD BEEN dancing and laughing for hours with an almost frantic intensity, keeping an eye out for the Fuller siblings as she made her way through the party, though she hadn't seen either of them in a while. She took occasional sips from a glass of champagne. The wine tasted sour in her mouth.

All too soon the night would be over, and Calliope would have to confess the truth to her mom: that she'd screwed everything up and they needed to leave, because Avery Fuller knew about them. Still, she sailed on through the crowds, her bright red mouth fixed in an inflexible smile.

She knew she was delaying the inevitable, but Calliope wanted to put off the conversation with her mom for as long as she could. Because once she said it—once she spoke the words aloud—Calliope Brown would be dead. *Here lies Calliope Brown, as beautiful as she was vicious. She died without anyone ever truly knowing her*, she thought bitterly.

For once, making up an epitaph for her lost alias wasn't particularly amusing.

She turned a wide loop around the dance floor, wondering if Elise might already be asleep, when she saw a couple on a terrace far below. Something about them seemed familiar, though they were too far away for Calliope to tell. They were ducked behind a NO ACCESS sign, where they probably thought they had utter privacy—and they would have, if not for her. No one else was looking in that direction.

For lack of anything better to do, Calliope craned her neck and zoomed in with her contacts. She was startled to realize that it was Avery and Atlas Fuller.

Avery had tilted her head up, and was talking emphatically to Atlas about something. Probably telling him the truth about Calliope and Elise.

Seized by a morbid sort of curiosity, Calliope zoomed in closer—and became aware of something distinctly odd that was going on between the siblings. The expressions on both their faces, the proprietary way that Avery stepped toward him, lifted the hairs on the back of Calliope's neck.

And then, to Calliope's shock, they flung their bodies together and kissed.

At first Calliope assumed she'd been mistaken. But the more she zoomed, the more certain she felt that it was definitely Avery and Atlas. She watched in fascinated horror as the kiss went on and on, Avery rising up on tiptoe, her hands in Atlas's hair.

Calliope blinked her vision back to normal and looked away. She took a few deep breaths, a dull roar echoing through her scorched brain. It all made an awful, twisted kind of sense.

She remembered Atlas telling her that he'd run away to Africa because he'd gotten himself into a "complicated mess." She remembered the bitter resentment Avery had shown her that morning after the Under the Sea party when she'd realized that Calliope had slept over. Even the way Avery and Atlas talked about each other, the way they always seemed to have a radar on what the other was doing; Calliope had assumed that was just excessive sibling fondness, but clearly it was so much more. All the pieces were fitting together into the truth, like shards of a warped, broken mirror that couldn't possibly depict reality. Except it did.

She stood there for a while, listening to the wind whistle around the corners of this extravagant tower—you could barely hear it beneath the music and gossip and laughter, but it was there. Calliope imagined that the wind was angry at being ignored. She understood the feeling.

She leaned forward on the railing, thinking of Avery and all the threats she'd delivered earlier, and smiled. There was nothing soft in the expression; it was a cold, calculating smile, a smile of victory. Because Calliope was done being pushed around by any of the Fullers.

So Avery Fuller wanted to play games. Well, Calliope could play games too. She'd played with the best of them, all over the world, and she had no intention of losing, now that she had something on Avery—something just as dangerous as what Avery had on her. She knew what she'd seen, and how she could use it to her advantage.

Avery could protest all she liked, but Calliope wasn't going anywhere. She was in New York to stay.

LEDA

HOLY SHIT, **LEDA** thought in a blurred daze. What was happening?

She was walking with the Altitude waitress—Miriam . . . Mariane . . . no, Mariel, she remembered, that was it. The other girl had one hand around Leda's waist and another on her forearm, closed tight around her like a vise. Somehow they'd walked along a service road far upstream of The Mirrors, and were down by the ocean. The dark waters of the Persian Gulf were there on her right, looking cold and implacable. Leda glanced around in every direction, but didn't see anyone.

"I want to go back to the party." She tried to pull on Mariel's arm, but the other girl was dragging her stubbornly forward. She looked down at her feet and realized they were bare. "What happened to my shoes?"

"We took them off, because you couldn't walk in them on the sand," Mariel said patiently.

"But I don't want to be on the sand. I want to go back to the party."

"Let's sit for just a minute," Mariel suggested instead, in a low, soothing voice. "You're too drunk to go back to the party."

It was true. Leda felt sleepy and disoriented, all her neurons firing at quarter-speed. Her feet tripped sluggishly down the beach toward the water. The wind whipped around them, its fingers reaching up into Leda's hair to tear her curls loose, but Leda hardly felt it. How had she gotten this smashed? The last thing she remembered was having that drink with Mariel . . . surely she'd had more than one, otherwise she wouldn't feel this way . . .

"Here." Mariel tried to guide Leda down a steep slope toward the shore. Leda shook her head in mute protest. She didn't want to step that close to the water. Its black surface caught the moonlight and reflected it back at her, shining and opaque, making it impossible to gauge its depths. "Come *on*, Leda," Mariel insisted, her tone brooking no argument, and pinched Leda's side through her filmy gown.

"Hey," Leda protested. She half slipped, half fell down the sand dune, landing on her side. She tried to stand, but wasn't strong enough. She gritted her teeth and just managed to push herself into a seated position.

A few buildings rose up out of the darkness like primordial monsters, full of angry-looking machinery and hydrojets. Leda suddenly longed for the pulse and laughter of the party. She didn't like this. What had happened to Watt? Did he know where she was?

"Here we go," Mariel said, trying to scoot Leda closer to the water. Leda shrank back uneasily, but the other girl was much stronger. One of Leda's bare toes accidentally touched a wave, and she let out a yelp. It was ice cold. Wasn't this a tropical ocean? Or was she so drunk she couldn't feel anything properly anymore?

"We need to talk. It's about Eris." Mariel's eyes bored into Leda's.

Something wasn't right. Every instinct in Leda's body was screaming at her to run away, to get out; but she couldn't move, she was trapped in this strange place as Mariel crouched there next to her.

"How do you know Eris?" she asked, and something menacing glittered in Mariel's eyes.

"She was my friend," the other girl said slowly.

"Mine too," Leda slurred. Her mouth found it difficult to form sentences.

"But what happened the night she died?" Mariel pressed. "I know she didn't fall. She wasn't even drunk. What happened that you aren't telling me?"

Leda burst into sudden tears—angry, ugly sobs that racked her body. She marveled at the clarity of her own emotion. What was happening to her? She was long past drunk; she was high, maybe, but this was unlike any drug she'd ever taken, as if she'd become detached from her own body and was hovering far above it. She was suddenly very afraid. Watt's face kept swimming up in her consciousness, the eerie way he'd listened to her confession, without blinking. He hadn't hesitated to hurt her. He didn't care about her. No one cared about her. She didn't deserve to be cared about.

"It's okay, Leda. I'm here," Mariel was saying, over and over, the repetition vaguely soothing. "I'm listening. It's okay."

"I want my mom," Leda heard herself say. She wanted to run into Ilara's arms, the way she had when she was little, and admit what she'd done. *My sweet Leda,* her mom would always say, tucking Leda's hair behind her ear, *you're too stubborn for your own good. Don't you understand that things won't always go your way?* And then her mom would punish her, but Leda always accepted it, because she knew there was love behind the punishment.

"It wasn't my fault," she whispered now, as if her mom were right here and listening. Her eyes were closed.

"What do you mean?"

"They were all there, Watt and Avery and Rylin. They knew it was dangerous. They should have pulled me away from the edge, shouldn't have let Eris get so close. I didn't mean to push her!"

"You pushed Eris off the roof?"

"I told you, it was an *accident*!" Leda cried out, rasping. A fire seemed to be kindling in her head, flames licking at the inside of her brain, where Watt kept his computer. She imagined the blaze burning everything, leaving nothing in its wake but ash.

"How did you keep the others from telling the police, if they were up there?" Mariel was shaking with disgust.

"I knew things about them. I told them that they had to keep my secret, or I wouldn't keep theirs." In utter horror, Leda heard herself telling Mariel everything. About Avery and Atlas. About Rylin stealing from Cord. And worst of all, Watt's secret, that he had an illegal quantum computer lodged in his brain.

Some dazed part of Leda knew that she shouldn't be saying these things; but she couldn't help it, it was as if someone else was saying the words, as if they were being pulled out of her of their own volition.

"You people are even worse than I thought," Mariel said at last, when Leda was through.

"Yes." Leda moaned, knowing she deserved this, welcoming it.

"You should never have brought Eris into all this. It wasn't fair," Mariel hissed, and Leda could hear the naked hatred in her voice. Mariel despised her.

A wounded stubbornness elbowed its way to the forefront of Leda's mind. "Yeah, right. Eris was part of it too," she protested. "She was fucking my dad, after all."

Mariel was deathly silent.

Leda tried to rise to her feet, but her body wasn't working properly, and she crashed violently to the ground. Her legs were bent at an awkward angle beneath her. The sand felt rough and grainy on her cheek. She closed her eyes, wincing at the pain, tears blurring her vision, but it had already been blurred anyway. "Please. Help me get back," she croaked. She still didn't understand how she'd gotten this drunk. "How many drinks did I *have*?"

Mariel leaned over her. Her face was as hard and unyielding as if it had been carved from stone. "Just the one. But I drugged it."

What? Why? Leda wanted to ask, but pushed that aside in favor of her more immediate problem. "Please, help me get back." The water was so close, and the tide was rising, creeping toward her with ice-cold fingers. She could see it, like a dangerous black mirror, as full of secrets as her own black heart.

No, she thought, she didn't have any secrets anymore, she'd given them all away. Even the ones that weren't hers to give.

Mariel laughed, a sharp laugh that had no mirth in it. The sound was like a million small slaps to Leda's face. "Leda Cole. You really think I'm helping you go back so that you can keep screwing with other people's lives? You *killed* the girl I loved."

"I didn't mean to . . ." Leda tried to say, but she wasn't sure if she'd really spoken the words, or just thought them. Her eyes were too heavy to keep open. Her hand was touching the water, but she couldn't move it. She felt a distant twinge of panic, imagining the water slowly flowing over her whole body, its darkness pulling insistently toward the matching darkness inside her.

"Before I leave, there's one thing you should know. Eris wasn't having an affair with your dad." Mariel spoke slowly, each word delivered with frosty clarity. "She was spending time with him, yes, but not for the reason you think. Which just goes to show how bad a person you are, that you assume the worst of people."

The words seemed to be coming from very far away, and Leda was falling, but with every last force of her being she listened, reaching up to hear what Mariel was saying, because it frightened her; and because she could hear the truth behind the hatred, ringing with the force of a gong.

"Your dad was Eris's dad too. You killed your sister, Leda," Mariel spat.

And then Leda did fall into the blackness, and there was nothing more.

WATT

WATT HAD BEEN looking for Leda for an hour now.

He'd circled the entire party at least three times, barreling clumsily into the thick of the dance floor, edging through the gardens alongside the Tower to check whether Leda might be in there. He'd gone upstairs to check the hotel room, but it was empty. Desperate, he'd even flickered Avery to ask whether she'd seen Leda, but Avery hadn't answered.

Normally, of course, he would've just gotten Nadia to hack Leda's contacts and determined her location that way. But her contacts feed was blank, which meant that wherever she was, Leda was asleep or passed out. *Or dead*, some horrible voice in him whispered, which he studiously ignored.

Any update, Nadia? She was doggedly searching through the contact feeds of everyone at the party, keeping an eye out for any hint of where Leda had gone.

This was all his fault. If he hadn't run away from Leda when she opened up to him, none of this would have happened. He couldn't imagine how rejected she must have felt—confiding in him, only to have him turn and disappear.

"Actually, I might," Nadia replied, and Watt sprung to alertness.

"I'm not sure it's Leda," Nadia hastened to assure him. "But there's a girl passed out on the beach, a couple kilometers north of the party. Someone just filed an anonymous report to security, saying the person was a threat."

A threat? Who would have reported that about Leda? Watt had already started running toward the northern exit. *When will security get there?*

"They haven't mobilized yet. I intercepted the report before it hit their monitors. Do you want me to wipe it from the log?"

Watt closed his eyes against the wind, feeling a cold sweat break out at his hairline. He had a terrible feeling that something had happened, something awful that Leda wouldn't want security to see. He remembered their visit to rehab, how well her recovery was going. If she'd done drugs tonight, and the Fullers' Dubai security brought her in, her parents would send Leda back to rehab for sure—and probably to a more intense place this time. Somewhere that Watt would never get to see her.

And if she'd truly done something threatening, she would need his help.

He felt suddenly selfish. What if Leda was in real danger, and by holding off the security bots, he risked her life?

"Watt?" Nadia prompted.

Keep it cloaked from security for now, he told Nadia, hoping he wouldn't regret this. *What's the fastest way to the girl's location?*

Nadia directed his gaze to a stray hoverboard that lay propped at the edge of the party. Watt had never ridden one of these before—they were an expensive highlier toy, but how hard could it be? He grabbed the board. It beeped in momentary protest, since it was registered to a different thumbprint and voice ID, but Nadia quickly hacked it, and the tiny micromotors whizzed to life. Ghostly arrows overlaid his field of vision, like some kind of real-life video game quest.

Watt inclined his weight onto his toes and the board leapt forward, responding to the command. He tried to make it go faster, but it bucked upward. He cursed under his breath.

Nadia, can you drive? Nadia obediently took over the hoverboard's directional system, pushing the board to max speed as it skimmed forward, just centimeters above the uneven surface of the ground.

The wind tore at his hair and the fabric of his tux, stinging Watt's eyes so hard that he was forced to close them, trusting everything to Nadia, but it wouldn't be the first time. He held his breath and crouched lower on the board, letting his fingers trace blindly along its aerodynamic surface.

Finally, it came to a stop and Watt half tumbled off. There she was—Leda, looking like some strange version of herself, crumpled unnaturally on the sand. Her white dress fanned around her like an angel's wings, a sharp contrast to her smooth dark skin. Her legs were already partially submerged in the rising tide of the ocean.

Oh god, oh god, he thought, scrambling down to pull Leda into his arms; and then his heart leapt with joy, because she was shivering, and that at least meant she was alive.

"Why is she freezing like this?" he said aloud, rubbing his hands on Leda's bare shoulders to create some friction, but her head tipped back alarmingly, forcing him to cradle it in one hand. "Is it the ocean?" He trailed one hand in the water, but it was a pleasant, tropical lukewarm, just as he'd expected.

"I believe she's taken some drugs," Nadia was saying. "I

would need a med-bot to do a full exam, but whatever they are, they've severely constricted her arteries. She's not getting any blood to her extremities."

Watt shrugged off his tux jacket and wrapped it around Leda like a cocoon. He cradled Leda in his arms and began to carry her back to the hoverboard, one hand still placed carefully behind her neck and the other under her knees. He managed to settle her sloppily onto the board, curling her on her side and then strapping her down with the emergency safety cord.

"Nadia," he said hoarsely, "how are we going to get her back?"

"We'll smuggle her into the hotel on the hover. Leave that part to me."

Into Watt's mind came the sudden realization that he and Nadia had gotten it all wrong. He'd set out to change Leda's opinion of him, but he was the one whose mind had ended up changing, about her.

What was it she'd said all those weeks ago? "We're the same, Watt, you and me." And she'd been right. He *knew* Leda, not just physically but mentally, emotionally—hell, he might know her better than he knew anyone else in his life. She was maddening and stubborn and tormented and deeply flawed, but so was he, and maybe the important thing wasn't finding someone without flaws, but just someone whose flaws complemented your own.

The hoverboard started toward the hotel, moving more slowly now, to keep Leda from falling off. Watt took off running in its wake.

"You really care about her, don't you?" Nadia asked him, oddly subdued.

Yeah. Watt couldn't believe it had taken a life-or-death crisis for him to realize it, but he really did.

AVERY

AVERY HAD LEFT the party. She'd returned to the hotel, but once she walked in the enormous entrance, all curved, carved stone and glittering tiles, she'd found that she wasn't ready to go upstairs. She didn't want to face her cold, solitary bed; a bed that would never have Atlas in it again. The prospect of a life without him stretched before her, empty and bleak and impossibly, torturously long.

She wandered over to the dramatic windows of the hotel lobby and stood there awhile, just looking out into the endless black of the sky. The stars were so bright here. She wondered when the next round of fireworks would begin.

An arrangement of mood-flowers on a table near her began to glow; stupid things never worked, Avery thought, because they were flashing a hot angry red when all she really felt was hollow. She kept working on her drink without registering what it was. Behind her she occasionally heard voices, the click of heels on the polished floor as people moved through the lobby on the way to their rooms.

Everything that had happened tonight—learning the truth about Calliope, confronting her, and then, worst of all, the way Atlas had told her good-bye, with that aching finality in his voice—had all left Avery strangely empty. Her mind had become a swirling, churning vortex with no bottom. She took another sip of her drink, hoping it would fill the void that threatened to break her in two.

"Avery?"

"Hey," she said, not even turning at the sound of Cord's voice. She just kept looking at the dark stretch of water below them, the bridges spanning the space, dotted with lights. Party guests moved back and forth across in a dance of scattered shadows. She wondered how many of them were with the person they loved tonight—and how many of them were alone, like her.

"What are you doing here?" he asked. She knew what he meant. What was she doing standing by herself, in the dim light of the window?

"Where have you been all night?" she asked, since she hadn't seen much of him.

Cord shrugged. "I only just got here. Guess I'm a little late to the party. It's a long story," he added, in answer to her questioning look, "but I was with Brice."

Avery nodded. They were both silent for a while, the only sound the occasional murmur of hotel guests, and the distant strains of music.

She couldn't stop thinking about Atlas, about the look on his face when he'd told her that they were through. She wanted to drown that memory out, pound it into oblivion until there was nothing left of it. She'd thought that alcohol would help, but all it had managed to do was sharpen her melancholy. She wondered if she would ever be able to forget.

"Avery, are you okay?" Cord asked. Startled, Avery turned to look at Cord—*really* look at him.

Driven by some foreign impulse, she rose up to kiss him.

For an instant Cord tensed, startled, not kissing her back. Then one of his hands was cradling her head, and the other was curled around her waist, and they felt scaldingly good on her numb, cold skin. The kiss was rough and insistent, a little frantic.

"Avery. What was that?" Cord finally asked, stepping away.

"I'm sorry . . ." Avery tried not to feel panicked, but the moment Cord's lips had left hers, the darkness was back, worse than before—tugging relentlessly at the corners of her mind, dragging her down into its endless, terrible depths.

She wasn't sure why she'd kissed Cord. Some logical part of her knew that there were plenty of reasons she should stay away. He was her friend, and it would ruin the friendship. And, of course, the biggest reason of all: she loved Atlas. But Atlas no longer wanted her, which was the only reason she was here with Cord, instead of in his arms.

No matter what she did right now, Atlas would still be gone.

She leaned in again, knowing she might regret this, knowing she was playing with fire, just as a message from Leda danced before the backs of her closed eyelids.

Where are you?

Avery hesitated. She didn't know what had prompted it, but the message was enough to make her step away—like a cosmic stroke of fate, protecting her from doing something with Cord that she could never turn back from.

Cord looked startled. He knew her so well. Avery wondered if he could read her right now, could see how hurt she was, how close she'd almost come to kissing him again.

"I'm sorry, but I need to go," she whispered, and ran toward the elevator bank without looking back.

RYLIN

WHAT A FANTASTIC night it had been, Rylin reflected as she walked through the enormous entrance to the hotel lobby. She couldn't decide which part had been her favorite. She'd listened to the music for a while, and wandered across the beautiful bridges. She and Leda had perched at a table to eat three full martini glasses of the bacon risotto. She'd even danced with a few of her classmates, the girls from English class she sometimes ate lunch with. Truthfully, the whole night had been perfect, except for the fact that she'd never found Cord. She wondered if for some reason he hadn't come, after all.

Rylin didn't feel too disappointed, though. They would see each other again soon enough, when they were both back in the Tower.

She'd started toward the hotel's private elevator bank when a shadow moved in her peripheral vision, and something about it gave her pause.

It was Cord. He was over by the windows with Avery Fuller; the two of them alone in the dimly lit, deserted lobby. Of course she would see Cord when she was least expecting it. Rylin swayed in her heels, debating whether to go say hi—

And then her body went cold all over as Avery leaned up to kiss him.

They stood there, their faces pressed together, clinging to each other. Rylin wanted desperately to look away but she couldn't; some cruel masochistic instinct forced her to watch. Her blood pounded through her body, close to the surface of her skin, like liquid fire. Or maybe liquid pain.

Then Rylin realized how she looked, just standing there watching Cord and Avery like a complete fool; and what if they glanced up to see her? She had the presence of mind to dart toward the elevator bank, where she began hitting the button furiously, blinking back tears.

How funny hearts were, Rylin thought, that she wasn't dating Cord—had no claim on him anymore—yet this hurt her as much as ever. More so, even, now that she knew the girl he'd chosen over her.

She'd been stupid to think that she could ever truly belong in this world. Oh, they let her attend their school, show up at their parties, but she wasn't one of them. Rylin realized with a startling clarity that she never would be. No matter how hard she tried.

Why would a boy like Cord ever pick a girl like Rylin, when he could have Avery Fuller?

LEDA

LEDA SCREAMED AND kept running down the corridor. It went on and on, no doors or end in sight, just the jagged floor beneath her and the shadows chasing her, flapping their great dusty wings above her face. They looked like harpies, scratching her with her claws, cackling maliciously. Leda recognized them for what they were.

They were all her secrets.

Her cruelty to Avery, her bitterness toward her father, the things she'd done to Watt . . . every last one of her misdeeds, her years of meddling and spying and plotting all coming home to roost at last . . . and foremost among them was what she'd done to Eris.

The harpies came closer, scratching at her face. They drew blood. Leda fell to her knees, wailing, and threw her hands up—

A sudden wetness on her face jostled her awake. She rubbed at her eyes. They stung a little. She put her hands below her, feeling the unfamiliar, lumpy surface. She was on a couch some-where.

"Leda! You're awake!"

Watt's face appeared before her, his strong jaw dusted with a shadow of stubble. "You've been out for hours. What happened? Nadia hacked a med-bot, got it to deliver adrenaline, which we've been feeding you in small doses—she thought you might be get-ting close to waking just now, which is why I threw the water on you—"

Poor Watt, Leda thought drowsily, he always rambled when he got anxious. It was so endearing.

And then her mind flagged to sudden, violent alert as she remembered. Watt couldn't be trusted—Watt was the enemy.

"Let me go!" she shouted, though it came out raspy and bro-ken. She tried to stand up only to tumble toward the floor instead. Watt swooped down and caught her.

"Shh, Leda, it's okay," he murmured, settling her back on the cushions, but not before she'd gotten a look at their surroundings. They were in their hotel room in the Moon Tower. She regretted not booking Watt his own room, the way she'd done for rehab. Where could she escape now?

"What happened?" he asked again.

Leda reached deep within herself, gathering every last shred of her strength. It wasn't much, because she felt as though she'd been crunched beneath the weight of the Tower itself. But she managed to lean back, her eyes half closed; and then in a quick, sudden motion she shot her fist upward toward Watt's head.

It hit his skull with a satisfying, resounding crack, right where she'd been aiming—at the spot where Nadia was implanted.

Watt yelped, momentarily blinded by pain. Leda took advan-tage of his confusion, pushing herself up and trying to run away—she staggered a few steps but the world spun off-kilter, the ground veering dangerously upward, and she fell heavily back to the carpet.

"What the hell, Leda! Next time your head might hit a table, okay?"

This time Watt kept his distance, crouching a few meters from where she lay on her side. He seemed to know better than to try to help her.

Slowly Leda sat up. Her head was pounding, and her mouth felt dry. The brightness hurt her eyes, and she lifted a hand to shade them, but the room was already growing dimmer. She looked sharply at Watt—she hadn't seen him make any motions for the room comp—then realized that, of course, his damned supercomputer had done it.

"I hate you," she managed to say, through her pain and her violent, rending grief. "Go to hell, Watt."

"Whatever happened to you, I didn't do it. What do you remember?" he asked urgently.

Leda pulled her knees to her chest. She didn't care that her gorgeous white gown was ruined, ripped at the hem, smudged with dirt and blood. It didn't matter. All that mattered was that she was here, still breathing, still alive. That bitch left her for dead—wanted her to fall into the ocean and drown—yet she'd survived.

"Have you sent me to jail yet, or were you waiting till I was awake?" she snapped. "Don't lie to me anymore, Watt. I know your computer is in your brain. You were recording me earlier, when I told you about Eris. Weren't you?"

Watt stared at her in evident shock, the color draining from his face. He reached unconsciously up to that same spot on his head, as if to check whether Nadia was still there. "How did you know?"

"So you don't deny it?"

"No. I mean, yes, I *was* recording," he stammered, "but I'm not sending you to jail, Leda. I wouldn't do that to you."

"Why on earth should I believe you, when you've been pretending to care about me this whole time?"

"Because I do care about you," he said softly.

She narrowed her eyes, unconvinced.

"Leda, are these yours?" he went on, reaching for something on a table behind him. He held out a handful of cheap drug vials, the kind that people shot directly into their veins.

Leda shook her head. "I've never taken anything like that."

"They were in your pocket when we found you," Watt said slowly. She noticed the *we*, and realized that he meant himself and Nadia, and her anger flared up again. "If you didn't take these, what did you take last night?"

"I didn't *mean* to take anything," Leda protested. "It was a girl named Mariel. She drugged me . . ."

She remembered how Mariel had bragged about slipping something in her drink—it had to be truth juice, the inhibition-reducing "chattiness" drug that Leda had given Watt when she convinced him to tell her about Atlas and Avery, what felt like a lifetime ago. God, talk about karmic justice. Leda had offered Mariel all her secrets, which she'd protected so carefully for so long, as casually as if she'd been remarking on the weather. She shivered, recalling the look in Mariel's eyes when she'd left Leda for dead. And that awful, final thing Mariel had said about Eris, that Eris was Leda's half sister—could it be true?

Leda wanted to explain, but for some reason she'd started crying. She wrapped her arms around herself, trying to make herself impossibly small, to contain this loud, awful grief.

She was mourning everything she'd done, and everything she'd lost. She was mourning the Leda she had been, long ago, before drugs and Atlas and Eris's death. She wanted to go back in time—to shake some sense into that Leda, to *warn* her—but that Leda was long gone.

Watt's arms wrapped around her, and he pulled her close, his head tucked over her shoulder. "It's okay, we'll figure it out," he assured her. Leda closed her eyes, relishing the feeling of safety, even though she knew it was temporary.

"You aren't sending me to jail?" she asked, her voice strained.

"Leda, I meant what I said. I wouldn't do that. I'm . . ." Watt swallowed. "I'm falling for you."

"I'm falling for you too," Leda said quietly.

Watt leaned forward—carefully, as if still not certain whether she might hit him again—and kissed her.

When they pulled apart, the winds of the ice storm tearing through Leda's mind had settled into a bright cold clarity. She knew what she had to do.

"We need Rylin and Avery," she said.

"I actually already had Nadia send Avery a message from you, when I was really worried," Watt said, sounding a little embarrassed for hacking her contacts yet again. "She didn't come."

"Then it clearly wasn't urgent enough." Leda nodded and spoke aloud, sending a flicker. "To Avery and Rylin. SOS. Room 175."

Then she looked back at Watt. "We need to tell them what happened. Mariel knows."

"What exactly does she know?" Watt asked quietly, and Leda hated what she had to say next.

"Everything."

WATT

WATT GLANCED AROUND the living room of their hotel suite. It was filled with pristine white furniture, fluffy white carpets, delicate white side tables, and blindingly white couches that Watt was almost nervous to sit on. Right now Leda was nestled in the corner of the couch wearing an oversized sweater, her bare feet pulled up onto the cushions next to her. Nadia was still keeping an eye on her vitals, tracking the pulse in the curve of her throat, the temperature radiating from her slight form.

He'd watched, just now, as Leda sent the SOS message to Avery and Rylin. "What's going on?" he'd asked, but she just shook her head and insisted that they wait for the other two.

"They need to hear this. They're involved, whether they like it or not."

Nadia sent a message across his vision, and Watt looked up at Leda. "Nadia says you can take a sleeping pill later, if you want. Your heart rate has evened out enough that it should be safe."

"I don't take pills anymore. I haven't had a single one since that night," Leda replied, hugging a white-tasseled pillow to her chest. She looked at the spot over Watt's ear where Nadia had been implanted. "Nadia, you can talk to me directly, you know. You don't have to go through Watt."

"Very well," Nadia said, through the room's internal speaker system. It made Watt jump a little. Leda noticed the movement, and shrugged apologetically.

"Sorry, but I'd prefer that Nadia talk aloud when I'm here, if that's okay. I know by now that if I'm dating you, I'm dating Nadia too."

Dating, Watt mused, trying out the word to see how it fit. He'd never dated anyone before. He didn't even know how to start. Hopefully Leda would need as much of a learning curve as he did.

Before he could say anything, the doorbell sounded. Leda nodded, and the room comp allowed it to swing inward.

"What happened, Leda?" Rylin asked without preamble. She was wearing a simple black gown, and looked very drawn and pale.

"It's a long story. I'll tell you when Avery gets here," Leda promised the other girl, sitting up a little straighter.

"That might be a while." Rylin perched on an armchair in the corner, sitting just barely on the edge of the seat, as if she might at any point change her mind and run off.

It was so late that it was almost morning. The sky seen through the curved flexiglass window was still dark, though far in the horizon Watt could make out the first tentative blush of dawn, quartz and rose and the soft gold of aged champagne.

The doorbell sounded again. Watt started to go answer it, but Leda nodded once more, and Avery hurried forward into the room. Her hair tumbled riotously about her shoulders, and she was walking barefoot on the white tufted carpet, holding her delicate beaded shoes in one hand. She seemed disoriented.

Watt saw Rylin shoot Avery a look sizzling with resentment, but Avery didn't pick up on it. She just ran straight to Leda and threw her arms around her friend. "Oh my god, what happened? Are you okay?"

"I'm fine, Avery," Leda assured her, gently shrugging off Avery's embrace. "Thanks to Watt. He saved me."

Avery turned her clear blue eyes to Watt, startled, and gave a tentative smile. *I didn't save her for* you, Watt thought, but he didn't resent Avery anymore, so he gave her a silent nod of understanding. After all, they both cared about Leda.

Rylin was still staring unabashedly at Avery, her face a mask of hurt and wounded pride. Watt wondered what had happened between them.

"I'm sorry I had to call you all here, so late at night. But you need to know what happened, and it couldn't wait," Leda began. The pillow was still in her lap; she kept fidgeting with the fringe, pulling at it until the pieces began to unravel. "Tonight I was confronted by a girl named Mariel. She's out to get us. All of us."

"Who is she?" Avery's flawless features creased into a frown.

Leda winced as she spoke. "I think she was Eris's girlfriend. She works as a bartender at Altitude, and came here tonight as part of the catering team. Apparently she's been on some kind of vigilante quest to find out what happened the night Eris died. And I gave her exactly what she wanted."

Nadia was already working at top speed, trying to put together all the pieces of the puzzle in a complete file for Watt. *Get her to tell it all. In detail,* Nadia requested, speaking directly in Watt's head now that the others were present. Watt nodded.

"Tell us from the beginning," he asked Leda. "Everything you can remember."

Slowly, Leda explained how Mariel had been there tonight, standing behind a bar right when Leda was upset, and alone. Watt knew why—because he'd abandoned her—and felt even more miserable at the realization.

Leda told them that she'd only had one drink, but the next thing she knew the two of them were out on the beach, and Mariel was pestering her with questions about Eris.

Found her, Nadia said, and a pic of Mariel—the official one, from her ID ring—appeared on the back of Watt's eyelids.

There was something familiar about her, though Watt couldn't place it. *Nadia, have we seen her before?*

You ordered a drink from her at the Hudson Conservancy Ball, Nadia reminded him.

Thank god for Nadia's photographic memory. *Maybe she was spying on us then too.*

"Is this her?" Watt asked aloud, pretending to use his contacts to send Leda the photo, since Avery and Rylin were watching.

Leda's jaw tightened in recognition. "That's her." She made a swishing motion with her wrist, and the pic projected onto one of the suite's enormous full-screen walls.

Avery gasped. "I met her at Eris's grave! She stared at me like she hated me."

Leda looked down. "After Mariel drugged me and kidnapped me, she asked me how I kept you all from telling the truth. I told her all your secrets." Her voice quavered, but she forged bravely on. "I told her what you did to Cord, Rylin—and, Avery, I'm so sorry, I told her your secret too." Watt glanced at Avery, waiting for a pained expression to cross her face at the reference to Atlas, but she just pursed her lips and said nothing.

Leda turned to Watt last of all. "And, Watt, I told her about Nadia . . ."

It's okay, Watt hastened to reassure Nadia, *we can figure this out—*

". . . I even told her where Nadia is," Leda finished.

Watt swallowed bravely over the horror that threatened to close up his chest. If Mariel told anyone that Nadia was in his brain, it was the end of both of them. "It wasn't your fault, Leda," he assured her.

Leda looked around the room, clearly waiting for the others to jump on her, to blame her—but neither Avery nor Rylin spoke up. Watt was surprised, and glad. Maybe he wasn't the only one Leda had made peace with recently.

Leda took a shaky breath. "Now Mariel thinks you all deserve to pay for Eris's death, since you helped cover it up. I wanted to warn you, because she's out for revenge, and there's nothing she won't do. She left me for *dead*."

"Let me get this straight," Rylin interjected. "This girl Mariel thinks we're all involved in the death of her ex-girlfriend, and she knows all our secrets, and she's out to make us pay?"

Hearing it said like that, Watt was overcome by a terrible wave of despair. In some ways it felt like he was reliving that terrible night on the roof, that nothing had changed in the last several months; but of course that wasn't true. Everything had changed. This time they were working together, instead of attacking one another.

They all looked around the room with hollow, terrified eyes. Watt kept hoping that Nadia would chime in with a suggestion, but she'd been frighteningly quiet. It wasn't a good sign.

"We have to do something," Leda finally spoke into the fractured silence. "We have to get rid of her somehow."

"Get rid of her? You don't mean *kill* her?" Rylin exclaimed.

"Of course Leda doesn't mean kill her," Avery interrupted, then glanced hesitantly at Leda. "Right?"

Watt chimed in. "I saw what Mariel did to Leda. I know what she's capable of. We have to do something before she does something to us. We have to keep her from ruining our lives."

They all looked around the room as the import of those words sank in. Through the window Watt saw fireworks explode into the night, the very last fireworks show before dawn, illuminated a searing, vicious red against the black sky.

Nadia? he asked, but she didn't answer, and he knew with a sinking feeling what that meant.

For the first time in his life, Watt had confronted her with a problem that she truly couldn't solve.

MARIEL

MARIEL WRAPPED HER arms tighter around herself and bent her head into the blistering wind, walking doggedly home from another of her cousin José's parties. She shouldn't have gone out tonight in the first place; should have known that all it would do was stir up memories of Eris. Tender memories that hurt like a bruise, but that she still kept pressing on, because it was better to feel the pain than to feel nothing at all.

She could have taken the monorail, but she liked this stretch of the East River, especially cloaked in the liquid inky shadows of nightfall. It was nice to have a moment to herself, to be alone with her thoughts in the wide-eyed darkness.

She still didn't understand what had gone so wrong in Dubai. After learning that Leda had killed Eris, Mariel had wanted nothing more than to leave Leda's life in tatters. Death was too good for Leda—she needed to watch her entire world fall apart, lose the people she loved, be locked away behind bars somewhere dark and hellish and lonely.

Mariel had planted drugs on Leda and abandoned her on the beach, in a spot known only to maintenance workers and drug-ferrying gangs. Then she'd sent in an anonymous tip about her, fully expecting Leda to go to jail for possession—or at the very least, to a rehab facility so miserable that it might as well be jail. She'd been floored when Leda had arrived safely back in New York and stepped into her old life as if nothing had happened at all.

Once again the upper-floor world had flung up an invisible, impenetrable wall to keep people like Mariel out—and to protect its own.

Except that it had failed to protect Eris, Mariel thought bitterly. Eris's death had been swept under the rug, just like the fact that Leda had been passed out, drugged, on a beach in Dubai.

The wind picked up, sounding almost hollow and mournful as it skittered over the water to batter uselessly at the Tower. It began to rain. Mariel hadn't realized it was a rain day; she rarely checked the feeds anymore, except to spy on Leda and the others. She shrugged deeper into her jacket and kept her head down, but she was already soaked to her skin.

As she stumbled down the street, her mind was spinning, reliving the final conversation she'd had with Leda. Mariel half wished she'd recorded it, though she would certainly never forget it. The shock of it was branded on her mind forever. Leda had thought Eris was having an affair with her father? How could she be so willfully blind to the truth?

She couldn't believe the things these highliers did to one another. Their world was a bright, dazzling whirlwind, but underneath the lights and the facade it was harsh and unforgiving: a world of hypocrisy and callousness and coldhearted greed. Leda had assumed the worst of Eris without asking any questions.

And then she'd *pushed* her, accident or not, and the others had all stood there and let it happen.

Mariel felt vindicated, finally knowing the truth about that night. She'd been mad with grief for so long, spinning wildly from one conspiracy theory to the next, trying to force the puzzle pieces into a narrative that made some kind of sense.

When she'd seen Leda and Watt together at the Under the Sea party, had heard Watt mention the roof and "that night," she'd known they were covering something up. She'd taken that catering job in Dubai—smuggling drugs there with her, and the expensive truth juice—just to prove she was right.

She may not have gotten her revenge, but at least she'd finally learned the truth. Now she knew exactly whom to blame.

I won't fail you again, Eris. So she'd slipped up in Dubai. It didn't matter. Mariel was nothing if not determined. Of course, she would have to tread more carefully now, since Leda would recognize her. She'd already quit her job at Altitude and started planning something new.

One by one, no matter how long it took, she would make all four of them pay.

A flash of light exploded in the sky, startling Mariel into stillness. Lightning? This wasn't just a rainy day, it was a storm. The rain came down even harder, as if each raindrop was hurled right at Mariel with vicious intent. They exploded against the pavement in little bursts, and where they hit her body, they stung her through her flimsy jacket like sharp-edged stones.

There was a shed near the water, with a tiny light glowing stubbornly through one small window. Mariel thought she heard a voice inside. Surely whoever it was would be okay with her waiting out the storm in there.

She started forward, wiping the water from her eyes, as a terrible roll of thunder sounded overhead. "Hello," Mariel tried to shout, but the thunder was angry and grinding and struck a primal terror deep into Mariel's chest. She was almost at the shed—

Something slammed into Mariel from behind, hard.

She staggered onto her knees, stumbling on the pavement near the water. Stars burst before her eyes, and a scream escaped her throat. But whoever—or whatever—it was hit her again, relentless. She scrabbled to grab on, but there was nothing there; she was tumbling out into the water. It was bitterly, bracingly cold.

Mariel couldn't swim.

She fumbled for a foothold, but the river was too deep. The rain kept falling around her, hissing angrily onto the water's turbulent surface, and she was sinking into a discordant, slippery blackness. The sky was wet and dark, and the water was wet and dark, and there was no way to tell which way was up.

Mariel tried to cry out again, but the sound was lost. The water dragged her limbs down, with cold dead fingers that would never let her go.

And then there was nothing more.

ACKNOWLEDGMENTS

IN SPITE OF my expectations, writing a second novel was no less terrifying, wonderful, nerve-racking, and thrilling than the first one. I'm grateful for the support and guidance of so many incredible people who've made this book possible.

I couldn't ask for a better publishing team than everyone at HarperCollins. Emilia Rhodes, my fearless editor—thank you for your sharp and thoughtful notes, your patience, and for believing in this series from the very start. Jen Klonsky, your enthusiasm consistently inspires me. Thank you for being *The Dazzling Heights*'s biggest cheerleader. Alice Jerman, I so appreciate all your editorial support.

Jenna Stempel, once again you have created an absolutely perfect cover. Thank you, thank you, for making this book so jaw-droppingly beautiful! Gina Rizzo, I am in awe of your publicity genius and your ability to stay organized in the face of chaos. Thank you for making it possible for me to meet so many readers and for all the creative ways you've spread the word about this series. Elizabeth Ward, you are nothing short of dazzling. Thank you for your boundless energy and your marketing brilliance. (I really am sorry for killing your favorite character—I promise to make it up to you somehow!) Huge thanks also to Kate Jackson, Suzanne Murphy, Sabrina Abballe, Margot Wood, and Maggie Searcy.

An enormous thank you is due to the entire team at Alloy Entertainment. Joelle Hobeika, I would be nowhere without your warmth, your enthusiasm, and your fierce editorial skills. Thank you for being on this journey with me every step of the way. Josh Bank, I am so grateful for your insights, your honesty, and your sense of humor. The best parts of this book came from laughter at our plotting meetings. Sara Shandler, you are as always the undisputed queen of romance—thank you for helping me deepen every relationship in these pages. Les Morgenstein and Gina Girolamo, thank you for all your efforts to make *The Thousandth Floor* into a television series. Romy Golan, we would all be lost without your thoughtful notes and magical scheduling abilities. Thanks also to Stephanie Abrams for managing the finances, Matt Bloomgarden for your legal expertise, and Laura Barbiea for making it all happen.

To the team at Rights People—Alexandra Devlin, Allison Hellegers, Caroline Hill-Trevor, Rachel Richardson, Alex Webb, Harim Yim, and Charles Nettleton—thank you for continuing to bring *The Thousandth Floor* throughout the world. To all the foreign publishers: thank you for believing in this series, and for sharing it with so many readers in so many languages. It feels like a dream come true.

Thanks also to my cousin Chris Bailey for my author portrait; to Oka Tai-Lee and Zachary Fetters for building a breathtaking website; and to Alyssa Sheedy for all your gorgeous paper designs.

To my friends and family, thank you for everything you have done to support this series. Mom and Dad, I know it was not the easiest year with my planning a wedding, graduating school, and writing a book all at once. I couldn't have managed any of it without your help. Thank you for your unwavering support, both logistical and emotional. Lizzy and John Ed, thank you for continuing to be my biggest champions and my earliest readers. And especially to Alex: thank you for the innumerable smoothie bowls, for the comic relief, and for helping me write myself out of various plot corners. Somehow you kept me (mostly) on-schedule and (mostly) sane throughout this process, and still we managed to get married!

Finally, to all the readers of the *The Thousandth Floor*—I am so grateful for your excitement, your ideas, and your passion for the story. This series only comes to life thanks to you.